THE PACE O...
HEATHER HA...
FOLLOWING...

"I have an idea. Why ... my shoes, and I'll guide you through the steps one more time. That way you'll be able to follow the motion of my body to anticipate the turns."

With his hands placed firmly on the small of her back, he pulled her in to him until she was flush with his body. Intense heat infused her entire being, and she started to object.

"Come on, Heather, you wouldn't tolerate such resistance from *your* students, would you?"

Tentatively, she placed the balls of her feet onto his toes. "Is this what you mean?" Her voice sounded shrill, and she hoped he couldn't detect her nervousness.

He inhaled the sweet rose-petal scent of her hair, felt the soft crush of full, firm breasts against his chest, and sighed. "Yes. You're doing it exactly right."

❧

Millie Criswell

Wild Heather

WARNER BOOKS

A Time Warner Company

WARNER BOOKS EDITION

Copyright © 1995 by Millie Criswell
All rights reserved.

Cover design by Diane Luger
Paper sculpture by Greg Gulbronson
Hand lettering by Carl Dellacroce

Warner Books, Inc.
1271 Avenue of the Americas
New York, NY 10020

Ⓦ A Time Warner Company

Printed in the United States of America

First Printing: July, 1995

10 9 8 7 6 5 4 3 2 1

To Judy DeBerry—sales rep. extraordinaire. Thanks for being my fan, my friend, and now my partner in publishing.

PROLOGUE

Salina, Kansas, Summer 1883

"Is he dead yet?"

Heather glanced up at the tear-stained face of her sister Rose, then back down at their father lying on the bed. For three days she and her two younger sisters had kept constant vigil by Ezra Martin's bedside. Doc Spooner had told them a week ago to expect the worst. Ezra's stomach ailment—most likely a cancer—had spread.

Before Heather could reply, her father's eyelids opened, and his blue eyes, bright in contrast to his ashen complexion, focused on Rose's anguished face.

"Quit wringin' your hands, Rose Elizabeth. I ain't dead yet. And I don't much appreciate your hurrying me off to meet my maker."

"Pa, I'm . . ." Rose stifled a sob and looked away.

"Hush, child," Ezra whispered, reaching for his youngest daughter's hand. Of all his girls, Rose looked the most like his beloved Adelaid, and it gave his heart a painful little twist, for he knew it wouldn't be much longer until he'd be meeting up again with sweet Adelaid in Heaven.

He wasn't sorry he had to go, though the thought of leaving his children alone lay heavily on his conscience. He hadn't done much for them in this lifetime. The farm barely eked out an existence, and Ezra knew it wasn't a place for three lovely, intelligent young women to spend the remainder of their days.

Dying gave a man wisdom, and recently he'd reached some conclusions. He was going to set things right for his girls.

Ignoring the pain in his gut, Ezra took a deep breath and turned his attention to his eldest child. Heather stared down at him, her face etched with grave concern, and he heaved a sigh of relief. She could be counted on to carry out his wishes.

Heather was used to being in charge; the girls always followed her lead. Since Adelaid's death nine years ago, the chore of raising the girls had fallen upon her slender shoulders. And she'd done a downright admirable job.

Ezra cleared his throat. "Where's Laurel? I want to speak to all of you at once. I don't have enough breath to chew my cabbage twice."

Heather sensed the urgency in her father's voice and exchanged a worried look with Rose before ordering her to fetch Laurel. She was outside, hanging up the wash and likely engaged in some fantasy about singing at a fancy opera house.

Heather didn't blame Laurel for dreaming about a better life. Living in a sod hut in the middle of a Kansas wheat farm left a lot to be desired. She lifted her gaze to the ceiling, then sighed with relief that no snakes or mice were slithering down from above. Rodents and vermin were a constant problem, and the grass roof gave easy access into their three-room abode, which had passed for a house these many years.

Pa always said he was going to build a real house one day, with a wood-shingled roof and smooth plaster walls. But there never was enough money. And though Ezra's intentions were always of the purest sort, his bank account never allowed him to carry out his plan.

Heather reached for her father's hand, holding on to his gnarled fingers tightly. Her father couldn't give them an abundance of material things. But he did give them love, and a great deal of encouragement to pursue their dreams, and for that she would always count herself rich.

"I'll need your strength, Heather. I'll need you to help me convince the others that what I'm about to suggest is the right thing to do."

"Hush, Pa," she said, brushing back the graying, sweat-streaked hair from his forehead. "You're not going to die. And you mustn't talk as if you are. It's bad luck to tempt the devil."

Ezra gave a weak little cough that could almost have passed for a laugh. "Child, the devil and me go way back, but I think I'm headin' for Heaven. No man who's produced such beautiful daughters could be denied access."

Before Heather could respond, Rose and Laurel entered.

Laurel rushed to her father's bedside, blinking back tears that threatened to drown them all. "I'm here, Papa. I came as soon as Rose fetched me."

He acknowledged his golden-haired daughter with a nod. "I don't have much time left, girls, and I'd just as soon not waste it by listening to you and that fool Doc Spooner assuring me that I'm going to live to a ripe old age. I'm ready to meet my maker, but before I go there are things that need settlin'. I've been doing a lot of thinkin' about what will happen to you girls after I'm gone."

"You know we'll be fine, Pa," Rose interjected with the confident air that was so much a part of her nature. "We have the farm. It'll see us through."

"Three hundred acres and a sod hut ain't much for a man to bequeath to his family upon his death, but it's all I got. But that don't mean that I have to leave it as it is."

Heather's forehead wrinkled in confusion. "You're not making much sense, Pa. How can you not leave it as it is? There's no way to change it."

"You girls deserve more in life than this miserable pile of dirt." He squeezed Heather's hand gently and with a great deal of love in his voice said, "You've got a rare talent with your picture drawin' and such. I wouldn't want you to waste it. And, Laurel . . . well, you've got your dreams about singing at a grand opera house someday." He and the good Lord knew that she didn't have the voice to match the dream, but he never mentioned that to his impetuous daughter.

With a sigh he turned to stare at the pretty, plump face of Rose, the youngest, who at eighteen was also the wisest. "I know my decision's goin' to be the hardest on you, Rose Elizabeth. I know you'd like nothin' better than to stay on this farm and work the land. You're too much like me for your own good."

"I love this farm, Pa."

"I know that, child, but this farm don't love you or anyone else for that matter, which is why I've decided to sell it."

"Sell it!" Rose's hand flew to her throat and a horrified look crossed her face.

Shaking her head, Heather cast her sister a warning look, and anything else Rose was going to say was swallowed up in stunned silence.

"I've put aside some money over the years. It ain't much, but it'll be enough to serve as a dowry for you three girls. It was something I promised Addy I'd do. And though it was mighty rough at times, I kept my promise to your mama. God rest her soul."

"A dowry!" Laurel exclaimed. "You mean like for marriage? I don't want to get married, Papa. I want to be an opera singer."

Heather empathized with her sister. She didn't want to get married either. She wanted to become an illustrator. That had been her dream ever since her mother had bought her her first pad of paper and a pencil. But she'd given her father her word that she would help convince her sisters of his wisdom, and she intended to do just that. Though she wasn't quite certain just how.

"Girls," she said finally, ignoring the shocked expressions on their faces. "Let's give Pa a chance to explain."

Ezra took several deep, painful breaths before he continued. "As miserable as this piece of land is, it's got to be worth something to somebody. As soon as I'm laid to rest—" he shook his head before any protestations could be voiced, "I want Heather to put the farm up for sale. With the money I've saved for your dowries, I want you girls to go your separate ways and pursue your dreams."

"But, Pa, I don't have no dream other than staying here on the farm!" Rose wailed, wringing her hands.

"I know that, Rose Elizabeth, which is why you're goin' to travel back East and attend one of them fancy finishing schools. They'll teach you to become a proper lady. You'll learn so much you'll be able to teach school one day. A genteel, educated woman has a much better chance of finding herself a rich husband."

"But . . ."

"I'm askin' you to do this for me, Rose. It's my dying wish."

The hand that grasped hers was large, gnarled, and liver spotted with age and infirmity, but it offered love and solace. Rose hesitated only momentarily before squeezing it, wishing she could somehow transfer her health and vitality to the dying man she cared for so deeply, whose death would create a void she would never be able to fill.

"Yes, Pa," she whispered, blinking back tears of despair.

"Laurel, you'll take your money and study singing. There'll be plenty of opportunities to meet a man of wealth at an opera house. Them refined gents always frequent those types of places."

Despite the somberness of the occasion, Laurel couldn't keep the joy she felt from lighting her face. Singing lessons. Opera houses. Marriage to a wealthy patron of the arts. Well, two out of three wasn't bad. and if she wasn't able to find a wealthy husband . . .

Finally, Ezra turned his attention back to Heather. "You've got lots of talent, child," he told her. "Mr. Pickens down at the *Salina Sentinel* says you should be able to find work painting portraits of well-to-do families. That could lead to a marriage proposal."

Heather did her best not to grimace. Portrait painting was too tedious and boring. She wanted excitement. She wanted to illustrate for a big-city newspaper or magazine.

And she wanted to see the ocean. The real ocean. Not the waves of Kansas wheat she'd watched ebb and flow for most of her twenty-two years.

"I could go to San Francisco," she suggested, trying to keep the excitement out of her voice. The city had been born for an extravagant destiny, and Heather had no doubt that hers led there as well. "The California gold rush left lots of rich men." And there was an abundance of newspaper publishers, though she didn't mention that fact.

"Then that's that," Ezra stated, a look of serenity settling over his face. "I'll be able to die in peace now, knowin' my three girls are going to be well taken care of and content."

Heather, Rose, and Laurel exchanged knowing glances with one another, then looked down at their father and smiled reassuringly.

"Yes, Pa," they chorused. "You can rest easy now."

CHAPTER 1

San Francisco, California, Late Summer 1883

"Are you deaf as well as dumb, miss? You come here yesterday asking for work, and I told you then, I ain't hirin' no woman illustrators. Now get yourself gone. *The Ledger* don't hire women."

Heather gasped when the large man grasped her arm, forcing her from the newspaper office building to deposit her shaking body on the street.

Her body filled with fury. No bald-headed Neanderthal man was going to treat her like a second-class citizen, especially in broad daylight, and in front of strangers, no less. She looked about her at the curious faces, silently daring anyone to say a word about her humiliation.

She was Heather Martin from Salina, Kansas. And she had talent, dammit. She knew it, too. Trouble was, no one else in this unfriendly town did, and it didn't look like anyone was going to give her the opportunity to prove it.

"Mule-headed barbarian," she called out, stifling the urge

7

to march back into the building and crack her art portfolio over the man's head. Her comment produced a chorus of laughs from passersby, and Heather suddenly realized that she was making a spectacle of herself—something she had always cautioned her two younger sisters never to do.

Good Lord, Heather thought, *I've only been in town a day and I'm already providing fodder for the gossip mill. What a sterling way to begin my new life and career. Keep it up, and maybe my name and face will be plastered across the front pages of the papers I want to work for:* HEATHER MARTIN TAKES SAN FRANCISCO BY STORM AND DROWNS IN HER OWN STUPIDITY.

Heather's temper had cooled slightly by the time she returned to her lodgings at Mrs. Murphy's boardinghouse. Actually, her pique was slowly working into a full-blown depression. As she stared out her window at the gray hills in the distance, she wondered if she would ever realize her dream of working for a newspaper. The possibility seemed remote.

A foghorn groaned its eerie warning at the same time as a knock sounded at the door. Heather met a smiling, apple-cheeked Mrs. Murphy, whose arms were full of fresh-smelling white towels.

"Good afternoon, miss. I've brought some clean linens. I'm sorry the room wasn't quite ready upon your arrival yesterday. I try to keep things neat as a pin for my guests, but my back's been ailing me, and I didn't get all the laundry done as I should have."

"No need to apologize, Mrs. Murphy." Heather smiled reassuringly, ushering the stout woman into the small, clean room.

Mrs. Murphy kept her house as tidy as her person. There wasn't a speck of dirt on the white apron that circled her thick waist.

"Your home is far grander than what I've been used to," Heather admitted, thinking that she hadn't had the pleasure of having a bedroom all to herself since she was a small child.

Her compliment obviously pleased the red-haired woman, for Grace Murphy's cheeks filled with color. "I do my best, dearie. Since Patrick up and died last year, it's been hard doing the chores by myself. I've a young boy who comes by twice a week to help with the firewood and such, but he's about as reliable as the weather." The proprietress set the linens down on the star-burst quilt that covered the bed. "You're from Kansas, ain't that right, dearie?"

"Yes, ma'am. Salina, Kansas. I've come here to make my mark in the world." Just saying the words filled Heather with pride and renewed determination, as if the mere uttering of them could somehow make her hopes come true.

"Well, you're pretty enough, that's for sure. I doubt it'll take long for some gent to pop the question."

"The question?"

"Marriage, dearie. It's the only sensible thing for a woman to do. Life's hard in this city. And dangerous. A good woman needs a protector. A man to keep the evils at bay."

"But you're all alone, Mrs. Murphy, and you seem to be doing all right for yourself."

Hanging the towels on the rod by the marble-topped washstand, the proprietress nodded. "I'm surviving, Miss Martin. But it ain't a happy existence to be alone in this world. I miss my husband something awful. The days seem to drag on. And the nights . . ." She shook her head sadly. "I can't even bear to think about the nights."

Not about to be dissuaded by the motherly warning, Heather confided, "I want more than just marriage, Mrs. Murphy. I want a career."

"A career!" The woman chuckled, shaking her head, clearly amused by the notion. "Land sakes, what for?" She seated herself on the edge of the feather bed, urging Heather to follow suit. "You've got looks, dearie. Get yourself married and have a passel of young ones. It's what God intended for us women. Though I'm sorry to say that I was never blessed with any children of my own."

"But I have talent, Mrs. Murphy. I can draw lovely pictures and sketches of people. Why would God give me the talent to do that if He didn't want me to use it?"

As Grace pondered the question, she patted Heather's hand in a reassuring manner. "You're young and full of adventure. I was like that once, too, when me and Patrick first set foot in this city. Gold fever had a strong grip on us, as it had on everyone out here. We almost ended up dying for our dreams. But we were one of the lucky ones. Patrick made enough off our claim to buy this house and set up his own business repairing clocks. We never got rich, but we were happy." A wistful smile crossed her lips. "Sometimes the dreams you seek are right before you, and you don't even know it."

The regulator clock on the wall gonged four times, and Heather was saved from replying when Grace Murphy rose to her feet.

"Pay me no mind, dearie. Old women like me ramble on. We've got little else besides our wisdom to give out." She paused by the door. "Go ahead and pursue your dream, dearie. You owe that to yourself. And if it don't work out, there're always plenty of men around this city looking for a pretty wife." She closed the door softly behind her, leaving Heather to ponder her words and wonder what would happen if she didn't succeed at finding employment as an illustrator.

The alternative was highly distasteful. Marriage was definitely not what she wanted. Not now, anyway.

She had dreams, plans to become the best illustrator the city had ever seen. And tomorrow she intended to make those dreams come true.

Clutching a well-worn copy of *Maxwell's Guide to San Francisco,* courtesy of Mrs. Murphy, and her leather portfolio of sketches, Heather made her way down Geary Street toward Market, the business hub of the city, where the majority of newspaper offices were located.

A stiff breeze blew in off the bay, chilling the morning air, and she wished she'd had the good sense to wear her wool coat. Shabby though it was, the gray, threadbare, moth-eaten garment was still warm.

The street was alive with activity. Fashionably dressed ladies and nattily garbed gentlemen drove by in bright-colored equipages, and Heather felt as dowdy as a brown wren dressed in her plain navy serge skirt and white cotton shirtwaist. *Dowdy but businesslike,* she reminded herself. As she walked, she kept her focus straight ahead, not bothering to acknowledge the admiring looks of the gentlemen who passed.

Rows of handsome two-story wooden houses with gardens set before them lined the street. She marveled at the intricacies and embellishments of their gaily painted gingerbread trim.

San Francisco was a far cry from Kansas, that was for certain. The hills alone were a testament to that fact. They reminded her of the bustles the society ladies were so fond of wearing—protruding for no special reason, incongruous with the natural lay of the land.

Arriving at Market Street, it was only a short walk to *The Chronicle* building, a solid mass of brick and concrete. Heather looked up in awe at the imposing structure. It was by far the tallest building she'd ever laid eyes on. Of course, there hadn't been much opportunity to view office buildings in Salina, she reminded herself: There weren't any. Squaring her shoulders, determined to succeed this time, she made her way to the newspaper's city room, where she'd been told she could find the editor, Mr. Maitland.

She paused in the doorway of the noisy room. Her eyes widened as she glanced about, trying to absorb everything at once. Every inch of wall space was covered with maps. Even maps of the remotest regions of the continent were displayed. On the back wall next to the water pail stood a small library of books relating to city affairs, and scattered about the room were reporters sitting at small green desks, their heads bent over their work as they scribbled feverishly to get out the latest news.

Excitement surged through her at the prospect of becoming part of such a profession. But that feeling was soon tempered by realism when a disheveled cigar-chomping gentleman with graying hair appeared out of nowhere.

"Can I help you?"

Though the man's question implied a willingness to be of assistance, his tone definitely did not. Despite her nervousness, Heather forced a smile and nodded, wondering if his scowl was a permanent part of his expression.

"Yes. I'm looking for Mr. Maitland."

"You found him, girlie. Now what can I do you for? This is a busy place, and I'm a busy man." His impatience was evident by his scuffed brogan tapping against the floor.

Busy he might be, Heather thought, *but rude is what he is.* Trying to keep the annoyance out of her voice, she hastened to explain, "I'm looking for work, Mr. Maitland."

The look he shot her clearly summed up his opinion: Annoying. Featherbrained. Woman! "This ain't the place for placing a classified, girlie. You'll have to—"

"You don't understand. I'm an illustrator, Mr. Maitland. I'm interested in finding employment with your newspaper." She pressed her portfolio at him, but his hands remained firmly tucked in his pants' pockets.

"We got all the illustrators we need, young woman. Even if I was in the hiring mode, which I'm not, I wouldn't be hiring a woman. There's plenty of men out of work—men who have families to support. You get my meaning?"

Having heard almost exactly the same thing yesterday, Mr. Maitland's meaning was all too clear.

"Are you saying that you won't hire me because I'm a woman?"

The idea was outlandish, barbaric, not to mention totally unfair. This was 1883, for heaven's sake! Women in Wyoming voted in elections. There were women doctors, lawyers. Why, she'd even heard of a woman dentist! And Mary **Anna** Hallock, who was somewhat of an idol, was already a successful illustrator in New York City, contributing to such prestigious publications as *Harper's Weekly* and *Scribner's Monthly.*

What on earth was wrong with the men in San Francisco?

Maitland blew a disagreeable cloud of cigar smoke in her face, and she wrinkled her nose in disgust. "Women belong at home, that's my firm belief," he said. "But if you've got your heart set on working at a newspaper, I could probably find you a job as a typesetter. That's the only position we're hiring women for. And even that's against my better judgment."

Heather's heart sank, but she squared her shoulders and looked the city editor straight in the eye, vowing to keep her temper in check this time. "I'm an illustrator, Mr. Maitland. If you'd taken the time to look at my drawings, you would see that I'd be wasting my talents as a typesetter, though I thank you for your generous offer."

The older man shook his head. "You're in for a big disappointment, girlie, if you think it's going to be different anywhere else. San Francisco's a man's town. And the newspaper business is a man's domain. You'd best go on home and learn to sew and such. Perhaps you'll be able to find work making ladies' dresses or hats." With that he left Heather to stare openmouthed as he walked away.

She turned on her heel and marched out the door and into the brisk morning air. Leaning against the post of a gas lamp, she took several deep breaths to calm her nerves and cool her heated temper. "I will succeed," she declared, receiving a strange, almost piteous look from a male passerby, which made her furious again.

Undaunted by the setback, and fueled with more determination than ever, Heather made her way down the street to the offices of *The San Francisco Star.*

A week later, Heather was no closer to finding employment as an illustrator than she'd been that first day at *The Ledger* offices. Everywhere she went the answer was the same: There was no work for a female illustrator, no matter how talented, no mater how qualified.

"Men!" she cursed, pacing back and forth across the pine-plank floor of her room, her high-button shoes beating a staccato rhythm as she walked off her anger. Men! They tried to rule the universe with an iron hand. And the pity was, they were succeeding.

Gazing at the rent notice held tightly in her hand, she fought back the tears that threatened to consume her. She had barely enough money to meet next week's accommodation.

San Francisco had proven to be an expensive city. Food was outrageous, and her purchase of two ready-made dresses to avoid further disdainful looks had been an even greater drain on her meager budget. Homemade calicoes and ginghams might not have attracted much notice in Salina, but in the business district of San Francisco, they stuck out like those bustles she had no intention of wearing.

Plopping down on the bed, she allowed her despair to wash over her, and tears formed in her eyes.

Failure. The word pricked at her. She had failed at very little up until now. But then, she'd never before tried to compete in a man's world.

Realizing that tears and self-pity would do little to put rent money in her reticule and food in her stomach, she reached for the afternoon edition of *The Examiner,* which she'd purchased that morning instead of *The Chronicle,* steadfastly refusing to add a cent to that horrible paper's coffers.

If she couldn't initially find a job at her chosen profession, than she would have to find a job doing something else in the meantime.

Spreading the newspaper out before her, she scanned the classified advertisements, frowning when she realized that she wasn't qualified to do much of anything. She had no idea how to operate a Remington typewriter. And though she was proficient with a needle, she'd never been trained on a Singer sewing machine, which was required for most of the seamstress positions advertised.

Her abilities centered on housework, gardening, cooking,

and the like. Evidently, not what one could call qualifications in demand.

Continuing to read, Heather came upon one advertisement that immediately piqued her interest. A position was being offered as governess to two children. Now that was something she was definitely qualified for, having almost single-handedly raised her two sisters.

But did she really want to burden herself with the raising of other folks' children again? And did she really have a choice?

The ad stated that they were looking for a mature, responsible woman with impeccable references. And they wanted someone to start immediately.

"Brandon Montgomery." Heather murmured the contact name mentioned in the advertisement, wondering where she'd heard it before. "Brandon Montgomery. Brandon Montgomery." She repeated the name several more times, then smiled when she realized who he was.

Brandon Montgomery owned one of the largest newspapers in the city, *The San Francisco Star*. She'd gone there last week to seek employment, only to be turned away by one of Mr. Montgomery's underlings, a most unpleasant little man who smelled of pomade and Sen-Sen.

Impeccable references. That could be a problem. But not for someone with her artistic ability and dire circumstances.

"God helps those who help themselves." Hadn't she heard her darling mama utter those very words countless times? And hadn't she read somewhere that San Francisco had burned to the ground six times within an eighteen-month period? And like a Phoenix, she had risen from her ashes to emerge as a bustling metropolis.

Determination fueled her, and, smiling confidently for the first time in weeks, Heather withdrew her writing pad and pencil from her portfolio, allowing her gaze to fall to her work. "There was more than one way to skin a cat." Her mama said that, too. And she aimed to prove Mama right on both accounts.

CHAPTER 2

The cable car climbed Nob Hill with a series of fits and starts, groaning as it made its way up the steep incline, and causing Heather's stomach to alternate between rising to her throat and plummeting to her feet.

Pressed firmly against the back of a wooden seat, she held on to the hand rope as if her life depended on it. She forced herself to concentrate on her surroundings rather than on the strange moving contraption she'd been forced to board to reach her destination.

Glancing out the open-sided car, she marveled at the magnificent mansions. They'd been built by wealthy "nobs," mining magnets who had spared no expense to create enormous and often ostentatious homes as testaments to their vast wealth.

The turreted palace of Charles Crocker, the railroad tycoon, amazed her. She'd read about such architecture in books from the Salina Lending Library, but she'd never actually seen one until now. Leland Stanford's home was no less splendid, nor was that of Mark Hopkins, whose Gothic chateau looked grand enough to qualify as a hotel.

When the trolley finally came to a screeching halt at the top of the hill, it was with a great deal of relief that Heather disembarked. But that relief was soon replaced by trepidation when she found herself only steps from the large stucco mansion of Brandon Montgomery.

It was obvious that *The San Francisco Star* was a profitable newspaper venture. The Montgomery estate indicated great wealth. The grounds were well cared for, the green velvet lawn neatly manicured. The distinctive odor of the eucalyptus trees bordering the lawn lingered in the air, mingling with the sweet scent of the roses that lined the brick walkway.

Heather's hand rested momentarily on the wrought iron gate as she took a deep, fortifying breath, hoping and praying that she could persuade Mr. Montgomery to hire her as governess to his children.

The massive oak front door displayed a shiny brass knocker. She banged it hard, waiting but a moment for her summons to be answered. A young woman dressed in a serviceable gray gown and white starched apron, who looked no older than Heather was, stood in the doorway. Much to Heather's relief, there was a welcoming smile on her face.

"May I help you, miss?"

Heather swallowed, thrusting in front of her the newspaper she carried. "I came about the governess position. The advertisement said to apply in person."

"Do you have an appointment?"

Heather's heart sank, and she shook her head, chastising herself for her inexperience. Of course, she should have made an appointment. All wealthy businesspeople maintained rigid schedules.

Her disappointment must have shown, for the young woman smiled kindly and said, "That's all right. Mr. Montgomery isn't home right now anyway. But you can interview with Mrs. Montgomery. Most likely she'll have to give final approval. She's very particular about the children."

Thanking the woman profusely, Heather was led into an
attractive sitting room to await the lady of the house. As she
stood there, she tried her best to hide her curiosity. This was
the grandest home she'd ever seen. It was attractively fur-
nished with heavy furniture of rosewood and mahogany. And
there were several sofas covered in expensive blue velvet.

The parlor was lit with colorful Tiffany gas lamps.
Heather was glad that Mr. Montgomery hadn't succumbed to
the temptation to wire his house with electricity, as so many
of the office buildings had. The gas lamps lent a much cozier
feel to the room, and in a house so large, coziness was probably not in great abundance.

At that moment the door slid open and an attractive
woman entered. Her dark hair, generously sprinkled with
gray, was fashioned into a bun at the back of her head. Mrs.
Montgomery was older than Heather had expected, and she
surmised that this was the reason the Montgomerys needed a
governess. Older folks tended not to have a great deal of patience where children were concerned.

Heather extended her gloved hand to the woman, who was
scrutinizing her person with a thoroughness Heather found
disconcerting. Glad that she'd worn one of her new dresses,
though she'd been unable to find one of the proper size, and
conscious of the fact that governesses were usually a great
deal older than she, Heather hoped the severity of the color
and style would make her appear more mature.

"Good afternoon, Mrs. Montgomery. I'm Heather Martin.
I've come about the governess position."

One of the woman's imperious, graying eyebrows arched,
but she took Heather's hand and shook it, her grip surprisingly strong. "You're rather young to be a governess, aren't
you, Miss Martin? It is miss, isn't it?"

"Yes, ma'am. I'm not married, but I do have a great deal
of experience raising young'n . . . children," she corrected
herself. *Young'ns* was not a proper term for San Francisco,
and she was trying her best to fit in.

"I've an adequate education, Mrs. Montgomery." All three
Martin sisters had attended school in Salina and received de-

cent educations. Her parents had insisted upon it. And what she hadn't learned in school, she had taught herself by reading almost every book in the Salina Lending Library, including the forbidden ones!

"I can read well, my cursive has always been praised for its clarity and neatness, and I consider myself to be intelligent. I admit to a weakness when it comes to mathematics, but I feel confident enough to instruct your children with their numbers." Having spoken so fast, Heather had to take a deep, calming breath.

The older woman's assessing gaze didn't waver. Indicating that Heather should sit, she said, "Please tell me a little bit about yourself, Miss Martin."

Heather lowered herself onto one of the matching embroidered wing chairs and began to explain how she had raised her two younger sisters after her mother had died. She told Mrs. Montgomery of her father's recent illness and death, omitting little except the fact that she had aspirations to pursue a career as an illustrator.

"Laurel, she's second oldest and as pretty as a picture, has gone to Denver to pursue a career in the opera. Pa was worried because Laurel doesn't have what you would call an entertaining voice," Mrs. Montgomery nodded, biting back a smile, "but she's determined to succeed. Rose Elizabeth, my youngest sister, has remained behind on the farm to await the new buyer. I've made arrangements for her to attend Mrs. Caffrey's School for Young Ladies in Boston. Rose is in need of a little smoothing out, if you get my meaning."

Her narrative at an end, Heather folded her hands demurely in her lap and waited, trying not to look as nervous as she felt.

"You seem intelligent enough, and you are charming, in an unusual way, Miss Martin," Mrs. Montgomery said, "but why is it you've never married?" She tapped her chin with her fingernail.

"No one ever asked me." At the older woman's surprised expression, Heather went on to explain. "Salina's a small town. I grew up with just about every eligible man, but there

wasn't any one gentleman in particular that I could see myself marrying." There certainly hadn't been anyone for
whom Heather would have considered giving up her art career.

"Are you opposed to the state of matrimony itself, Miss
Martin?"

She shook her head. "No. If I find the right man someday,
I would like to settle down."

Mrs. Montgomery was impressed by Heather Martin's di-
rectness. She was a comely young woman. Though her dress
was baggy and ill suited to her—she was much too young to
wear black—Harriet could tell that Heather had a good figure. Her skin was flawless, and there was an intriguing,
bright sparkle in the depths of those lovely amethyst eyes.

"Do you want to have children of your own one day?"

Surprised, Heather blushed becomingly. "I hope to have a
family one day, Mrs. Montgomery. I love children, and they
seem to take to me. But I have no plans to marry in the im-
mediate future."

"That could always change, my dear," Harriet said, almost
to herself, and Heather thought the comment quite odd but
nodded politely anyway.

"You might find my grandchildren a bit—"

"Your grandchildren?" Heather's eyes widened at the disclosure. "I thought the children were your own."

Harriet laughed, and a tinkling sound like a music box
filled the room. "Heavens, no! I'm much too old to have six-
year-old twins. Jennifer and Matthew are my grandchildren,
and Brandon is my son, not my husband.

"No. My son and his wife divorced when Jennifer and
Matthew were still babies. The children have been without a
mother these many years, Miss Martin, and I don't mind
telling you that it's been hard on them. My son is well meaning, and he loves them in his own way, but the children need
the love and attention of a woman. I've done what I could,
but it's not been enough. They crave the affection only a
mother can provide."

Heather's eyes filled with sadness. "I understand how they

feel. Even though I was nearly fourteen when Mama died, it was still hard growing up without her guidance. I had all sorts of questions that needed answering about . . ." she blushed, "well, you know. Naturally I couldn't go to Pa, so I spent a great deal of time at the library." It hadn't been easy sneaking by eagle-eyed Thelma Tucker. The ancient librarian had guarded the adults-only section as zealously as a miser did a pot full of gold.

The older woman smiled knowingly, and a spark of amusement lit her kind brown eyes. "Doing research on growing up, I take it?"

"Rose Elizabeth was only nine when Mama died. She took Mama's death real hard. I tried to make up for it, but being young myself, I didn't always know the right thing to say or do."

As she listened to the girl talk of her past, Harriet's admiration for her grew by leaps and bounds. Heather had a great deal of compassion for one so young. And she didn't doubt that Heather possessed a great deal of love—love that could balm three anguished souls.

"I would need whomever I hire to move into this house on a full-time basis. Would that be a problem, Miss Martin?"

"No, ma'am," she said, smiling with relief. "In truth, I'll be needing a place to stay. My funds have nearly run out, and I've been at wit's end trying to decide what to do."

Heather's honesty touched Harriet. "As I'm sure my maid, Mary-Margaret, informed you, Brandon is not at home and won't return for several days. But I feel confident that in his absence I can offer you the position of governess to the children. He usually relies on my opinion where the twins are concerned." That wasn't quite the truth, but why burden the young woman with details about Brandon's perverse nature now? Besides, if she knew how difficult Brandon could be, she'd probably turn tail and run.

Heather smiled widely. "I'm very grateful."

Especially for the fact that the woman hadn't asked to see her references. For in truth, Heather had none to give. When push came to shove, she just couldn't bring herself to lie and to falsify documents, as she'd previously been tempted to do.

Honesty had been drilled into Heather since birth. It was a trait she hadn't quite been able to relinquish. She was oftentimes honest to a fault and said things a bit too bluntly. Tactfulness was not her strong suit.

"I promise you won't be disappointed, Mrs. Montgomery. I'll do my best to teach the children proper behavior."

Harriet rose to her feet and Heather followed. "My grandchildren know proper behavior. Miss Martin. I'm of the opinion that they know it all too well. What they need is love and laughter. They need nurturing. They need someone to listen to their childish dreams, answer their endless questions, read to them. In short, they need a friend.

"I'm not suggesting that they don't need a proper education. Society will demand it of Matthew, and, the way things are progressing, Jenny will have need of one too. Of that I'm certain."

"I understand completely, Mrs. Montgomery. I promise you I'll do my best."

"That's all I ask. If you have no objection, I'd like you to move in tomorrow. I want you to be firmly ensconced in your new position before my son returns home."

The steely glint of determination lighting the older woman's eyes went unnoticed by Heather, who nodded enthusiastically, feeling happier than she had in weeks.

Exiting the mansion with a much lighter heart than when she'd entered, Heather couldn't suppress her grin. Everything was working out just wonderfully. In fact, things would have been downright perfect, if only she didn't have to ride that darn cable car again!

Eager to begin her new position, Heather arrived at the Montgomery mansion early the following morning. Too early, judging by the surprised but amused expression on Mary-Margaret Feeney's face.

"Come in, Miss Martin. I was told to expect you," the maid said, ushering Heather into the front hallway.

"I apologize for arriving so early," Heather said, removing her coat. "But . . . well . . . after packing my bag, and telling my landlady good-bye, there didn't seem much point in lingering any longer."

The maid nodded in understanding, hanging Heather's garment on a brass coatrack. "You're a practical one, I'll give you that. The rest of the household is still abed, but I can show you up to your room. It'll give you time to unpack and settle in before the others come down for breakfast. Have you eaten?"

Color flooded Heather's cheeks, and she was reluctant to admit that she didn't have money to spare for a meal. And even though Mrs. Murphy had offered to extend her a bit of credit, she couldn't bring herself to take the kind woman up on her offer, knowing that Mrs. Murphy's financial situation was not much better than her own.

"I'm not all that hungry," she finally replied.

"You've got the same look on your face that my boy, Jack, gets when he's about to tell a whopper."

Mary-Margaret's comment brought two bright pink blotches to Heather's cheeks, and the maid chuckled good-naturedly.

"Me and Jack know what it's like to be down on your luck, miss. If it wasn't for Miss Harriet's generosity and warm heart, I don't know what we would have done. You just follow me up the stairs. Once you're settled, come down to the kitchen at the back of the house and I'll have the old Chinaman fix you something to eat."

Mary-Margaret continued to talk in her soft Irish brogue all the way up the stairs, barely pausing to take a breath, and Heather felt as if she were riding on the tail of a Kansas tornado. When they reached the room that would be hers, the maid threw open the door.

"Here you go, miss. There's fresh water in the basin on the dresser, though the bathing room's at the end of the hall, if you prefer taking a full bath."

"That won't be necessary. I indulged myself at Mrs. Murphy's." And what an indulgence it had been to bathe in scented hot water in a room set apart just for that purpose, after all the lukewarm baths she'd taken in the old tin tub in the kitchen of the sod hut.

Turning up the gas lamp on the nightstand, Mary-Margaret wiped her hands on her apron. "I'll leave you to unpack. And don't take too long to come down for breakfast. I'm fairly starved myself." With a wink and a smile, the young woman disappeared out the door, closing it softly behind her.

Feeling almost exhausted from listening to Mary-Margaret's steady stream of conversation, Heather plopped down on the bed, pushing the palm of her hand against the mattress. She marveled at how downy soft it felt. Then she took a good look at her surroundings, pinching herself to make sure everything she saw was real.

Her bedroom was beautiful. The walls were papered in a delicate floral pattern. Tiny violets repeated over the walls and on the fluffy comforter. Exquisite white lace curtains hung at the windows. One of the windows was bow-shaped, which would allow plenty of sunlight to enter even on the dreariest days, and there was a window seat beneath it covered with a purple velvet cushion.

Closing her eyes for a moment, she pictured herself sitting there with her sketchbook on her lap, then smiled happily. This had to be a dream, she thought. Everything was working out, even if she hadn't found a job as an illustrator.

"First things first, Heather Martin," she told herself. And the first thing she had to do was unpack. She was hungry and Mary-Margaret was expecting her for breakfast. And two children she'd never set eyes on were waiting to pass judgment on her.

She would not fail. Not at becoming an illustrator. Not at becoming a governess.

Mary-Margaret was seated at the long, oak kitchen table when Heather entered. A boy of about ten years was seated next to her. He had a shock of yellow hair, almost the same color as Mary's, and Heather assumed he was Jack, the one who told the "whoppers" on occasion.

"Good morning," she said, advancing to the table. "I hope I haven't kept you waiting long." The odor of frying bacon and freshly brewed coffee scented the air with a heady fragrance and caused her stomach to rumble. She blushed, hoping no one had heard it.

A wizened little man with a long black pigtail trailing down his back turned away from the stove to point his wooden spoon at Heather. "Missy, sit down and eat. I make dang good grub."

Mary-Margaret smiled indulgently, offering Heather a seat. "Mr. Woo likes to pepper his speech with western words. He thinks it'll make him fit in better."

The Chinaman was dressed in the strangest garments Heather had ever seen. Over loose-fitting black pants, he wore a smock-type shirt of the same color and fabric, and on his head a tight little black silk cap cupped his crown.

"Excuse me for staring, but I've never seen an Oriental person before." What she had read about them in books now struck her as totally unfair.

A year ago the United States had closed its doors to Chinese immigration for a period of ten years. Hatred and distrust of the Orientals had infiltrated the highest reaches of the government.

"Chinamen are as common as fleas in San Francisco, ain't that right, Mr. Woo?" Jack interjected, smiling to reveal two missing front teeth.

"Many Chinee come here to work on railroad," the cook explained, setting down delectable-looking platters of bacon, eggs, and fluffy biscuits. "White man no likee Chinamen, but we stay anyway. We stake claim here." He crossed thin arms over an equally sparse chest, looking quite pleased with himself.

Mary-Margaret reached for a biscuit. "It's true, Miss Martin. There're a whole bunch of Mr. Woo's relatives living over in Chinatown, that's the part of the city they congregate in."

"Not good place for white lady to go alone, especially at night." Mr. Woo's expression grew serious. "Too doggone dangerous."

"He's right about that, Miss Martin. Them people do heathenish things that ain't fit for a lady's ears," agreed Mary.

Heather swallowed her coffee in one large gulp. Deciding that she didn't really want to know just what those "heathenish" things consisted of, she changed the subject. "Please, won't you call me Heather? I'd feel more at home if you would."

"And you must call me Mary-Margaret, or Mary, if you like. And this ill-mannered ruffian is my son, Jack." She tousled the boy's hair. "And you've already met our cook, Mr. Woo."

"And when will I be introduced to the children?" Heather asked, wondering at the odd look Mary exchanged with her son.

The maid shrugged. "That's hard to say. The twins have a routine of sorts they're expected to follow."

"A routine? Isn't that a bit much to expect from a pair of six-year-olds?"

"Miss Harriet don't make the rules, Mr. Montgomery does. And she don't see fit to deviate from them when he's gone."

"Mr. Montgomery's got a mean temper," Jack offered with a child's honesty.

"Jack!" his mother scolded. "You mustn't speak of your elders that way. And it's not polite to gossip at any rate."

Looking not the least bit contrite, Jack smiled impishly, reaching for another biscuit. "Well, he does."

Shooting her son another scathing look, Mary said, "Don't worry about a thing, Heather. I'm sure you'll be able to manage the children quite nicely."

Heather didn't doubt that for a moment. But she did wonder how on earth she was going to manage Brandon Montgomery.

• • •

Harriet Montgomery's summons came a short time later. Heather entered the rear sitting room, which the family used for informal entertainment, to find Harriet and the children waiting for her.

The twins, Jennifer and Matthew, were the most adorable children Heather had ever seen. Both had dark brown hair and brown eyes, which, she noted, didn't light up when they saw her.

"Children, I'd like you to meet your new governess, Miss Martin. Miss Martin, these are my grandchildren, Jennifer and Matthew." Having made the introductions, Harriet excused herself, leaving Heather to get better acquainted with the children.

Realizing that it had been a good long while since she had conversed with any six-year-olds, Heather seated herself on the sofa between the two children. "What do you two like to do for fun?"

They both stared oddly at her, then Jenny said, almost in a whisper, "We don't do much of anything, Miss Martin."

Slightly taken aback by the admission, Heather smiled nonetheless. "Why don't you call me Heather? Miss Martin seems so formal, don't you think?"

The little boy shook his head, a grave expression on his face. "Father says we're to address our elders with respect. He wouldn't like it if we called you by your first name."

"I see," Heather replied, thinking that was an awful lot of wisdom for a six-year-old to possess. It was unnatural, as was their solemn disposition, and it bothered her. They were like miniature adults rather than carefree children.

Where were the impish grins? The mischievous twinkles that should be lighting their eyes?

Perhaps they were just shy around strangers, she thought. Hoping to lighten their mood and gain their confidence at the same time, she suggested a game of hide-and-seek. Most children couldn't resist that. It had been a favorite of Rose Elizabeth's when she was young.

"Would you children like to play hide-and-seek?" She waited for their eager, enthusiastic responses, but all she got were confused looks.

"We've never played that game before, Miss Martin," Jenny confessed, smoothing the skirt of her crisp, white pinafore.

Heather's glance drifted between the two children, and she marveled at how neat they looked. There wasn't a smidgen of dirt on their clothing, nor was there a hair out of place on their heads. Matt's hair was neatly combed—"slicked down like a greased axle," as her father used to say—and Jenny's curled in springy, coiled ringlets.

Taking hold of their hands, Heather urged them onto the floor. They hesitated momentarily, then followed her to sit on the red and gold Aubusson carpet. "Hide-and-seek is probably better played outside anyway," she explained. "Perhaps we could start with something a little simpler, like ring-around-the-rosy."

"Don't know that one either," Matt said, a deep frown etching his face. He turned to his sister for confirmation, and she nodded, her sigh almost imperceptible.

Frowning, Heather wondered what kind of childhood these two had had and grew more determined to teach them the game. "Everyone stand up and join hands, please," she directed, helping them to form a circle. "Follow me and sing what I sing, do what I do." She began to skip. "Ring-around-the-rosy, pocket full of posies, ashes, ashes, all fall down." She yanked on their small hands until they dropped to the floor beside her.

At first they stared at her curiously, then Jenny began to giggle, and Matthew followed suit. Soon they were laughing uproariously and playing the game again.

"Ring-around-the-rosy, pocket full of posies . . ." The game went on for the better part of an hour, and Heather was glad that she'd been able to bring some laughter into their lives.

They continued to skip about in a circle, laughing gaily

and noisily, repeating the verse, then dropping down to the floor.

Absorbed in the children's pleasure, Heather was unmindful of the dark brown eyes glaring at her from the open doorway, until a deep, angry voice drew her attention.

"What the devil is going on here?"

CHAPTER 3

An instantaneous pall fell over the room. Wide-eyed, the children scrambled nervously to their feet at the sound of their father's voice and rushed toward the sofa.

Heather, still seated on the floor, glanced up slowly, taking in the highly polished shoes, the dark navy pin-stripped pants that housed a pair of long, muscular legs. Her gaze rose to a waistcoated chest of appreciable width, passed shoulders that seemed to fill the doorway with their massive breadth, until her eyes landed on the angriest expression she'd ever encountered.

The man's lips were thinned in displeasure. His dark brown eyes flashed furiously at her. His large, powerful hands, which could probably snap a neck in two if they had a mind to, rested on his narrow hips, as he pinned her to the floor with his gaze.

For the briefest of instants, Heather felt as if she had just laid eyes on the devil himself. But the devil couldn't possibly be as handsome as this man was, and the devil probably had a much better disposition than this man appeared to possess.

Glancing at the children to make sure they were all right, Heather winked at them reassuringly, then smiled up at the man, who, having advanced farther into the room, now loomed over her like a specter.

"I repeat: What the devil is going on here? And who, may I ask, are you?"

Heather's smile slid off her face, and she held out her hand to him. "Would you mind helping me up?"

With no pretense at politeness, he assisted her to her feet. She half expected him to haul her over his shoulder like some prehistoric caveman, carry her outside, and dump her on her backside on the front porch.

But he didn't.

Instead, he just stood there staring, waiting for her explanation.

Mustering up what was left of her courage, Heather took a deep breath. "I assume you are Mr. Montgomery? Mr. Brandon Montgomery?"

His scowl deepened, though she didn't think that was possible. "That's right. I'm Brandon Montgomery. And who, I repeat, are you?"

She was standing eye to chest with him now. He was tall, much taller than she was, she realized, as she stared at the diamond stickpin in his tie. It winked at her mockingly.

"I'm Heather Martin, Mr. Montgomery, your new governess," she said, holding out her hand again. He refused to take it.

"The hell you say!" His face reddened as he continued to stare openmouthed at her, then his jaw snapped shut so hard that she could hear his teeth click together, before he turned to shout over his shoulder, "Mother! *Mother!* Come down here, please."

Harriet Montgomery entered the room so quickly that Heather was certain she'd been eavesdropping outside the door. She looked anything but pleased by her son's behavior.

"What on earth is all this shouting about, Brandon? None of us are deaf. Though we soon might be if you don't desist in your bellowing."

"This woman," he flung his hand in Heather's direction, "claims to be my new governess. Can you explain how that is possible, since I haven't hired a new governess?"

Casting her son a fulminating look, Harriet turned toward Heather. "I apologize for my son's rudeness, Miss Martin. Brandon isn't usually lacking in manners. In fact, most times he has an overabundance of them."

Heather had the impression that Brandon Montgomery was counting to ten under his breath, but she couldn't be certain. His face looked purple. She feared he was on the verge of an apoplectic fit.

"There's no need to apologize, Mrs. Montgomery. I quite understand the situation." Though she didn't. She had no idea why this man was so furious with her. Unless, of course, he already had someone else in mind for the position Mrs. Montgomery had filled without his permission.

Heather noted the frightened expressions on the children's faces and frowned. "If we're going to continue this discussion, perhaps we should ask the children to leave the room for a few minutes. I don't like exposing young'ns . . . children to arguments."

"Are you proposing to tell me what to do with my very own *young'ns*, Miss Martin?" he asked snidely, mocking her apparent lack of formal education. "And in my own house? That's rather presumptuous of you."

"Miss Martin is right, Brandon." Harriet turned toward her grandchildren, smiling kindly at them. "Children, please go to your rooms and study your sums. I'll be up shortly to check on you."

Without a thought to defiance, the children marched out of the room like good little soldiers, closing the door quietly behind them. As soon as they were out of earshot, Heather, who'd had quite enough of Brandon Montgomery's rude behavior, turned on him.

"Since I was hired as the children's governess, Mr. Montgomery, I feel it's my duty to look out for their best interests. I'm afraid subjecting small children to a shouting match is not in their best interests." She folded her arms across her chest, daring him to deny it. The quelling look he flashed her would have crumpled lesser souls, but Heather stood her ground.

Brandon Montgomery stared at the woman before him, clenching and unclenching his fists, a vein in his neck throbbing wildly. No one in his employ had ever spoken to him like that. There was defiance in her eyes—her most extraordinarily violet eyes, he noted. And there was a definite stubborn tilt to her chin. It was obvious that the woman needed to be taken down a peg or two.

"Your so-called position here as governess is a tenuous one at best, Miss Martin. I don't allow my employees to speak rudely to me under any circumstances."

"Then perhaps you shouldn't address your employees in a like manner, Mr. Montgomery. I assure you, I can be civil when addressed the same way."

Harriet's head turned back and forth so quickly as she watched the heated exchange that she feared she would have a crick in her neck by evening. Miss Martin was holding her own under Brandon's unreasonable assault, and she admired her for that. It also reinforced her opinion that Heather Martin was the right person for the job. The very right person.

It was truly a stroke of bad luck that Brandon had finished up his business and returned home earlier than expected. She hadn't had time to explain to Miss Martin about Brandon's perverse nature. Not that anyone would understand it. She certainly didn't!

"I don't believe you should be taking Miss Martin to task, Brandon." Harriet smiled apologetically at the young woman. "I hired her, and I will stand by my decision. The children need a governess, and Miss Martin is amply qualified for the position."

Not wishing to intrude on what was obviously a family disagreement, Heather said, "Perhaps I should go up and check on the children, Mrs. Montgomery, while you and Mr. Montgomery talk this over. I wouldn't want Mr. Montgomery to hold back any of his opinions for fear of hurting my feelings." She cast Harriet a meaningful look, saw that she understood her sarcasm, then smiled prettily at Mr. Montgomery. "I'm sure you will excuse me." Picking up her skirts, she exited the room as regally as any countess.

When the door closed behind her, Brandon turned to his mother, outrage and disbelief etched clearly on his face. "I can't believe you did such a thing, Mother. Why, this woman you've hired is hardly more than a child herself. I can't possibly allow her to have supervision over my children. She's obviously unqualified. Find someone else."

Harriet raised herself up to her full five-foot, three-inch height. "There is no one else. If you remember, every governess you've hired over the past six years has quit. Your reputation for being difficult has made finding a suitable woman next to impossible." Ignoring his surprised expression, she continued. "Heather Martin is perfect for the job. She's intelligent, kind, loving, not to mention quite lovely. And the children are already taken with her."

"They were all sitting on the floor together when I came in, Mother, playing and rolling around like a bunch of Indians—Miss Martin included." He folded his arms across his chest. "Is this the type of governess you want for your grandchildren? I shudder to think what she could possibly teach them."

"Miss Martin is suitably educated to instruct the children in their lessons, Brandon. She's well read, articulate, and knowledgeable about a great many things. She's familiar with geography and agriculture."

She had to keep her face perfectly impassive on that last one. Brandon might not agree that being raised on a wheat farm would qualify as agricultural wisdom, but Harriet thought it should count for something.

"And most important, Brandon, Heather could teach Jenny and Matt about love and patience. She could teach them to be children. God only knows I'm too old to do it."

From the open doorway she had watched Heather and the children playing their game, and her heart had warmed at the joyous looks on the twins' faces. The children had actually enjoyed themselves today, and by all that was holy, she was not going to allow Brandon to ruin it for them. This was their chance to grasp on to a bit of normalcy. They needed it, the poor dears!

Brandon wasn't swayed by his mother's vehement argument. "Children need a firm hand, Mother," he insisted. "We have rules in this house. You know very well that I won't abide frivolity. Education is what's important. Education and manners and—"

"Yes, yes, dear." Harriet waved away his explanation with a flick of her wrist. "I know all about what you think is important. You drill it into the children every chance you get."

A dark eyebrow arched imperiously. "Do I detect a note of censure in your voice?"

She sighed, unwilling to be too critical, but knowing that Brandon needed to understand. "I think you've done an admirable job of raising the children thus far, Brandon. I know it hasn't been easy since your divorce from—"

"Don't say her name, Mother. I don't want to hear it." Lydia's betrayal was a wound that still festered. Time might heal all wounds, but it hadn't healed the mockery Lydia had made of their marriage. Even now, six years later, Brandon couldn't believe he had misjudged her so.

"As much as we've tried to make up for the loss of Jenny and Matt's mother," Harriet went on, putting an end to Brandon's ruminations, "the children still feel the pain of growing up without a woman's influence."

"Nonsense. They have you. You're very kind and loving."

She patted Brandon's cheek. "Thank you, dear. But it isn't my love and affection they crave. I'm an old woman. Jenny and Matt need someone younger. Someone they can share things with, play games with, someone who'll shower them with undivided attention and love. You're too busy, Brandon, and I'm too old for the task. Heather Martin is the logical choice."

He shook his head. "I don't think—"

"Please, Brandon," Harriet implored, placing her hand on his forearm. "Just give it some consideration. The girl has already moved into the room upstairs."

His face whitened. "Not . . ."

"No. She's in the guest room. The one that overlooks the rear of the house and the ocean." The panicked look left his eyes. "She doesn't have anywhere else to go, dear, and she's completely out of funds. She moved out of her boarding-house this morning, at my direction, I might add. Please say you'll think it over. Give her a chance. I know she'll be perfect for the job. I feel it in my bones."

Brandon paced back and forth across the carpet, rubbing the back of his neck as he walked. The whole affair had given him an enormous headache. And he feared that with Miss Heather Martin in residence, his headaches were only just beginning.

He believed Heather Martin was far too young for such responsibility. She was far too outspoken to behave as a proper employee. She had a stubborn streak in her a mile wide. And she gave as good as she got. Even though she possessed large violet eyes and a mass of auburn hair that shone like velvet in the morning sunshine, the corners of his mouth still turned down as he remembered how she'd taken him to task.

"Well?" Harriet prodded, keeping her fingers crossed behind her back, praying that for once in his life, Brandon would be flexible.

"All right, Mother. We'll give her a try. But only for three months. If she doesn't behave, doesn't conform to my standards in that time, she's out. Is that understood?"

Harriet beamed with pleasure. "Do you wish to tell her, or shall I?"

"As Miss Martin's employer, I feel it's my responsibility to advise her of just what is expected of her."

He had every intention of laying down the law to the chit. When he got through with her, she'd most likely run back to wherever she'd come from. That thought brought him a great measure of satisfaction. He didn't need some young, inexperienced woman turning his well-ordered existence into a chaotic mess.

Order was what he needed. What he lived by. A place for everything and everything in its place. For six long years he had strived to establish stability in his and his children's lives. Now that he had rid himself of the chaos his life had once been, he had no intention of ever slipping back into that frenzied place where feelings ruled and common sense took a backseat to emotion.

"Shall I send her down to your study?" Harriet asked, interrupting his thoughts.

"Yes," he answered quickly, then shook his head. "No, wait. I want to go up and visit with the children awhile." He hadn't missed their looks of apprehension when he'd intruded on their play or the joyous look on their faces as they frolicked on the floor with their new governess. The thought made his frown deepen. "I'll speak to Miss Martin while I'm upstairs."

"Very well, dear. I'm so glad you decided to be reasonable about this."

He shot her a quelling look. "I'm always reasonable, Mother. I pride myself on being reasonable."

Harriet smiled softly. "Yes, dear. If you say so."

After checking to make certain that the children were all right, Heather went to her room and stared at her battered brown leather suitcase. She'd flung it onto the bed in a fit of temper, and now she wondered if she shouldn't just repack all her belongings and get the heck out of the Montgomery mansion.

Brandon Montgomery was going to be impossible to work for. He was rude, arrogant, opinionated . . . Not to mention the fact that his stupid newspaper had refused even to give her an interview!

"Botheration!" She punched the pillow clutched in her hands, wishing it were Brandon's Montgomery's head that she squeezed with such vigor. She counted to ten, then counted to ten again, trying to regain control. Her temper could be formidable at times. Laurel and Rose Elizabeth had always said so.

But Heather knew she needed this job. As she'd painfully

discovered, jobs for women with her qualifications were few and far between. It was just by a stroke of luck, and Harriet Montgomery's generosity, that she'd landed this one.

Her mind made up, she tossed the pillow back onto the bed, snapped her suitcase shut, and stuffed it beneath the bed.

Brandon Montgomery was not going to get rid of her that easily. Besides, those children needed her. Having had the misfortune to have been raised by *him* for the last six years, she could see why they were so withdrawn and sullen. It was her Christian duty to help Jenny and Matt, to bring some laughter into their lives. Obviously they weren't going to get that from their father.

Father, ha! she thought. She'd seen dogs with more paternal instincts than Brandon Montgomery exhibited toward his children. They certainly hadn't rushed to greet him when he'd come home from his trip. Rather, they'd huddled together on the sofa as if they were frightened to death of him.

She was going to make some changes around here, starting with getting those darling children to trust her. She would show them that not all adults were loud, overbearing brutes.

A knock on the door interrupted her silent diatribe. Heather was surprised to see Brandon Montgomery standing there in his impeccable, lintless navy suit and white starched shirt. He looked every bit as formidable as he had downstairs. Not one of his dark graying hairs was out of place. There wasn't a wrinkle in his necktie. It didn't take a genius to figure out who the twins had patterned themselves after.

"Mr. Montgomery, what a surprise." She didn't add an unpleasant one.

"Miss Martin." He nodded perfunctorily. "May I come in? I would like to speak to you about your new position."

She let out the breath she didn't know she'd been holding. "Then you've decided to allow me to remain as your governess? How generous."

He left the door open and entered, not bothering to comment on her sarcasm. "I see that you're all settled in." His gaze fell on the thin, lawn nightgown tossed carelessly at the foot of the bed, and his eyebrow arched ever so slightly. Heather felt her cheeks warm.

"I hope the room is satisfactory?"

"It's perfectly lovely. Nicer than any I've stayed in." Why on earth had she admitted that to him? He already thought she was some country bumpkin, and now she'd only helped to confirm his opinion.

"Really?" He glanced at the tiny violets on the wallpaper, noting that the color matched her eyes exactly. "I guess it does suit you." He'd never before noticed the pattern on the wallpaper. Perhaps it was new. He made a mental note to ask his mother about it.

Uncomfortable with his scrutiny, Heather cleared her throat. "You wanted to talk to me?"

"I think you should know, Miss Martin, that I only consented to your employment to please my mother. I have agreed to a three-month trial period, during which time I shall ascertain your suitability. I don't believe you are qualified for this position, nor do I believe that you are old enough for such responsibility."

Well, he certainly didn't mince words. "I assure you, Mr. Montgomery, that I'm adequately educated to instruct two six-year-olds. I've also had years of experience in raising children. My mother died when I was young, and the responsibility of raising my sisters fell to me."

"Raising a pair of siblings and raising two motherless children are hardly the same thing, Miss Martin. I don't see the correlation at all."

"I'm sure there's a lot you don't let yourself see, Mr. Montgomery. Like the fact that your children are afraid of you." His face grew florid, and Heather feared she had overstepped her bounds.

"I would hardly equate respect with fear, Miss Martin. My children are well aware of what is expected of them, of the proper behavior they should exhibit. I won't have you undermining all the good I've done these past six years."

Heather rolled her eyes heavenward. Those children were

starved for love and affection. Didn't this impossibly stubborn, inflexible man realize that? "I will do my best to teach the children proper behavior, Mr. Montgomery." *I will also do my best to teach them how to be children,* she added silently.

Her answer seemed to placate him for the moment. "As long as we see eye to eye, Miss Martin."

"I doubt that will ever be the case, Mr. Montgomery."

His lips tightened. "If you fail to carry out my wishes, Miss Martin, you will be tossed out on your attractive little backside."

Heather glanced up at Brandon Montgomery's self-satisfied smirk. Her violet eyes narrowed. "You and your children need me more than you know, Mr. Montgomery. And I'll thank you kindly to keep your eyes and your comments off my backside."

His laugh was anything but kind. "Don't worry, Miss Martin. There's nothing I've seen here that interests me. I assure you, my tastes run to the refined."

"Where I come from, Mr. Montgomery, a man as rude as you would never be considered refined. Refinement isn't something you attain just because you have money. It comes from in here." She tapped her finger on his chest, directly over his heart. "Unfortunately for you, Mr. Montgomery, the space usually occupied by a heart is vacant."

His eyes glowed like black coal. "You, Miss Martin, are treading on thin ice. Very thin ice."

She smiled, gesturing toward the window. "Why, how can that be, Mr. Montgomery? As you can see by the sunlight pouring in, we're still in the throes of summer."

With a sharp hiss of breath, Brandon stalked out of her room, slamming the door behind him.

Heather winced at the sound, then bit down hard on her lower lip. The battle lines had been drawn.

She'd won the first skirmish.

But who would win the war?

CHAPTER 4

"We're glad Father didn't make you leave, like he made all the others, Miss Martin," Jenny told Heather the following morning.

They were standing in an empty bedroom which had been converted into the schoolroom. Earlier this morning it had been made clear to Heather that she was expected to teach the children their sums and letters in accordance with Mr. Montgomery's strict edicts. Apparently he didn't put much faith in the public school system. Of course, he didn't put much faith in her abilities either, as he reminded her before leaving for *The Star*.

"I trust you are educated enough to see to the rudiments of my children's schooling, Miss Martin. I prefer them to use proper language, correct grammar, and neat penmanship."

His arrogance had galled her, especially in light of the fact that she'd gone out of her way to make it perfectly clear to him that she was suitably educated.

"I'll do my gall-darnedest best, Mr. Montgomery," she

had replied in her best cracker imitation. "But I ain't promisin' no miracles."

He had exited the schoolroom much the same way he had left her bedroom yesterday—with a scowl and a slam.

Jenny's tug on her skirts brought Heather's attention back to the present. "I'm glad, too, Jenny," she replied. "I hope you and Matt will like having me for a teacher and a friend."

Silent up until now, Matt scoffed. "A friend? How can you be our friend? You're all grown-up."

"Sometimes even grown-ups like to feel like children on the inside, Matt. Why, there are lots of things I still do that I learned when I was a child." Playing poker, for one. Her father had absolutely loved the game, and Heather and her sisters had become fairly proficient at winning the meager pots. Sometimes it was only a hair ribbon or a piece of licorice, but the victory was sweet all the same.

"Really, Miss Martin?" Jenny asked, wide-eyed. "Would you tell us what they are?"

Heather instructed the children to sit at their wooden desks, while she did the same. "First, I think you should know that all adults, including your father and grandma, started out as children, just like you."

Matt thought that over for a moment, then shook his head. "Grandmother may have, but I don't think Father did. Nope. I'm pretty sure he didn't."

Heather smiled affectionately. "Yes, he did, Matt. He's just forgotten how to reach the child still inside of him." They seemed totally in awe of that possibility. "All children possess magical qualities. They can pretend to be anything they want. They can use their imaginations to travel to far-off places and perform all kinds of exciting feats."

"Really, truly, Miss Martin?" they asked in unison.

"When I was little I used to dream of sailing the ocean, of being a fairy-tale princess who was captured by pirates, then rescued by a handsome prince."

"Yuk!" Matt scrunched up his nose in disgust. "That's girl stuff."

"It's not either, Matty," Jennifer admonished. "It's no different than you pretending to be a cavalry soldier fighting Indians."

The little boy's face reddened. "You promised not to tell!"

"It's perfectly all right to pretend, Matt. Everyone does it, even grown-ups," Heather quickly reassured him. But she could see by the determined set of his chin that he wasn't the least bit convinced.

"Father wouldn't like it. He says we need to be real . . . realistic and not trust in make-believe or fairy tales. You won't tell on me, will you, Miss Martin?"

Heather sighed and shook her head, wondering how on earth she was going to counter all the misinformed teachings these children had been subjected to over the past six years. Who in their right mind would tell children not to make-believe? That was like telling them that there was no Santa Claus.

Obviously for these children, there wasn't. There was only Scrooge. And Scrooge had taken the very distinct form of Brandon Montgomery. Her frown deepened.

"Would you children excuse me for just a moment? I'll be right back."

Though there were ample history and geography lesson books in the schoolroom from which she could instruct the children, there were no books to stimulate their imaginations or to read for pure enjoyment. Heather aimed to rectify that oversight immediately.

Hurrying to her room, she found just what she needed: a large volume of *Grimm's Fairy Tales.* Heather clutched the precious volume to her chest. It had been her favorite book as a child, her most treasured possession. She still read it frequently, though now her motives were strictly professional. She liked to illustrate the stories between the pages.

Back in the schoolroom, she held up the volume to show Jenny and Matt. "This book is filled with all sorts of magical stories. There's 'Little Red Riding Hood' and 'Jack and the Beanstalk.' " Her voice filled with animation. "I've had it ever since I was your age."

Two pair of brown eyes widened in disbelief. "Really, Miss Martin?" Jenny asked. "It must be ancient."

Heather laughed. "It's seen better days," she admitted, flipping through the dog-eared pages. "But time hasn't lessened its magic." And magic, she knew, was something these children needed in abundance.

Settling down on her chair, she began to read.

The soft knocks on the door brought a frown to Brandon's lips. He pulled his attention away from the editorial he was composing for Wednesday's evening edition of *The Star* and replied in an impatient voice, "Yes? What is it?"

As Heather looked at him tentatively from the doorway, his eyes widened in surprise. After the lethal stares she had directed at him throughout dinner, the last thing he expected was a visit from her. But then, who else could it have been? Everyone else in residence knew better than to disturb him while he worked.

Heather took a small step into the room, and Brandon's gaze flitted over her in an instant. She was still dressed in the unbecoming black dress that was two sizes too big for her and made her complexion look sallow. He supposed she might have an attractive figure hidden beneath it. Annoyed by the direction his thoughts had taken, he greeted her less than cordially.

"Come in, Miss Martin. Don't hover near the doorway. If you've got something to say, just spit it out. As you can see, I'm quite busy."

He tapped his pencil on the pile of papers in front of him, and again Heather thought he was the rudest, most arrogant man on the face of God's earth. She was tempted to "spit it out" all right, but she wasn't sure he would like where it landed. Taking a deep breath, she bit back the scathing retort on the tip of her tongue.

She needed something from her surly employer, and an insolent attitude wasn't going to get it for her. *For the children,* she amended. Wild horses couldn't have dragged her into Montgomery's private study, if it hadn't been for Jenny and Matt.

Her gaze roamed over the very masculine room, and she decided that it fit him to perfection. A solid stone fireplace hugged the wall behind his massive walnut desk, where he was seated in a forest-green leather wing chair studded with brass tacks. The drapes were heavy green velvet, so dark that they almost appeared black. The pine-paneled walls made the room seem much warmer than the man who occupied it.

"I'm sorry to disturb you, Mr. Montgomery, but I'd like to talk to you about the children. I assume you have time to discuss them." She couldn't help the note of sarcasm.

He waited till she'd taken the seat he proffered, then replied, "I'm a patient man, Miss Martin. If you have a legitimate subject to discuss about my children, then I have all the time in the world to listen." He folded his hands atop his desk and stared at her with an intensity that made her uncomfortable. His dark, fathomless eyes bored into her as if he could see into her soul and beyond.

Brushing off that fanciful notion, she said, "I've discovered after my first day in the schoolroom that the books you've selected for the children's instruction are not quite satisfactory. I need to purchase additional ones, as well as some other supplies."

His right eyebrow arched. "I'm quite surprised to hear that, Miss Martin. The math primers and readers I've purchased conform to what the public schools are using. I've even included G. P. Quackenbo's *American History for Schools,* and Swinton's *A Complete Course in Geography.* What is it that doesn't meet your criteria?"

"There are no storybooks, Mr. Montgomery. No works of fiction to expand the children's horizons." Before he could issue the rebuke she saw forming on his lips, she rushed ahead. "I'd also like some art supplies. Drawing paper and pencils, which the children can use to express themselves. There's more to life than learning correct grammar and doing mathematical equations, Mr. Montgomery. There's a whole world out there, and I feel the children are missing out by not experiencing more of it."

He leaned back in his chair, steepling his fingers in front of his chest while he studied her. Heather Martin was a damned attractive woman when her face lit up in animation. Her eyes flashed violet fire, and she seemed imbued with a vitality sadly lacking in most of the society women of his acquaintance. Of course, most of the women he knew were refined, genteel creatures, he reminded himself, quite unlike the farm-fresh girl before him. Still, there was something about her. . . .

"Before you say no, Mr. Montgomery, I just want you to know that Jenny and Matt are very bright, inquisitive children. Reading important works of literature"—there was no way she was going to tell him that her important works consisted of *Grimm's Fairy Tales* and *Mother Goose*—"can only increase their vocabulary. I'm sure you'll agree that the readers who avail themselves of your daily newspaper can attest to the same benefit."

Brandon had to keep himself from smiling. She was smart, this Heather Martin, and clever, too. The corners of his mouth twitched despite his best intentions. "Have you ever thought of running for politics, Miss Martin? I daresay you'd be quite good at it."

Heather's eyes widened a fraction. "Actually I hadn't considered it. But now that you mention it . . ."

Though he'd known her only a short time, the prospect of Heather in politics was a daunting one. No doubt she'd be zealous, demanding, and headstrong in trying to right the wrongs of the world. He shook his head at the horrifying thought.

"In order to spare our fair city that eventuality, Miss Martin, I'll allow you to purchase the items you need. I guess a few storybooks can't hurt. Though I insist that you include some proper works of fiction as well, like Shakespeare and Dickens."

"Oh, I intend to, Mr. Montgomery. Dickens's *Christmas*

Carol is one of my favorites." And the children could certainly benefit from hearing it.

In a very un-Scrooge-like gesture, he said, "Make me a list of everything you want. I'll have the items delivered tomorrow." Thinking the interview concluded, Brandon returned to his paperwork, but Heather didn't seem inclined to leave. After a moment he looked up again. "Was there something else you wanted?"

"Actually there is, Mr. Montgomery."

"I trust you don't desire a menagerie to teach the children about animal husbandry?"

She shook her head and smiled, wondering if the man might actually possess a sense of humor after all. It was unlikely, but still, there was a remote possibility.

"I'd like your permission to include Mary's son, Jack, in my schoolroom," Heather said. "He's a bright boy who's starved for learning. Mary tells me he's had some problems in public school, but I know with a little extra help, he can learn to read and write."

Brandon was clearly appalled by the revelation. "You mean he doesn't already know?" He was ashamed to admit that he'd never paid much attention to Mary-Margaret Feeney or her son. He'd always been too busy to bother with domestic problems and had turned such affairs over to his mother, who handled them quite capably.

But his conscience couldn't allow any child to go without an education. If there was one thing he wanted to change about the world, it was to wipe out illiteracy. There was no excuse for it, in this day and age.

Frowning, he said, "I don't understand why this wasn't brought to my attention before now. I wonder why I didn't notice the problem myself."

"Perhaps your attention was focused on more important matters, Mr. Montgomery." Heather stared meaningfully at the silver-framed photograph of the lovely woman on his desk: Cecelia Whitten, his fiancée.

Mary had told her all about the pretty blond socialite, and, Heather had to admit, Cecelia fairly reeked of refinement and money. She was just the type of woman who would appeal to Brandon Montgomery.

Brandon didn't miss where Heather's attention was focused or the implication of her words. His face reddened. "You may include Jack Feeney as one of your students. But my children must be your top priority. Is that understood?"

Heather rose to her feet, and she couldn't quite contain her triumphant smile. "Of course, Mr. Montgomery. You can be assured that I will do everything in my power to satisfy your demands."

Slowly Brandon's gaze fell from the softness of her lips to the soft swell of her breasts, and back up to her creamy complexion, now tinged pink in embarrassment. He looked into eyes widened in confusion, and his smile seemed to mirror the erotic thoughts rushing through his brain.

"I don't doubt it for a minute, Miss Martin. And perhaps someday we'll put it to the test."

Mary-Margaret grasped Heather's hand across the kitchen table and gave it a gentle squeeze. "I can't tell you how grateful I am that you've convinced Mr. Montgomery to allow Jack to attend school with the Montgomery children." She shook her head in disbelief. "You're truly a miracle worker, Heather."

Jack, who was totally emersed in his bowl of hot oatmeal, didn't seem to mirror his mother's opinion, and Heather smiled at that. Children were honest creatures, which is what she loved most about them. They never saw the need for pretense or the necessity to hide their feelings.

"I'm not sure Jack feels as charitably toward me as you do, Mary. Isn't that right, Jack?" She patted his shoulder and gave the disgruntled young man a wink. "Don't worry. You'll like my school. It won't be like the others you've attended."

His face lit. "You mean we won't have to do all those math problems?"

She smiled inwardly, readily able to empathize with Jack's

dislike of mathematics. Heather had always figured that if God had wanted folks to do mathematics, he'd have given them more than ten fingers and toes to count with. "Sorry. You'll still have to do mathematics, but I'll try to make learning more fun."

"I'm too dumb to learn, Miss Martin. I heard the teachers at the school I used to attend say that no amount of schooling could teach me a thing. The other kids used to laugh at me."

"Jack Feeney, I'm ashamed to hear you say such a thing," his mother admonished, shaking a finger at him. "Why, you're just as smart as all them other children. It just takes you a little bit longer to learn, that's all."

The look of defeat on Jack's face tore at Heather's heart. She wanted to march down to that school and shake some sense into those insensitive clods who called themselves teachers. "Your mother's right, Jack, and I'll make you a wager right now that you'll know how to write all the letters of the alphabet before the month is at an end."

"But there's only another week, Miss Martin!" His brow wrinkled in confusion. "Are you sure?" With his two front teeth missing, the word came out as *thor*.

"Of course I'm sure. Learning just needs to be made fun. When it is, children soak it up like a sponge."

The old Chinaman wandered over to the table, a look of rapt interest on his face. "Missy teach Woo?" he asked. "Woo want to be smart as spit."

Heather's eyes widened, and she glanced at Jack, who was grinning from ear to ear. "I don't see why not, Mr. Woo. If you'd like to join the children in learning to read and write English, then please do. I'll arrange for those lessons to be taught after lunch, so you'll have some free time to attend."

"Missy make Woo happy as fly on pile of dog shit."

Mary-Margaret choked on her coffee, and a brown stream of liquid flew across the table at Heather, who'd had the good sense to move out of its path and cover Jack's ears all at the same time.

When the color had receded from her cheeks, she shook her head at the Chinaman. "Lesson number one, Mr. Woo:

We don't use certain words in mixed company or in front of children. Dog . . ." she paused for emphasis, "is one of those words."

Mr. Woo hung his head in shame. "I sorry, missy. I feel worthless as tits on boar."

Heather rolled her eyes heavenward and wondered what she'd let herself in for.

Staring at the charcoal drawing she'd just finished of the two children, Heather smiled in satisfaction. She had captured the very essence of their personalities. Jenny had that look of wonderment on her face that always surfaced when she discovered something new and exciting in her textbooks.

And Matt, precious Matt, had a look of skepticism tempered with hope. He resembled his father a lot; both children did, in fact. But Heather was determined that they wouldn't resemble Brandon Montgomery in temperament or in personality.

The knock on the bedroom door made Heather look up, and she wondered who could be calling at this late hour. It was nearly ten o'clock, and by all rights she should have been in bed herself. She was already dressed in her nightgown, hardly appropriate attire for receiving callers.

What if it was Brandon Montgomery? She hadn't been able to get his veiled threat out of her mind. Okay, so maybe it wasn't a threat. But the way he'd said, "Perhaps someday we'll put it to the test," certainly sounded sordid.

"Heather, dear, it's me, Harriet. May I come in?"

Relief mingled with surprise, and Heather quickly snatched her wrapper off the bed and donned it before opening the door. "Mrs. Montgomery, this is a surprise."

Harriet's smile was full of apology. "I'm sorry to bother you, dear. But I saw your light beneath the door, and wondered if I might ask a favor of you."

"Of course. Please come in?"

Harriet entered, her eyes zeroing in on the sketch, which Heather suddenly realized she had left lying on the bed.

"Oh, my!" Harriet exclaimed, staring in wonder as she picked up the drawing. "This is absolutely marvelous. Did you draw this, Heather?"

Should she lie or tell the truth? Deciding to choose middle ground, she said, "It's a hobby of mine, Mrs. Montgomery."

"You're extremely talented, dear. Why, you've captured my grandchildren to perfection." Tears misted the old woman's eyes. "They are delightful children, aren't they?" she asked almost absently, continuing to stare at the picture.

"Yes. They've taken to schooling like fish to water, and, surprisingly, so has Jack. He's nearly mastered the alphabet, and in only a week." There was a great deal of pride reflected in Heather's voice.

"I heard about the wager you placed. A child will do a lot for the chance to eat an entire chocolate cake by himself. Actually most grown-ups would, too. I confess to having a real weakness when it comes to chocolate. But Mr. Woo rarely bakes desserts. Brandon thinks sweets will rot the children's teeth and take away their appetite for wholesome, nutritious food. But I'm glad to see that your method of motivating Jack Feeney has worked. You're very clever."

"I just dangled the carrot, or rather the cake, Mrs. Montgomery. Jack did the rest."

"Please, won't you call me Harriet? Mrs. Montgomery makes me feel every bit my sixty-four years."

Heather offered Harriet a seat in the cane-backed rocker by the fireplace. "You mentioned my doing you a favor, Mrs. . . . Harriet. What is it you wish?"

"My son's birthday is coming up, dear, and I was wondering if perhaps you'd care to assist me with the arrangements. It's going to be a tedious affair. He insists on inviting that fiancée of his, as well as her overbearing father." She sighed deeply. "I wanted a family party, but . . . well, it's Brandon's birthday, after all."

Heather didn't miss the look of distaste that crossed Harriet's face when she mentioned Brandon's fiancée, and she couldn't help wondering what had put it there. "Don't you and Cecelia Whitten get along? It's only natural for a man to want his fiancée to attend his birthday party."

"I suppose. But Cecelia is just . . . well, she's just Cecelia, is the kindest way to put it. To be perfectly honest, Heather, I don't believe Cecelia is right for Brandon. I think she'll make him a terrible wife, and I shudder to think the kind of mother she'll make for my grandchildren." She rubbed her arms as if chilled by the notion. "The girl is self-centered and horribly immature. After her shopping sprees, frivolous parties, and pretense at charity functions, I doubt she'll have the time to devote to Brandon's needs, let alone Jenny and Matt's.

"Also, Cecelia is too quick to agree with everything Brandon says. She never gainsays him anything. Everything is always, 'Yes, Brandon . . . of course, Brandon . . . anything you say, Brandon.' It's as if she doesn't have a mind of her own. Which, I'm sorry to say, she doesn't. Feathers hold more weight than her brains do."

Heather bit her lower lip to keep from laughing. "I've never met Miss Whitten, so I can't say whether or not I agree with your assessment of her. But I will say this: Your son is not an easy man to deal with. Perhaps Miss Whitten doesn't have the strength of will to argue with him. It does take a bit of energy to constantly do battle."

Harriet laughed. "You are truly delightful, Heather. And you've got backbone, which Cecelia sadly lacks. It's what I admired most about you the first time we met."

"Thank you. But what you call backbone, I just call good old-fashioned midwestern stubbornness. And I'm quite positive Mr. Montgomery wouldn't agree with your glowing compliment."

"My son wasn't always as difficult to deal with as he is now. Sadly, events which have transpired over the years have hardened him into a rigid individual. I swear, sometimes his spine's so stiff it just has to be made of steel."

"I'm sure it couldn't have been easy for him raising two small babies, even with your help."

"No," Harriet replied, barely above a whisper, her eyes

filling with sadness. "Lydia's defection and the subsequent divorce were the straws that broke the camel's back, so to speak. But it wasn't the only thing."

Harriet realized that she was rambling on about things Heather knew nothing about and smiled apologetically. "I'm sorry to go on like this, dear. Please forgive me. I don't usually discuss family matters, but I feel like you're already one of us. Which is a sneaky way of cajoling you into helping me with a family event."

"I'd be happy to help, Harriet. And in return, there's something you can do for me."

"Would this something have to do with my grandchildren?"

Heather smiled mischievously. "I'm planning some rather unorthodox activities over the next few weeks, and I'm going to need your support when Mr. Montgomery finds out about them."

The brown eyes widened. "Nothing dangerous, I hope?"

Heather shook her head and laughed. "Only if you consider fishing and trips to the zoo dangerous."

Rising to her feet, Harriet held out her hand to seal their bargain with a handshake. "My dear, I'll be only too happy to supply the support you need."

"And you'll see to it that my battered body is safely delivered back to Salina when Mr. Montgomery gets wind of my plans?"

Harriet chuckled, and replied with a delighted look on her face, "I'm happy to see that my son, despite his good intentions and the fact that I love him to distraction, has finally met his match. Hallelujah!"

CHAPTER 5

The blue gingham dress looked perfectly adorable on Jenny. Heather adjusted the puffed shoulders a bit, then stood back to admire her handiwork. She'd spent the better part of the past week sewing play clothes for the children, and she was pleased with the results.

"Father isn't going to like this dress, Miss Martin," Jenny told her, unable to mask the apprehension in her voice. "He's going to be awfully upset that Matt and I aren't dressed like a proper young lady and gentleman."

Matt's dark head bobbed in agreement as he stared down at the sturdy denim pants and blue checkered shirt he wore. "Father's going to be awfully mad."

"Do you children like the new clothes I've made for you?" They nodded enthusiastically, the concern melting off their faces, and Heather breathed a sigh of relief. "Well then, that's all that matters. You can't very well go on picnics and fishing trips dressed in velvets and lace." She patted their cheeks. "Don't worry about your papa; I'll take care of everything."

She spoke with far more bravado than she felt. Brandon Montgomery was going to be madder than a wet hen when he found out what she'd been up to. Ginghams and denims were definitely not his idea of refinement.

Oh well, she thought, sighing, she would just have to make sure that he didn't find out.

"Hey, you guys look pretty good," Jack said from the doorway of the schoolroom, his eyes widening as he took in the twins' informal appearance. "Does this mean we're still going fishing, Miss Martin?"

"Indeed it does, Jack. We're going to have an outdoor science lesson today. Since fish are aquatic animals, it'll be a wonderful chance to study them."

"But how are we going to catch them, Miss Martin?" Matt wanted to know. "We don't have any fishing poles."

"Yeah. And where are we going to fish? There's no rivers close by that I know of." Jack scratched his head.

"That's true," Heather admitted. "But there's that lovely ornamental fish pond . . ."

Jenny gasped, clearly appalled by the idea. "Father's fish pond! Oh, no, Miss Martin." She shook her head. "Those fish are Father's prized possessions. They're rare. He had them shipped all the way across the ocean from Ha . . . wa . . . Hawaii."

Herding the children to the door, Heather swallowed, trying not to appear nervous. How on earth was she supposed to have known that the pond was full of rare fish?

It couldn't be helped. She had promised the children they were going fishing, and she wasn't one to back away from a promise. Besides, they didn't have to eat the fish, they only had to catch them.

It was a glorious September day. The air was warm with just a hint of a breeze ruffling the treetops, and puffy white clouds danced across the azure sky.

With her knees drawn up under her chin, Heather tilted her face toward the sun while listening to the children's delighted screams as they played a game of tag. A smile touched her lips, but her heart ached for everything they'd missed in their short lifetimes.

Biting an apple, she glanced at the exquisitely landscaped rear yard. Like his house, his children, and everything else Brandon Montgomery possessed, it was neat and orderly. The bushes were sculpted into rounded forms, the trees perfectly trimmed. The lawn was cut so even that it looked as if someone had taken a ruler to it. And Heather was pretty sure that the pink blossoms on the rose bushes wouldn't dare wilt!

"Can we have our fishing lesson now, Miss Martin?" asked a breathless Jack, pulling up short in front of Heather. The twins followed, adding their own excited pleas.

Heather rose to her feet, tossed her apple core into the wicker picnic basket, and wiped her hands on her faded green calico skirt. "Mr. Woo and I made these makeshift poles for you," she explained, reaching for the rods. "He was kind enough to supply us with bamboo and fishing line." She handed one to each of the children. "Jack, fetch the worms, please."

Jenny made a face. "We're not going to have to touch those slimy things, are we, Miss Martin?"

"Quit being such a sissy, Jen." Jack shook his head. "Me and Matt are going to bait our own hooks. Aren't we, Matt?"

Looking just a bit queasy at the idea, but relishing the idea of being on an equal footing with the older boy, Matt nodded. "Sure we are. Jenny's just being a big baby."

Heather put her arm around the distraught little girl, who looked as if she was about to burst into tears. "Don't worry, honey. I'll help you bait your hook. I used to go fishing with my papa all the time."

Jenny sniffled a few times, her face brightening. "Really, Miss Martin? Your father took you fishing? Did he play other games with you, too?" There was a wistfulness to her questions that touched Heather. She almost hated to tell the child the truth.

"I grew up on a farm. There were more opportunities for my sisters and I to do things with our papa."

Heather could tell by the disturbed expression on the little girl's face that she was doing a quick comparison of her father and Heather's. Brandon came up painfully short.

Oh, Brandon, how could you have failed these children so miserably?

The time passed quickly as the children cast and recast their fishing lines into the small pond. Fortunately, none was skilled enough to catch anything, which was a relief to Heather. By the position of the sun, Heather judged it to be well past three o'clock. Not wanting to risk Brandon catching her and the children at play, she clapped her hands together, instructing them to pull in their lines.

A moment later, Jenny stomped her foot in frustration. "Mine's caught, Miss Martin." She pulled hard on her line to demonstrate. "What shall I do?"

Taking the bamboo pole from the vexed child, Heather yanked on it, trying to free the line. It wouldn't budge. "Botheration!" she said softly under her breath. There was no way she would leave any evidence behind for Brandon to find.

"I'm going to wade into the pond to release your line, Jenny. I need you to hold the pole tight while I go in."

Matt's eyes widened. "You're going to go into that fish pond, Miss Martin? What if one of the fish bites you?"

"Yeah," Jack said solemnly. "My pa was killed by a shark . . . eaten alive."

Rolling her eyes heavenward, Heather made a mental note to speak to Mary about Jack's overactive imagination, then proceeded to remove her shoes and stockings. "I haven't seen one shark this entire afternoon, Jack Feeney. And those fish don't look mean enough to bite," she assured Matt.

Lifting up her skirt, she brought it through her legs and tucked it into the waistband, as she had done a thousand times when she was a child.

Ezra Martin had been quite the fisherman in his day, and all three of his girls had been schooled in the art of angling.

Wading into the water, Heather was surprised to find it warm. Grabbing hold of Jenny's line, she followed it into the middle of the pond until she discovered the source of the problem: The hook was wedged beneath a sizable rock. As she bent over to free it, she heard Jenny's loud gasp.

"I'll just be another minute, Jenny. I've almost got this dang hook free. Don't worry."

"Well, isn't that just *dang* peachy, Miss Martin."

At the sound of the voice, Heather turned her head and her heart sank. Standing on the edge of the pond, hands on his hips, was Brandon Montgomery. He looked not at all pleased.

"I hope you have a suitable explanation for wading in my fish pond and my children being dressed like ragamuffins."

Trying to think of an explanation that might placate him, Heather pulled the hook free and tossed the line to Jenny. Then, as she opened her mouth to reply a long, snakelike creature clamped its sharp teeth around her ankle. A blood-curdling scream escaped her instead, and she plopped into the water with a splash, prompting the eel to swim away.

"My God!" Brandon said, sounding as concerned as he did irritated. Without a thought to the expensive suit and fine leather shoes he wore, he waded in after his errant governess, knowing that eels were not too particular when it came to their prey and would devour any animal food, living or dead.

Jenny started to cry, and Jack came forward to put his arm about her shoulder, doing his best to comfort her, while Matt continued to stare wide-eyed at the fish pond.

"Damn foolish woman!" Brandon said upon reaching Heather, who looked up at him with a sick smile.

"Thank you for coming to my rescue, Mr. Montgomery," she said as he lifted her effortlessly into his arms, making her feel as if she weighed no more than a feather.

"Father rescued Miss Martin, just like that prince in the fairy tale," Jenny said, staring in awe at her father, who had carried Heather to the edge of the pond and was now depositing her on the grass, frowning at the nasty bite on her ankle. "He's your hero, isn't he, Miss Martin?" she asked. "Father's like the handsome prince in the story you told us about."

Unable to look Brandon in the eye, Heather blushed furiously, nodding at the impressed child.

"What nonsense is this?" Brandon looked sternly at the three children, having no idea what they were talking about. "You children get back to the house. I'm sure you have schoolwork to finish."

"But Miss Martin said—"

"It's all right, Matt. We'll finish our science lesson some other time. You, Jenny, and Jack go up and study your geography. I'll be there shortly."

"Yes, Miss Martin," the three chorused.

Brandon scowled as he watched them depart. "I notice they don't argue when you tell them to do something."

"Perhaps it's not what you say but the way you say it, Mr. Montgomery," she replied, wincing as he touched her wound. The eel's bite hadn't drawn blood, but her ankle was beginning to swell.

Kneeling beside her on the grass, Brandon did a thorough examination of Heather's ankle and lower leg. Everywhere his fingers touched she experienced the strangest tingling sensations. When his hand made contact with the sensitive flesh at the back of her knee, she jerked in response.

Her reaction caused his eyebrow to arch. "There doesn't seem to be any damage to your extremities, other than the nasty bite. You're lucky it was only an eel that took a bite out of your ankle, Miss Martin. There used to be piranha in that pond. They would have loved nibbling on such sweet meat."

His gaze traveled upward to find the woman's blouse wet and nearly transparent. He sucked in his breath and had to restrain himself from staring at the two protruding dark nipples pressing against the clinging fabric. Swallowing with a great deal of difficulty, he tried to concentrate on her wound, but the sight of all that bare flesh was playing havoc with his usually disciplined nature.

Heather watched Brandon's gaze move up and down her bare legs and swallowed nervously at the odd look on his face. She'd read about that kind of look in *The Adventures of Tom Jones*. It was called lascivious, and it shocked her. She yanked down her dress. "Thank you for your assistance, Mr.

Montgomery. I'm sorry to have entered your fish pond without permission."

"I doubt that." He rose to his feet, pulling her up with him. "Most likely, the only thing you're sorry about is getting caught."

She smiled sheepishly. "That's true."

"Can you walk?"

"I think so."

Though her ankle was throbbing as wildly as her heart, she took a step forward and would have collapsed if Brandon hadn't been there to steady her. Without another word, he lifted her into his arms again, cradling her against his chest.

"Really, Mr. Montgomery, there's no need . . ."

"Just relax. I'll have you upstairs in no time."

Wrapping her arms about his neck, Heather wondered why it felt so right to be held in his arms. It was a secure feeling—a safe, warm feeing. Until his hand moved beneath her buttocks to hoist her to a more comfortable position. She let out a small little yelp.

"I'm not hurting you, am I, Miss Martin?" he asked solicitously.

She swallowed, shaking her head emphatically. "Oh no, Mr. Montgomery. I'm not the least bit disturbed." So why, she wondered, was her voice two octaves higher?

Brandon wished he could say as much. He'd thought the sight of Heather's bare legs as she bent over in the pond a test of his self-control. But holding her close, feeling her breasts pressed against his chest, smelling the wildflower scent of her hair, was just too much to ask of one man. He drew a ragged breath.

Good Lord, this woman was a handful . . . in more ways than one! She was chaos and disorder, the embodiment of disaster. And he was more determined than ever to get rid of her.

"Absolutely not! I won't hear of dismissing Heather, and I'm surprised that you would suggest it over such a trifling matter. In case you've conveniently forgotten, Brandon, you agreed to give her a three-month trial period. And we are nowhere near the end of that." Harriet glared at her son as he paced back and forth across the expansive office.

He rubbed the back of his neck. "Miss Martin is not going to make a suitable governess, just as I feared, Mother. I don't know why you're so insistent upon keeping her. Maybe it's the fact that you enjoy seeing your grandchildren running about like wild Indians."

"No harm was done, and they enjoyed their fishing experience immensely. They told me so themselves." In fact, they had fairly gushed with the story of their first real adventure, opening up to her in a way they'd never done before. Harriet had been touched, elated, and very grateful to Heather, for she knew that the young woman had been responsible for this change in her grandchildren.

"No doubt they enjoyed tormenting my exotic fish, too."

"Sit down, Brandon." Harriet pointed to the leather sofa in front of the window and sat beside him.

"What is it, Mother? Do you have more reasons why I shouldn't dismiss Miss Martin? Are you going to plead on her behalf?"

Seeing the implacable expression on her son's face, Harriet's voice filled with sadness. Why God had seen fit to change this once-smiling man into such a martinet, she would never know.

"You are rigid and quite demanding of everyone in this household, Brandon. I have kept my opinions to myself up until now, but my conscience begs me to speak, to try to reach the man I used to know."

His eyes widened in disbelief at her outburst. "What nonsense is this?"

"It isn't nonsense, son. It's sadness. I'm sad for you, for your children, and for what life has done to you. I never realized until now how deeply scarred you are. Why can't you let go of your past and live your life as it was meant to be lived? You have two beautiful children who need you, Brandon. You're on the brink of beginning a new marriage"—though she wasn't entirely certain he was over the first one—"and now you've finally found a governess who can bring a little pleasure and fun into your children's lives.

"You weren't raised in such a strict, suffocating manner, Brandon." She smiled in remembrance. "Why, you and your father used to spend—"

"I don't want to hear about him." An anguish look pinched his features. "He's dead. Leave him buried."

"Charles may be dead, but I don't think you've ever buried him, Brandon. He was weak. Alcohol made a good man into an insensible drunk, but that doesn't mean that by letting down your guard and enjoying life, you're going to turn out the same way. Why, I haven't seen you take a sip of wine or brandy since I've been living here. And you used to enjoy having wine with your meals."

Brandon rose to his feet, and there was a pained look on his face as he turned to stare out the window. At one time his father had been his idol. He'd been everything to Brandon—parent, friend, confidant, and the main reason Brandon had entered the newspaper business.

Charles Montgomery had been a distinguished small-town editor in his day. He had even won an award of distinction from *The Santa Clara Courier,* before his addiction to alcohol had ruined his reputation, his health, and finally his relationship with his son. He'd died of liver disease on Brandon's twentieth birthday, and Brandon had never forgiven him for his weakness.

"My father has nothing to do with me. He hasn't for years."

"Then why won't you let yourself be a true father to those children of yours? They love you. They want to please you. But I don't believe there is any pleasing you, Brandon. I used to think you were a man with vision, but I can see now that your sight is limited. You see only what you want."

With a spent sigh, Harriet stood up and crossed to the door. "You've become an inflexible, harsh individual with no room in your life for anything or anyone but your work. When was the last time you took a walk in the park, or played a game with the children?"

"My children are given everything that money can buy. They are perfectly happy and content. And if I'd thought that the mention of firing Miss Martin was going to bring on this diatribe, I would have kept my mouth shut."

Pausing by the door, Harriet looked back. "You're a good man, Brandon, but you're a foolish one. You may have given your children everything money can buy, but you haven't given them the one thing they desire above all else."

He snorted contemptuously. "What's that, Mother? Miss Martin?"

She shook her head sadly. "No, son. Your love." Harriet walked out of the room and closed the door softly behind her.

Taking a seat behind his desk, he stared down at the mound of work before him, but he couldn't concentrate. His mother's words kept pounding at him. She'd never said such things to him before. And the children had never behaved so badly before.

Before Heather Martin came.

She was to blame for the mess his life had become. She'd been there only a short time, but already his orderly world was turning topsy-turvy.

And he didn't like the way she made him feel when he was near her. He'd become cognizant of her fresh, clean scent, of the way her slight body felt nestled in his arms, how satiny soft her flesh felt beneath his hands. And those firm, lush . . .

He slammed his fist down on the desk. What the hell was wrong with him? He'd never carried on about Cecelia before, and she was his fiancée.

Cecelia. He stared at the photograph on his desk, at the serene smile hovering about her lips, and at her face, which bespoke refinement and breeding.

She was a trifle immature, and terribly spoiled, but with the proper guidance Cecelia would make a suitable wife for a man in his position. She was malleable. She could become the type of woman he wanted. Unlike Lydia, she had no desire for a career. She'd be perfectly content to stay at home and raise his children, to be the perfect hostess when the occasion called for it, and to warm his bed when his need dictated.

He knew that Cecelia wasn't passionate in nature; the few times he'd kissed and fondled her had proven that. Nor was she an overly demonstrative woman. When the time came for them to make love, she would be poised and contained, the perfect lady.

Brandon also knew with certainty that Heather would never be like that in bed. She'd be wild, untamed. That glorious auburn hair would fan out over the pillow, and she would cry out in ecstasy when he brought her to fulfillment. She would tell him over and over again how much she wanted him, needed him.

And she would control him.

Just as Lydia had controlled him with her feminine wiles and sweet smiles. Lydia had been lusty and wanton in bed. There'd been times when he'd had to stifle her cries of pleasure with his lips, for fear of waking up the rest of the household.

But Lydia had also played him false, pretending to love him, to desire nothing more than marriage and family. He'd eventually found out about the secret life she'd been leading. About her career on the stage.

She'd been an actress. A charlatan. All the time they'd been married, she had led another life. And because he'd been wrapped up in his own career, and had been trying to make a better life for them by getting his newspaper started, he'd never suspected a thing.

He'd castigated himself for a fool when that newspaper clipping of her stage performance showed up in the mail one morning. There'd even been a note attached, congratulating him on his wife's acting accomplishments: "Her finest performance," it said.

But it hadn't been.

No. Her finest performance had been in the role of Mrs. Brandon Montgomery. And Brandon had vowed that day that no woman would ever dupe him again. No woman would ever tear out his heart the way Lydia had.

Cecelia wouldn't. Which was why he wanted to marry her. Though he liked her, he didn't love her. Cecelia would never control his heart. And she would never completely satisfy him in bed.

But Heather would.

Just the thought of making love to her made him hard as a brick. He was losing control, he realized with disgust. And that was the one thing that he would never allow to happen to him again.

CHAPTER 6

"I just knew it was a bad omen when I looked out the window this morning and saw the rain." Harriet stared morosely out the kitchen window at the heavy downpour. Droplets bounced noisily off the slate roof, threatening to drown out her softly spoken words.

She turned to face Heather, who was still at the table eating a breakfast of buttered toast and coffee, and waved a piece of notepaper at her. "This note from Mr. Woo's niece confirms my worst fears. He's sick and won't be here today to prepare Brandon's birthday dinner."

A look of concern flashed across Heather's face. "I hope it's nothing serious."

"Mr. Woo is something of a hypochondriac, I'm afraid." Harriet sighed deeply. "He always manages to get sick when we have a dinner celebration or party. Though we haven't had many of those in the five and half years I've lived here," she added absently. "I think it makes him nervous to cook for large numbers of people. And he's not particularly fond of Gerald Whitten. But then, who is?"

66

Heather could not envision Brandon hosting a party where guests were expected to enjoy themselves. He didn't take pleasure in frivolity, as he'd so readily pointed out on numerous occasions.

Heather did a quick survey of the cupboards and larder. "It looks as if Mr. Woo has already laid in the supplies for tonight's dinner. I don't think it'll be that difficult for me to take over the cooking." She glanced at the stove.

The cast-iron range, which contained a large oven, grill, and hot plate with burners, was grander than anything she'd ever used before. Mr. Woo kept it blackened and polished, so that it sparkled like the copper pots hanging on the metal rack above it. Though she'd always cooked on a smoky old wood stove back in Kansas, Heather was sure she'd have no trouble using this one.

Harriet's face brightened. "Do you think you could, dear? That would be just marvelous. I'd hate to cancel the affair at this late date. Cecelia would be sure to remark on it if I did. The woman's a notorious gossip."

"I'm not a fancy cook, mind you. But I believe I can make a suitable meal for tonight's celebration, as well as a scrumptious chocolate cake." Heather's eyes twinkled as she caught the look of rapture on Harriet's face.

"Oh my! That would be just wonderful. Chocolate, you say?"

"Why don't you fetch Mary-Margaret? She can help prepare the vegetables and side dishes, while I get started on the cake. I believe she's still upstairs making the beds."

"All right. And I'll keep an eye on the children. It's Saturday, so they'll probably sleep for a while yet."

Harriet continued talking to herself as she hurried from the room, and Heather shook her head at the older woman's jittery mood. You'd think they were entertaining President and Mrs. Arthur, not Brandon's fiancée and his future father-in-law, Heather thought.

But she had to admit that the prospect of meeting Cecelia for the first time did make her a trifle anxious. She wasn't schooled in the niceties of polite society. Oh, she'd read Mrs.

Ward's book on the subject, *Sensible Etiquette of the Best Society,* and knew that it was impolite to leave a teaspoon in a coffee cup. But she didn't know how to make small talk, didn't possess a decent wardrobe, and wasn't quite certain which forks were used for what.

The place settings at the Montgomerys' dinner table had proven quite a challenge the first time she'd sat down to eat with them. There had been three forks to the left of the plate and more spoons than any practical person needed for one meal. If it hadn't been for the gentle nudge of Harriet's foot beneath the table, she'd never have gotten through it.

The only sensible thing for her to do this evening was to stay hidden in the kitchen. She'd have a good excuse with the dinner preparations and all. And it wasn't likely that Mr. Montgomery would want to introduce a mere governess to his guests anyway.

He'd already made it perfectly clear that he thought her totally inept as a governess. There was no way he would take the chance of her humiliating him in front of his guests with her country-bumpkin antics. But the idea did have merit, she thought, smiling wickedly to herself.

Heather was just putting the finishing touches of frosting on the birthday cake when Mary-Margaret burst through the doorway of the kitchen, looking fit to be tied.

"That bitch!" she said, pulling out a slat-backed chair and plopping down on it. "I feel like taking that birthday cake you're fixing and dumping the whole thing on top of Miss High-and-Mighty's head. I've never heard such rude things out of a guest's mouth before."

This wasn't the first time that Mary had stormed into the kitchen from the dining room in a fit of temper. It seemed Miss Whitten had made some nasty remarks about Heather's cooking, though everyone else, including Gerald Whitten, had commented on how good the food was.

There wasn't a lot you could do to destroy baked ham, candied yams, and green beans, Heather knew, though the cloverleaf rolls might not have been as fluffy or as pretty as Mr. Woo's, but then, she made excellent buttermilk biscuits.

"Don't worry about it, Mary. Miss Whitten is probably used to a fancy French chef preparing her meals. Her criticisms don't bother me."

"Well, they bother me. And me dear departed mother would have rolled over in her grave if she'd heard her. She used to tell me and my brothers: 'Like shoes and stockings, good manners must be worn at all times.'

"But Miss Whitten is just a snotty hoity-toity who enjoys making annoying comments when she should be keeping her mouth shut. And I know Mr. Montgomery doesn't like her causing problems at the dinner table. He hates disagreements at mealtimes."

When does he like them? Heather thought. Brandon Montgomery did not favor dissension of any kind, especially opinions directly opposed to his own.

"We'd best get back to the dining room, Heather. Miss Harriet asked that you bring in the cake while I serve the coffee."

A look of panic crossed Heather's face. "I can't go into the dining room dressed like this." She glanced down at her dress. "I look a fright." Though she was wearing one of her ready-made dresses, it was hardly appropriate for a fancy dinner party. Even little Jenny's dress was made of crimson velvet.

"Here, put this on over your dress," Mary said, handing Heather a clean white apron from the drawer. "With the black dress you've got on, you'll look just like a serving maid."

That's what I'm afraid of, Heather thought, picking up the sterling silver tray that held the birthday cake. Shoulders squared, she followed the outspoken maid into the dining room.

Mary had done a fine job of setting the table. An ecru lace cloth served as a lovely backdrop for the Waterford crystal and the blue and gold Limoges china, which matched the colors in the floral-print wallpaper. A pair of matching brass candelabra flanked a colorful arrangement of yellow roses and white chrysanthemums.

The Montgomerys and their guests were seated around the oval table. Brandon sat at one end, Harriet at the other, and the children occupied the seats directly opposite the Whittens.

Cecelia Whitten's dress was positively indecent. Her bosoms threatened to overflow the bodice of her blue satin evening gown, and Heather could see that the voluptuous woman would never have need of Egyptian Regulator Tea, which added graceful plumpness to flat-chested women. She'd never actually tried it herself, but Laurel, who despised being scantily endowed, had. Her sister's results had been inconclusive. At least Heather hadn't noticed any difference.

"Come in, Heather." Harriet urged the young woman forward with a wave of her hand. "The meal you prepared tonight was just wonderful. Wasn't it, Brandon?" She looked at her son for confirmation.

"A fine meal, Miss Martin. Thank you for filling in for Mr. Woo in his absence. I appreciate it."

Setting the cake on the table before him, Heather smiled softly, pleased by the compliment. "Happy birthday, Mr. Montgomery." Beneath lowered lashes she caught the malevolent stare of Cecelia and the leer of her father, and felt annoyed by both.

"Well, I do hope that cake isn't as greasy as the ham," Cecelia remarked, sniffing the air like a preening feline. "No doubt my stomach will be suffering the effects of all that grease for days to come."

"Perhaps you could try taking Hostetter's Celebrated Stomach Bitters, Miss Whitten," Heather offered in a solicitous fashion. "My father swore by them."

Brandon frowned. Hostetter's Bitters were nearly 50 percent alcohol. Had Miss Martin's father suffered the same addiction as Charles Montgomery? Brandon was aware that with Kansas prohibiting the sale of liquor two years before, many went to great lengths to satisfy their craving for drink, including the purchase and consumption of patent medicines.

At Heather's suggestion, Cecelia stiffened in her seat. "Really, Brandon! Since when do you allow your servants to converse with the guests? My Wanda would never dream of doing such a thing. It's highly improper."

Thoroughly humiliated, Heather began to back away from the table, but Harriet reached out and gently caught her wrist, staying her departure. "Miss Martin is not a mere servant, Cecelia. She's governess to the children, and we think of her as part of the family, don't we, Brandon?"

Brandon noticed at once how his mother was staring daggers at his fiancée and decided that this was not the time or the place for a confrontation. "That is true, Mother. Miss Martin is the governess, not a servant."

"My mistake," Cecelia said, though her snide smile belied anything resembling an apology. "How was I to know? The way she's dressed in that hideous gown, I just assumed she was one of the maids."

Color crept into Heather's cheeks as she listened to Cecelia malign her as if she weren't there. Silently she counted to ten. "If you'll excuse me, I need to get back to the kitchen."

"Why not join us, Miss Martin?" Gerald asked, his gaze lingering over the soft swells of Heather's bosoms, a gesture that did not go unnoticed by Brandon, whose frown deepened.

"Please, Miss Martin," Jenny begged, patting the chair next to her. "Come sit by me and Matt."

"Children should be seen and not heard," Cecelia remarked, staring at the children so intently that Matt lowered his gaze to his plate, finding renewed interest in his yams as he tried to be inconspicuous.

"Do join us, Miss Martin," Brandon said. "I'm sure whatever chores await you in the kitchen can be delayed a little while longer."

The fierce look on Cecelia's face filled Heather with a great deal of satisfaction. "Thank you, Mr. Montgomery." As she took the seat Jenny had offered, she winked at Harriet. "I admit to having a real weakness for chocolate. My sisters and I didn't get to indulge ourselves much on the farm."

"You were raised on a farm, Miss Martin?" Gerald inquired. Then he rushed on, not giving her a chance to respond. "So was I. Born and raised in Missouri. But that was a long time ago. Poverty didn't agree with me, so I came west to make my fortune. Did a bang-up job of it, if I say so myself."

Cecelia beamed at her father. "Father is a very successful businessman. He has shipping and manufacturing interests all over the city."

"All over the world," he corrected in a booming voice. "And speaking of business, Brandon, what do you think of this Labor Day holiday coming up on Monday? It's just another way for the government to pick our pockets, if you ask me. Next they'll be expecting us to give paid vacations and sick leave."

"I don't think giving employees a paid day off is going to bankrupt any of us, Gerald. Besides, it's the law now, and there's nothing to be done about it."

"Does your family still live on the farm, Miss Martin?" Cecelia asked. She wasn't really interested in anything having to do with the attractive governess, but she hated it when her father and Brandon discussed business and moved the center of attention away from herself. "I guess that would explain your obvious lack of polish."

"My parents are dead," Heather said, ignoring the insult. "Our farm has been sold, and my sisters have both left Kansas to pursue other interests." At least she hoped Rose Elizabeth had left. She hadn't had a letter from either of her sisters, though she'd written to Miss Caffrey's School several times.

Brandon listened intently, realizing that he didn't know anything of a personal nature relating to Heather Martin. His mother had done the initial interview and had filled him in on only the barest of details. "What brought you to San Francisco, Miss Martin?" he asked. "It's an odd choice for a farm girl from Kansas, is it not?"

Though she was dying to impress Brandon with her abilities as an artist, she didn't think he would appreciate knowing that she had secured employment with him under false pretenses. "I've always wanted to see the ocean, Mr. Montgomery. After living in the middle of a Kansas farm surrounded by nothing but wheat, I thought San Francisco would be a nice change of pace."

"And you probably thought you'd meet your prince charming here, too," Cecelia remarked.

"Miss Martin's prince . . ." Jenny began. But whatever else Jenny was about to blurt was stifled by the gentle pressure Heather exerted on the child's chubby knee.

"You shouldn't have any trouble finding a husband," Cecelia went on as if no one else had spoken. "I've noticed the men here aren't too choosy about whom they marry."

Looking first at Cecelia, then at Brandon, Heather nodded. "I've noticed that too." Cecelia seemed oblivious to the insult, but Heather thought she saw the corners of Brandon's mouth twitch. She added, "I don't believe marriage is the only choice for a woman."

Heather decided she must have been mistaken about Brandon's previous amused reaction. Now he was glaring at her so fiercely that his nostrils were actually flaring, and she half expected smoke to pour out of them at any moment.

"Heather's right. Women should have a mind of their own in this day and age." Harriet peered directly at Cecelia, ignoring her son's rude look. "Look at the strides women have made in medicine and business. Why, I recently read that a female attorney by the name of Laura Gordon has been allowed to practice before the Supreme Court."

Cecelia gasped. "I'm shocked by your attitude, Mrs. Montgomery. I would be lost without a man in my life. God put woman on this earth to please man." She smiled softly at Brandon, patting his cheek. "And I like to think that I please Brandon to no end."

Gerald beamed proudly at his daughter, nodding, obviously in concurrence with her beliefs. Beliefs that he, no doubt, had taught her himself. Heather exchanged an appalled glance with Harriet, then turned to stare down the table at Brandon, whose face was turning red.

"I'm not feeling too well, Miss Martin," Matt confessed, patting his stomach and diverting the attention away from his father, much to Brandon's relief.

"Me neither," Jenny added. "My face feels all hot."

Placing her palm on each of the children's foreheads, Heather grew immediately concerned. Their skin was very hot to the touch.

"The little gluttons probably had too much birthday cake," Cecelia remarked, and Brandon cast her a quelling look.

"The children are burning up with fever, Mr. Montgomery. I need to get them up to bed immediately."

"Oh, my goodness!" Harriet's face became a mask of worry.

"I'll help you, Miss Martin." Brandon pushed back his chair, and his mother smiled with approval.

"Brandon!" Cecelia wailed. "What about us? We came over to celebrate your birthday. You can hardly leave in the middle of the festivities. We haven't opened presents yet."

"I apologize for the inconvenience, but my children have taken ill."

Gerald cast his daughter a reproving look. "Of course, Brandon, my boy. Think nothing of it. Your children should take first priority. My Cece always did."

That was as obvious as the bulbous nose on Gerald Whitten's bearded face, Heather thought, gathering Jenny into her arms, while Brandon did the same with Matt.

His "Cece" was a spoiled brat! And every bit as annoying as Harriet had said.

Spare the rod and spoil the child, Heather thought, recalling her mother's favorite adage, usually repeated before Heather or one of her sisters received a whipping. She wished she could take a rod to Cecelia Whitten. If there was ever anyone that needed it, it was that irksome, immature woman!

• • •

"Should I call the doctor, Miss Martin?"

Heather glanced over her shoulder to find Brandon standing at the foot of the bed, staring helplessly down at his daughter, a distraught look on his face. Matt, asleep in the adjoining bed, didn't stir, but Jenny remained awake and fretful.

"I think I'm going to be sick, Miss Martin," the frightened child said, slapping her hand over her mouth.

"Quick, Mr. Montgomery—hand me the basin!"

Brandon thrust the basin into Heather's outstretched hand just in time to catch the first eruption of Jenny's stomach. He looked horrified and as sick as his daughter.

"Haven't you ever seen anyone vomit before, Mr. Montgomery?" she asked, amazed.

"I . . ." He shook his head. "It makes me sick to watch."

"Then turn around and face the wall. I don't have time to clean up after both of you."

She glanced over her shoulder, surprised to find that he had followed her instructions. The thought that a grown man who ran a successful newspaper business could not stand something as trivial as vomit almost brought a smile to her lips.

"I feel better now, Miss Martin," Jenny said. It could as easily have been her father who had spoken, his look of relief was so great.

Setting the basin down on the floor, Heather adjusted the child's bedding. "Close your eyes and go to sleep, honey. I'll wait here until you do."

"I'm not going to die, am I, Miss Martin? I sure feel like I could."

Brushing back the strands of hair from Jenny's forehead, Heather said, "No, honey. You're going to be just fine. Most likely the cake didn't agree with you. Or maybe Miss Whitten was right—maybe the food was too greasy."

"The food was just fine. And don't believe anyone who says differently," Brandon said in an authoritative voice as he approached the bed, making Heather's eyes widen in surprise. He patted his daughter's head. "Miss Martin is going to take good care of you, Jenny."

Jenny reached out to touch his hand, and a strange look passed over his face that almost brought tears to Heather's eyes. It was a look of surprise, and she guessed that Brandon wasn't used to having his children reach out to him like this.

"Will you sit by my bed until I fall asleep, Father?" She brought his hand to her face, rubbing it against her cheek.

"Of course I will, if Miss Martin says it's all right."

Heather nodded, and Brandon lowered himself onto the mattress, looking ill at ease and out of place beside his daughter.

After a few minutes, Jenny's even breathing indicated that she had fallen asleep.

"Perhaps I should notify the doctor, Miss Martin. Neither of the children looks very well. It might be more than indigestion."

"Why don't we wait until morning to decide. If their fevers haven't subsided by then, we should definitely call a doctor. I've spent many a night nursing my sisters and father, but I don't profess to know all that much about medicine, Mr. Montgomery."

He nodded, seeming to think her decision a wise one, and rose to his feet. "Since my daughter is finally asleep, I will bid you good night, Miss Martin. But first I would like to thank you again for your efforts this evening."

"There's no need to thank me, Mr. Montgomery. I only did what anyone would do faced with similar circumstances."

Brandon didn't think it at all likely that Cecelia would have gone out of her way to volunteer to cook, and to care for his sick children, but he refrained from saying so. "I will compensate you for your efforts in your next check, Miss Martin."

"That won't be necessary. But if you truly want to repay me, you can do so by calling me Heather. I would prefer it."

"Very well. And you may call me Brandon, if you like. Since we are living in the same house . . ."

The room seemed to close in around Heather as she stared at the enigmatic expression on Brandon's face. He would be a terrific poker player, she thought. There was no telling what he was thinking. Unlike him, her thoughts were reflected all over her face; the heat was already creeping into her cheeks. She was grateful for the darkness of the room.

What was it about this man that put her on edge? The mere mention of "living in the same house" had started her imagination soaring in directions it had no right to soar. Brandon Montgomery was betrothed to another woman. They were total opposites in personality and nature. And they'd hardly spoken a civil word to each other since she'd arrived.

Still, there was something about him that attracted her. He was the most complex man she'd ever met. The hardest, certainly the most cynical. And yet she sensed that deep beneath all that hardness lay a warm heart and a vulnerable soul.

When he'd looked at his children tonight with love and concern, Brandon had almost appeared to be a real father.

What had made him shut himself off from the world? From his children? she wondered. In her heart, Heather knew that she had no right to interfere.

But she had a soft spot for lost causes and puppy dogs. And Brandon Montgomery was the saddest creature she'd come across in quite some time.

CHAPTER 7

Heather trudged up the stairs, carrying a tray laden with bowls of oatmeal and two large glasses of water. She'd done a lot of trudging these past few days, ever since Dr. Lipscom had diagnosed Jenny and Matt's illness as measles.

Measles! She should have known, she thought, shaking her head at her stupidity. All three of the Martin sisters had succumbed to the disease at about the same age as the Montgomery children were now.

It was a childhood disease few children had the good fortune to escape, and apparently Jack Feeney was no exception. Mary-Margaret had sent word that her son was sick and that she wouldn't be in to work this morning.

One by one the troops were abandoning ship, and just when she needed them most. Upon hearing of the children's illness, Mr. Woo had sent word that he wouldn't enter a house filled with pestilence. Woo's niece had written a note stating as much, using the dictionary Heather had loaned him only last week.

Even Harriet had deserted her. The poor woman had confessed to never having had the disease and had taken up residence at the elegant Palace Hotel, promising to return when the "coast was clear."

That left only her and Brandon to care for the children. And having Brandon for help was like having no help at all. He was absolutely useless. He couldn't cook, he didn't know how to change beds, and his efforts at entertaining the twins were proving dismal. Last evening he'd spent the better part of an hour reading the editorial from his newspaper to them. The man was not only useless, he was hopeless!

When she entered the sickroom, Heather found Jenny and Matt reading quietly in their beds. They looked up from their books and smiled happily at her, though the effort was piteous. Their little faces were still puffy and blotched with red spots, but thankfully their fevers had finally subsided.

"Hello, Miss Martin," Jenny said between coughs. "I'm feeling much better today. But I've got red spots all over me, and they itch something terrible." She scratched her belly to prove her point.

"Me too. Having the *missiles* is no fun," Matt said.

"You're not to scratch, no matter how much you itch," Heather cautioned. "It'll only make it worse. I'll bring up calamine lotion later and dab it all over you. That'll help the itching some. And perhaps in a day or two you can have a bath in saleratus." She made a mental note to check the kitchen cupboard for a box of Arm and Hammer Baking Soda.

"Where's Father? Is he going to read to us again?" Matt scrunched up his face at the memory of Brandon's last effort to amuse them. "Do you think he might read us a storybook this time, instead of the newspaper, Miss Martin?"

"Your father has gone to work. I don't expect him home until later this afternoon. But if you're patient and allow me to get my chores done, I'll come back and read you a story. Now eat your breakfast." She placed the tray of food on the table between the two beds. "Dr. Lipscom said your fever was down, so now all we have to worry about is getting you measle-free." From the looks of their rashes, that would take several more days.

"How much longer are we going to have to stay in bed?" Matt glanced longingly at the window, though the drapes had been drawn against the sunlight to protect their sensitive eyes. "I hate being sick."

"I'm afraid that until your eruptions dry up, you're both contagious. Jack's sick, too. And most likely he's going to come down with the measles same as you two. So it's very important that you remain in this room and in your beds. Is that understood?"

The children nodded, and Heather breathed a sigh of relief, for she didn't have the energy to argue. She'd forgotten how trying and tiring it was to care for sick children—children, who, even when they were sick, had far more energy than she did.

Already burdened with the cooking, the laundry, and the housecleaning, Heather didn't think she could deal with one more crisis. But that evening her resolve was tested by yet another dilemma.

Glancing over her shoulder as the kitchen door swung open, Heather caught sight of Brandon and knew immediately that something was wrong. His eyes were red and watery, and he was dabbing at his nose with his handkerchief.

Moving away from the sink, she dried her hands on her apron and said in a tone that brooked no refusal, "Brandon, come in here and sit down. You look as if you're about to fall." She helped him into the chair.

"It's probably just a cold. It came upon me suddenly this afternoon. How are the children?" he asked, wiping his nose again.

She placed the palm of her hand on his forehead, ignoring the way his eyes widened at the gesture. It was just as she suspected: Brandon was feverish. "Have you ever had the measles?"

Looking at her as if she were crazed, Brandon nodded. "Of

course. I'm sure I did. I must have had them. Besides, grown men do not come down with children's maladies."

She crossed her arms over her chest. "Want to bet?"

Her question made him look even sicker. "What are you saying?"

"I'm saying that you're going to go upstairs and get into bed. I'm saying that I'm ninety-nine percent sure you have the measles."

"Impossible."

"Mr. Montgomery, I already have my hands full with the care of your children. I will not tolerate your stubbornness, nor will I put up with any of your arguments. When you're feeling better, and I have more time, perhaps we'll discuss this. Until then, I want you to go upstairs. I'll be up in a moment to check on you."

Shaking his head, Brandon cast her a disagreeable look and rose to his feet. He said, "I do not . . ." then promptly collapsed onto the floor.

It was only by the grace of God that he didn't crack his thick, obstinate skull, Heather thought ungraciously.

Laboring every step, Heather finally managed to haul Brandon up the stairs and deposit his large, heavy body onto his bed. She was breathing rapidly from the exertion, and she was drenched in sweat, but at least they had made it.

Now all she had to do was get him undressed and under the the covers. She frowned at the prospect. She had performed that task countless times with her father when he was ill, but the thought of stripping Brandon naked was downright unsettling. Her mouth was suddenly as dry as parched soil, and she felt a large lump in her throat. Staring down at his long, masculine form, she took a deep breath and set to her task.

As Heather stared down at the naked man, a strange, tingly feeling formed in the pit of her stomach. It was as if she had a hundred butterfly wings flapping wildly inside of her. Her face suddenly felt hot, and she knew it wasn't caused by any fever.

As her gaze traveled over Brandon's muscular body, her

eyes widened. Who would have guessed that beneath all those somber business suits was such a stunning man? A man so powerfully built it made her throat ache.

His chest was muscular and lightly covered with dark hairs. Tentatively she reached out to touch them. They were soft as a downy chick.

Climbing onto the wide, mahogany-framed bed, she straddled his body, well aware of the impropriety, but telling herself that she was only doing her Christian duty, and grasped him under the arms, trying to pull him onto the pillows. It took several big tugs, but she finally managed to get him situated. The bulging biceps beneath her hands made her throat tighten again.

Sitting at the side of the bed, her eyes wandered shamelessly to the area between his legs, and she gasped aloud. His male member was enormous, even in a state of nonarousal! She had the strangest urge to touch it, to see if it was as velvety soft as it looked, but she didn't.

Instead, she jumped up and lightly slapped the sides of her face, silently admonishing herself for her audaciousness. She felt her cheeks glowing like a flat iron.

What would Pastor Bergman say about her behavior if he knew? The rheumatoid old clergyman back in Kansas would no doubt give an entire Sunday sermon directed at her moral turpitude and lack of restraint.

Knowing there was nothing more she could do for Brandon at the moment, Heather pulled the bedcovers up to his chin, blocking out the tantalizing sight of his nakedness. At the windows, she pulled the drapes shut against the waning twilight, then headed for the door.

Jenny and Matt would be waiting for their supper and another bedtime story. She would need to get them settled down for the night before she could concentrate her efforts on their father.

The thought of spending hours on end in close proximity with Brandon Montgomery filled her with unease. Gazing back at his sleeping form, a feeling of foreboding washed over her. For some strange, inexplicable reason, she felt her life had just been subtly altered, but she had no explanation as to why.

"Water."

Heather came instantly awake at the sound of Brandon's hoarse cry and glanced toward the window. It was pitch black out. From her seat on the rocker, she leaned toward the nightstand and turned up the lamp just a bit, knowing that too much light would bother Brandon's sensitive eyes. Filling a glass with water from the pitcher resting there, she brought it to his lips and supported the back of his head while he drank.

"Not too much at first," she cautioned when he tried to drink too greedily. "You'll make yourself ill."

"I'm already ill," he croaked. "And I'm hot." He tried to throw off the covers, but Heather, who knew what lay beneath them, grabbed the blanket before he could expose himself.

"The fever's got a grip on you. It'll most likely get worse before it gets better." She placed a cooling hand on his forehead and discovered that he was burning up. "I'll get a damp cloth."

"No!" he said when she tried to remove her hand. He clutched at it, keeping it firmly in place with his own. "Feels good."

She smiled to herself, thinking that no matter how old or large the man, they were really all children at heart. "I suspect you'll have a rash in three or four days."

He groaned. "I don't have time to be sick. I've got a newspaper to run."

"Ssh. Your paper will be fine without you for a while. Just concentrate on getting better. The measles have to run their course."

"How long?"

"I'd say two, maybe three weeks, depending on how good a patient you are." Childhood diseases were oftentimes harder on adults. Dangerous complications could develop—

pneumonia, for one. But there was no need to burden him with that knowledge just yet.

He groaned again. "You shouldn't be in here. You could get sick."

Absently her hand trailed to his cheek, which was lightly stubbled with a day's growth of beard, and she caressed it, gentling her voice as if she were talking to a small child. "I've already had the measles. Once you've had them, you can't get them again."

He nodded, then closed his eyes. "Tired."

"Go to sleep. I'll be close by if you need me."

She was surprised by the satisfied sigh that escaped his lips before he drifted back to sleep.

Distinct, mournful cries jarred Heather into wakefulness once again, and she bounded from her bed, not bothering to don her wrapper as she headed for the hallway.

The children were her first thought, and she rushed to their room. Both were sound asleep.

The crying sounds continued, and she hurried down the hall to Brandon's room to find him thrashing wildly on the bed in the throes of some hideous nightmare.

"Lydia!" he called out when she approached the bed. He held out his arms, seeing her, but not really knowing who she was.

"Ssh, Brandon," she said soothingly and placed a comforting hand on his forehead. He was burning up with fever. "It's the fever. You must lie down and rest."

He quieted for a moment, then grabbed on to her shoulders, pulling her toward him. "Why did you do it, Lydia? Why? We could have had a good life, you and I."

Heather's heart ached at the anguish she saw on his face, at the remnants of tears streaking across his cheeks. She had left the lamp burning when she went to bed; now she wished she hadn't. His pain reflected a soul wrapped in torment.

Smoothing the deep crease between his eyes with her

thumb, she wondered what had happened between Brandon and his wife. Something horrible, judging by his sorrow.

"Brandon, it's me, I've brought you some water."

He didn't release her, but pulled her down on top of him. The instant her breasts touched his chest, Heather's nipples hardened, despite her best intentions to remain perfectly detached.

In the space of a moment she told herself that this man was her patient, that he was sick, that he didn't know who she was or what he was doing. But the feel of her breasts touching his rock-hard chest made her painfully aware of the fact that she was a woman—a woman who had never felt this way before.

"Lydia, kiss me. Don't play coy. You know how good it is between us."

Heather resisted the pull of his plea, the tug of his arms, but at the moment she was too weak both physically and emotionally to offer more than a token struggle. Telling herself that the best thing she could do was to go along with him, she placed her lips against Brandon's, allowing him access to her very anxious, inquisitive mouth.

"Oh, my darling," he whispered. "It's been so long." He thrust his tongue into her mouth, tasting and teasing, devouring the honey he found, while his fingers slid up and down her back, sending currents of desire racing through her.

Heather, who'd never been kissed before, was at first appalled by the invasion of Brandon's tongue. But as he continued to probe, his mouth suckling hers, her blood heated to a fevered pitch, and she felt as if liquid fire poured through her veins.

His member hardened beneath her, and the realization that he was as excited as she filled her with a heady elation. Her womanhood pressed down on the hardened bulge, and she couldn't resist the compelling urge to rub against him. It felt so incredibly good, so very right, and she wished that the covers separating their bodies would somehow melt away.

"I knew you wanted it, darling." He reached for the front

of her nightgown, tearing it open in one deft movement and freeing her breasts.

Heather knew a moment of panic, but then he began to caress her breasts, and the sheer ecstasy of it took away all thought of resistance. She moaned in pleasure.

"You've got such beautiful breasts," he said, and she felt warmed by the praise. "I remember how sensitive your nipples are." He pulled at the hardened nubs with his fingers. "They're so large, so very sweet." With a strength she didn't know he possessed, he pulled her up until her breasts were positioned next to his mouth, and he began to suckle.

Heather's body surged at the intimacy. She reveled in it, loving the way his tongue caressed her sensitive, swollen nipples. Ripples of pleasure darted through her, traveling all the way down to the core of her femininity.

Her torn nightgown hung about her waist in tatters, revealing every glorious naked inch of her, and Brandon couldn't remember anyone quite so lovely or so giving. Somewhere in the fogged recesses of his mind, he sensed that something wasn't quite right, but he was too wrapped up in his pleasure to take much notice of it.

Heather, caught up in her own newly found passion, didn't notice when their positions changed. She now found herself lying beneath Brandon's body. He was thoroughly exploring her breasts with his tongue, while his hands moved down to cup the swollen area between her thighs.

The touch of his hands against her most private of areas made Heather gasp both in pleasure and shock at the exquisite sensations he created. It also made her realize with frightful clarity that what she was doing was wrong.

Bolting upright, she pushed against his chest, rolling out of his reach.

"Darling, what's wrong?"

She stared at the passion she saw burning in his eyes and shook her head in disbelief. *Oh, God! What have I done? I practically allowed Brandon Montgomery to make love to me. No! Not to me. He thought he was making love to his ex-wife. Oh, God! Oh, God!*

On her feet, she pulled the edges of her nightgown together and reached for the glass of water on the nightstand. When he grabbed for her, she threw the water in his face. It had the desired sobering effect.

"What?" Brandon shook his head, looking stunned, dazed, as if just waking up from a wonderful dream or hideous nightmare.

"You were delirious," she explained, unsure if he knew what she was saying or what they'd been doing. "I had to do it." Fortunately, it looked as if his fever had peaked and receded and the dousing hadn't done him any real harm.

He blinked several times, as if trying to focus, then zeroed in on the torn nightgown, the way she was holding the frayed edges of it together. Like a curtain lifting, his thoughts cleared.

"Miss Martin? Are you all right? Did I hurt you in any way?" She was trembling, and there was a distraught look on her face. Shocked, he realized he couldn't remember what he had done.

With one hand still clutching her nightgown, she pushed him back down onto the pillow. "I'm fine. You . . . you just got a little carried away." *We both did.* "No harm done. I believe you were having a nightmare, probably induced by your high fever."

"But your nightgown . . ." He looked at her again, and he could see the outline of two dark, very prominent nipples. He tried to swallow but his mouth was cotton dry.

She colored fiercely. "I was trying to restrain you. You probably thought I was out to do you harm, so you . . . you came at me. I'm perfectly all right. There was no harm done."

"I'm terribly sorry. I didn't realize. . . ."

"It wasn't your fault; it was mine. I shouldn't have put myself in such a compromising position." That was the understatement of the century!

Flashes of memory darted through Brandon's mind. Plump breasts and pebble-hard nipples. Moans of passion.

He shook his head. He'd been dreaming. That was the only possible explanation. Wasn't it?

"I apologize if my behavior was anything but gentlemanly."

With her free hand, she removed a towel from the washstand and mopped at the droplets of water on his face, at the sweat beading on his forehead. "I must go to my room and change."

"Is my fever gone? I feel a little better."

She placed her hand against his forehead, then touched his lips with her fingertips; he was slightly cooler, but still warmer than normal. But then, she already knew that from a much closer observation. "It's down for now, but it will probably go up again. The fever lasts a few days, until the rash develops."

"I'm not sure I can take another few days of what I've just experienced. It seemed so real. I . . ." An erotic smile touched his lips, making Heather's cheeks burn anew. "It seemed so real," he repeated in wonder.

"Yes, well . . ." She swallowed. "I'd best go and change." She moved away from the bed toward the window, and the moonlight streaming in silhouetted her naked body beneath the thin gown she wore.

At the sight, Brandon felt his member stiffen, and clearly remembered his hands caressing those firm, lush breasts, and the way her woman's mound had throbbed wildly beneath his fingers. He moaned in agony.

Jesus! Another dream like that could kill him.

And what the hell was he doing dreaming about Heather Martin anyway?

The following morning, having spent a miserable night tossing and turning, and dreaming of things she had absolutely no moral right to dream about, Heather went through the motions of preparing breakfast as if she were dazed.

She dreaded the prospect of facing Brandon. She had

hardly been able to look at herself in the mirror, and she prayed fervently that everything that had transpired between them last night would be eradicated by the fever that had possessed his body.

Unfortunately, the fever that had possessed *hers* still gripped her strongly. She had only to close her eyes to experience the magic of his lips on her breasts, to feel his mouth on her own.

"Botheration!" She had to put this behind her or she would go crazy. She was governess to Brandon Montgomery's children and nothing more. She would go about her duties in an efficient and circumspect manner. She would forget all about kissing and fondling, and the way a man's hard member felt pressed against her. . . .

She slammed the pot of mush down on the burner, shaking her head in disgust. What was the use? She was forever doomed. In the space of a few fleeting moments, she had become a wanton, wanting woman.

And, to her eternal mortification and damnation, she wanted more of Brandon Montgomery!

After checking to make sure the children were still occupied with the art supplies she had brought them, Heather entered Brandon's room. He was asleep. Relieved that she wouldn't have to face him yet, she began tidying up the room.

It was a mess. Brandon's clothes were strewn about haphazardly where she'd tossed them yesterday. Gathering up his suit and fine linen shirt, she brought them to her nose and inhaled deeply. His spicy cologne still lingered on the fabric. The manly scent made her pulse skitter.

Cursing herself for her foolishness, she dumped the garments on the chair and paused to look out the window. The sun shone brightly, as if nothing on earth had been altered.

But it had. She had.

"What the devil are you doing in my room?"

She spun around. Brandon was sitting up in bed, looking

at her with that outraged expression she knew only too well. Her face flushed with her own guilty thoughts.

"I'm straightening up your room, Brandon. I've brought fresh water for you to drink, and . . ."

He looked down at his naked chest, then back up at her, pulling the covers up to his chin. "Where the devil are my clothes? Where is Mr. Woo? You must send him to me at once."

She knew that he probably had to relieve himself, and she wasn't exactly sure how to handle that problem. "Mr. Woo's not here. No one is but me. You've been feverish and out of your head. I . . . I had to undress you and put you to bed yesterday. Don't you remember?"

He stared at her intently. "You undressed me?" He peeked under the covers, his cheeks turning a bright red. "But I'm naked!"

Her cheeks grew even hotter at the distinct memory of just how naked he was. Trying to remain perfectly poised, though she was anything but, she explained, "You were feverish. It was necessary to bathe you several times during the night with cool water." Fortunately, he'd been asleep during those times.

"Then that explains it."

Cautiously, she asked, "Explains what?"

He wasn't about to confess all those lurid dreams he'd been having about her. Staring at Heather this morning in her prim and proper blue gingham gown, he couldn't fathom that she was the siren in his fantasy. Funny, though, he thought he knew exactly what she looked like naked beneath that dress.

"It's nothing. I must have had a nightmare." *But oh, it seemed like the most delicious dream.*

"You did," she stated matter-of-factly, trying to keep all traces of emotion out of her voice. "Last evening I came in to find you in the midst of one. You calmed down after a few moments."

"I see." But he really didn't. Something seemed strange, but he couldn't quite put his finger on it. "Thanks for taking care of me. I thought Mr. Woo had put me to bed, but now I remember that he was afraid to come to work for fear of catching the disease."

"Is that all you remember?" She waited anxiously, wiping her sweating palms on her apron, wondering if any traces of their encounter lingered in his mind.

Visions of her full white breasts and dusky nipples flashed before Brandon's eyes, and he stared intently at Heather's chest, then shook his head, his mind unwilling to make the connection. "That's all," he finally said. "I'm starved. What have you brought me to eat?"

She sighed with relief. Brandon didn't remember. But somewhere in the deepest part of her soul, she wished that he did remember the gloriousness of their passionate encounter. She would never forget it.

"Is something the matter? You have the oddest look on your face."

She shook her head emphatically. "I've brought you some toast and tea. You'll need to eat lightly until we're sure your fever has subsided."

"You seem very knowledgeable about nursing, Heather."

"I took care of my father when he was ill. And I nursed my sisters through several childhood diseases."

"And do you desire to nurse children at your breast?" he asked, wondering where the intensely personal question had come from, but knowing for a fact that nursing at her breasts would be extraordinarily pleasurable. He shook his head to clear away the absurd thought.

What the devil is wrong with me?

She reddened instantly. "I hope to have children some-day."

"Sounds to me like you've had a lot put upon those slender shoulders of yours."

Her hand went up to touch her shoulder, and, remembering the way his hands had gripped them last night, she swallowed with difficulty. "One does what one must."

He nodded, thinking of the way he'd taken over during his father's illness and after his death. Brandon had been plunged into manhood, saddled with responsibility at an early age, just as he suspected Heather had.

"It appears we have something in common after all."

More than you know, Heather thought. *More than you know.*

<u>CHAPTER 8</u>

Laurel's letter arrived early that morning, and Heather was relieved to finally receive word from her family. Stealing a few minutes for herself, she sat down at the kitchen table to read it.

Just as every other morning for the past few weeks, she was alone. Brandon and the children were still asleep, and she thanked the Almighty for that.

The children were much improved. Their rashes were clearing, and she'd allowed them out of bed on several occasions to exercise and play a few games. Brandon, unfortunately, was not faring as well. His body was covered with measles, of which he complained constantly. And though his fever hadn't completely subsided, there hadn't been any further episodes of nightmares. Thank the good Lord!

She felt drained, both physically and emotionally. The latter had more to do with tending to Brandon's needs than the children's. It was a struggle every day to enter his bedroom, engage in small talk as if nothing at all had transpired between them, touch his body while administering sponge baths and calamine lotion, and remain completely detached and impersonal. It was not only a struggle, it was an impossibility.

Pouring herself a cup of hot coffee, she sighed deeply and cocked her head toward the stairs to make sure everyone was still asleep, eagerly ripping open the lilac-scented envelope and smiling to herself. Laurel's penchant for the dramatic and romantic was a well-known fact.

> Dearest Heather,
> I trust this letter finds you well and situated in the position of your choice. I've no doubt that you succeeded at becoming an illustrator. You were always the most determined of us three girls.

Heather frowned, wondering what Laurel would say if she knew that Heather was working as a governess. And a nursemaid! Laurel had always looked up to her with an adoration Heather found difficult to live up to. Rose Elizabeth, who was grounded more firmly in reality, would no doubt chalk up Heather's recent experience to a run of bad luck. She was pragmatic and practical to a fault.

Thinking of her youngest sister deepened Heather's frown. Why hadn't she heard from Rose? It had been many weeks since they'd parted company. A long enough time for her sister to have written. Pushing the disturbing question to the back of her mind, she continued to read.

> As of yet, I have not secured employment at an opera house, though I am not without hope that I will do so soon. Please don't be shocked, but in order to support myself, I have taken employment singing in a saloon.

A saloon! Heather swallowed at the image of dainty little Laurel in a saloon filled with rowdy men. It just didn't fit. And it alarmed her to think that her sister was consorting with ruffians, though she knew Laurel could handle herself.

Their father had made certain that all the Martin sisters could take care of themselves.

> The owner is an insufferable man by the name of Chance Rafferty. He's the rudest, most horrible man I've ever met.

Now who did that sound like? Heather smiled to herself.

> But I am determined to triumph here, as I'm sure you are already doing in San Francisco. Does the ground truly shake there? Mr. Rafferty assures me it does, but then, I don't believe much of what he tells me. The man is an absolute scoundrel.
> I've had only the briefest of notes from Rose, who still remains on the farm. She promised to write you the entire account of her reasons for staying, so I will not elaborate on her predicament now.

Heather cursed softly under her breath. Rose had defied both her father and Heather by staying at the farm. What possible reason other than illness could have prevented her sister from traveling to Boston?

> The odious Mr. Rafferty is summoning me to work, so I must end this letter. Please write to tell me all about your adventures in the Paris of the West (that is what Mr. Rafferty calls San Francisco). I miss you dreadfully.

Laurel had signed her name in that childish scrawl so familiar to Heather, and it brought a small tug to her heart and tears to her eyes. "I miss you, too, Laurie," she whispered.

The slam of the back door roused Heather from her melancholy thoughts, and she turned to find Mr. Woo marching through the doorway, his arms filled with groceries. Her eyes widened at the unexpected sight. Overjoyed, she jumped up from the table and rushed to help him.

"Mr. Woo, I'm so happy you've come back to work," she said, taking the sack of potatoes from his arms and depositing it on the table.

The Chinaman stared down at the toes of his shoes. "Woo powerful sorry, missy. I scared to come. But niece, Soon Ye, tells me you work all alone. I feel like yellow-bellied varmint and come to help."

Startling Mr. Woo considerably, Heather threw her arms about the contrite man and hugged him to her breast. "Thank you, you dear little man. You don't know how much I've missed you."

Woo giggled like a schoolboy, covering his mouth with his hand. Then, looking over his shoulder to make sure no one had seen them, he sobered instantly and said in a conspiratorial fashion, "You no tell Woo's wife about this, missy. She crazy, jealous woman. She cut off more than Woo's pigtail."

Laughing for the first time in days, Heather hugged the man again, then fairly skipped out of the room as she headed for the stairs.

Heather's excitement was short-lived. Three hours later, Cecelia Whitten decided to grace the Montgomery household with her presence.

Having heard the disturbing news that her fiancé was indisposed with some dreadful disease, Cecelia had rushed home from a visit with her great-aunt in Portland and was now cooling her heels in the mansion's hallway.

Obviously annoyed by waiting for over ten minutes, Cecelia was pacing rapidly when Heather entered. The elegantly gowned woman seemed to be wearing a hole in the carpet runner as she muttered something about dirty heathens. Her arms were folded across her chest, and she had the angriest look on her face. It reminded Heather of a firebreathing dragon she'd seen in a picture book.

"Miss Whitten." Heather nodded in greeting, though there was no pretense of a welcoming smile on her face. "Sorry to keep you waiting, but I've been attending to Brandon's and the children's lunches. Mr. Woo only just informed me of your arrival."

Cecelia didn't miss the informality with which Heather had referred to Brandon; her nostrils flared even wider. "It's most inappropriate for hired help to refer to their employers by their given names, Miss Martin. Perhaps your upbringing didn't allow for the instruction of correct comportment for a woman in your position."

Heather bit the inside of her cheek to keep from saying what was uppermost on her mind: that Cecelia was a snooty bitch! "If you'd like to see *Brandon*," she said, "I'll be happy to escort you up."

"That won't be necessary. I've been in his bedroom before." She smiled snidely at the governess's shocked expression.

Heather recovered quickly. "Well, I doubt you've been in it when Brandon's had the measles. You have had them yourself, haven't you? They're highly contagious."

"Of course I've had them. Do you think I would risk my health? I just knew those dreadful children were going to be the death of Brandon," she said.

Heather glared at the woman. "I hardly think the twins can be blamed for contracting measles, especially when there seems to be an epidemic of the disease throughout the city." Using the utmost self-restraint, Heather added; "If you'd care to follow me, I'll show you up to Brandon's room."

They entered the room to find Brandon propped against a stack of pillows, reading the morning edition of his newspaper. He didn't look up.

Assuming that it was only Heather who'd entered, he said, "I'm not ready for my sponge bath yet. We can wait until later, can't we?"

A loud gasp made him lower the paper. His eyes widened as he saw Cecelia standing at the side of his bed. Her face was as red as his, and she was glowering at him.

"Really, Brandon, the impropriety of what you just said is shocking! How can you allow this . . . this woman to attend to your personal needs? As your fiancée, I must strenuously object to this familiarity."

Brandon ignored her pique. "It's nice to see you, Cecelia. How have you been?"

Heather bit the inside of her cheek to keep from smiling. She was not about to explain to Cecelia that Brandon was partially clothed during his sponge baths. Let the aggravating woman think what she wanted!

Like a chameleon, Cecelia camouflaged her irritation. "Why, I've been just worried to pieces over you, darling," she purred. Then she wrinkled her nose in disgust. "My goodness, Brandon, you look positively awful. I hope those bumps all over you will not leave scars. They're positively hideous."

Casting Brandon a commiserating look, Heather excused herself and left the affianced couple alone.

As soon as the door closed, Cecelia's annoyance became clear. "Your governess has taken much upon herself, Brandon. She treats you with a familiarity I find shocking. How can you allow it?"

"If it weren't for Miss Martin, I might not be here now, Cecelia. She's nursed me and my children day and night, with hardly a thought to her own well-being. I owe her a great debt of gratitude."

The blond woman scoffed rudely. "She's a servant, Brandon. She's only done what she's been paid to do. I hardly think she deserves a medal." She crossed to the mirror, obviously pleased by what she saw, and smiled at her reflection.

"And if she hadn't?" Brandon asked. "Would you have been willing to come over and risk your health to care for me? My own mother and cook took off in fear of contracting the measles. Heather . . . Miss Martin was the only one who stayed to help."

"You're not being fair, darling." Cecelia spun around and sat on the chair by his bed. "You know perfectly well that I was in Oregon visiting my Great-Aunt Penny when you took ill. Why, the woman is old and infirmed. I couldn't very well be at your bedside to care for you, when I had to take care of my aunt. She needed me, Brandon."

And I didn't? And wasn't it quite a coincidence that Cecelia's aunt had taken sick the very day the children had been diagnosed with measles? But he didn't ask those questions. Instead, he held out his hand to the lovely woman.

"I've missed you, Cecelia. Come and give me a kiss."

Cecelia's eyes rounded, and she pulled back, horrified at the prospect of touching him. "Honestly, darling, how can you expect me to kiss you when you have sores all over your body? I can't bear the thought of touching you like that. You look like a leper."

Brandon thought of all the times Heather had bathed him, shaved him, applied soothing ointments to his rash, rubbed his neck when it was stiff and aching, and he had a difficult time accepting Cecelia's reticence. But then, realizing she was a lady and gently reared, he made allowances for her behavior.

"I guess I'm a sight to look at."

Cecelia rose to her feet. "Why, you'll be yourself in no time at all, darling. Then we'll be able to resume some of our former activities." She smiled seductively, and Brandon felt obliged to smile back, though he wasn't in the mood for her teasing games.

Cecelia loved to tease and torment. She allowed him to kiss her, to fondle her full, ripe breasts, but she'd made it clear from the beginning that there would be no consummation before their wedding night. That was one area where Cecelia was inflexible.

"I'm looking forward to it, my pet."

"I'm sure you are. It must be just awful having that farm woman around you all day. Her hands are no doubt chafed and reddened, and I've yet to smell the scent of French perfume on her person. It must be such a trial for you."

Cecelia blew Brandon a kiss and floated out of the room, closing the door behind her. Sighing with relief, Brandon closed his eyes and recalled her remarks concerning Heather.

Funny, he'd never noticed anything unpleasant about the way Heather smelled. Quite the contrary, in fact. She smelled clean and fresh, like wildflowers growing in a meadow. And her hands had always been gentle when they'd caressed . . . attended to his needs.

As if conjured up by his thoughts, Heather reentered the room a moment later. "I hope your visit with Miss Whitten didn't tire you out too much."

She came right to his bedside, with no thought to the rash that covered him, and began adjusting his pillows. She placed her palm on his forehead, as she had done so many times before; her hand felt cool and comforting and not the least bit chafed.

"You're cool to the touch, Brandon." she smiled, obviously pleased by the discovery. "I think you're making progress. Perhaps tomorrow I'll allow you to get out of bed for a while to stretch your legs." She pulled down the blanket to look at his chest. "Your measles are drying up some. I think we'll need to apply a bit more calamine lotion to them, however."

Suddenly feeling ill at ease at her suggestion, Brandon tugged the blanket up to his chin. "I'm fine. I don't think that'll be necessary."

She shook her head, yanking the blanket back down to his waist. "Nonsense. You do want to get well, don't you?"

"Of course I want to get well. Do you think I enjoy lying in this bed day after day, having you wait on me hand and foot?" he answered, his voice harsher than he'd intended. "I need to get back to work."

Ignoring his surly mood and protestations, Heather dabbed the lotion onto a small bit of cotton, then applied it to his chest in a smooth, circular motion. "If Miss Whitten's visits are going to put you in a snit, I won't allow her to come again."

Brandon sighed, but he didn't dispute her opinion that Cecelia's visit had worked him up. He wasn't going to admit that the touch of Heather's hands on his chest and arms was doing strange things to his insides. That if she had the inclination to pull the covers back a little bit farther, she would find his manhood standing straight up at attention, begging for something she wasn't likely to supply.

With that distressing thought, he closed his eyes and submitted to the torture.

CHAPTER 9

"Thank goodness that's all over with." Mary-Margaret poured a dollop of cream into her cup of steaming coffee and stirred it absently with her spoon. "I never thought Jack was going to get rid of those awful spots. I guess you're quite relieved that the children and Mr. Montgomery are back to normal."

Heather sighed, knowing she should be delighted that Brandon had finally gone back to work, but sorry he'd seen fit to return to his former nasty self. Apparently his gratitude had dried up along with his measles.

Just this morning before leaving for work, he had informed her in his contemptible, superior manner that now that the crisis was over, he expected things to return to normal. And she knew exactly what he meant by normal—proper behavior, strict rules, and adherence to all his dictums. The man was insufferable!

"Heather, are you feeling all right? Your face is flushed. I hope you're not coming down with something."

"I'm fine, Mary," she quickly reassured the maid. "And

yes, it was quite a chore tending to so many sick people at one time, but the house seems rather empty now that everyone is off and about."

"It was sweet of Miss Harriet to take the children to the zoo. She admitted to me that she's been riddled with guilt for abandoning you."

Smiling, Heather thought of all the beautiful things Harriet had brought back with her upon her return yesterday. Heather now possessed a lovely new wardrobe, including two exquisite evening dresses that made her feel like a fairy-tale princess whenever she gazed at them.

"Harriet's not the only one feeling guilty. I didn't want to accept all those fine clothes she bought me." Especially since she knew who had paid for them. No doubt, Brandon would be upset when he received the bill.

"Never you mind," Mary said, patting her hand. "You deserve all those pretty things. This family'd be lost without you, Heather. Surely you know that. I know me and Jack would be. Jack's doing so much better with his lessons. Why, he's actually starting to like school. And that's nothing short of a miracle."

Refilling their coffee cups, Heather paused as she listened to the quiet. Even knowing she should be occupying her time with something other than idle chitchat, it felt wonderful to sit and do absolutely nothing.

"You look like you're gathering wool again, as me dear mother used to say."

"I'm just enjoying the quiet. It's so refreshing after all those shouts of, 'Miss Martin, I itch. Miss Martin, I need another glass of water.'" *Heather, would you please rub my back. . . .*

Mary laughed, nodding in understanding. "I know what you mean. Jack nearly drove me out of my mind. He's such an active boy. And it was difficult at times keeping up with his demands."

At the mention of Jack, Heather was reminded of something the child had said that day at the fish pond. "You've never told me about Jack's father, Mary. I was wondering . . . did he really die from a shark attack?"

Mary smiled ruefully, patting the wisps of golden hair that had escaped her bun. "No. That's just what I told Jack. It seemed kinder than telling him that his father run off like a scared jackrabbit when he found out I was pregnant. I haven't seen John Feeney since that fateful day, and I say good riddance to him."

Mary's eyes clouded in sadness, and Heather grasped her hand, squeezing it gently. "I'm sorry for prying, Mary. I had no idea you were divorced."

"I ain't divorced, Heather. I was never married to begin with. I took the bastard's name 'cause I figured I deserved it." With a shrug of her shoulders, she said, "I guess I'm just a fallen woman."

Gazing at Mary's innocent face and sweet smile, Heather shook her head. "You're about as fallen a woman as I am. I guess I'd rather be a fallen woman than a virgin," Heather found herself admitting.

Mary clamped a hand over her mouth, and her eyes widened in disbelief. "Heather Martin, you are not!"

Heather looked chagrined. "As pure as newly fallen snow."

"My word. I done lost my virginity at fifteen. And here you are going on twenty-three." She shook her head, clearly amazed by the news.

"Well, you needn't make it sound as if I have the plague or something. There weren't a whole lot of eligible men to choose from in Salina, and Pa watched us girls like a hawk. As far as I know, Laurel and Rose Elizabeth are still virgins, too. At least they were before they left home."

"Three virgins and all from the same family. I've never heard of such a thing."

"Well, I'm likely to go to my grave as one. I'm on the way to becoming a spinster, and living here hasn't afforded me the opportunity to meet many men. Unless you count Mr. Woo, who's already saddled with a jealous wife, or balding

Pete Cooper, the butcher who delivers the meat once a week."

"Pete's happily married with five children," Mary informed her, almost apologetically.

"See, there you go. I'm doomed." She'd never given much though to marriage before coming to work at the Montgomery mansion. But taking care of Jenny and Matt . . . and their father . . . on a daily basis had given her new insight into motherhood and family life. She hadn't given up her dream of becoming an illustrator—that aspiration was too firmly entrenched in her soul to abandon—but perhaps children and a husband could be melded together with a career.

"What about Mr. Montgomery? You haven't mentioned him. He's a very eligible bachelor."

Heather's face turned various shades of scarlet as she recalled her one passionate encounter in Brandon's arms. *Yes, there was a lot to recommend about marriage.* She swallowed with a great deal of difficulty before answering.

"Are you forgetting that Mr. Montgomery is engaged to the divine Miss Whitten?" A generous amount of sarcasm laced Heather's words. "And besides, we don't suit each other at all. In case it's escaped your notice, he and I don't agree on much of anything."

"If there's a God in Heaven, and I'm sure there is because I was raised on believing it, Mr. Montgomery will come to his senses long before he saddles himself to that shrewish witch, Cecelia Whitten. And I'm of the opinion that people who have such strong reactions to one another, like you and the mister, would be perfect. Me and John had what one might call a love-hate relationship. I just loved to hate him." She grinned impishly.

Heather laughed, shaking her head. "You're a tonic, that's for certain, Mary-Margaret Feeney."

"Having sex with someone you care about is a whole lot better than a tonic, Heather me girl. Think about it." With a laugh at Heather's shocked expression, Mary exited the kitchen and left Heather to do just that.

•   •   •

"Dammit, Frank! I'm gone for a couple of weeks and in my absence *The Chronicle* scoops us on an important news item."

Managing editor Frank Burnside shook his head at the irate look on his employer's face. "Your temper ain't improved a whole hell of a lot, Brandon. If you ask me, those measles only made it worse."

Sinking into the big leather chair behind his desk, Brandon's scowl deepened. He should be used to the old man's caustic remarks by now—Frank had been with him for years, and he wasn't one to hold back his opinions—but they rankled just the same.

"Last May we missed out on the news about the completion of the Brooklyn Bridge, a singularly important piece of news. And now I'm not supposed to be upset to find out that we've missed the story of Joseph Pulitzer's acquisition of *The New York World.* Anything involving Jay Gould is news, Frank, especially when he stands to make close to three hundred and fifty thousand dollars for the sale of his newspaper."

Frank ceased his pacing in front of Brandon's desk and stared his employer straight in the eye. Frank prided himself on being a straight shooter, and he didn't mince words. And there weren't many at *The Star* who dared to question his judgment. But Brandon was an entirely different matter, for he was the one man whose opinion mattered to Frank.

"I didn't think the Hungarian's activities were all that newsworthy," the managing editor explained.

"Don't let professional jealousy cloud your judgment, man. Pulitzer is brilliant. He's a goddamn success story—the American dream personified. 'Immigrant Who Joined Union Army to Fight for U.S. Freedom Buys *New York World.*'

"Christ, Frank! I can see the headline as clearly as those snow-white chin whiskers of yours."

Absently pulling on those whiskers, Frank digested Brandon's reasoning and, with an apologetic look on his face, said, "I'm sorry, Brandon. I really blew it. I must be slipping in my old age."

"You're a damn good editor, Frank, so there must be another reason. You're not hitting the bottle again, are you?" Brandon's eyes narrowed slightly at the thought.

After what he'd been through with his father, he wasn't going to tolerate that weakness in another human being, especially one who was in his employ. He'd already made one exception for Frank, because he liked him and because he was a damn good newspaper man. But if he'd slipped off the wagon, Brandon wouldn't hesitate to fire him on the spot.

A hurt look crossed the editor's face, and the frown he wore only added to the age lines around his eyes and mouth.

"Not a drop in over a year, Brandon," he said, shaking his head emphatically. "I've just been preoccupied. Clara's not been feeling well lately, and I'm worried about her. The doc says it's female trouble, but I've got my doubts."

Brandon's relief was tempered with concern for Frank's wife. Clara was a good Christian woman, and the single most important reason why Frank was able to quit drinking.

"If there's anything I can do, you let me know. We can always get another doctor's opinion. My own doctor, Henry Lipscomb, is very good, very thorough."

Frank expressed his gratitude, then added, a teasing note to his voice, "Guess you were lucky to have received such fine nursing care, huh, Brandon?" The old man's eyes twinkled. "Gerald Whitten tells me your new governess is a pretty little thing. Said he wouldn't mind being tended to in bed by the likes of her."

Brandon was immediately incensed at the remark. Nostrils flaring, he banged his palms on his desktop, making Frank wince and take a step back in retreat. "Gerald should learn to keep his remarks to himself. And so should you! Now get back to work and find us something newsworthy to print. Check with the Associated Press. Perhaps something's come in."

With a sheepishness not usually associated with Frank Burnside, he slunk out the door. Sighing, Brandon leaned back in his chair, staring out the large window behind his desk. A faint drizzle was coming down, making the day as gloomy as his disposition at the moment.

Damn Gerald! No doubt Cecelia was behind his impertinent comments. Her jealousy of Heather had been all too obvious, and he knew that the time had come to placate his indignant fiancée.

Due to his recent illness, they hadn't spent much time together. And knowing Cecelia's possessive nature, her sour disposition had no doubt been caused by the same thing he'd been plagued with of late: Heather Martin.

What the devil am I going to do about that woman?

His close, constant proximity to his children's governess was driving him to distraction. She'd been nothing but a problem since first stepping into his house, and he'd spent an inordinate amount of time thinking about her instead of concentrating on his newspaper.

There was no denying that she was the best damn governess his children had ever had.

There was also no denying that she was getting under his skin like an itch that needed scratching.

Well, he'd had enough itching to last him a lifetime, thank you very much! And he had a feeling that, unlike the measles, which lasted only a couple of weeks, the itch Heather caused would last a whole lot longer and be a lot more difficult to cure.

"Miss Martin! Miss Martin!"

Heather looked up from the papers she was grading, and her eyes widened in disbelief. "Good heavens, Matt," she scolded, frowning at the disheveled child as he came barreling into the schoolroom. "Where on earth have you been? You're fifteen minutes late for class, and you're a mess."

She was certainly glad that Brandon wasn't here to see his son's appearance. No doubt it would prompt a few choice words about Heather's methods of child rearing. But despite the child's slovenliness, she had to admit, it was gratifying and worth raising Brandon's ire to finally see Matt coming out of his shell. He actually looked like a normal little boy for a change!

His face was smudged with dirt, the right sleeve of his shirt was torn, and two buttons were missing from his jacket. The knees of his pants were caked with mud.

"Jack and I were playing outside for a few minutes, Miss Martin," Matt confessed.

She glanced over at Jack to find him staring innocently up at the ceiling, and her suspicions were immediately confirmed.

Matt cast his co-conspirator a secretive smile, then handed Heather an envelope. "Sorry I'm late, but Grandmother said to give you this letter. It just arrived, and I had to wait until she finished talking with the postman." He rolled his eyes. "Grandmother likes to talk a lot."

Biting back a smile, Heather glanced at the envelope and was relieved to see Rose's distinctive handwriting scrawled across it. She decided to let Matt's inappropriate behavior slide.

"I want you children to study the vocabulary words on page fifteen of your *McGuffey's Reader*. There will be a test at the end of today's lesson."

A chorus of groans filled the air, and Heather looked pointedly at each child. "There could also be a math test . . ." She left the remainder of the threat unsaid, as three heads bowed diligently to their books.

Tearing open the envelope, Heather read her sister's descriptive paragraph about the unusual warm spell they'd been having in Salina and felt her face flush red in anger.

Salina, not Boston! she thought. *Dammit Rose Elizabeth, why are you still in Salina?*

Apparently the new owner had arrived a few weeks back. An English gentleman. A duke, no less!

Rose went on to say:

It was obvious from the moment that his lordship stepped onto our property that I wasn't about to leave this farm in his inept hands. Alexander James Warrick—the Duke of Moreland, or the Duke of Disaster, as I call him—knows absolutely nothing about wheat farming. In fact, he knows absolutely nothing about a great many things. I've never seen a grown man so lacking in basic skills!

Alexander's more interested in riding to the hounds and taking part in shooting matches. I don't have to tell you that he's made quite an impression with the townsfolk. But they're just impressed by his title, cultured speech, and fancy clothes. But I am not fooled one little bit by his refined manner and pretty words.

I hope you'll forgive me, but I couldn't possibly leave our farm and Ma and Pa's graves in the hands of someone so totally irresponsible and live with myself.

The duke has threatened to bodily evict me from the premises, but so far I've been able to stand my ground. To set your mind at rest, he is occupying Pa's old room, while I am still situated in ours.

I will write again to keep you apprised of my situation. It shouldn't be too much longer until I can convince Alexander that he's made a big mistake by coming to America. Please don't be disappointed in me, but I'm happy living here, despite the fact that I must share our home (temporarily) with an Englishman!

Despite her fury at her sister's antics, Heather couldn't contain her smile. She almost felt sorry for that poor English duke. Rose Elizabeth was going to make his life a living hell, if she hadn't done so already.

Once Rose took the bit between her teeth, she was like a racehorse that wouldn't quit until it crossed the finish line. She was a very single-minded woman.

Of course, there was an obvious flaw in Rose's plan to rid herself of Alexander Warrick. The money he'd paid for the farm would already have been deposited by their business factor in the Salina branch of the Farmer's and Merchant's Bank.

Heather sighed, shaking her head in disgust. "Rose Elizabeth," she whispered to herself, "for such a sensible, level-headed woman, you have turned out to be one major pain in the bustle!"

The rose satin evening gown shimmered in the late afternoon sunlight, and Heather smiled happily at her reflection in the long cheval looking glass. "I do look like a fairy-tale princess," she murmured, holding out the sides of the dress as she pirouetted about like a ballerina.

"My goodness, child, but you do look lovely in that gown! I knew from the first moment I laid eyes on it that it would be perfect with your coloring." Harriet had bustled into the room without bothering to wait for an invitation. "I hope you don't mind that I came in," she said as an afterthought.

Surprised by the intrusion, Heather's hand flew to her throat, and she took a deep breath. "No, not at all. I was just trying on some of my new clothes."

"I'm so glad you like them, my dear. And I hope you don't think it too presumptuous of me to have bought them. But those other dresses of yours left much to be desired."

"I made most of them myself, except for the black ones; they were store bought."

"I'm not saying they weren't practical, Heather, or well made, but they did absolutely nothing for your figure. And you have such a splendid shape, even without a corset."

Heather blushed to the tips of her toes, which she realized were quite bare. She scrunched them up beneath the hem of her gown.

"Mellon's Mercantile didn't have much variety to choose from," she explained. "Mostly ginghams and calicos. There's not much use for satins in Salina."

"Well, there most definitely is in San Francisco. I've just heard that Leland Stanford will be giving a birthday ball in his son's honor, and we're sure to be invited. We are practically neighbors, you know."

A panicked look crossed Heather's face. "Surely you're not including me in that invitation, Harriet? I'm merely a servant in this house, despite my fine wardrobe."

"Of course you're invited! And quit talking like you're not suited to society. You have much to recommend. You might have been reared on a farm, my dear, but you're better educated than most and far more intelligent than you-know-who."

Heather knew exactly *who*. "That may be true. But I'd venture a bet that Cecelia can dance, which is something I've never learned."

"Not dance!" Harriet's eyes widened in disbelief. "Heavens! That is a problem." She tapped her finger against her chin, then said, "I guess we'll just have to get Brandon to teach you."

"Oh, no, Harriet." She shook her head emphatically. "Please don't say anything to him. I'd be mortified."

"Nonsense. My son is an excellent dancer, and he owes you that much for caring for him while he was ill."

"But . . ."

"Leave everything to me. It's time you were introduced into San Francisco society."

"But I'm only a governess, Harriet. I'm not in the same social class with those women." Women like Cecelia.

"Thank heavens for that!" Harriet quipped before shoving Heather aside and making her way to the closet. "Now where to begin . . ." She began tapping her chin again, a gesture that instantly alarmed Heather. Harriet's tapping meant she was plotting, and that didn't bode well for governesses, farm girls, or the general population of San Francisco.

"You'll need shoes to match everything. And underclothing. A corset is a must. And, of course, a bustle."

Heather groaned and shook her head, trying to make the older woman understand. "Brandon will never approve of this." She stabbed herself in the chest with her finger. "*I* don't approve of this!"

"Nonsense, my dear." Harriet turned to face her. "By the time we're through, my son is going to be stunned into acceptance, devastated by your beauty, and overwhelmed by your charm."

Heather's laughter bubbled up at the effusive comments. "Brandon's already been charmed by Cecelia, Harriet. Surely you haven't forgotten?" Heather herself certainly hadn't.

"*Hmph!* That woman couldn't charm a snake soaked in an aphrodisiac. Whereas you could melt the heart of a polar bear."

Heather's right eyebrow shot up. "Are you comparing your son to a polar bear?"

Taking Heather's hands in her own, Harriet sighed deeply. "Brandon's heart is encased in ice, his emotions frozen beyond anything Cecelia Whitten could hope to reach. She doesn't have the capacity to love anyone other than herself. I've seen her with the children; she can hardly stand to be in the same room with them. No doubt she feels she will have to compete with Jenny and Matt for Brandon's affections.

"But you, dear Heather, are different. You have the power to melt the ice around my son's heart and the capacity for great love. You will make a far more suitable wife for Brandon and mother to his children than that odious woman he has chosen for himself."

Heather's mouth opened wide in astonishment. Then she snapped it shut and said, "Harriet, I'm honored by your opinion of me, truly I am. But it's Brandon who must choose his wife, not you, and he has chosen Cecelia."

Undaunted by Heather's reasoning, Harriet replied, "Nonsense. Brandon can't see the forest for the trees. Or in this case, what is right before his eyes. I only want what is best for him and my grandchildren. Surely you can understand that?"

Heather understood perfectly. But Brandon was an entirely different matter. Somehow, she had to make Harriet understand this. She had to convince the determined woman to give up her preposterous, however delightful, dream.

"What makes you think I would consider marrying your

son, Harriet? Why, I don't even like him most of the time. He's rude and arrogant. We have absolutely nothing in common. Certainly nothing to base a marriage on."

Harriet studied the young woman for a moment. "You have the children. Do you deny that you care a great deal for them?"

"Of course I care about Jenny and Matt. I adore them like they were my own."

"And they adore you. And so will my son. Mark my words."

Sighing in frustration, Heather held out her hands beseechingly. "Harriet, you're not listening to a word I'm saying."

"I've heard every word, my dear." She patted Heather's cheek, as if she were a small child incapable of comprehension. "It's you who aren't listening. You aren't hearing what your heart is telling you." Harriet kissed the startled young woman on the cheek and marched to the door, leaving Heather to stare openmouthed after her.

CHAPTER 10

With a lump in her throat almost the same size as the one in her stomach, Heather paused before Brandon's study door and took a deep breath. She'd been dreading this moment since this afternoon when Harriet had happily informed her of Brandon's decision.

For some reason known only to Brandon, he had agreed to his mother's ridiculous demand that he teach Heather the rudiments of dancing. Arrangements were made for them to meet precisely at eight o'clock that evening, after the children were in bed.

The clock in the hall began tolling the hour at the exact moment Brandon's bellow sounded through the thick oak door. "Quit standing out there debating, Heather, and come in. I haven't got all night."

Irritation replaced nervousness and she opened the door to find Brandon with his broad back to her. Annoyed that he'd guessed she was cowering outside his door, it suddenly occurred to her that if he had a bull's-eye attached to him at that very moment, she might be tempted to find herself a bow and arrow.

"Your mother said I was to meet you this evening for the dancing lessons."

He spun on his heel, his eyes widening in appreciation. Arriving home late from the office, he hadn't yet seen Heather in all her new finery.

She was dressed in a lilac and green taffeta gown. The ruched bodice molded her breasts to enticing proportions, and the skirt bustling out in back delineated her curves. Her hair, which was usually worn back in a chignon, had been left down to form soft curls about her shoulders. Her beauty took his breath away, and he thought that perhaps this odious chore of dance instruction might have its rewards after all.

"You look stunning."

She blushed, toying nervously with the skirt of her gown. "Thank you. It was very generous of you and your mother to provide me with such a fine wardrobe. I don't know how I can ever repay you." But it was worth all she possessed to see that admiring glint in his eyes.

"Just seeing you in that dress is payment enough," he said without thinking, then cleared his throat self-consciously. "Besides, as my mother judiciously pointed out, it was the least we could do after all you've done for us."

"It wasn't my idea about the dancing lessons," Heather was quick to point out. "I just wanted you to know, I wouldn't dream of overstepping my bounds. But Harriet has this ridiculous idea that I should learn how to dance."

"As you're probably already aware, my mother has very definite ideas about a great many things."

If you only knew the half of it.

He motioned her forward until they were an arm's length apart. "Since we don't have the benefit of an orchestra, we'll just have to improvise and pretend to hear the music."

That wouldn't be hard. Bells were already ringing in her ears. And what was that strange strumming in her chest?

She stepped into his outstretched arms, swallowing as he placed one hand gently on her waist and grasped her hand with his other. His warm breath on her face when he spoke made her heart flutter madly.

"I will guide you in the steps, counting as we go. You merely have to follow my lead. Do you understand?"

Afraid that if she spoke her words would sound breathless and foreign to her own ears, she merely nodded, allowing him to guide her in the rudiments of the waltz.

"It's simple really. One, two, three . . . one, two, three." He counted out the steps as they danced. "I'm surprised you never learned. You're knowledgeable about so many things."

His compliment pleased her. "We didn't do much dancing in Salina. Unless you count barn dances or the Fourth of July picnic. Then we mostly danced reels or square dances."

"It's much nicer when you actually get to hold on to your partner," he remarked, twirling her about and pulling her tighter against his chest.

Yes, much nicer. But it's a whole lot safer to dance three feet apart, she thought.

The pace quickened and Heather had a difficult time following Brandon's lead. Twice she landed on his foot, and once she nearly knocked them both over when she tripped over the hem of her gown.

"Sorry," she said, blushing with embarrassment.

"I have an idea. Why don't you stand on the toes of my shoes, and I'll guide you through the steps one more time. That way you'll be able to follow the motion of my body to anticipate the turns."

"Step on your toes?" She laughed. "Haven't I been doing that already?"

With his hand firmly placed in the small of her back, he pulled her into him until she was flush with his body. Intense heat infused her entire being, and she started to object.

"Come on, Heather. You wouldn't tolerate such resistance from *your* students, now would you?"

Gazing into his face, she tried to discern an ulterior motive for his unorthodox suggestion, but as always his expression was perfectly impassive. Tentatively she placed the balls of her feet onto his toes but soon found that she had to grasp his shoulders to keep from falling off.

"Is this what you mean?" Her voice sounded shrill to her own ears, and she hoped he couldn't detect her nervousness.

He inhaled the sweet rose-petal scent of her hair, felt the soft crush of full, firm breasts against his chest, and sighed. "Yes. You're doing it exactly right."

They began to move as one. Heather was standing so close to Brandon that she could feel his heartbeat mingling with her own. "You'd better clasp your hands about my neck," he instructed. "It'll be easier for you to hang on that way." His hands came down to wrap about her waist, and each time they turned, he pulled her into him. As their bodies melded, he bent her backward, groaning aloud at the exquisite torture.

"Am I too heavy for you?" she asked, instantly alarmed. "Am I hurting you?"

He shook his head, too afraid to speak, too afraid to let her know that the feel of her soft, pliant body wrapped about him so trustingly was creating havoc below his waist. He wasn't sure if her skirts prevented her from feeling how hard she made him, or if she had any idea how utterly desirable she was. He doubted it. She lacked the artifice so many women took years to perfect.

The feel of Brandon's rigid erection pressing into her abdomen gave Heather a pretty good indication of his reaction to her. It brought back memories of another time when their bodies had been pressed together in a passionate embrace. She remembered his soft lips suckling her swollen nipples, his hot hands caressing that area between her legs now throbbing wildly in anticipation. Heat like molten lava surged through her veins.

Frightened of her ardent, uncontrollable response, she backed out of his embrace, taking a deep breath.

Her violet eyes locked with his brown ones and they stared at each other for what seemed an eternity. His eyes were burning with the same intensity as her own. His face looked as flushed as hers felt. She fought desperately to regain her composure as the tension between them grew palpable. The grandfather clock in the corner ticked off the seconds, matching the erratic, erotic rhythm of her heart.

The door opened suddenly and Harriet entered, breaking the spell. "How are the lessons going?" She looked first at Brandon's tortured expression, then at Heather, who was rubbing sweaty palms against the skirt of her gown. Better than expected, Harriet deduced, smiling inwardly.

Brandon cleared his throat. "Heather's a fast learner, Mother. She's already mastered the steps of the waltz."

"Yes," Heather said a bit too quickly. "Brandon's an excellent teacher. Very thorough."

Her eyebrow raised, Harriet glanced at her son, noting the uncharacteristic pink tinge to his cheeks. "I always say— Brandon is nothing if not thorough. And his expert tutoring will be put to good use in two weeks' time. The invitation to the Stanfords' gala arrived this afternoon.

"I'm sure there'll be plenty of eligible men only too happy to benefit from Brandon's instruction. I expect you'll be quite the belle of the ball, Heather. What man could resist such fresh, unblemished beauty?"

As the words sunk in, Brandon's face darkened like a thundercloud, Heather's cheeks turned crimson, and Harriet smiled in satisfaction, tapping her chin. . . .

If the Astors were the richest people on the East Coast, than surely the Stanfords were the richest on the West. Their wealth was clearly evident in every room of the lavish Nob Hill mansion. Heather was astonished at the opulent surroundings.

Priceless objets d'art filled the brass étagères. The walls displayed paintings that rightfully belonged in a museum. Rare Persian rugs graced inlaid parquet floors, and exquisite crystal chandeliers, which had been electrified, were suspended from ornate plaster ceilings.

The effect was beautiful, ostentatious, and cold.

"Close your mouth, my dear," Harriet whispered, placing

a gloved hand on Heather's forearm. "We wouldn't want the Stanfords to think you're unaccustomed to wealth."

Why not? Heather wondered. She wasn't. And she disliked having to pretend to be something she was not. It wouldn't take the Stanfords long to discover they had an impostor in their midst. Despite Harriet's tutoring and Brandon's dance instruction, she was still Heather Martin from Salina, Kansas. And nothing was ever going to change that.

Standing in the receiving line waiting to be introduced to Leland Stanford, his wife, Jane, and the guest of honor, fourteen-year-old Leland Jr., Heather had plenty of time to make comparisons.

This birthday party was very different from the ones she'd attended in Salina. Those parties consisted of homemade ice cream, a cake, if they were fortunate enough to have the ingredients, and an assortment of small but thoughtful gifts, either handmade or purchased at the mercantile.

Leland Jr. was likely to get his own department store, she thought, or at the very least his own railroad car to play with.

"The house is impressive, is it not?" Harriet asked.

"I haven't seen anything like it before," Heather whispered. "Except for yours, of course." Though Brandon's mansion was nothing compared to this one, she liked the Montgomerys' much better. It, at least, looked lived in. The Stanfords' home resembled a museum.

"Leland's a former governor of this state," Harriet said. "And there's talk that he's going to run for United States senator in the next election. But he made his money in the building of the transcontinental railroad, along with Crocker and Hopkins.

"We're next to be introduced. I wonder where Brandon took off to." Turning her head, she frowned when she spotted him three couples back, standing with Cecelia and Gerald Whitten. "I can't imagine why he would rather be with that woman instead of his family."

Heather sighed, not wanting to point out the obvious. She wasn't part of Brandon's family, and men Brandon's age usually didn't cling to their mother's apron strings. No one would ever accuse Brandon Montgomery of being a mama's boy.

Patiently, she said, "Cecelia's his fiancée, Harriet."

"Hmph! Not for long. Mark my words." Suddenly her tone changed, and Heather knew it was time to be presented. Pasting on a smile, she extended her hand to Jane Stanford.

Standing beneath a large potted palm in the ballroom, listening to the melodious strains of a Strauss waltz, Heather felt more like a duck out of water than ever. She didn't belong here, any more than these city folks would belong on a wheat farm in Kansas.

She might be dressed in satins and lace, but she didn't fool herself into thinking that twenty yards of rose satin could conceal the fact that she didn't fit in. As her mama used to say, you couldn't turn a sow's ear into a silk purse. And at the moment, Heather was feeling very much like that misguided porcine creature.

Her gaze latched onto Brandon, who looked resplendent in his formal black evening attire. The cut of his jacket emphasized the width of his broad shoulders and the strength of his arms, which were presently wrapped around the waist of his fiancée as he glided Cecelia about the black-and-white tiled dance floor. She was smiling up at him, batting her eyelashes in a coquettish manner, as if he were the only man in the room.

Heather frowned, knowing that she was incapable of using such artifice. Well, at least she didn't have to worry about spilling out of her gown the way Cecelia did, she consoled herself. The woman's large bosoms looked dangerously close to taking flight every time Brandon spun her around the floor.

"Brandon and Cece appear to be having a good time. Wouldn't you say so, Miss Martin?"

Gerald Whitten's voice startled Heather out of her observations. Turning to find him sidling up next to her, she did her best not to groan aloud. She didn't like Gerald much. He was too loud, too much a braggart. And there was something about the man that she didn't trust.

He was very rich, yet no one could explain how he'd acquired his wealth. Mary-Margaret said he was a gambler. Harriet hinted that his dead wife had been an heiress. But no one knew for certain, and it only compounded Heather's distrust of the man. There was something terribly sleezy about Gerald Whitten, like the way his reptilian gaze snaked over her, as if he could actually see what she looked like beneath her clothing.

"I told my gal that her dress was cut too damn low. But Cece says if you've got it, flaunt it. And Brandon doesn't seem to mind." He chuckled in such a suggestive manner that shivers of revulsion darted up Heather's spine. "That boy's eyes have been glued to her . . ."

"Have you known the Stanfords long, Mr. Whitten?" Heather interrupted rudely, not caring to discuss Cecelia's glowing attributes. *If only her brains were as big as her bosoms,* she thought unkindly, smiling up at Cece's doting father.

"Not long. I've attempted to do a couple of business deals with Leland, but he hasn't been interested. I haven't found the chink in his armor yet, but I will. You've got to know a man's weakness before you can best him in business."

She tried to keep the aversion she felt out of her voice. "What exactly is it that you do, Mr. Whitten? I don't recall you ever having mentioned it."

"Well now, I don't usually discuss business with women. I find they don't have a head for such matters. But since you asked—I'm in the import/export business. I have some very influential customers scattered all over the world." They paid a damn high price for the quality of goods he exported, he thought, smiling to himself, and the price for those goods was only going to increase. "Supply and demand, Miss Martin. It's an extremely profitable business."

"I'm sure you're quite adept at what you do."

His chest puffed out, reminding her of a strutting peacock. "Damn right. You've got to be hard as nails in this day and age. I don't pamper and mollycoddle my people the way Brandon does." He pulled his chin whiskers. "I don't know what this world's coming to, but I'm damn tired of the government sticking its hands into my pockets. I've told Brandon he should write some editorials on the subject."

"Have you and Brandon known each other long?"

"About a year, I guess. Cece and I moved here from Oregon not long after her mama died. It didn't take my girl long to set her cap for the handsomest man in Frisco. She's like her daddy. Once she sees what she wants, she goes after it."

He grasped Heather's hand, his head bending down so close to her face that she could smell cigar smoke on his breath. "Did I mention how lovely you look tonight, Miss Martin? I'd be honored if you'd dance with me."

She'd rather eat prunes from morning till night than be held in Gerald Whitten's arms—and she hated prunes!—but she couldn't think of a polite way to refuse the invitation. After all, he was her employer's future father-in-law, and it wouldn't help her future if she insulted Mr. Whitten, which would make Brandon mad at her.

She hadn't given up on her plan to approach Brandon about an illustrator's position, and now that she'd proven herself capable with his children, he just might be willing to give her a chance.

"Thank you, Mr. Whitten," she said. "I'd be delighted."

Brandon's gaze remained riveted on them the entire time Gerald and Heather were out on the dance floor. What could Heather be thinking of, to dance with that old coot? Didn't she know his reputation when it came to the ladies? Gerald was a notorious womanizer. He prided himself on it, bragging about his conquests to anyone and everyone who would listen. Remembering Frank's remark about what Gerald had said regarding Heather, his frown deepened.

"Darling, what's put that dark scowl on your face?" Cecelia inquired. "You look positively fierce, and you're supposed to be having a good time." She pressed her breasts into his chest. "I'm looking forward to later, Brandon, when I can have you all to myself."

Cecelia had made the momentous, self-sacrificing decision this morning that it was time to give herself to Brandon. She couldn't risk the chance of losing him, especially to someone like his new governess. She'd noticed the looks Brandon had been casting at Miss Martin all evening. There was no mistaking the admiration in his eyes when he looked at her. And knowing just how passionate a man Brandon was, she wasn't going to allow that passion to be channeled to a light-skirted servant.

If anyone was going to bring Brandon Montgomery to the altar, it would be Cecelia Whitten. She'd enticed him with her charm, ensnared him with her beauty, and would bring him to her bed. What better way to ensure their marriage? Her daddy would likely kill any man whose intentions were not purely honorable. And she'd make sure her daddy knew the exact moment she lost her virginity.

Distracted by the fact that Gerald's hand was moving below Heather's waist, Brandon's step faltered and he landed on Cecelia's foot. She yelped in pain, taking a step back.

"Honestly, Brandon, what is wrong with you? You've been distracted this entire evening. Is there a problem at the newspaper?" she asked coyly, feigning interest in his work.

Apologizing for his carelessness, Brandon shook his head. "No. Not at the newspaper." The problem was much closer to home. The problem was at that very moment twirling about the dance floor in the arms of yet another man. Chad Stuart, this year's most eligible bachelor, had just cut in on Gerald. Brandon's eyes darkened to match his mood.

"I can't imagine why your mother insisted on allowing that governess of yours to attend this important social event." Cecelia glowered at Heather when she laughed at something Chad Stuart said. "Harriet is just too kind to her inferiors, Brandon. You really should have a talk with her. When servants start rising above their station . . ." She shuddered in dread. "Why, total chaos could develop."

"I doubt Miss Martin is going to start any social insurrections by attending this ball, Cecelia." Though she had certainly started a riot of his emotions. Emotions he'd thought dead and buried a long time ago.

"You always defend her." A petulant pout formed on Cecelia's lips. "I hope you're not falling for that fresh-farm-girl act. Women of her social standing usually have been around the block a time or two."

Cecelia's disparaging comment irritated the hell out of Brandon, but he smiled nonetheless, unwilling to let her know that she had scored a direct hit with it.

"You talk as if you're jealous of Miss Martin. There's no need to be," he lied.

"Not in the least, I assure you." Cecelia smiled like a feline on the prowl, pressing her breasts into his chest. "I've been thinking, darling, that perhaps it's time we . . ." She paused, forcing a maidenly blush. "We *are* going to be married soon. And I've decided that it's silly for us to wait when we both want each other so desperately."

Brandon's eyes widened, and he wanted to laugh aloud. So Cecelia was jealous. He'd figured as much. For her to offer herself like a sacrificial virgin, she must really feel threatened. And who could blame her? Heather was a beautiful woman.

"Are you suggesting we celebrate our wedding night a little early?" That idea no longer held much appeal, Brandon realized.

"Father's meeting his mistress tonight after the party. I heard him tell Wanda that he wouldn't be home until morning." She boldly caressed his thigh. "We'd have the house all to ourselves."

At that moment, Heather twirled by in the arms of another handsome swain. She was smiling up at him, looking like she was enjoying herself immensely. Jealousy ripped through him, and he realized that Cecelia wasn't the only one suffering that malady this evening.

Pulling his fiancée into his chest, he nuzzled her ear and heard her sharp intake of breath. "Your offer sounds too tempting to resist, my pet. I'm getting hard just thinking about it."

Cecelia gasped. "Brandon, really! That is a shocking thing to say."

It sure as hell was, Brandon thought, especially considering the fact that it wasn't even true.

It was nearly two in the morning when Brandon staggered into the house. The faint humming noise from the kitchen drew him, and he paused in the doorway to see Heather, dressed only in her nightgown, waltzing about the room. Her eyes were closed, and she had a dreamy expression on her face that made his gut tie into knots as she danced about with some imaginary partner.

He watched her for a moment. The full moon shining through the windows cast a spotlight of sorts, and he could see the outline of full breasts and naked limbs through the thin material of her gown. That image was relayed quickly from his brain to the swelling organ straining against his trousers.

Quietly he strode forward and took her into his arms. "I believe this is our dance."

Heather's eyes flew open, and she gasped, her face flaming red. "Brandon! I . . . I didn't know you were home."

"Well, I am. And I believe this is our dance." He wrapped both arms about her waist and pulled her into him, making Heather realize what a scandalous and vulnerable position she'd been placed in. She was naked beneath her nightgown!

Unable to sleep, she'd come down to the kitchen for a glass of warm milk. But the moonlight pouring through the windows had filled her with the crazy, irresistible urge to dance once again. Tonight at the gala she had felt like Cinderella at the ball, and she wanted to recapture that feeling, if only for a few moments. But she hadn't expected anyone to catch her in her momentary madness. Certainly not Brandon!

She fought desperately to regain her composure. Not an easy task when her breasts were crushed against the hard planes of his chest. "Brandon, you must release me. This is hardly proper."

"I watched you dance with all the other men tonight. How many partners did you have? Fifteen? Twenty? I lost count after a while."

She smiled in remembrance, not hearing the angry tone of his voice, not realizing that his comments were far from complimentary.

"I had a wonderful time. Did you? You seemed to be enjoying yourself with Cecelia," she reminded him, trying to keep the smile on her face as she remembered the disturbing sight of them dancing together.

Ignoring her comment, he waltzed her about the room, holding her so tightly that she could barely catch her breath. "I didn't have a chance to dance with you, and as your instructor, I need to be certain you've learned everything just the way I taught you."

"I performed reasonably well, and I didn't need to stand on anyone's toes."

"See that you don't," he said harshly, and she smelled brandy on his breath.

"Brandon, have you been drinking?" She was shocked by the discovery. Harriet had confided that Brandon never drank, and she had never seen him touch so much as a drop of liquor.

"I had a couple of brandies," he said, despising himself for the weakness that had suddenly overtaken him tonight. But he'd needed the alcohol to fortify himself for his liaison with Cecelia.

As it turned out, it had been totally unnecessary.

The pent-up passion and frustration of watching Heather in the arms of all those other men tonight had driven him to strip Cecelia naked as soon as they'd entered her bedroom. But it had also prevented him from consummating the act.

Much to his complete and utter mortification, he'd been unable to perform the sex act for the first time in his life. He'd left a panting, teary-eyed Cecelia lying ready and willing in the middle of her bed, citing alcohol as an excuse for his inadequacy.

He didn't know if she believed him, nor did he really care.

He dressed quickly and departed, cursing himself a thousand times for being all kinds of a fool.

It was Heather he wanted, goddammit! And he despised himself even more for that.

Heather felt frightened. Brandon wasn't acting anything like his usual, reserved self. She knew what seething passions bubbled beneath his calm exterior; she'd experienced them firsthand. He was like a volcano that could erupt in a hot shower of emotion, scalding everything in its path, igniting the burning embers of her desire.

She couldn't allow herself to succumb to them again. She might have been able to excuse herself that first time, when he'd been delirious with fever and she'd been curious and overcome by her inexperience. But now she knew the dangers. She knew what exquisite joy could be found in his arms. And he was promised to another.

"You must release me, Brandon," she said with more conviction. "I'm not suitably attired to be dancing about the kitchen with you. What if someone were to come?"

A delicious idea, he thought wickedly, palming her buttocks. "God, you're so soft, and you smell good." He inhaled the rose scent of her hair. "I love the feel of your hair." He threaded his fingers through the thick auburn mass, fanning the strands out over his hands and arms. "It's lush, satiny soft, just as I imagine are your breasts."

She swallowed, hardly able to believe what he was saying, wondering if he had any subconscious memory of that time in his bed. "You're drunk, Brandon! And you'll hate yourself in the morning for losing control of yourself like this. You must stop. Please stop!" she begged. Before she was unable to.

His hands were moving over her back, her buttocks, and she could feel the moisture gathering between her thighs. Her breasts, full and aching, were pressed against his chest; her nipples, hard points of desire, yearned to be stroked and suckled.

"I haven't been drunk for a long time, Heather. I haven't

felt the need for liquor up until now. But seeing you tonight dressed so beautifully, I . . ."

He could feel her firm, naked flesh beneath his hands, despite the thin layer of cloth that separated them. His gaze moved to the long kitchen table and he pictured her there, naked, her legs spread wide, vulnerable to him. He could see the thatch of hair between her thighs, feel its soft coarseness between his fingers, beneath his mouth, as he plunged his tongue deep into her warm, wet cleft.

Sweat broke out on his forehead and upper lip, and he fought desperately to regain control. He was hard and throbbing. All he had to do was back her up a few feet and lay her down on the table. He would kiss her, caress her, and then he would take all the sweetness he knew existed within her.

But her soft, frightened cries jolted him into sobriety. He could never hurt her like that. No matter how much he wanted her, how much he needed her.

He held her at arm's length and with his fingertips wiped the tears from her face. Her lovely eyes held no hatred, only confusion, and he was relieved by that.

His voice thick with equal amounts of desire and self-derision, he said, "Christ, Heather, I'm sorry! I had too much to drink tonight. I hope you'll forgive me. I don't know what came over me. I'll understand if you want to slap my face. In fact, I wish you would. It would make me feel better."

She brought her palm up, but she didn't slap him. Instead, she smiled softly, caressing his cheek with gentle fingers. She wished she could take away his pain, remove the torture from his past, so that he could be free to enjoy the present.

Gazing into his eyes, Heather smiled reassuringly and decided two things: She would do everything in her power to help Brandon Montgomery, help him with his children, help him find the way to ease the torment within him.

And, more important, she would find a way to make him love her. Love her as she loved him.

CHAPTER 11

Brandon stared down at the pink vellum paper and cringed. Heather had requested a meeting at ten o'clock this morning. No doubt she would seek retribution for his unconscionable actions of the night before. She might even sue him for molesting her. God, that would surely cause a stink!

Wouldn't his competitors love to get their hands on that headline? He thought of Peter Glendenning, star reporter of *The Chronicle,* and sighed deeply. The man could dig dirt out of concrete. He had a nose for scandal and was one of the best damn reporters in the city. Brandon had been trying to steal him away from his rival, Michael De Young, for months. He could imagine Peter's headline now:

SAN FRANCISCO STAR OWNER ACCUSED OF MOLESTING GOVERNESS.

Heather had been right about one thing, he thought, hanging his head in a self-deprecating manner: He hated himself this morning.

Though he'd asked himself a hundred times how he'd come to lose control, the answer that came back to him was always the same. Heather made him behave in a totally irrational manner, as if she were a sorceress who'd cast a spell over him.

The soft knock on the door filled him with dread. He looked up and took a deep, fortifying breath.

"Come in."

Heather's smiling face surprised him. She was escorted by Jenny and Matt. They were all dressed in their outerwear, and it was obvious that she and the children were on their way out.

"Good morning, Father," Jenny and Matt chorused, swinging their arms as they held on to Heather's hands. He stole a quick glance at their governess, then smiled at the children's eager expressions, noting that Jenny and Matt smiled a lot these days.

"Good morning. You two are up bright and early for a Sunday morning. Are you going to church?"

Heather had taken it upon herself to see to his children's religious upbringing, telling him plainly that she didn't care what denomination of church they attended, as long as they attended one. He'd decided on Methodist, since that was how he'd been raised. Though it had been a long while since he'd set foot inside a church. He'd found no solace or comfort within its walls and so considered attending a total waste of time.

"That's why we've stopped by, Brandon. We thought perhaps you might like to accompany us this morning." She smiled in such a way as if to say that he might be in need of some religious instruction after the way he'd behaved last night. "After the services I thought I might take the children to the park."

The three hopeful faces were smiling and eager as they waited for his response. It would be small and churlish of him to refuse, he decided, especially since he needed to get back in Heather's good graces. She was, after all, the children's governess. And it was only good business practice to maintain a cordial atmosphere for Jenny and Matt's sake, he told himself. And, since she had chosen to forgive him, the least he could do was humor her by going with them.

Pushing himself up from his desk, he said, "Since I have nothing pressing this morning, I believe I can spare the time."

Squealing with delight, the children ran ahead to wait on the front porch. Heather stepped forward and placed a gloved hand on Brandon's forearm. Her touch burned all the way through the sleeve of his wool suit coat.

"Thank you so much for agreeing to go, Brandon. It's made the children very happy." Her smile was so ebullient that it fairly took his breath away. "They really cherish the moments you spend with them."

His eyes lit with an undefinable emotion. "And I cherish the time I spend with . . ." he paused, staring at the way she licked her lips nervously, the way she moistened them with the tip of her little pink tongue; he swallowed with some difficulty and finished, ". . . them."

It was nearly one o'clock when they finally entered Woodward's Gardens. The sermon had been unduly long, and Heather had sensed Brandon's unease and impatience the entire time she was seated next to him in church. He'd fidgeted with the hymnal, cleared his throat so regularly that she could have timed it with a stopwatch, and his deep sighs had expressed his boredom more eloquently than words could have done. Even Matt had been better behaved than his father.

Perhaps making Brandon attend church services on their first outing had not been such a good idea, especially since the entire sermon had been about fornication, lustful hearts, and mending sinful ways.

She hadn't dared look over at him, but had stared straight ahead, wondering if the reverend's words had been directed squarely at her. *Or was it just my guilty conscience that made it seem so?* She certainly had enough lust in her heart to qualify as a sinner.

When the benediction had finally been given and their souls secured for another week, Heather said a silent prayer that her plan to include Brandon in the children's activities would work.

The briny smell of the Pacific filled the air as they strolled down sandy lanes toward the merry-go-round. Jenny and Matt tugged eagerly on their father's hands as they propelled him toward the amusement. Expecting him to be displeased by her selection of entertainment, Heather was pleasantly surprised to find Brandon actually smiling as he paid for the tickets and put the children atop the two wooden horses.

The tinkling tune of the carousel made a joyful accompaniment to Jenny and Matt's excited squeals of pleasure. Brandon and Heather took a seat on a nearby bench to watch, waving at the two as they whirled by.

"They seem to be having a marvelous time," Heather commented, smiling at Matt's pleasure. The happy boy's grin seemed a mile wide. "Have you brought them here before?" His chagrined expression told her the answer even before he said it.

"Uh, no. There never seems to be enough time."

"When it comes to children, time is something you never have enough of. They grow up so fast, and suddenly you wonder where all the time went. One day they're babies, and the next grown men and women."

"Is that how it was with your sisters? You said you'd helped raise them after your mother died."

Heather stared off in the distance, remembering. "I was only fourteen myself, but I felt so much older, having had the responsibility of raising Laurel and Rose Elizabeth. Papa tried to help, but he was busy with the farm, trying to make ends meet. And his grief over Mama's death often blinded him to the needs of three growing girls.

"The day-to-day routine of managing the household fell to me. I cooked, cleaned, refereed fights between Laurel and Rose. . . ." She shrugged. "You know, all the normal things a mother would do."

She smiled at him. "I missed part of my own childhood, so I enjoy watching Jenny and Matt revel in theirs."

"They didn't have much of one until you came along."

The admission shocked not only Heather but Brandon as well. Perhaps he had been a little too hard on the children. The thought that his mother may have been right about his inflexible behavior was quite unsettling. But not as unsettling as the soft hand covering his.

The realization that he was enjoying his time with Heather confounded him. He'd never enjoyed such idle amusements before. At least, he hadn't for a very long time. But Heather was fun to be around. Her sunny disposition never failed to warm even the gloomiest of days. And he found himself able to relax in her presence.

Jenny and Matt certainly adored her, and with good reason. She was kind and patient with them. He'd never once heard her raise her voice in anger. Heather had many fine qualities to offer and would make some lucky man an excellent wife.

The disturbing thought made Brandon frown. The image of her in another man's arms, in his bed, of her nursing another man's baby at her breast, did not sit well at all. However, he chose not to ask himself why, afraid of what the answer might be.

"Well, we're going to change all that, aren't we?"

Her question startled him. He was about to respond in the affirmative, then thought better of it, reminding himself that he was affianced to another woman. Though at the moment, he couldn't imagine why.

They rambled among shady groves until they came to a small stream. As Jenny and Matt ran ahead to skip rocks, Brandon and Heather seated themselves on the grass beneath a tall live-oak tree, but only after Heather had judiciously spelled out a series of safety rules to the children.

"If I had known this place existed, I could have spared your goldfish a traumatic experience."

A mischievous smile lit her face, and Brandon threw back his head and laughed. The throaty, masculine sound made gooseflesh rise on Heather's arms, and she was grateful for the long sleeves of her shirtwaist, which hid her reaction.

"God, the sight of you in that fish pond, with your skirts up and your blouse plastered to your—" He stopped suddenly, gazing at her breasts, his eyes smoldering with desire, and she blushed furiously.

Uncomfortable with the vivid memory, Brandon cleared his throat, trying to dispel the image. "I could have paddled your backside that day. You do have a way of bringing out the worst in me."

Stunned by Brandon's uncharacteristic good humor, and discomforted by the erotic picture his words created, Heather tried to make light of his remarks. But her eyes kept straying to his lips, and she wished with all her heart that he would kiss her.

"You're very lovely, you know." He lifted her hair off her shoulder, sifting the auburn strands through his fingers. His fingers itched to caress much more than her hair. "I'm glad you decided to leave your hair down today. I love the way it feels, so soft and silky."

His words were a caress against her cheek, making her feel breathless and weak-kneed. "I know. You told me so last night."

Reminded of his indiscretion, Brandon stiffened and pulled back his hand; as if she were Medusa, her hair teeming with wily serpents.

Heather could have kicked herself for her stupid remark. "I wasn't mad about last night, Brandon. I realized you weren't quite yourself."

His frown deepened. "I haven't been myself since you moved into my house."

"Do you wish I'd never come?" She waited anxiously for his answer, wondering, now that he'd gotten to know her better, if he still regretted his mother's decision to hire her.

His arm came around to clutch the back of her head, drawing her toward him. "God no!" he said. And then he kissed her with all the pent-up passion that the months of yearning had created.

Heather was stunned by the intensity of Brandon's kiss, by the way his lips moved over hers in tantalizing possession. His tongue traced the soft fullness of her lower lip, sending the pit of her stomach into a wild frenzy.

He had kissed her before, when he thought she was someone else, but it hadn't felt like this. This kiss sizzled and seduced. When his tongue sought entry into her mouth, she opened, allowing him to taste her, possess her, brand her with his masculine heat.

Time seemed to stand still for Brandon. Nothing mattered but the sweet taste of this woman in his arms, the feel of her pliant body soft and warm against his hard-muscled planes. He was lost, drowning in a whirlpool of desire. He wanted to caress her, to touch the velvet softness of her breasts, feel the wet, throbbing mound he knew would welcome him. . . .

The sound of children's laughter jolted him back to reality.

"Father, Father, what's wrong?" Matt ground to a halt, trying to catch his breath. A concerned look drew his brows close together. "Is Miss Martin sick? Is that why you're holding on to her?"

Brandon jerked back quickly, as if Heather's clothes had suddenly caught fire. Only, it was he who had been seared.

The horrified expression on his face at having been caught in a compromising situation by his own children filled Heather with compassion. She thought quickly.

"I was feeling a little faint, Matt. Your father was trying to comfort me, but I'm fine now."

At least that much was true. Brandon's kisses had made her faint with desire. She fought the urge to lick her lips, knowing that if she did, she'd find them as sensitive and swollen as her nipples.

"You do look a little funny, Miss Martin," Jenny pointed out. "Your face is all red, like you've got a fever. And you have a rash on your face."

Brandon turned and saw the whisker burns he'd left on Heather's tender cheeks, and his own face reddened. "Miss

Martin has fully recovered, children. I suggest that you go on to the museum. We'll meet you there shortly."

After they'd left, Brandon rose to his feet and extended a hand to help Heather up. He looked angry and confused, but Heather couldn't tell whether he was angry at her or at himself.

"Once again I must apologize for my behavior." The words were as stiff as his spine, and oh so very proper.

"Why?" she asked, irritated by his need to explain. "I'm not complaining."

Heather walked away in search of the children, leaving Brandon to ponder her words and to curse himself for his own stupidity and lack of restraint.

There was no denying the bulge in his pants.

There was no denying the attraction between them.

And there was no denying that he couldn't and wouldn't do a damn thing about either!

"Miss Martin! What the devil are you doing? And why is there a pile of mud on my kitchen table?"

As he took in the children's disheveled appearance, Brandon's face tightened. But he could hardly blame Jenny and Matt for the disgraceful way they looked. Not when their role model looked far more slovenly.

Heather was dressed in one of those old, ugly gowns he abhorred. The dress was splattered with a brown gooey substance that looked like something right out of the barnyard. There were traces of it on her face and in her hair, too. Even Mr. Woo was up to his elbows in the stuff. It was no surprise that she had corrupted the cook as well, he thought.

At Brandon's angry expression, Heather sighed in disbelief. He'd been in a bad temper since their kiss three days ago. Obviously it hadn't settled as well on his conscience as it had on hers. She'd reveled in it, replaying over in her mind every minute of their passionate embrace. Of course, she wasn't engaged to be married, she kept reminding herself.

"This is sculptor's clay, not mud, Brandon," Heather ex-

plained with far more patience than he deserved. "Mr. Woo
has been kind enough to help us with our project today." She
smiled at the little man, who quaked under Brandon's gaze,
looking as if he might slide beneath the table at any moment.

"Missy need help. Woo learn to make wild breasts."

"It's *beast,* Mr. Woo. Beast," Heather corrected, feeling
her cheeks warm. "You're learning to make a sculpture of a
mountain lion."

Brandon stared at the mound of clay before Woo, his eyes
widening. Mountain *breasts* indeed! The large lump of clay
hardly resembled a catamount, and it did have two very dis-
tinguishing points at the top, which looked suspiciously
like. . .

He lifted his gaze to meet Heather's. "Miss Martin, when
you have cleaned that god-awful mess off your arms, I would
like to see you in my study."

Jenny and Matt exchanged worried looks, then Jenny said
hurriedly, "This is part of our art project, Father. Miss Martin
is teaching us to be well-rounded indiv . . . indiv . . . people."
The little girl smiled. "Isn't that right, Miss Martin?" She
looked at Heather for confirmation.

Before Heather could respond, Brandon banged his hands
down on the table, causing everyone to jump in their seats.
"Children should be seen and not heard."

Knowing exactly where he'd heard that line before—it
was one of Cecelia's favorites—Heather cast him a fulminating look.

"You and your brother go upstairs and clean up," Brandon
ordered his misty-eyed daughter. "Miss Whitten is coming
over this evening to entertain us on the piano, and I want
both of you to be on your best behavior."

Matt screwed up his face, looking like he'd just swallowed
a whole bottle of castor oil. "Why do we have to be there?
Miss Whitten doesn't like us, and she can't play the piano
worth beans."

At Brandon's outraged look, Heather quickly interceded.
"Matt, I'm sure Miss Whitten likes you very much. And you
must remember to be tolerant of those who are not as tal-

ented or as smart as you. Remember what Reverend Jessup said about judging others lest ye be judged?"

"Sorry," he said, looking suitably chastised, before climbing down off his chair and slipping out of the room. Jenny followed close on his heels.

"Five minutes, Miss Martin," Brandon reminded her before stalking out of the room.

Heather entered the study to find Brandon pacing back and forth like a caged lion. His arms were clasped behind his back, and he looked like a world-weary politician about to make a speech. Things did not bode well for her.

"You wanted to talk to me, Brandon?" She paused in front of his desk.

"Please have a seat, Miss Martin."

"So, it's 'Miss Martin' again. What happened to 'Heather'? I thought we'd decided a while ago to dispense with such formalities." She sat down, crossing her legs primly at the ankles while resting her hands on her lap. Though she presented a calm demeanor, inwardly Heather seethed with indignation.

Would Brandon ever allow himself to feel honest emotions? He disguised his affection as easily as a chameleon changed colors. He did it with his children, and now he was doing it with her.

Brandon stopped behind his desk but he didn't sit, grasping the back of the chair instead. "Perhaps we've bent the rules a little too much," he said by way of explanation, unwilling to elaborate.

Heather had a pretty good idea where all this hostility and guilt had come from, and she didn't bother to mince words. "It's much easier to keep me at a distance if you call me Miss Martin, isn't it, Brandon?" She rose, placing her palms flat on the desk while impaling him with fury-filled eyes. "I think we both know what this is all about, but I won't be unladylike enough to bring it up and embarrass you. Since it seems you already are.

"But I won't go back to the way things were before, Brandon. I will continue to call you by your first name, and you may call me whatever you damn well please. Now, if you'll excuse me, I'll go up and see that the children are made presentable for your fiancée, who you so conveniently dismissed from your mind the other day."

Brandon purpled, the pulse in his neck throbbing so violently that Heather feared it might burst. It didn't. Instead, his temper exploded. "I should fire you for your insolence. And for the way you are turning my children into sassy street urchins."

His remark rankled, igniting the embers of a temper Heather could no longer hold in check and turning it into a raging inferno. "I'm turning your children into children. I'm trying to undo all the harm you've created by your rigid behavior and ridiculous rules over the past six years.

"And you won't fire me, Brandon, because no one else in this city will work for you. Your mother told me that much. Apparently I wasn't the first governess to grace the halls of this mansion." She was face to face with him now, breathing so hard that her chest hurt. "Take care that I don't turn the tables on you and quit, *Mr. Montgomery*. It's no more than you deserve."

"Lord have mercy! I can't take another night of Miss High-and-Mighty's caterwauling. Three nights it's been of her singing and playing the piano. How does Mr. Montgomery stand it?"

"Ssh! They'll hear you," Heather cautioned Mary-Margaret, though the woman's sentiments mirrored her own. Cecelia's musical abilities left a lot to be desired. But then, she was fairly certain it wasn't her voice that had attracted Brandon.

Shoving the plate of freshly baked oatmeal-spice cookies across the kitchen table toward Mary, she filled their cups with hot coffee from the blue speckled enamel pot. The scents of cinnamon and clove teased her taste buds as she sunk her teeth into the chewy morsel.

"At least Harriet had the good sense to make herself scarce

tonight," Heather whispered, wiping crumbs off the corners of her mouth with her forefinger.

Mary's eyes sparkled with merriment. "To get Miss Harriet to volunteer for the Red Cross is quite an accomplishment. She hates being around all those do-gooders, as she calls them. But it's for a good cause, so she offered to help collect clothing and money for last week's fire victims."

The chemical plant on Battery Street had exploded in a burst of flames. Four people had been killed and sixteen injured. There was talk that the fire that had caused the explosion had been deliberately set, though the culprits had yet to be caught.

Brandon's newspaper had featured several human-interest stories on the victims and the survivors.

"It was kind of Harriet to help out," Heather said.

Mary snickered. "I think Miss Harriet's volunteering had more to do with you-know-who," she jerked her head in the direction of the family parlor, "than anything else. Did you know Matt threatened to put cotton balls in his ears this evening?"

Heather covered her mouth to stifle her laughter. "That's horrible! You don't think he really did such a thing, do you?" There'd be hell to pay if Brandon got wind of it.

"Jack was sworn to secrecy. But my Jack don't know how to keep a secret. He's like his mother in that respect."

"What do you think Brandon's motives are for bringing Cecelia over here every night? Do you suppose he actually enjoys her recitals?"

Mary cast Heather a look of disbelief before reaching for another cookie. "Not on your life. Miss Harriet said, with quite a bit of disgust, I might add, that Mr. Montgomery is trying to acquaint Miss Whitten with the children. He feels he's done her a disservice by not allowing her and the children to spend more time together."

A lump rose in Heather's throat, but she swallowed it. She'd guessed as much, but hadn't wanted to face the truth. Obviously, the kiss they'd shared had frightened Brandon straight into Cecelia's waiting arms.

"She's to be their stepmother," Heather finally said. And the admission tore straight into her heart.

"That one's got about as much mothering instincts as a stray cat." Mary sniffed disdainfully. "If Mr. Montgomery marries up with that woman, the children are going to be the ones to suffer. She'll pack them off to one of them fancy boarding schools back East quicker than she can spit."

Heather covered her mouth again, but this time it was to stifle a scream of despair. *Jenny and Matt in boarding school? Those two trusting, innocent children ripped away from their family?*

That was not going to happen, Heather vowed, her eyes filling with determination. Not as long as she had a breath left in her body. If Brandon was too wrapped up in Cecelia to see her for what she was—a manipulative, social-climbing . . . then she would just have to do something about it. She might not have borne Jenny and Matt, but she was more a mother to them than Cecelia could ever hope to be.

CHAPTER 12

"Father, this ice cream is yummy. I wish we could bring some home for Miss Martin." Jenny smiled happily at Brandon, who had surprised her and Matt with a trip to Benton's Ice Cream Parlor for getting perfect scores on their geography test. The children's only complaint had been that Miss Whitten had been included in the outing instead of Miss Martin.

Her red lips pursed at the child's suggestion, Cecelia glared at the little girl, making Jenny squirm nervously in her chair. The children's dislike of her was obvious, as was their devotion to the redheaded governess who cared for them.

Well, that dislike was mutual, Cecelia thought. She didn't enjoy sharing Brandon's time with anyone, especially his two bratty children, and she hoped they wouldn't embarrass her in front of the Ponds, a very influential family who were listed in the *Elite Directory,* a "guide" to more than six thousand wealthy families, and who were seated in the far corner of the parlor.

Benton's was a popular gathering place on Saturday afternoons. Cecelia cringed, wondering who else might stop in to see her in her new, unwelcome role of surrogate mother.

Lorna Pond had already cast her a catty smile. The fat biddy was obviously envious of Cecelia's success in snaring the most eligible catch in San Francisco. Of course, Lorna wouldn't be quite so envious if she knew that Cecelia had also netted Brandon's young twins in the bargain.

This plan of Brandon's to acquaint her with his children was proving far more trying than she'd expected. The only flaw in her relationship with the handsome newspaper owner were the two brats seated next to him at the table.

They looked angelic sitting there with grateful, adoring smiles directed at their father, but Cecelia knew them to be spawns of the devil, especially the girl, Jenny. Cecelia knew firsthand how easy it was for a daughter to cajole whatever she wanted out of her father. She'd done it numerous times with her own dear daddy.

Well, she wasn't about to let either of the little *darlings* interfere with her plans to become the next Mrs. Brandon Montgomery. Once the wedding ring had been slipped on her finger, she had plans for both of them. Consoling herself with the notion that the Montgomery children were only temporary inconveniences, she pasted on an insincere smile.

Cecelia was trying her damnedest to look motherly. Not an easy chore dressed as she was in a red velvet box-pleated skirt and braided Hussar jacket, which made her look more like a commanding military leader than a motherly figure.

The ostrich plume cascading from the side of her jaunty hat didn't help her image one bit. It had come close to blinding Matt on one occasion and had very nearly landed in Jenny's ice cream on another.

"Are you enjoying your ice cream, children?" she asked.

Matt looked up at her question, unsure of the correct response. It seemed that no matter what answer he or Jenny gave Miss Whitten, it was never the right one. He tried anyway: "Yes, ma'am." He licked the chocolate cream off his lips with relish. "I like it just fine."

Nervous at having been addressed by her father's lady

friend, Jenny accidentally dropped her spoon on the floor. It clattered noisily beneath the table.

"Be careful, you silly thing," Cecelia lashed out, forgetting for the moment that Brandon was seated next to her, watching her every movement with rapt interest. "Don't get any of that ice cream on your dress or mine," she scolded the distraught child, sighing deeply, as if the whole incident was just too much for her to bear. "Children need to learn proper eating habits when they're out in public. And, Matt, quit wiping your hands on your pants. That's what napkins are for."

She cast an apologetic smile in the Ponds' direction, hoping that gossipy Lorna wouldn't repeat this horrible incident to anyone. But knowing she would, Cecelia's tone was that much harsher when she added, "Didn't that governess of yours teach you two anything?"

Brandon frowned at his fiancée's excessive annoyance but said nothing, allowing Cecelia some latitude in dealing with the children. If she was to be their mother, Jenny and Matt would have to get used to dealing with her reprimands on occasion. But she certainly didn't have to be so damn vehement about it, he thought.

"Miss Martin always teaches us correct behavior," Jenny blurted in Heather's defense, and Brandon shot her a reproving look, making her eyes well with tears.

He sighed inwardly and wondered, not for the first time, if his idea to have Cecelia spend more time with the children was such a good one.

The children's animosity toward their future stepmother was evident. Matt hadn't bothered to hide his hostility and had refused to take Cecelia's hand the few times she'd offered it, saying that he was too big to be treated like a baby. But Brandon had seen him swinging on the end of Heather's hand numerous times, and he knew how much Matt loved to sit on her lap while she read him a story.

But then, Cecelia wasn't Heather.

His fiancée had neither the experience nor the patience Heather had in dealing with small children, but he couldn't fault her for it. As an only child, Cecelia had little understanding of children's ways. It was only natural for her to be reticent in her dealings with Jenny and Matt.

And Cecelia did have other qualities to recommend her. True, she wasn't as patient as Heather, but she did possess the social skills and standing necessary to a man in his position. That was an asset that couldn't be overlooked.

Cecelia was like an expensive piece of crystal whose brilliance shone in a flattering light.

Heather was more like a comfortable quilt you could wrap around yourself to keep warm on a winter's evening.

One sparkled, able to make witty conversation.

One laughed, her face lighting up an entire room.

Both women were dangerous in their own right.

But it was Heather who scared the hell out of him.

Sitting in the window seat in Heather's bedroom, Harriet looked down at the scene below, and a pinched look drew her brows together. Brandon and Cecelia were strolling hand in hand, oblivious to the two unhappy children trailing after them.

"You'll have to face this way, Harriet, if you want me to continue with your portrait," Heather instructed, wondering how on earth she had allowed the older woman to talk her into painting her portrait in the first place. Harriet was nothing if not persuasive.

"I'm sorry, my dear. But it just breaks my heart to watch my grandchildren suffer so. They've looked so miserable these past few weeks. And with good reason, I might add. If I had to share Miss Whitten's company for any length of time, I'd go stark raving mad."

Heather dabbed silently at the canvas with her paintbrush, hoping that Harriet couldn't see how her words affected her. She too had noticed the children's unhappiness. They were reverting back to morose behavior and introversion, and it broke Heather's heart.

It hurt almost as much as the fact that Brandon had chosen to spend an inordinate amount of time lately with his fiancée, virtually ignoring Heather in the process. His obvious denial of the feelings between them had wounded her.

"Look how she leads Brandon around by his nose," Harriet said with disgust. "My son is nothing but a fool."

"Quit scowling, Harriet, or this surprise Christmas gift you've planned for your fool of a son is going to turn out just dreadfully."

"It's really quite good of you to do this for me, dear. And it was really very clever of you to suggest that we keep this a secret between us. I do so want to surprise Brandon with something special this year."

Knowing the real reason for her suggestion of secrecy, a guilty flush filled Heather's cheeks, and she decided to change the subject. "How is Mr. Woo coming along with the plans for the party Brandon is giving? I understand there's to be quite a few newspaper people invited."

Brandon's announcement of the party had come as quite a shock to everyone, especially Mr. Woo, whose dislike of the idea was made crystal clear when the Chinaman let out a string of curses as soon as Brandon had exited the kitchen:

"Woo no likee give party. Woo madder than sore-titted itch."

It was supposed to be sore-titted *bitch*. Heather had heard her father use the expression countless times when he'd been angry, but she hadn't corrected Woo on it. She'd never heard anything quite so unusual as the Chinaman uttering profanities.

"Brandon is very fond of his managing editor, Frank Burnside," Harriet explained. "Mr. Burnside's sixtieth birthday is coming up, and Brandon wanted to do something extra special for him. Apparently Frank's wife, Clara, has just been diagnosed with a terminal illness. The cancer's centered in her breasts, and she's not expected to live out the year."

Heather's hand stilled over the canvas. "How dreadful!"

She remembered her father's battle with the disease and felt deep pity for Frank Burnside. Ezra's vitality had dissolved along with a hundred pounds of his weight. He'd been a shell of his former self when he'd finally succumbed to the sickness.

"How is Mr. Burnside holding up?"

"Not well, I'm afraid. You see, Frank was an alcoholic. It was Clara who pulled him up from the depths of his despair, and Brandon's worried that once she dies, he'll go right back to the bottle."

"Like Brandon's father?" Heather asked softly.

Harriet's shoulders slumped as unhappy memories washed over her. "Brandon told you about Charles?"

"Not directly. But I've pieced things together from some of the remarks he's made."

"Brandon doted on his father. We both loved Charles Montgomery to distraction. I think that was part of the problem. We continually made excuses for his behavior, instead of admitting his drinking problem. The liquor eventually destroyed Charles's liver, and Brandon never forgave his father for falling off the pedestal he'd placed him on."

"Brandon expects a lot from those he loves."

"Yes, he does. Which is why I have never understood his attachment to Miss Whitten. Surely she could never live up to his expectations."

"Love is blind, as they say," Heather replied, ignoring the pain twisting her heart as she wiped the paint from her brushes.

"You're the one who's blind, my dear, if you think my son is in love with Cecelia." Harriet's gentle smile softened the reprimand. "Brandon wants to marry her for exactly the opposite reason."

Putting aside her paints and brushes, Heather came to stand before Brandon's mother, who looked lovely in the periwinkle-blue gown they had chosen for her sitting. But as bright as her dress was, Harriet's eyes were dark with sadness and resignation.

"You must be mistaken, Harriet. I've seen Brandon and Cecelia together. They appear to be very much in love, and I think you should learn to accept the inevitable." *I have.*

"I know my son better than you think, my dear. Brandon's

marriage to Cecelia is a convenience, nothing more. He needs a hostess and a mother for his children. Though his motives for marrying might sound selfish, to Brandon they make perfect sense. He views it as a practical arrangement. He'll have all the benefits of marriage, without endangering his heart in the process.

"You see, Brandon's first wife hurt him very deeply. I'm not sure he will ever recover from that blow to his ego and self-confidence. His judgment, trust, everything he prided himself on knowing and believing was shattered in one fell swoop."

"Lydia sounds like a terrible woman," Heather remarked, remembering how Brandon had cried for his ex-wife in his delirium. He had loved her a great deal, and she wondered what it would feel like to have someone—no, not "someone"—*Brandon* love her like that.

"Lydia wasn't terrible. She just wanted something out of life that Brandon wasn't able to give her." Harriet didn't elaborate. Instead she sighed and waved her hand, as if that could wave away all the unpleasantness of the past. "But that's enough of that. This whole topic has made me terribly depressed and hungry. Why don't we go down to the kitchen and whip up one of those chocolate cakes you're so famous for?"

Heather laughed, holding out her hands to help the older woman up. "I'm not sure feeding your depression is the best way to deal with it."

"No," Harriet agreed, wrapping her arm about Heather's waist. "But it's the only solution I can come up with at the moment." Glancing toward the window, she tapped her chin. "But give me time. I'll think of something. . . ."

Heather was just taking the cake out of the oven when a bloodcurdling scream rent the air.

Harriet gasped and ran toward the window. "My goodness! I hope the children are all right."

Fearing that something dreadful had befallen Jenny and Matt, Heather's face paled. Dropping the cake and pot holders on the wooden table, she dashed for the back door.

At a sprint, Heather covered the rear yard in moments. Spying Jenny and Matt standing by the fish pond, looking none the worse for wear, she breathed a deep sigh of relief, and was about to call out to them when another horrible scream filled the air.

The wail was unmistakably Cecelia's.

"Help me, Brandon! Help me!"

Heather skidded to a halt, and Harriet, who'd been hurrying to catch up with her, nearly collided into her back. They looked at each other, stared at the pond, then covered their mouths to stifle their laughter. Cecelia had fallen into the fish pond.

Dripping wet, her scraggly blond hair hanging down over her face, Cecelia emerged from the pond looking like some hideous sea creature from a Jules Verne novel. A dead goldfish clung to her green silk gown, and several cattails decorated her once-impressive coiffure.

"They did it," she said, pointing an accusing finger at Jenny and Matt, who stared wide-eyed at their future stepmother. "Those horrible children tried to drown me by pushing me into the pond."

Heather caught Brandon's gaze, and unless she was very much mistaken, he too was doing his best not to laugh. She then looked at the children, who were cowering behind their father as if this might be their last day on earth.

Stepping toward them, Heather asked in a calm voice, "Jenny, Matt, were you responsible for Miss Whitten falling into the fish pond?" She already knew the answer. Jenny and Matt didn't possess a mean bone in their dear little bodies. Unlike Cecelia, who fairly reeked of venom.

Two pair of wide, innocent eyes stared up at her. "No, Miss Martin," Jenny said, wagging her head. "We were all looking at the fishes, bending down close to the water so we could see them good. Miss Whitten just bent too far over."

"And you didn't do anything that might have caused her to fall in?"

"It wasn't the children's fault," Brandon said in their defense. "I saw the whole thing. Cecelia just leaned over a bit too far, and gravity did the rest."

"How dare you take their side against me, Brandon!" Cecelia screamed, her eyes flashing with fury. "I have never been so humiliated in my life." The dead fish fell off her dress at that moment, belying her contention, and Heather had to restrain herself from smiling. Harriet wasn't as generous.

"Come into the house, Miss Whitten, and I'll provide you with something dry to wear," she offered with far more kindness than she felt.

Cecelia stamped her foot, and a squishing sound erupted, pond water slowly seeping out of her shoe. "I certainly will not! I demand to be taken home at once, Brandon. I have had quite enough of these incorrigible brats for one afternoon. They would benefit from an extended stay at boarding school, where they might be taught some manners. I say 'might' because nothing short of a good beating is likely to do any good where those two are concerned."

Harriet gasped, Brandon's lips narrowed, and Heather saw red.

"The children possess excellent manners, Miss Whitten," Heather retorted. *Unlike yourself.* But Heather refrained from verbalizing that thought. If she got too worked up, she was likely to punch Miss Cecelia Whitten smack dab in her nasty mouth. "They are delightful children who behave quite normally for six-year-olds. Perhaps you are not familiar with small children, Miss Whitten. Perhaps you are placing the blame on them instead of where it belongs . . . on yourself."

Unaware of Harriet's delighted smile and the sickly red tinge now occupying Cecelia's cheeks, Heather grasped the children's hands and hauled them across the yard, away from their crazed future stepmother.

She didn't see the spark of admiration in Brandon's eyes.

Entering the house feeling frustrated and depressed, Brandon wished he were a drinking man. After what he'd just been through, he could certainly use a stiff shot of something.

Cecelia's ranting and raving about the incident at the fish pond had given him an enormous headache. The sound of her whining, complaining voice on the carriage ride to her home had filled him with an uncontrollable desire to tape her mouth shut!

When had the woman become such a shrew?

Heather had certainly responded to her dunking with far more grace and dignity. And she hadn't tried to blame her predicament on two innocent children.

God, what a mess! He brushed impatient fingers through his hair, hanging his coat on the hall tree. *The children despise Cecelia. It's obvious she can't tolerate them. So why am I planning to marry her?*

The sound of sobbing drew him forward. Brandon paused in the doorway of the family parlor and saw Heather and the children seated on the rug in front of the fireplace. Heather's arms were wrapped about Jenny and Matt's small shoulders, offering comfort while they cried. It was a touching scene, even to someone as embittered and callous as he.

He'd learned long ago that tears were a sign of weakness. He deplored the womanly use of them to get their way and had forbade his children to express their emotions in such a manipulative manner.

Tears, like excuses, never solved anything.

But there was something about his children's heart-wrenching sobs that tore through his beliefs and stabbed at his heart.

Moving behind the door to shield himself from their view, he eavesdropped on their conversation.

"She hates us, Miss Martin." Matt wiped his nose on the sleeve of Heather's dress, and she seemed not to mind at all. "We don't want her for our mother. She's not like mothers are supposed to be. She don't bake cookies . . ."

"Doesn't bake," Heather corrected automatically.

"Doesn't bake cookies. She doesn't read stories. And she doesn't know how to make school fun like you do, Miss

Martin. Miss Whitten makes us recite our ABC's, and if we miss one, she calls us stupid and makes us start all over again."

Brandon frowned deeply at that disclosure.

Jenny's tears spiked her dark lashes like diamonds. "Why can't you be our mother, Miss Martin? Me and Matt love you. We want you to stay and live here with us and be our mother forever and ever."

Brandon sucked in his breath, waiting for Heather's response.

"Your father and I don't love each other, Jenny. He's in love with Miss Whitten, and you must do your best to get along with her." She smoothed the child's tears away with her fingertips. "I love both of you very much. But I can't be your mother. That very great honor has already been given to someone else."

Did he detect a note of sadness in Heather's voice? Or was that just wishful thinking on his part?

"Don't you want to stay here and be our mother?" Matt asked, hugging Heather about the waist until she wanted to cry, to scream: *Yes, yes, I do! With all my heart, I do.* But she couldn't. That wouldn't be fair to Brandon, or to the woman he had chosen to give his heart to.

Her voice gentled. "Matt, you mustn't try to wish for things that cannot be. You must accept things the way they are and try to make the best of them."

"Why, Miss Martin?" Jenny countered, tilting her chin in a defiant manner that Brandon was starting to recognize. "You taught us to believe in fairy tales, magic, and make-believe. You said if we believed hard enough, whatever we wished for would come true. Don't you remember, Miss Martin? That's what you said. Isn't it, Matty?"

Matt nodded solemnly. "It sure is. You said we had the power to be whatever we wanted to be. That we could make the world a better place to live in by fulfilling our po . . . po . . ."

"Potential," Heather supplied, sighing as the words she'd uttered were thrown back in her face.

The twins nodded.

Feeling totally helpless for the first time in her life, Heather shook her head. "You don't understand. If you were a little older, you would. I don't have the power to make your father love me. He's in love with another woman. Nothing I can dream or wish for can make him change his mind."

"Maybe *we* could, Miss Martin," Jenny offered, her eyes brightening. "Maybe we could tell Father that we've chosen you for our mother and not Miss Whitten."

The suggestion horrified Heather, and her voice grew stern, though she hated herself for it. "You'll do no such thing! You and Matt will respect your father's wishes and do as you're told. You are only six years old. Far too young to be dictating to an adult, especially someone like your father."

"But . . ."

She held up her hand. "So you want your father to fire me? Do you want him to accuse me of putting these ideas into your head?" Which is just what Brandon would think, she had no doubt.

The children's tears began again as they shook their heads, and Heather had to concentrate very hard to keep herself from joining in their misery. "It's enough for now that we can be together," she said. "No one knows what the future holds in store. Only God has the power to predict which way our lives will go."

"What if God decided you could be our mother?" Matt asked.

Ruffling his hair, Heather smiled softly. "Then that's what would happen. If God decides something, no one can tell him any differently. He's much too powerful."

Digesting this important piece of information, Jenny and Matt put their hands together and conferred, then Jenny reached out to take Heather's hands in her small ones.

"If that's so, Miss Martin, then me and Matty are going to pray really hard that God will choose you to be our mother."

Heather smiled sadly and kissed them both on the cheek. And Brandon, still concealed behind the door, felt her lips on his face as surely as if she'd kissed him too.

CHAPTER 13

Despite the fact that it was the second week of November, it was an absolutely glorious day for an outdoor party. It never failed to impress Heather that the weather in California was so much more temperate than Kansas's wintry climate. It was probably snowing there now, or at least sleeting. It was doubtful that the sun would be shining as brightly as it was here, or that roses and daisies would still be blooming in such mass profusion.

But this was San Francisco, not Salina, she reminded herself. "Sunny California" as the guidebook stated. And the warmth of the autumn day couldn't dispel the truth of that claim.

A half-dozen tables graced the lawn of the rear yard, where many of Brandon's guests were already seated. The tables had been draped in white cloths, and in the center of each stood a lovely bouquet of wildflowers. The caterer Brandon had hired, after Mr. Woo had pitched another fit, had done a marvelous job of making the arrangements and preparing the food.

Champagne flowed out of cherub-looking fountains, and exquisite caviar canapes and hot mushroom and crab hors d'oeuvres were served on shiny silver trays. A small string quartet entertained atop a makeshift bandstand, and several of the guests amused themselves with a game of croquet.

Everything was perfect, just as Heather knew it would be. Brandon would have tolerated no less.

"There you are, my dear." Harriet approached on the arm of a very handsome gentleman, looking radiant in a silver satin day gown that picked up the silvery highlights of her hair, which peeked out beneath the brim of her enormous hat. Harriet was forever fearful of getting too much sun on her face.

The gentleman escorting her was nattily dressed in a brown and gold houndstooth jacket and brown slacks. His flaxen hair glinted in the afternoon sunlight, and his eyes were the prettiest sapphire blue.

"There's someone I'd like you to meet," Harriet said. "This is Peter Glendenning. Peter works for *The Chronicle* as their star reporter."

Heather held out her hand to the stranger and smiled. "Welcome, Mr. Glendenning. It's an honor to meet a man of your immense talent."

"Mrs. Montgomery exaggerates, I'm afraid," Peter Glendenning said, his smile displaying two charming dimples. Heather thought it was sinful that a man could possess such even white teeth and long black eyelashes.

"Peter's too modest," Harriet countered. "Brandon's been trying to lure him away from that other newspaper for months. He constantly bemoans the fact that Peter's insightful articles are stealing away his customers."

"I believe I've heard Brandon mention as much." Charmed by the way Peter blushed under Harriet's praise, Heather added, "And I admit to sharing his opinion. I've read your work, and I'm very impressed by it."

Harriet's gaze drifted between the two and a calculating gleam entered her eyes. "Well, if you two will excuse me, I must mingle with the other guests."

"Do you wish me to do anything, Harriet? Perhaps pour champagne? Or pass the canape trays?"

"No, dear. Your only task is to keep Peter amused. Perhaps your charm can lure him to work at *The Star*." She winked at the young man and patted him on the cheek in a motherly display of affection.

Peter laughed, his blue eyes twinkling. "You may be right, Mrs. Montgomery. Your governess is every bit as lovely as you indicated."

Embarrassed by the compliment, Heather blushed under Peter's praise. But she was pleased, too. After the bruising her ego had sustained from Brandon's indifference, it was nice to have a handsome man pay her tribute. "Thank you, Mr. Glendenning."

He linked his arm through hers. "Call me Peter, because I certainly intend to call you Heather. Now, are you going to give me a tour of the grounds? I understand Brandon has an Oriental fish pond that's been making news of late." His eyes twinkled mischievously.

"You've heard?" Heather asked in surprise.

Chuckling, Peter nodded. "Cecelia Whitten's dousing is all the talk in the newspaper community. I don't mind saying, it couldn't have happened to a more deserving person. Unless, of course, it had been her father." His eyes narrowed slightly.

Loyalty to Brandon prevented Heather from commenting, but she was secretly delighted to hear Peter's opinion. At least there was one man who hadn't been taken in by Cecelia's charms.

The woman had had the audacity to show up at the afternoon party wearing a formal velvet ball gown studded with precious gems. Like most of her gowns, this one showed off a generous amount of Cecelia's anatomy. She reminded Heather of those women Mary had told her about, the ones who frequented the street corners of the Tenderloin district.

"Tell me about your job, Peter. I'm fascinated by the workings of newspapers."

"Then you must come down to *The Chronicle* and let me show you around sometime."

"I've been there," Heather replied without thinking. "I met a horrid little man by the name of Mr. Maitland." She grimaced at the memory of that nasty city editor.

"George?" Peter laughed. "He's not so bad, once you get to know him. What brought you to the newspaper in the first place? It's not a place most women would choose to visit."

"I . . ." Heather was not quite sure what to say. She hemmed and hawed for a few moments, then decided to trust Peter Glendenning. He had the sort of face that bespoke honor and confidence, and she felt extremely comfortable in his presence, as if she'd known him all her life. It was the oddest sensation.

"Will you keep my confidence, if I tell you, Peter? I could lose my position if the Montgomerys found out my reason for visiting your offices."

A teasing quality to his voice, he asked, "You're not Montgomery's spy, are you?"

Giggling at the absurd notion, Heather shook her head. "Heavens no! I applied for a position as an illustrator. It was when I first arrived in the city and was desperate to find work."

Peter arched an inquisitive eyebrow. "If you don't mind my asking, why are you working as a governess if you're qualified to illustrate?"

Heather paused beneath a huge eucalyptus tree, inhaling its pungent odor as she scraped at the bark with her fingernail.

"Your Mr. Maitland made it quite clear that he wouldn't hire a woman for what he considered a man's position. After making the rounds of all the other newspapers, I found that they felt the same way."

"Why didn't you inform Montgomery of your abilities? I hear he's pretty open-minded about most things. Perhaps he would have given you a job."

Heather stared at Peter as if he'd lost his faculties. *Bran-*

don? Open-minded? Were they talking about the same Brandon Montgomery?

"That's a word I'd never associate with Brandon." She shrugged. "Anyway, I did apply at *The Star*, but I was turned away by one of Brandon's underlings."

"And I take it Montgomery doesn't know of your abilities?"

A look of chagrin crossed her face. "I didn't want him to think I had taken the governess position under false pretenses. Though, to be perfectly honest, I did think it might help me secure a position with his newspaper after I proved myself."

"And have you proven yourself?"

"As a governess, yes. But I've never had the courage to reveal my real avocation. No one knows, not even Harriet. She's aware of my artistic ability, but she believes it's only a hobby."

"And it isn't?" He studied her intently, noting the way her eyes lit with an inner flame.

"Oh, no, Peter. It's what I want most in the world. I've always wanted to paint pictures and illustrate stories. It's part of who I am."

"I'm impressed by your dedication, Heather. But can you draw?"

"Yes, I can," she replied without hesitation. "I can draw extremely well."

Heather's ebullient smile was like a prizefighter's punch to Peter's gut, and he felt as if all the air in his lungs had been expelled. Heather Martin was truly lovely. And he had an appreciation for pretty things, especially when it came to women.

He loved women. No matter the shape, size, or color of hair or eyes. It was fortunate, however, that Heather was pleasingly packaged. But more important, she was intelligent.

Why would Brandon Montgomery bother with a dimwit like Cecelia Whitten when he had pretty Miss Martin living under his roof? There was just no accounting for taste, he decided. Fortunately, Peter prided himself on having excellent taste.

Enveloping Heather's hand in his, he caressed it lightly. "Perhaps you would allow me to take a look at some of your illustrations. I would be happy to offer a professional opinion."

She smiled in gratitude. "You're very kind."

"I confess to having an ulterior motive."

Her eyebrow arched. "Which is . . . ?"

"I would very much like to take you out to dinner. I find myself extremely attracted to you."

A moment of silence stretched between them, making the birds' chirping overhead seem unnaturally loud to Heather. Swallowing with some difficulty, Heather extricated her hand from Peter's, wiping her damp palm on the skirt of her violet taffeta dress.

"I don't know what to say. We really don't know each other very well."

"Are you involved with someone else?" He held his breath, suddenly realizing that her answer was very important to him.

She thought of Brandon. She thought of how much she loved him, desired him . . . and of how that love would go unrequited because of his engagement to Cecelia.

"No. It's nothing like that. I'm just terribly busy with the children."

He smiled easily, not at all put off by her rebuff. "I quite understand if you're not attracted to me. Though it does do a bit of damage to the ego."

Dismayed at having hurt his feelings, Heather replied quickly, "Oh, it's nothing like that. I find you very attractive. How could I not? You're a very handsome man."

Chuckling, he tipped up her chin. "You know, Heather, honesty like yours could get you in a great deal of trouble. You're lucky that I'm such an honorable chap. Now, will you have dinner with me? Say tomorrow evening? I know a wonderful place by the ocean. It's called The Cliff House, and I'll arrange for us to have a table by the window. The view is magnificent."

Heather couldn't contain a surge of excitement flowing through her. "The Cliff House. I've read about it in my guidebook. It sounds wonderful. And if it's by the ocean . . . Well, the ocean is one of the main reasons I moved here from Kansas."

"Then you'll go?"

She wondered momentarily if Brandon would have any objections, then decided she really didn't care. Tomorrow was Sunday, her day off.

"I'd love to. And I'll bring along some of my sketches. That way we can consider this a working engagement." She laughed at the wounded expression on his face.

Peter leaned against the tree, both hands resting on either side of Heather's head as he stared into her eyes. He was so close, Heather could feel his breath on her face, and she found it wasn't a completely unpleasant sensation.

"Once I ply you with wine and a dinner of succulent Dungeness crabs, you won't be thinking about business, only of pleasure and me."

He was teasing her. She could tell by the way the corners of his mouth twitched. Her uncontrollable giggles dissolved the romantic moment.

Peter shook his head, a look of mock disgust on his face. "You really know how to hurt a guy, you know that?"

"I think you and I are going to be good friends, Peter Glendenning," Heather said, taking hold of his arm to lead him back to the party.

"I had something a whole lot more interesting in mind, sweet thing. But friendship's as good a beginning as any."

Laughter stole Brandon's attention, and he gazed across the yard to where Heather and Glendenning were engaged in a lively game of croquet. Heather was laughing at something Peter had said, holding up her mallet as if she were going to strike him with it. Some perverse part of Brandon's nature wished she would.

Jealousy reared its ugly head, ripping into his gut. His mother's words a moment later didn't help to alleviate the alien emotion.

"Heather and Peter are having the most marvelous time, Brandon. I'm so happy I thought to introduce her to him. They make such a handsome couple, don't you think?"

Harriet bit the inside of her cheek to keep from laughing aloud at the sick expression on her son's face. If Brandon thought he was feeling ill now, just wait till she got through with him.

Brandon shrugged in a noncommittal manner. "I hadn't noticed."

"Really? Well, I don't know how you could miss the obvious adoration on Peter's face. It's quite apparent to me that he's smitten with our Heather. But then, that's not surprising. Heather's a lovely young woman. Any man would be proud to call her his wife."

"I hardly think a game of croquet constitutes a marriage proposal, Mother. Don't you have anything better to do than play matchmaker and interfere in other people's lives?"

Harriet patted his arm, ignoring the gruffness of his tone. "Why, yes, dear, I do. Heather's just informed me that Peter's invited her out for dinner tomorrow evening. I'm going to help her decide which of the lovely dresses you purchased for her she should wear."

The pulse in Brandon's neck began to pound. More than delighted with her afternoon's work, Harriet excused herself and headed toward the champagne fountain, wearing a very self-satisfied smile.

Peter Glendenning, San Francisco's most notorious rake, was going to take innocent Heather Martin out for dinner tomorrow evening! The idea was abhorrent, impossible, Brandon decided, scraping the toe of his shoe into the grass. She couldn't go. He wouldn't allow it. But how could he not? Tomorrow was Heather's day off.

"Dammit to hell!" he cursed under his breath, hoping he'd

be able to convince Glendenning of his foolhardiness at their meeting later today. Glendenning had finally consented to discuss the possibility of coming to work for *The Star*. It would be Brandon's golden opportunity to discuss Peter's intentions regarding Heather. And they'd better be strictly honorable, or he'd . . .

Before Brandon could conjure up any dire punishments for Peter, Frank strolled up, laughing at the fierce expression on his employer's face. "You look mean enough to chew nails, Brandon. I take it you've had some bad news."

Wrapping his arms about his managing editor's shoulders, Brandon smiled smoothly. "Nothing to concern yourself about, Frank. This is your birthday party. I want you to enjoy yourself. But not too much." He stared meaningfully at the full champagne glass in Frank's hand. "How are you holding up, old man?"

"I guess as well as can be expected under the circumstances." Frank's gaze flitted across the yard toward his wife, who was engaged in conversation with Brandon's mother. Clara looked pale and thin. Having lost twenty pounds, her eyes were sunken, her cheekbones prominent. "I don't know what I'm going to do with myself after she's gone, Brandon." His words were choked with sadness.

Guiding his editor to a secluded corner of the yard, Brandon removed the glass from Frank's shaking hand. "For one thing, you don't need any more of this. Alcohol's not the answer, old man. You know that. Don't ruin what little time you have with Clara by reverting back to old, self-destructive habits. Clara wouldn't want that, Frank."

Tears filled the older man's eyes, bringing a lump to Brandon's throat. He loved the irascible old goat, despite all Frank's failings.

"I've tried to prepare myself for the worst, Brandon. I've tried to tell myself that I'll be able to carry on once she's gone. . . ."

"You will, Frank. I promise you that."

Frank shook his head. "You lost the only woman you ever loved, Brandon. You know the kind of hurt I'll feel."

Brandon flinched at the reminder but said nothing.

"But this is worse. To never see Clara again, to never hold her in my arms . . . Our hearts beat as one, Brandon. When she dies, part of me dies with her. It's like that when you lose someone you love."

Brandon stared across the yard at the smiling woman in violet taffeta, and his heart ached. Heather epitomized everything good about life. Like bubbly champagne, her effervescence tickled his senses, leaving him drunk with emotion.

If he allowed something as precious as Heather to walk out of his life, would he ever be able to forget her? More important, would he ever be able to forgive himself?

"It was a great party, Brandon." Peter leaned back in the leather wing chair, his hand draped lightly over his knee. He had the look of a man well pleased with himself, and knowing what had put that look on his face grated Brandon's already frayed nerves.

"For Frank's sake, I'm glad it went off without a hitch," he replied, trying to get his thoughts off Heather and back to the matter at hand.

"If this is how you treat all your employees, Montgomery, I'd be crazy not to take you up on your offer to work for you."

"I reward those who do a good job. There would be no exception in your case. If you write the kinds of stories for *The Star* that you're presently doing for *The Chronicle*, you'll be more than compensated, monetarily and otherwise."

The easy smile melted off Peter's face, and his expression sobered. "I'm not sure if you're aware of what I'm presently working on, Brandon. When I tell you, you may have a change of heart about wanting me to work for you."

Brandon leaned back, studying the man before him. Peter was handsome. And young. It wasn't surprising that Heather would find him attractive. He had that dashing sort of air about him that most women found appealing, especially one as young and inexperienced as Heather.

But Peter also had a serious side, and that side was now

displayed as worry on his face. "Why don't you let me decide, Glendenning. If you're on to something hot, then, by all means, you'll continue to work on it."

"Even if that something has to do with your future father-in-law?"

"Gerald?" Brandon's brow arched in question. "What's the old fool done now? I didn't think bedroom farces were your cup of tea. What'd he do this time? Get caught in the mayor's bedroom again?"

"I'm afraid Gerald Whitten is involved in a lot more nefarious activities than bedroom farces," Peer explained, despite the look of disbelief on Brandon's face. "I've been doing a great deal of research into his activities over the past few months. And I intend to keep right on investigating the rumors I've heard until I can substantiate them. When I've completed my investigation, I mean to write an exposé on Whitten.

"How would you feel about that, Brandon? After all, you're engaged to be married to his only daughter. It might prove quite an embarrassment to have your future father-in-law's dirty linen aired in public."

Silence ensued while Brandon digested everything Peter had said. Gerald's vast wealth had always been something of a mystery. Brandon had taken his explanations of importing and exporting Chinese porcelain and other valuable artifacts at face value, but others engaged in similar enterprises hadn't acquired the wealth Whitten had. Of course, in fairness to Gerald, he may have been more astute at business than the others, which would explain his ability to make more money.

If Gerald was involved in something nefarious, as Glendenning had claimed, Brandon's conscience dictated that the man be exposed, no matter the consequences. And marriage to Cecelia, if that marriage did in fact take place, would not enter into his decision.

"I've never let my personal feelings interfere with my objectivity in reporting the news. If you have sufficient facts to back up your story, *The Star* will print it. The truth must prevail above all else. That was the one thing my father drilled into me when I started in this business.

"And I learned on my own that the kind of articles you're proposing to write are immensely popular with the reading public. Circulation and sales benefit from scandal." Disapproval etched his face. "No matter how distasteful, the public seems to thrive on it."

Pleased by Brandon's answer, Peter smiled. "I can't believe Heather thinks you're close-minded, Montgomery. You seem inordinately fair to me. If you still want me on your staff, then I'll give notice and report to work first thing Monday morning." Peter stood, holding our his hand to seal their agreement.

"Welcome aboard, Glendenning. There's just one more thing. . . . What did you mean when you said my governess thought I was close-minded?"

Why on earth would Heather think that? Brandon wondered. True, he was a bit opinionated at times, maybe even a bit hardheaded. But close-minded? His brows furrowed. And why had Heather discussed him behind his back? And with Peter Glendenning? Did she truly feel so close to the reporter that she'd discuss her employer with him?

"It was nothing." Peter quickly brushed aside the query, not wanting to get Heather in trouble. "Just something we were discussing." His shoulders lifted. "You know, idle chitchat."

Brandon decided to let the irksome matter drop to pursue a more important one. "I understand you'll be taking Miss Martin to dinner tomorrow evening." He tried his best not to scowl, though there was a definite downturn to his lips.

Smiling widely, Peter nodded. "That's right. The pretty lady agreed to a dinner date."

"I trust you'll have her back at a decent hour. Heather does have to work the next day," he added quickly, at Peter's surprised expression.

"Your fatherly interest in Heather is commendable, Brandon. But rest assured, she'll be safe with me. I've taken quite a liking to the girl. I intend to shower her with attention and affection." Peter winked as he crossed to the door, and Brandon got the sickest feeling in the pit of his stomach. Actually, he felt like he'd just been slapped in the face.

Father figure! When it came to Heather Martin, his feelings were anything but paternal.

Pausing, Peter looked back to find Brandon's woebegone expression still directed at him. "Don't wait up for us, Montgomery. I'm planning to take Heather on a romantic carriage ride in Golden Gate Park after dinner."

Brandon's hands fisted, and he shoved them into his pants pockets, lest he slap the stupid smile off Glendenning's face. He'd heard that the brash reporter was something of a ladies' man; this merely confirmed it.

"It's a bit chilly out for that sort of thing, isn't it?"

"Never fear, Montgomery"—Peter's cocky grin set Brandon's teeth on edge—"I'll keep the little lady warm enough. See you Monday. And thanks for the job, and for the opportunity to meet the sweetest gal in Frisco." Whistling Peter Glendenning shut the door on his way out.

Brandon paled, dropping heavily onto the leather wing chair. The cushion made a whooshing sound, deflating almost as much as his spirits.

Peter Glendenning is going to take Heather on a romantic carriage ride; he's going to keep her warm!

"Mother!" he shouted, banging his fist into the palm of his hand. "What the hell have you done?"

CHAPTER 14

Pacific breakers crashed against the jagged rocks and beach below the stilted structure of the Cliff House restaurant, throwing a salty spray against the darkened window.

Heather peered out, hoping to catch a glimpse of the aquatic seals who inhabited the seaweed-draped rocks, while trying to keep her attention diverted from the man seated across the table from her. Peter studied her sketches with an intensity she found unnerving, and she couldn't gauge as she surreptitiously peeked out of the corner of her eye what his opinion was of her work. Finally, he spoke. And she released the breath she didn't know she was holding.

"These are quite good! You're a very talented young woman." He flipped through the book again, pausing as he studied the portraits of Jenny and Matt. "You've got a talent for capturing the intensity of the moment, Heather. I can actually see the mischievous twinkle in young Montgomery's eyes."

"Th-thank you," she replied, reaching for her glass of

water and taking a large gulp. "I was worried you wouldn't like them."

"You're wasting your talents working as a governess. You should be illustrating for a top-notch newspaper or magazine."

Her heart filled with joy, and she smiled. "You really think I have the talent to do that?"

"You could probably make more money painting portraits for wealthy nobs, but I'd hate for you to waste your talent on such trivial work. The world should see what you create."

"I don't know what to say, except thank you. I always thought my drawings were good, but to hear someone of your stature confirm my beliefs . . . Well, it's just too much to take in all at once." She felt giddy, as if she'd just devoured a whole bottle of champagne.

Peter reached for the bottle of red burgundy resting on the table. "Care for more? You hardly touched your dessert."

She shook her head, color filling her cheeks. "The meal was delicious, but I was so nervous watching you study my drawings, I couldn't eat a bite when the cherry pie was served."

He clasped her hand. "You've got talent, as well as great beauty, sweet thing. I've got a proposition for you."

A soft gasp escaped her, and she pulled back her hand. "I hope I haven't misled you by having dinner with you tonight, Peter. I'm not that sort of—" His laughter halted her maidenly protestation in midsentence.

"It's not *that* sort of proposition." He winked. "That one will come later. What I'm proposing is a job . . . an illustrator's job."

Her mouth gaped open for a second. "An illustrator's job? But who would hire me? I've already told you, I've been to every newspaper in this city."

"I would."

"You? You don't even own a newspaper. You work for *The Chronicle.*"

"Not anymore. As of tomorrow morning, I work for Brandon Montgomery at *The Star.*"

"You accepted his offer?" Heather's astonishment blossomed into a smile of radiance. "That's wonderful, Peter! Congratulations. I'm so happy for you. And for Brandon. I know how much your coming to work for *The Star* means to him."

Peter glanced over his shoulder to make certain no one else could hear what he was about to reveal. They were quite alone in their secluded corner of the restaurant. It was nearly ten o'clock, and most of the other patrons had left. He lowered his voice anyway.

"I'm working on a new series, Heather. I've been conducting a covert investigation into a prominent member of San Francisco society. It's still quite confidential at the moment. I wouldn't want my subject to get wind of what I'm doing. But when it hits the streets it's going to explode. It's big, Heather, very big." He could barely contain the excitement in his voice, which made Heather's eyes widen in wonderment.

"It must be so thrilling to do what you do."

"You could be part of it, Heather. You could do the illustrations for the articles I intend to write. A couple of more weeks and I'll be able to begin."

She shook her head in disbelief, not sure she'd heard him correctly. "You want me to illustrate your articles? But . . . I've never done anything like that before."

"You have to get your feet wet sometime, and the Whitten exposé . . ."

Her head jerked up. "Whitten? Did you say Whitten?"

"Ssh! Not so loud. I don't want anyone to get wind of what I'm doing. Whitten has spies everywhere."

She leaned across the table, her voice lowering to a conspiratorial whisper. "Are we talking about the same Gerald Whitten? The father of Brandon's fiancée?"

"One and the same. The old man's up to his elbows in dirty dealings. I'm convinced he was the one responsible for that chemical fire on Battey Street a few weeks back. And just last night two prostitutes were murdered in a bordello on O'Farrell. Women who were willing to talk for a price."

Gasping, Heather's hand flew to her throat. "You're not serious!"

"Didn't you ever wonder what Gerald did to make a living? Where he got the money to buy that big mansion? To outfit his daughter in all those satins and jewels?"

"Mr. Whitten told me he had business interests all over the world. Something about import/export. He said it was very lucrative."

"He does, and it is, I'm afraid," Peter admitted, his distaste obvious. "Whitten's into the importation of drugs—opium and cocaine. He deals in white slavery, prostitution, gambling. He's got his finger into just about every dirty operation and illegal activity you could think of in this city and beyond. It's going to be my pleasure to expose the corrupt bast . . . businessman," he corrected at Heather's shocked expression.

"But how do you know all of this? Do you have proof?" It was just too fantastic to believe. But it did confirm her inexplicable distrust of the man, and it explained how Gerald Whitten was able to make so much money.

Peter nodded. "I have sources who are willing to supply me with the proof. I've almost got enough evidence to go to press. The murder of the prostitutes set me back, but I've got others who'll talk."

"But what about Brandon? Does he know what you're planning to do?"

"Montgomery's got more integrity than most. I told him flat out that if I came to work for his newspaper, I'd want the freedom to write the story."

"What did he say?"

"That the truth was the most important thing. Damn! It made me feel proud to be a newspaper reporter when I heard him say that. Not many men would risk the embarrassment he's sure to face when the story breaks."

Heather sat back in her chair, too stunned to speak. Brandon knew of Peter's plans, and yet he still gave him the go-ahead to write the story? It was too noble to be true. And too totally Brandon. Her heart swelled with pride.

"Will you come to work for me? Will you illustrate the articles?"

The questions ricocheted inside her, filling her with excitement. This was her chance to fulfill her life's dream to illustrate for a big-city newspaper.

But what of her job with the Montgomerys? She couldn't just abandon Brandon and the children. Especially now, knowing what she knew of Gerald Whitten.

"I understand there are reporters and illustrators who work on an independent basis, supplying their input outside the realm of the newspaper office. Would it be possible for me to do that? I wouldn't feel comfortable leaving the Montgomerys right now. Not under the present circumstances. This could be a difficult time for the children." And for Brandon. "They'll need me now more than ever."

He rubbed his chin, contemplating her idea. "I think that could be arranged. I'll make plans to stop by the house and pick up—"

"No!" she blurted, horrified at the prospect of Brandon's finding out what she was planning. "I don't want Brandon to know of my participation. He would never approve of my involvement. We'd have to meet at a prearranged place, where you could supply me with your articles, and I could drop off my drawings to you."

"Sort of cloak-and-dagger stuff, heh?"

"I'll have to illustrate under a different name to conceal my identity."

"This really is getting to be a bit melodramatic. I like it." He grinned, taking a moment to think about it. "How about using the name Martin Heath? It's sort of an abbreviated version of your real name."

"That's wonderful! No wonder you're so talented a writer. You're very good at making up things."

"I doubt that Gerald Whitten will express those same sentiments when he sees his name smeared all over the front pages of *The Star*."

"But you won't be making that up. You'll be writing the truth. And the truth shall set you free."

"Sweet thing," he said, bringing her hand to his lips for a kiss. "I'm going to enjoy our new association."

"Just as long as you remember it's strictly business, Mr. Glendenning," Heather reminded him.

"Spoilsport." He kissed her hand again, making her giggle. "It's a good thing I have such a big ego, or I'd never survive those barbs you constantly throw at me."

"My sisters claim I have a fierce temper, that I'm someone who shouldn't be tangled with."

"Are these sisters as pretty as you?"

"Prettier. Especially Laurel. She's blond and blue-eyed, just like you."

"I'd love to hear more about them. Perhaps the next time we have dinner you can tell me all about these paragons of womanhood."

"Is that an invitation, Peter?"

"I have a feeling you and I will be spending a lot of time together, sweet thing. After all, we are going to be working together. And I do so enjoy your company."

"As long as you understand that I'm not looking for anything more than friendship from you."

"Your feelings are crystal clear. I understand perfectly, sweet thing."

Despite his admission, Heather didn't think Peter Glendenning really understood her feelings on the matter. She liked Peter a great deal. He was loads of fun, and he made her laugh. But her heart was otherwise engaged. And there was nothing and no one that could make her change her tender feelings toward Brandon.

More exciting than the arrival of *Harper's Weekly Magazine* or *The Ladies Home Journal* was the appearance of Laurel's letter the following Friday morning.

Scented envelope clutched in hand, Heather dashed up the stairs to her room to read the latest missive from her sister. She'd despaired of hearing from either of her sisters before the Thanksgiving holiday, which was only four days away, so this little touch of home was a welcome surprise and a very great relief. She did so worry about the girls.

Plopping down on the fluffy comforter, Heather tore open the envelope.

Dearest Heather,

I pray this letter reaches you before Thanksgiving day. I'm feeling rather nostalgic these days and wanted to let you know how much I miss you and Rose Elizabeth.

Denver has turned out to be a disappointment, as far as my opera career is concerned. The opera house refuses to audition me another time—I've already tried eight times in the past. Finally, I've reconciled myself to the notion that my talents must lie elsewhere.

The notorious Mr. Rafferty thinks I'm talented for only . . . Well, he does run a saloon, after all! I have left his employ to join a group of God-fearing Christian ladies whose goal it is to rid this town of sin, corruption, and alcohol.

Chance's saloon is at the top of my list for such an undertaking, though I don't expect he'll be easily convinced to change his sinful ways. As Hortensia Tungsten, our intrepid leader, constantly reminds us members of The Denver Temperance and Souls in Need League: the leopard does not readily change his spots. We have urged Mr. Rafferty to turn over a new leaf, but I'm afraid he'll need to upend the entire tree to make an appreciable difference.

No word lately from Rose Elizabeth. Has she written to you? I do worry about her living on the farm with that eccentric duke and no real protection. I've heard those Englishmen are notorious rakes and lechers. But then, most men are!

My thoughts and love are with you this Thanksgiving holiday. Perhaps by next we will all be together again.

In righteous temperance, I am your loving sister,
Laurel.

Staring at the missive, Heather was hardly able to comprehend that her flighty little sister, who usually had no more concerns than which dress to wear on a particular day, or which beau would escort her to a party, had written it.

Laurel a temperance worker? She couldn't imagine such a thing, and she sincerely hoped that her sister hadn't been sucked into something she'd soon regret. No doubt her former employer, Mr. Rafferty, was not pleased by her decision to join forces against him and his saloon.

Most men did not like to be crossed or gainsaid. She was fairly certain that if Brandon ever got wind of what she planned to do with his ace reporter, Peter Glendenning, she'd be bounced out of his house and onto her rear without so much as a by-your-leave.

A quick peek at the clock told her that Harriet would be returning home soon. She'd taken all three children to the lending library for this week's "Grandmother's Outing," as she called them. Harriet had made it a point each week to treat the children to a special event. She wanted the opportunity to spend time alone with them, away from the house and Brandon's irascible moods.

The man had been positively surly of late, his disposition nastier than usual, if one could believe that! Brandon had taken Heather to task only last evening, when he'd discovered her and the children in a chewing-gum contest with Mr. William Wrigley's newest invention. The fact that Matt had blown a very large bubble, which had exploded all over his hair and face, had not helped matters one bit.

At least Harriet's outings with the children provided Heather with time to practice her art. The recent charcoal sketches she'd done from memory of Brandon and the children she would keep close to her heart forever, as a reminder of her time spent with them.

Crossing to the window, she stared out at the ocean in the distance. How like those churning blue-gray waters were her moods of late. She hated the idea of deceiving Brandon and Harriet, but she knew that she might never have another chance to prove herself as an illustrator. Opportunities to work on a story of such magnitude came along only once in a lifetime.

Like true love.

She'd missed out on one; she couldn't allow herself to miss out on the other.

"I hope I'm not intruding, but I knocked before entering."

Heather spun around to see Brandon framed in the doorway. Her heart gave a queer little lurch, before it surged all the way up to stick in her throat. "I'm sorry," she replied, hoping she didn't sound as breathless as she felt. Brandon's presence always had that effect on her. "I didn't hear you knock. I guess my mind was a million miles away."

No doubt dreaming about her latest conquest, Peter Glendenning, Brandon surmised, his lips turning down in a frown. The man had been a frequent visitor at the house this past week, and he hadn't come to talk newspaper business with Brandon!

"I came up to visit with the children, but they're not in their room."

It was a small lie to conceal the real reason for his visit. He missed Heather's company. He missed her quiet companionship in the parlor of an evening while they read, missed her infectious laughter when she and the children rolled around on the floor, playing one of their many games, and he missed her intelligent questions when he'd written an editorial that didn't coincide with her opinion.

He missed her.

"Your mother took them to the library," Heather explained, wondering at the odd expression on his face. It seemed a look of regret or sadness. She hoped nothing terrible had happened at the newspaper or to Mr. Burnside's wife.

"Ah, that explains it then." He stepped farther into the room, unable to control the pull she had over him. When he was an arm's distance away, he stopped. "You've been keeping yourself busy of late."

"I . . . Yes. I've had several occasions to tour the city with Mr. Glendenning. But always after my duties were completed for the day. Is there a problem?"

Yes! he wanted to yell. *There is. Why are you seeing Peter Glendenning? What do you feel for him?* But of course he said nothing like that. It wasn't his place to interfere in her life. He had no right. He had no reason to feel the jealousy and anger that tortured him. He was, after all, engaged to another woman. And he suddenly realized that that was something he would have to rectify immediately.

Gazing into Heather's soft violet eyes, he knew he could never marry Cecelia. He could rationalize a million reasons why he couldn't. But there was really only one: He was in love with another woman. The woman who now stood before him, looking confused and uncertain as to what he was doing in her bedroom.

Before he could talk himself out of it, he reached for Heather and drew her into his arms. His voice was low and seductive when he began, "Heather, I . . ."

"Heather?" Harriet called out, and Brandon stepped back quickly, his arms dropping to his sides. "There you are, dear," Harriet proclaimed upon entering. "Hello, Brandon." She turned to smile at her son, as if his presence in Heather's bedroom was an everyday occurrence and no cause for concern. Brandon wasn't certain whether or not to be insulted by her reaction.

"The children and I had the most delightful time today. I wish you could have been there with us. Each child checked out three books."

Her emotions in a turmoil, Heather forced a smile. "That's wonderful, Harriet," she said, feeling confused by Brandon's actions, and disappointed that they'd been interrupted so abruptly before he had a chance to complete his enigmatic sentence.

"Oh, I completely forgot." Harriet shook her head at her

own forgetfulness. "Mr. Glendenning is waiting for you downstairs. I believe he's come to ask you out for dinner."

"Again?"

Both women turned their heads to stare at Brandon, who was glowering.

"I mean . . ." His face filled with color. "Heather was just out to dinner with Peter last evening. Perhaps she would enjoy staying in tonight. I'm sure the children miss her presence."

"If it's a problem, then of course I'll tell Peter that I can't . . ."

"Nonsense, my dear! Brandon didn't mean to say that you shouldn't go out with your young man, did you, Brandon?"

Her young man? At that very moment, Brandon wished for a needle and thread to sew his mother's lips together! He looked from the interfering woman to Heather, who stared at him expectantly. "I didn't mean to imply that you couldn't go out with Glendenning, if that is what you wish to do."

"If you'd rather I didn't . . ."

"It doesn't matter to me. I'm not your keeper."

Turning on his heel, he stalked out of the room, slamming the door behind him.

CHAPTER 15

"Will Heather be much longer, Mrs. Montgomery?" Peter asked, sipping his brandy, completely unaware that his innocent question had irritated the man seated across the room from him.

Brandon glared at his handsome new employee, annoyed that his mother had seen fit to invite Glendenning to dinner tonight. That in itself was bad enough. But his eager, wide-eyed, puppy-dog adoration of Heather was just too damned disgusting!

"I'm sure she'll be down when she's ready, Glendenning," Brandon replied gruffly, not bothering to mask his annoyance.

"Heather wanted to look especially pretty for you tonight, Peter," Harriet explained, ignoring her son's rude snort.

"Heather always looks presentable, Mother." Brandon eyed the Waterford brandy decanter with longing, wishing he'd had the presence of mind to pour himself a drink. He'd been longing for alcohol a great deal lately and wondered if he was growing as weak-natured as his father. He took a deep breath to dispel the craving, and almost choked on his breath when Heather stepped into the room.

She was half-naked! The low cut of her velvet gown exposed the majority of her very ample bosom. Her full, white breasts overflowed the bodice, looking dangerously close to spilling out at any moment. Brandon was about to protest the outrageous display when Glendenning stood, smiling like a hyena, his eyes riveted on Heather's breasts.

"You look stunning this evening, Heather, like a juicy purple plum good enough to eat."

The vein in his neck pulsating ominously, Brandon made a beeline for the brandy decanter. *Juicy purple plum, my ass!* Why, he ought to shove his fist down the man's throat for saying such a thing.

"Good evening, everyone," Heather said, swallowing her nervousness. Feeling mortified at having been put on display so blatantly this evening, she eyed Brandon's outraged face, wondering what he must be thinking of her. Probably not much better than she thought of herself—a Tenderloin trollop displaying her wares.

No matter how many times she'd tried to explain to Brandon's mother that the dress she insisted Heather wear was cut too low, was much too small, was totally inappropriate for an at-home dinner party, Harriet refused to be swayed. And Heather had no difficulty figuring out from whom Brandon had inherited his stubbornness!

Smiling like the Cheshire cat in Lewis Carroll's novel, Harriet came forward to wrap her arm about Heather's waist, drawing her farther into the room. "Why don't you sit on the loveseat next to Peter, my dear? Brandon," she turned toward her son, "would you please fetch Heather a glass of sherry?"

"Of course." His clipped tone belied the polite smile on his face as he poured the golden liquid into a cut-crystal wineglass and offered it to Heather.

At that moment one of Heather's earrings slipped off, falling to her feet, and she bent over to retrieve it. Brandon sucked in his breath as his eyes fixed on the shadow of a nipple rising above the bodice of her gown. Mesmerized by the dark protrusion, he stared at it, his tongue coming out to lick absently at his lips, forgetting for the moment everyone else in the room.

"Are you feeling all right, Brandon? Your eyes look glazed, like you might have a fever."

Heather's question snapped Brandon back to attention, and his cheeks filled with color. "I'm fine," he replied in a hoarse whisper, finally handing Heather the glass. "Just famished."

He turned away from her questioning gaze to find his mother and Peter still deep in conversation and breathed a sigh of relief that they hadn't noticed his unorthodox behavior.

Intrigued by Brandon's discomfort and odd conduct, Heather studied him beneath lowered lashes. His forehead and upper lip were beaded with perspiration, and he constantly dabbed at the moisture with his handkerchief. He'd been staring at her bosom with rapt interest, as if he'd never seen one before, though she was sure he'd had ample views of his fiancée's on more occasions than Heather cared to think about. His interest was flattering, disconcerting, and intriguing enough to make her wonder. Perhaps Brandon's obvious annoyance at Peter meant that Harriet's assessment of her son's jealousy was correct.

Despite the fact that she had absolutely no intention of leading Peter on, Heather couldn't resist the opportunity to conduct a little experiment to see if Harriet's theory held water.

She scooted closer to the unsuspecting subject of her test, and a low growl, like a wounded animal's emanated from Brandon's direction. It confirmed her suspicions, and she smiled inwardly.

Harriet, bless her heart, knew her son better than Heather had given her credit for.

Peter brought her hand to his lips for a kiss, and Heather thought Brandon might hurl his fist at the poor man.

"Was there something you needed, sweet thing?" Peter asked, arching a blond eyebrow.

At the endearment, Brandon's empty brandy glass slipped from his fingers and crashed to the floor—shattering, much like his composure.

"Sorry," he said, bending over to retrieve the broken fragments, stifling the urge to cut Peter's throat with a particularly jagged piece.

Peter, oblivious to his employer's nefarious thoughts, asked, "How's that piece Fred Turner's been working on, Brandon? The one about the Olympic Club gymnasium on Broadway?"

Taking a seat in the wing chair next to his mother, Brandon was grateful that Peter had introduced the subject of work into the conversation. Work was the one thing that might take his mind off Heather's abundant charms.

Though Brandon fought to keep his eyes focused on the blond man, they couldn't help but stray to the two delicious mounds so enticingly displayed to his left. Heather was so close he could almost reach out and touch her, caress those luscious . . . An uncomfortable stiffening suddenly emerged in his lap, and, as unobtrusively as he could, Brandon placed his hand there to conceal it.

"It's about done," he replied, clearing his throat. "I'd never have thought a piece on physical tits . . ." Brandon's face flamed at the slip, and Heather's gasp filled the room. "Physical *fitness*," he amended quickly. "Fitness is the thing these days," he said, trying to cover his blunder.

Jesus! What the hell is wrong with me? I sound as incoherent as Woo.

Biting her lower lip to keep from laughing, Harriet felt triumphant and totally vindicated by Brandon's predictable behavior. She could have leaned over and kissed him, she was so happy.

"I think Mr. Woo has dinner on the table, everyone," she announced, a devilish gleam in her eyes. "Shall we adjourn to the dining room? I understand the breast of duck is especially succulent tonight."

Noting the mortified expression on Brandon's face, Peter attempted to smother his amusement with a cough, but

Heather had caught the twinkle in his eye and nearly choked on the sherry she was sipping.

Heather's choking sound alarmed Peter, prompting him to render assistance by patting her gently on the back, which immediately caused her breasts to jiggle like two soft mounds of quivering gelatin.

Brandon jumped to his feet. "Good God, man! Quit doing that," he ordered.

His demand so shocked Heather that the spasm in her throat suddenly subsided, and she was able to breathe regularly again.

"Are you ready to go in to dinner now, Heather?" Brandon reached for her hand, hauling her to her feet before she had a chance to respond.

"I . . ."

"Good. Because I've suddenly developed a voracious appetite." And it had little to do with pressed duck!

Brandon paced the width of the hallway impatiently, waiting for Heather to bid Peter good night.

He could just imagine what they were doing. It didn't take fifteen minutes to say a simple good-night to someone. And it certainly hadn't been necessary for her to accompany Glendenning outside to his carriage.

Visions of Heather locked in Glendenning's arms for a passionate kiss propelled Brandon down the hallway. He had just reached out to grasp the brass knob on the front door when it swung open and Heather stepped in.

Her cheeks were ruddy from the cold. As were her lips. But were they red for the same reason, or from the one he suspected?

"Brandon!" Heather came to an abrupt halt, nearly colliding with him. "What on earth are you doing here? I thought you had already retired for the evening, along with everyone else."

"Was it really necessary to escort Glendenning to his carriage? He's a grown man, for heaven's sake. I'm sure he could have made it on his own."

Hanging her coat on the hall tree, she shrugged. "I can't really see how that's any of your business, Brandon." Turning for the stairs, Heather was caught in midstride when he grasped her arm.

"I'd like to have a word with you in my study. I believe there are a few things you should be made aware of."

She glanced down at the possessive hand on her forearm, then back up at the perturbed look on his face. "Really? Something to do with the children? It's rather late, Brandon. Perhaps it could wait until tomorrow."

She had a sneaking suspicion what Brandon wanted to talk about, and she didn't have the energy to get into a discussion about her supposed relationship with Peter. Brandon had been staring daggers at the man all evening, his surly behavior bordering on rudeness. Perhaps, as Harriet had said, he was a bit jealous of the time she'd been spending with Peter. He'd certainly acted out of character.

"It can't wait," he reiterated, unwilling to release his hold on her arm.

Heather had no choice but to allow him to escort her to his study. When they stepped inside the room, he shut the door firmly behind them, and the finality of that act sent an apprehensive shiver up her spine.

A fire roared in the hearth, and she stepped toward it to warm herself. "I trust this won't take too long, Brandon. I'm really very tired."

His lip curled derisively. "What's the matter? Did Glendenning wear you out? Perhaps you should stay at home more often and rest, instead of gallivanting all over this city on the arms of that blond lothario."

Heather stared at Brandon as if he'd gone completely insane. "I would hardly call Peter a lothario. He's been nothing but a perfect gentleman, which is more than I can say for the way you've behaved on occasion."

The barb hit; he reeled back on his heels as if slapped, his eyes darkening. "Don't be deceived, you innocent fool. Men like Peter Glendenning devour little girls like you for lunch. The man has a reputation a mile long. His only interest is getting you into bed."

Heather's cheeks crimsoned, but it wasn't humiliation causing the heat, it was anger. Her voice shook with outrage. "How dare you say such a thing to me? What I do and who I do it with are of no concern to you. You are my employer, not my keeper. And I'll thank you to remember that."

"As my children's governess I expect you to behave in a seemly fashion, not like some harlot."

Gasping, Heather's eyes sparked fire as she advanced on Brandon, who had the good sense to take a step backward.

"Harlot, am I!" Her arms waving wildly, she added, "Aren't you confusing me with your simpering fiancée, Cecelia Whitten?"

His gaze roamed over her insultingly, landing with undisguised interest on her breasts. "Your dress is totally inappropriate for your role as my children's governess. Why. . . you've exposed yourself for all the world to see. It's disgraceful. You should be ashamed." He folded his arms over his chest, daring her to deny it.

She ground her teeth at the pompous gesture. "I would hardly call Peter and your mother 'all the world.' And what about that big-breasted cow you call your fiancée? Cecelia's dresses are always indecently low cut. I don't notice you taking her to task over it. Quite the contrary! You practically drool all over her massive bosoms."

"That's different. You're different. You shouldn't be displaying yourself like Cecelia." He didn't want another man looking at what he constantly craved, but he couldn't admit that. "You're my children's governess."

"And she's to be their mother," Heather practically shouted, her chest heaving in indignation, drawing Brandon's eyes to the creamy mounds once again.

"You're being unreasonable and irrational," he accused, swallowing with a great deal of difficulty. Removing his handkerchief, he mopped at the beads of perspiration dotting his brow. "I forbid you to dress in such a fashion again. And

I'd prefer that you didn't encourage men who are in my employ. It isn't good for business."

"Why, you . . . !" Propelled by anger and frustration at Brandon's high-handedness, Heather launched herself at him, pounding on his chest for all she was worth, but her blows failed to make an impression. "How dare you tell me how to dress and who to see? You're not my father! You're not even my husband! You're nothing but a tyrannical, stiff-necked, opinionated . . ."

Grasping her hands, Brandon pulled Heather tightly against his chest, grinding his lips down over hers in a kiss meant to punish, effectively shutting off her tirade.

Incensed at being physically restrained, Heather fought like a wildcat, kicking at Brandon's legs, pulling his hair, trying to break free of his hold on her. But she succeeded only in throwing them both off balance. They landed with a thud on the rug, Heather atop Brandon, who had come within inches of hitting his head on the stone hearth. Their fall broke the contact of the kiss, but only for a moment. With a single-mindedness that shocked her, Brandon recaptured her mouth, shutting off any further protestations.

The fire blazed near where they lay, but the heat from the glowing flames was nothing compared to the blood now boiling through her veins.

Brandon's lips were hard and demanding as they played upon hers, sending spirals of ecstasy swirling through her. His tongue, when it entered, was urgent and exploratory, wiping all thoughts of resistance from her mind. Returning his kiss with reckless abandon, she gave herself up to the total joy of it, the exquisite ecstasy, the sweet tenderness of the moment, completely forgetting her anger.

Her hands came up to toy with the hairs on the nape of his neck, and she heard a contented growl rumble from low in his chest. She protested but a moment when his lips left her mouth to trail burning fire down her neck to the wide expanse of exposed flesh below.

Brandon tugged hard at the bodice of the gown, eager to remove the material separating him from the points of pleasure he so desperately ached to taste. Molding the heavy globes with his hands, he brought them to his mouth and feasted like a starving man at a banquet, unable to get his fill. He lapped at her dusky nipples with his tongue, surrounding the protruding buds with his lips, nipping gently with his teeth, until Heather's moans of pleasure urged him to suckle harder.

"Brandon!" she cried, her head rolling from side to side, as the painful pleasure he elicited created a desperate need in the core of her femininity.

Brandon stilled, gazing into eyes glazed with wonderment and passion. "I want you, Heather. I want you more than I've ever wanted another woman." The veracity of that statement overwhelmed him. He loved Heather, as he had loved no other woman before her.

She didn't answer with words, but tugged at his shirt until the studs holding it together came apart, scattering in all directions, like her inhibitions and common sense. With exploring hands, she caressed every inch of his naked chest. The rippling muscles excited her; the soft mat of hair tingled beneath her fingers as she stroked and explored his body.

Heather wanted nothing more than to give pleasure, to make Brandon feel as glorious as he made her feel. She wanted to communicate with actions the words she would never get a chance to say: She loved him.

Tentatively her tongue came out to taste his nipples. She heard his sharp intake of breath and felt triumphant at the response.

Stripping out of his jacket and shirt, Brandon unfastened the button on his trousers, his eyes never leaving hers for a moment. "You're so beautiful. I've tried to resist you, tried to tell myself I didn't want you, but you've cast a spell over me that I'm powerless to resist. Feel what you do to me." He placed her hand over his hard, throbbing member. "You have bewitched me."

Brazenly, Heather's hand trailed up and down the long length of him, then slipped inside the opening of his pants to feel the silken flesh.

"I want to feel you, Brandon. I want to know the truth of your words." In gentle exploration her fingers glided up and down the turgid shaft, pausing at the tip to feel the moistness of his desire. A feeling of power surged through her, and she felt her own need as powerfully as the one she held in her hand.

"Touch me, Brandon. Make me feel as you feel."

Reaching behind her, Brandon grasped the two sides of Heather's dress, splitting the delicate velvet material in two. He drew the gown completely off her, feasting his eyes on the flimsy undergarments, which did little to conceal her delectable body. Then he removed those as well.

Heather lay naked and writhing beneath him, like a perfectly sculpted porcelain statue. But the hardened tips of her breasts and the dewy moisture between her thighs told him she was not an inanimate object, but all flesh-and-blood woman. His woman.

"You are perfection," he whispered, kissing each swollen nipple, trailing his tongue down her chest, her stomach, moving down the length of her to the soft nest of auburn curls that drew him like a magnet. His fingers separated the dewy folds of her cleft, circled the exposed bud, and then with the tip of his tongue he tasted her.

"Oh, Brandon!" Heather cried out. "Brandon, I've never felt anything so exquisite. Please . . ." She gasped, gripping the rug beneath her, wanting the torture to go on and on, praying it would never end.

Her response pleased him, excited him, stealing whatever fragile control he still possessed. "Easy, my darling," he crooned, easing his finger into her tight crevice to ready her for their joining, pleased to find proof that no man had gone before him. "You're tight, so very tight. We need to stretch you for our coupling," he explained, inserting a second finger into her, then moving them gently in and out.

Heather knew a moment of fear, but it was soon forgotten under the exquisite onslaught of Brandon's fingers and tongue. Over and over he laved at the tiny bud, caressing it, urging it to hardness, until she thought she would die of the need he created. "Please! I can't stand any more." She bucked her hips, trying to communicate the urgent need inside her.

Stripping out of his pants, Brandon positioned himself on top of her, his turgid member resting between her thighs. He sucked her nipples, his hands exploring, searching for the telltale moistness that would indicate her readiness.

Slowly and carefully he entered her, inching his way in until he reached the barrier of her virginity. Immediately he stopped, though it cost him dearly, allowing her time to adjust to the size of him.

Taking several deep breaths, he instructed, "Relax," then covered her lips once again.

"Oh!" Heather cried out at the stab of pain, then felt herself widen and expand to accommodate his huge member. His fierce pumping continued, deeper and deeper, harder and harder. She pushed up her hips to meet the thrusts, reaching for that ultimate pleasure she knew awaited her.

Like a bubbling volcano, the pressure built. She grew taut, climbing higher, higher, until she thought she would scream with the ecstasy of it. Finally, she exploded, singing out Brandon's name in breathless little whispers.

"Oh, Jesus!" Brandon groaned, releasing his seed deep within her, feeling more replete and satisfied than he'd ever felt before.

Spent, he lay there stunned by his reaction, and by what had occurred between them. Heather looked equally as confused but happy. Brushing the damp strands of hair away from her face, he kissed her tenderly. "I'm sorry if I hurt you. It can't be helped the first time."

She smiled an achingly sweet smile, caressing his cheek with her hand. "It was the most marvelous thing I have ever experienced. I don't know quite what to say." She felt such love, such total devotion for this man. She wanted to shout her feelings for all the world to hear, but knew she could not.

Rolling off of her, Brandon retrieved his pants and put them on. She watched him pace, observing the uncertainty and regret on his face, and feeling none of those emotions herself. She was happy—joyously, ecstatically happy.

"Heather," he began, rubbing the back of his neck, then handing her what was left of her dress. "I'm sorry about your gown. I'll buy you a new one."

Holding it up in front of her, she stood. "As long as that's all you're sorry about, Brandon, I'll forgive you for the dress. As you pointed out, it was much too small in the bust anyway."

At her words, regret washed over him, and he looked as if he might jump into a long list of recriminations for what they'd done. Not wanting to give him the chance, Heather did the only thing she could think of to divert his attention: She dropped her dress to the floor.

Brandon could only stare. The firelight played over Heather's naked body in waves of light and darkness, burnishing her skin to a golden hue. She stepped toward him, wrapping her arms about his waist, pressing herself into him, and he fought against the sweet torture.

"Heather," he said in a choked voice, unable to keep his body from responding in the most elemental way.

"Ssh." She placed her fingertips against his lips to silence the protest. "Tonight you are mine. Tomorrow we'll worry about what is right or wrong. Tonight I only want to make love with you again."

Her words humbled him, and he wrapped his arms about her, kissing the top of her head. "Your body is much too tender at the moment, love. You'll be sorry if we make love again so soon."

"You are a foolish man if you think that, Brandon. Making love with you is something I will never be sorry about. Not tonight. Not ever."

CHAPTER 16

Brandon was nowhere to be found the next morning. When Heather inquired as to his whereabouts, Mary-Margaret informed her that Mr. Montgomery had gone calling on Cecelia Whitten.

The news was devastating to Heather, bringing questions of uncertainty to her mind. Questions that had no suitable answers.

Had Brandon gone straight from her arms into the arms of his fiancée? *Apparently.*

Hadn't their lovemaking made any difference to their relationship? *Obviously not.*

Didn't Brandon possess even the tiniest bit of feeling for her? *Definitely, No!*

"Fool," she silently admonished herself. But she still wouldn't trade last night for a million tomorrows. She would never regret what had transpired between them. No matter the consequences.

Heather stared at Mary, who had borne a child out of wedlock, and wondered if she'd be as brave as the Irish woman if circumstances warranted. She might very well find herself pregnant and unmarried, which would render her an outcast in society.

"You look like you've lost your best friend, Heather," Mary said, sitting down next to her at the kitchen table. "Aren't you looking forward to Thanksgiving? Me and Jack always have such a good time preparing the pumpkin pies. Though Jack gets a bit carried away, throwing the seeds all over the place." She laughed good-naturedly.

Tossing a handful of the cranberries she'd sorted into a large ceramic bowl, Heather forced a smile. "Of course I'm looking forward to it. I adore turkey. And Mr. Woo has promised to make all the traditional fixings. With your pies, it promises to be quite a feast." She wondered where Laurel and Rose would spend their holiday and hoped they'd found the happiness and contentment that seemed to have eluded her.

"Then why are you wearing such a long face today? I'd think you'd be happy Miss Harriet's gone off with the children on another one of her adventures. I think she's taking them to the petting zoo to look at the turkeys. God help us if they won't eat Mr. Woo's dinner because of it." She frowned at the disturbing notion.

"We've already covered the Pilgrims first Thanksgiving in our history lesson. I've explained about the turkeys, and I think the children are looking forward to eating the bird, whether friend or foe."

"Did you have a good time last night?" Mary leaned forward, waiting eagerly for Heather to regale her with the events of last night's dinner party.

Heather's guilty thoughts made her face turn florid, and she swallowed. "Very nice."

"Miss Harriet said you were the belle of the ball. She said Mr. Glendenning is quite taken with you. I wished I'd been here to see it. But my landlady took ill, and I felt I should sit with her in case she took a turn for the worse."

"You really didn't miss much, Mary. My dress was too tight, and I could barely eat I was so uncomfortable. And you know how Harriet likes to play matchmaker. Peter is just a friend."

A look of disbelief crossed the blond woman's face. "I wish I had friends like that. The man is absolutely gorgeous. If he was falling at my feet, the way I hear he's falling at yours, I wouldn't think twice about taking him to my bed. A woman's entitled to her pleasure."

Lowering her voice so that Mr. Woo couldn't overhear, Heather asked, "Do you really think so, Mary? I mean . . . we're taught just the opposite. Do you think it's sinful to enjoy the pleasures of the flesh?" Because if it was, she had sinned something awful. She'd never known such pleasure existed. Before last night, she had only guessed, from the little Mary had told her, that the carnal act between a man and woman could be so wonderfully fulfilling.

"Sinful . . . ly delicious." Chuckling at Heather's surprise, Mary patted the innocent young woman's hand, her expression suddenly sobering as she looked intently at her friend. "I don't know why I didn't recognize the change in you when I walked in this morning, Heather. You look different somehow, and I'd bet money on why that's so."

"Mary!" Heather's cheeks filled with heat, and she turned to look over her shoulder at Mr. Woo, who was occupied in the preparation of cloverleaf rolls for tonight's dinner. "Please keep your voice down. Mr. Woo might not speak very good English, but his hearing is excellent."

"You did it, didn't you? You went and lost your virginity to that handsome newspaper reporter, Peter Glendenning." Mary squealed in pleasure, clapping her hands, bringing a curious glance from Mr. Woo, who shook his head disdainfully at the excited maid.

Heather's eyes widened. "No." She shook her head emphatically. "It wasn't Peter." She slapped her hand over her mouth, aghast at what she'd just admitted.

Mary sat back in her chair, too stunned to speak. When she finally did, she exclaimed, "You mean . . . ? Lord have mercy! I just knew you and Mr. Montgomery were destined for one another."

"It's not like that. It just . . . just happened."

"I'll bet. There's been talk about Mr. Montgomery. They say he's like a smoldering fire and once he's lit . . . *Boom!*"

Mary threw her arms wide to indicate an explosion, and Heather practically jumped out of her seat. The "boom" didn't even come close to describing Brandon's lovemaking. It had been more like cannons blasting, fireworks exploding, and a twenty-piece orchestra simultaneously.

"What's he like? Was it good? Did he give you orders? Instruct you how to behave? Make you keep your clothes on?"

Heather's hands flew to her cheeks to still the burning there. "Please, Mary! You're embarrassing me. I should never have said anything."

The maid giggled. "You didn't. I guessed." Patting Heather's arm, Mary attempted to reassure her. "Don't worry. Your secret's safe with me. But there's something I don't quite understand. If you made love with Mr. Montgomery last night, how come he went calling on that snooty Miss Whitten this morning?"

Heather's face fell, wishing she knew the answer, but not really sure she wanted to.

"Why, Brandon, this is a surprise!" Cecelia tightened the gold-fringed sash about her green satin day gown in a gesture she hoped was provocative. Smiling sweetly at her fiancé, she said, "I wasn't expecting you quite so early, darling," and bussed him on the cheek.

Stepping into the Whitten's formal parlor, Brandon removed his hat and coat, tossing them on a chair. "I apologize for the earliness of the hour, Cecelia, but this meeting couldn't wait."

"Come in and sit down." She pointed to the Louis XVI sofa, which was garishly upholstered in red brocade to match the fringed drapes at the window. The room was oppressive, Brandon thought, much like the cloying gardenia-scented French perfume Cecelia was so fond of wearing. Quite a contrast to the clean, wildflower scent of Heather's skin.

God! Heather had been so responsive last night. So in awe of what she'd experienced at his hands. They'd made love into the wee hours of the morning. And after she'd fallen into an exhausted sleep in his arms, he'd carried her upstairs to her bed, wishing for all the world that he could crawl in beside her and never let her go.

"Would you care for coffee? Wanda's just brought in a fresh pot."

Brandon's head snapped up at the question.

Without waiting for a reply, Cecelia filled a delicate, rose-patterned china cup and handed it to him. Dutifully, he took a sip, then set the cup on the marble-topped tea table. He hadn't come to make polite chitchat, and she might as well be apprised of that fact now.

"We need to talk, Cecelia. Something's happened, and it's going to affect our relationship."

Cecelia's stomach knotted into a tight little ball, but she tried to keep a serene smile on her face, unwilling to face her worst fears. She'd found that if she ignored trouble, it usually went away. Or Daddy fixed it. Either way, she didn't like hearing anything that might upset her. Filling her with dread, the look on Brandon's face made it clear that the subject was serious.

"If you want to postpone the wedding again, Brandon, I'll certainly understand. I'd much prefer holding the ceremony in spring anyway. Winter's such a . . ."

"Cecelia, don't you understand? We've already postponed the wedding five times. Didn't you ever wonder why that was so? Why I continue to get cold feet?"

A trembling hand tightened around her heart. "But you said it was because of business. You said you didn't have the time to devote to our marriage and wanted to wait until you could spend more time with me."

Brandon stood and began to pace, rubbing the back of his neck to ease the tension headache that had started pounding there. "I lied. I postponed our wedding because I didn't feel right about it. I still don't feel right about it."

At the time, he'd thought it was merely nervous apprehension because of what had happened with Lydia, but now he knew it had been much more than that. His heart had been telling him what his mind had refused to accept: Cecelia would never make a good mother for his children.

Cecelia rushed to his side and wrapped her arms about his waist, pressing herself into him. Desperation laced her words. "I told you we could consummate the marriage before the wedding, Brandon. I understand men's urges better than you think. Father has gone to a great deal of trouble to discuss the matter with me, and I'm perfectly reconciled to going to bed with you . . . darling." She rubbed his thigh, but Brandon pulled back, gripping her shoulders to distance her from him.

Brandon could see by the confusion on Cecelia's face that she didn't fully comprehend what he was telling her. He didn't want to hurt her, but he had to make her understand that it was over between them.

"I can't marry you, Cecelia. Though I like you, care about you a great deal, I don't love you. And the children will never accept you as their mother."

It took a moment for his words to sink in, and when they did, her eyes filled with tears. "The children?" She shook her head, unwilling to believe his words. "What do they know? They're only six years old, Brandon. I told you that they should be placed in boarding school. It would be the best thing for everyone concerned. That governess of yours has had undue influence over the children. She's poisoned them against me. I don't know why I didn't see it before."

"I'm positive that Heather has never said a word against you to the children. It's not in her nature to be unkind."

The truth suddenly dawned, and Cecelia's eyes turned glacial. "It's her, isn't it? You're in love with that governess. Oh, Brandon, can't you see? She's put some sort of spell on you. We were happy before she came into your life. We could be happy again. All you have to do is fire her, and then things can resume between us. You love me, Brandon. You know you do."

"You're not listening, Cecelia. I admit I have feelings for

Heather." He was not about to tell this agitated woman that he was in love with the other woman. Cecelia wasn't taking the rejection well; he doubted that she could take the whole truth any better. "But Heather isn't the only reason I'm breaking our engagement. My children need stability in their lives, Cecelia. I couldn't possibly marry someone they don't care for. It wouldn't be fair to them. Jenny and Matt have already had too much unhappiness in their lives."

Cecelia threw herself down on the sofa and began to cry, deep heart-wrenching sobs that made Brandon feel lowlier than the smallest insect. Taking a seat next to her, he patted her back in a consoling gesture, trying to offer comfort. "We can still remain friends, Cecelia."

Raw hurt glittered in her eyes, and she turned on him, snarling. "Never! Never. Do you hear me? I don't want to be your friend, Brandon. You have humiliated me in front of this entire city. When my friends hear of my broken engagement, I won't be able to hold my head up." Lorna Pond would have a field day with the news. She was ruined. Totally ruined. And it was that redheaded governess's fault. God, how she hated her!

"You can tell them it was my fault, Cecelia. You can lay the blame for our broken engagement at my door."

Her eyes narrowed, and a strange, eerie light entered them. "The blame will be laid at your door, Brandon." *And it will be your sweet-talking governess who'll bear the brunt of my wrath.*

The sound of heavy footfalls coming down the hallway alerted Heather and Mary-Margaret to Brandon's presence.

"He's back," the maid whispered, pressing a comforting hand on Heather's shoulder, squeezing gently. She'd just spent the better part of an hour consoling her friend about Brandon's betrayal, counseling her on the evils of the male gender as a whole.

Heather's tears had touched Mary as nothing else could have. The kind woman was her friend, and she'd be damned if she was going to allow Mr. Montgomery to hurt her again. "I'm going to give him what-for," she promised.

Alarmed by the maid's vehement expression, Heather shook her head. "Don't say anything, Mary. It's best you keep out of it. I knew what I was getting myself into. I only have myself to . . ."

Heather paused in midsentence as the door swung open, her heart fluttering at the sight of Brandon's weary face. He looked as exhausted as she felt, and because she knew they were tired for the same reason, her cheeks warmed.

"Heather." He approached the table, wondering at the nasty look Miss Fenney passed his way. "I'd like a word with you in the study."

Heather swallowed. "In the study?" She couldn't bear to go back to the sight of her recent humiliation. Not when she knew he was going to tell her to pack her bags and leave. Mustering what was left of her courage, she managed a tight smile. "Of course."

He walked out, and as Heather rose to follow, Mary grabbed her hand. "You don't have to go. I won't allow him to seduce you again, then run back to that piece of fluff he's engaged to."

Woo, who'd been silent as a church mouse during their entire conversation and crying jag, came forward. With his hands on his slender hips, he looked at Heather. "Missy, go into study now. Woo have good feeling about this. You soon be happy as possum in cow carcass."

Deciding that she already felt as dead inside as a cow carcass, Heather sighed with resignation.

"What do you know about such things, Mr. Woo?" Mary lashed out at the Chinaman. "I'll have you know that matters between Miss Heather and Mr. Montgomery are quite serious at the moment."

Folding his arms across his chest, Woo glared at the maid. "Woo know plenty. Woo know you have blabbering mouth." And to Heather, who stared wide-eyed at the outburst, he said, "Go, missy. Woo feel good things in gut." He pressed his stomach. "You help Woo learn English. You teach Woo to make pretty breasts. I no stare you wrong."

"It's *steer,* you silly Chinaman," Mary said.

Heather didn't wait around to listen to the rest of their argument. As unobtrusively as she could, she backed out of the kitchen and marched slowly to the study, much like a condemned prisoner trudging to the gallows.

Opening the study door, Heather was immediately assaulted by the provocative scents of sex and her own stale perfume. She paused, praying for the courage she would need, hoping she wouldn't break down in hysterics when Brandon told her her services were no longer required.

God! What would she tell the children? How could she leave, knowing she would never see them again?

Brandon turned, smiling tenderly at her, and a painful lump of remembrance rose in her throat. "You wanted to speak to me?"

"Come in, Heather, and sit down. We need to talk."

Crossing the room to take the chair in front of the desk, Heather avoided looking at the rug, and at the fire, which still crackled and hissed. She did not want to be reminded of what had transpired in this room last night. The memories burned brightly, but only ashes remained in the cold light of day.

Seated behind his desk, Brandon looked every inch the hard, no-nonsense businessman. He fumbled with the silver letter opener and cleared his throat several times before saying, "I've just come from seeing Cecelia. I thought under the circumstances—"

"Brandon, you don't have to explain," she interrupted, unable to bear his rationale. "What happened last night wasn't your fault. I understand completely about . . ."

"Apparently you understand nothing, Heather." He tapped the end of the opener on the desk, and the sound mimicked the anxious thumping of her heart. "I have broken my engagement to Cecelia. We are no longer to be married."

Disbelief and astonishment touched her pale face, and her eyes widened at his startling announcement.

"I felt, under the circumstances, that the correct and proper thing to do is offer you my hand in marriage."

"Marriage." Heather whispered the word, unable to believe her ears, or the unromantic proposal Brandon had just delivered. She sat back heavily against the seat, unsure she'd be able to formulate a response.

"It's an honorable offer for a woman in your position. I'm well aware that you came to me as a virgin and that you might in fact be carrying my child at this very moment. A marriage between us would be the practical solution to everything. The children adore you. You're already like a mother to them."

That pleased her, if nothing else did, and she felt tears burning behind her lashes.

"I realize this is rather sudden, but then, these things usually happen that way, or so I'm told."

Jesus! He was making a royal ass of himself. He could tell by the confusion on her face, the total disbelief, that she thought he'd lost his senses. Well, he had. He was crazy in love with her. But he couldn't risk telling her that. Not until he was sure about her, about her devotion. He couldn't tell her everything that was in his heart and have her throw it back in his face as Lydia had done.

When Heather finally found her voice, it was to say, "I'm honored by your proposal, Brandon, though totally taken aback by it. I thought you'd called me in here to dismiss me."

He looked quite surprised. "Dismiss you? Why would I do that? You're the best governess the children have ever had. I'd be pretty stupid to do such a thing."

Heather wanted to scream at him. To ask him where the romance was. The heartfelt declaration that usually accompanied a marriage proposal. The love.

She'd always dreamed of a marriage like Ezra and Adelaid Martin had shared. Years filled with love and commitment. A bonding of souls that could endure the good times and bad. Apparently that wasn't what Brandon had in mind. He made marriage sound like a business merger, not a romantic joining of two hearts.

Hurt and disappointment filled her, and she wanted to wound him as he had her by his unfeeling proposition. "I believe you're correct, Brandon. Marriage to you would solve many things. My father's deathbed wish was that I marry a man of wealth and position, who could provide me with a stable home and security." Ignoring his shocked expression, she went on. "As you already know, I'm terribly fond of Jenny and Matt. I love them like they were my own children. And marriage to you would mean that I could continue on in my role of surrogate mother and friend. Their happiness is very important to me."

His lips thinned in irritation. "I see. Well then, that settles it. Since this arrangement suits both our purposes, we shall be married immediately. I'll make all the arrangements, put a suitable announcement in the paper, and notify the reverend of the date."

"Which is . . . ?" She could barely contain her excitement, and it was difficult to sustain her detached demeanor. Her hands perspired profusely, and she secured them between shaking knees.

"I don't want to wait. The sooner the better." He certainly didn't want to wait a second longer than he had to to make love to her again. He'd replayed last night over and over again in his mind, remembering the soft feel of her skin, the musky taste of her. The rapidly stiffening member between his legs was telling him more plainly than words that he couldn't wait.

"Let's make it the second Saturday of December. That will give you a little over two weeks to make the necessary preparations."

Heather pushed herself to her feet, though she had to steady her rubbery legs by holding on to the edge of the desk. "I . . . I think a marriage between us can work out very well, Brandon. I . . ." Her face flushed bright red. "We seem to be very compatible in many areas."

Rising to his feet, Brandon came around the desk to draw

her into his arms. "Shall we seal our declaration with a kiss?"

She nodded mutely, her hands moving up his chest to twine about the back of his neck. When their lips touched, sparks of desire shot through her, and her blood heated to a fevered pitch, bringing back all the glorious feelings of last night's lovemaking. Pressing herself into him, she felt his answering desire against her belly, felt the same need in him as she felt in herself.

Locked in each other's arms, lost in their hunger for more, they didn't hear the study door open. But they did hear the startled gasps of surprise coming from the two women standing in the doorway.

The newly affianced couple broke apart guiltily to find Mary-Margaret and Harriet staring openmouthed at them.

"I told you he was up to no good, Miss Harriet. I told you he was trying to seduce our poor Heather." Mary pointed an accusing finger in Brandon's direction, and his face flamed at the maid's condemning words. Heather bit the inside of her cheek to keep from smiling.

"Doesn't anyone in this house ever bother to knock?" he asked, wondering what his mother and the maid would have thought if they'd walked in on them last night. That image brought a smile to his lips.

Noting the sparkle of laughter in Heather's eyes and the delicate pink tinge to her cheeks, Harriet knew all was well and felt a deep sense of relief.

"I'd been led to believe that you were in the process of ravishing this poor, innocent young woman," she said to her son, casting her maid, who had the grace to blush, an annoyed look. "I trust your intentions are strictly honorable, Brandon. You are, after all, engaged to be married to another woman."

Brandon wrapped his arm about Heather's midsection in a possessive gesture, prompting the older woman to smile knowingly. "I've broken off my engagement to Cecelia. Heather has done me the honor of accepting my proposal of marriage."

"Praise the saints!" Mary-Margaret shouted, waving her hands wildly in the air. "Our Heather's getting married."

Harriet shut her eyes to say a silent prayer of thanks to the Almighty, then rushed forward to embrace both her son and her future daughter-in-law and gave Heather a kiss on the cheek. "I couldn't be happier for both of you." Tears of joy filled her eyes, and she wiped at them with the back of her hand. "I'm delighted and so terribly surprised by this turn of events."

Brandon looked at his mother in disbelief. "Really, Mother! You don't expect me to believe that, do you?"

A secretive smile touched Harriet's lips and she nodded. "Why yes, dear. I believe I do."

CHAPTER 17

"Psst!"

Glancing up from the book she was supposed to be reading, Heather looked down the long stacks of books marked "U.S. History" and saw Peter signaling to her. Checking to make certain no one had seen or heard him, she gathered up her reading material and headed in his direction.

Peter was leaning casually against an oversized tome on the life of Ulysses S. Grant, his arms crossed over his chest, looking as if he didn't have a care in the world. His eager smile told her how happy he was to see her, and that observation filled her with dread.

She hadn't had the opportunity to inform him of her engagement and upcoming marriage to Brandon. And she wasn't at all sure how he would react to the news.

Peter had made his interest in her obvious from the first day they'd met. And though she hadn't encouraged him beyond friendship, she didn't want to hurt him. Their relationship meant a great deal to her.

"Is this meeting clandestine enough for you?" he quipped,

grinning boyishly at her, though Heather was too nervous to join in the amusement.

She'd had a devil of a time departing from the house today. Finally she had used the trip to the library to return overdue books as a plausible excuse to meet Peter. Fortunately, Mary-Margaret had unwittingly aided her departure by offering to bake cookies with the children. Heather hated the subterfuge, but there was no help for it.

"This really isn't anything to joke about, Peter. I could get into serous trouble if anyone knew I was involved with your article on Gerald Whitten."

Clasping her by the elbow, he led her toward the back of the library, where they were concealed by stacks of books and out of earshot of the other patrons. "I've finished the first article of the series," he whispered, his eyes alive with purpose and excitement as he thrust a manila envelope at her. "You'll need to read it, then supply me with your illustrations. I need them no later than Friday. Is that going to be a problem?"

Only one of many, she thought. She was up to her elbows in wedding preparations. The announcement had been made only two days before, and Harriet had already begun interviewing caterers, dressmakers, and so on. Brandon's mother had taken command of the affair like a military leader about to engage the enemy. It was enough to make one's head spin.

"I can have them finished, but there's something else we need to talk about."

He stroked her cheek with his fingertip. "How about telling me at dinner tonight? I've been dying for a chance to . . ."

She took her head. "I can't. That's what we have to talk about."

His eager expression melted into one of concern. "Something's happened." It was a statement, not a question, but Heather nodded in response.

Picking nervously at the spine of a book with her fingernail, Heather considered what she could say to Peter, how she might explain this abrupt change of circumstance. She liked him too much to hurt him.

"I take it that this important matter you want to discuss is something other than what we're working on?"

Realizing that tact was not her strong suit, and not knowing a kinder way to break the news, Heather took a deep breath and blurted, "Brandon has asked me to marry him, and I have accepted."

The shock of her announcement registered first as disbelief, then as resignation, as Peter leaned back against the stacks, shaking his head, dismayed by his lack of foresight. "I sort of suspected you were interested in Montgomery, but I kept hoping my intuitions were wrong. They rarely are, you know. It's been Brandon all along, hasn't it? That's why you tried to keep me at arm's length?"

"When I agreed to go out with you, Peter, I never realized that there could be anything between Brandon and myself. He was engaged to Cecelia. I never meant to lead you on."

Gently he clasped her hand and smiled with understanding. "There isn't a dishonest bone in your entire body, sweet thing. You made your position clear to me from the start. I was just too blinded by your beauty to believe what my brain kept telling me. I'm afraid I let my emotions rule my good judgment. And that's death for a reporter."

"I care for you a great deal, Peter, and I hope nothing will ever change our friendship. I love you as the brother I never had, and I hope you'll want to maintain our present relationship. It's very important to me."

"You really do know how to hurt a guy, Heather." He tweaked her nose, trying to make light of his disappointment. "Jeez. A brother? Well," he said, shrugging, "it'll take some getting used to, but I guess that's better than nothing." A mischievous grin suddenly split his face, and he wiggled his eyebrows lecherously. "Do brothers get to kiss their sisters?"

Heather laughed at his antics, pointing to her cheek with her fingertip. "Only on the cheek."

His expression sobering, Peter asked, "What about the article? You still want to do the illustrations, don't you? You have a lot more at stake now, you know."

Her brows knitting together in worry, Heather gnawed her lower lip. There was much truth to Peter's words, and she'd debated many times whether she should confide to Brandon her talents as an illustrator and inform him of the role she intended to play in Peter's investigation. But fear of Brandon's reaction when he found out that she hadn't been completely honest with him, and the knowledge that he might not want a woman working on his newspaper staff, much less his fiancée, had kept her silent.

She had a great deal at stake. Even more than her marriage to Brandon. She had something to prove, if only to herself: that her abilities were every bit as proficient as a man's, that she could compete on a professional level in the newspaper industry.

She'd waited twenty-two years to test herself under fire. She could not back away from it now. Once she had proven herself worthy, once she had succeeded, then she could give up her dream to pursue the other, more important goal of marriage and family. But not until she had at least finished what might be her only chance. It was, after all, the reason she had ventured to San Francisco in the first place.

Brandon was a self-made man with dreams of his own. Heather was positive that she could make him understand what motivated her, if the need arose.

"You look lost in contemplation. You're not having second thoughts, are you?" Peter asked.

She clutched the article to her chest, shaking her head emphatically. "This is something I've got to do for myself. I don't want to spend the rest of my life wondering and having regrets. Papa always said that a body could live on hope, but that it couldn't live with regret."

"Smart man, your father. I wonder if those sisters of yours might still be available?"

Heather smiled, and a calculating gleam entered her eyes. "Why don't you stop by the house tonight? There's someone I'd like you to meet."

"Oh, no," Peter said, shaking his head. "You've got that matchmaking look in your eyes that my mother always gets when she's about to introduce me to some horse-faced friend of hers."

"Mary-Margaret Feeney is a far cry from horse-faced. And she just happens to be my very best friend."

Peter's eyebrow arched in interest. "You mean the little blond with the sassy mouth and big—"

"She thinks you're gorgeous."

Her words were a balm to his ego, and Peter smiled. "Never let it be said that Peter Glendenning wasn't interested in meeting a woman with impeccable taste. What time do you want me?"

Strolling through the print room, the large, high-speed cylindrical presses humming like music to his ears, Brandon snatched a new piece of newsprint off the roller and smiled proudly.

The capture of Black Bart headlined the morning's edition of *The Star*, scooping the other newspapers with the disclosure that the bane of Wells Fargo and Calaveras County had finally been caught. The dapper outlaw and stagecoach robber, Charles E. Boles, who had robbed twenty-eight Wells Fargo stages in less than ten years, had been traced through a San Francisco laundry mark and apprehended late last evening.

"This is a fine piece of work, Frank," Brandon said, entering the city room, where his managing editor was standing hunched over his desk as he studied an article. "Thanks for putting in the extra hours last night to get it ready for this morning's edition."

Frank nodded, looking more haggard and weary than Brandon had seen him in a long time. The man had been pushing himself. Frank was using work to keep his mind off his wife's illness, and it was taking a toll.

"You should take a few hours off and go home; get some

rest. Check on Clara. Has there been any change in her condition?"

At the mention of his wife, Frank's face twisted in pain. "Doc says it'll be a miracle if she lives out the year. As much as I hate to see her go, I can't bear to see her in pain. The medicine doesn't come close to easing her discomfort."

"You take as much time off as you need, Frank. You know your job will always be here for you."

"I've taken your advice and kept away from the bottle, Brandon. Though there's been many a day that it's been damn hard. I get that old, familiar craving, and I want a drink so bad I can taste it. But then I think of how I'd be letting my Clara down if I do, and I resist the temptation. I just pray the good Lord will see fit to help me when she's gone. I'm going to need it."

"You won't be alone, Frank. You'll have me and . . . and Heather." He said the latter almost self-consciously. "You'll always be welcome in our home."

For the first time that day, Frank smiled, dropping down into the swivel chair behind his desk. "I'm pleased by your decision to marry that little gal, Brandon. She's going to make a wonderful wife and mother to your children."

"Jenny and Matt are very fond of her."

A graying eyebrow arched. "And what of their father? Are you fond of her, too?"

Heat crept up Brandon's neck and he brushed at it with the palm of his hand. "Our marriage is more of a business arrangement than a love match, Frank."

Heather had made that quite clear the day she'd accepted his proposal. And though he had thought her levelheaded and sensible for having made such a decision, he couldn't help but wish that her feelings for him were a bit more amorous.

Tugging on his beard, Frank snorted in disbelief. "Boy, you may have led that gal to believe such a thing, but I know you better than most. Your marriage to Cecelia Whitten would have been a business arrangement, but not this marriage to Heather. Your heart's involved, and don't go trying to deny it. I've lived too long, and I know you too well."

"You're crazy, you know that, old man? You'd better just tend to the newspaper business and forget about interfering in my personal affairs."

Chuckling, Frank replied, "Now what kind of friend would I be if I did that? Any fool can see you're in love with that gal. She must be blind as a bat not to see it herself."

Not caring to debate the feelings he had for Heather or her lack of vision, Brandon turned and fled the room, annoyed that Frank had made him care whether Heather loved him.

Theirs was a business arrangement, nothing more, he told himself as he eased behind the massive walnut desk in his office. But when he stared down at the calendar and saw the large red circle around the date of their wedding, he knew it was much more than that. At least on his part.

Despite everything, his heart had become involved. If Heather realized how much he cared for her, she would use it against him, the way Lydia had. She would tear him to pieces with loving words and kisses, then she would leave him with bitter memories and longing and despair.

"No!" he said, smashing his fist down on the red circle. Not again. Not ever again.

Brandon glanced up from his editorial to find Jenny and Matt hovering in the doorway, anxious expressions on their small faces. They were dressed for bed, and Matt was fidgeting nervously with the hem of his pajama top. Jenny's countenance was a bit more determined.

"Is there something you need, children?" With a crook of his finger, he motioned them toward the desk, wondering what had prompted them to interrupt his work. They looked so serious that Brandon decided not to take them to task over it.

Her hand firmly clasped around Matt's, Jenny marched in, towing her brother behind her. "Me and Matt wanted to thank you for asking Miss Martin to marry you. She told us that she was going to be our new mother, and we're real happy about that." The words came out in a rush, as if she'd been storing them up for days and suddenly had the need to expel them.

A chagrined look crossed Brandon's face. "I've been meaning to discuss my decision with you."

He felt foolish and embarrassed that he hadn't had enough nerve to tell his children about his plan to marry their governess. Communication between them had been sadly lacking of late. That was something he needed to rectify immediately.

"Miss Martin told us you were very busy, Father," Matt said matter-of-factly, bringing a twitch to Brandon's lips. "She said you were just waiting for the right time to tell us. But we got tired of waiting, and thought we'd better come in ourselves to hear what you had to say." Matt looked so grown-up standing there in his striped pajamas that a lump formed in Brandon's throat.

Rising from his chair, he came around the desk to perch on the edge of it, hoping he would appear more accessible and less threatening. He remembered what Heather had said those many months ago about his children being afraid of him. It seemed she'd been right about that, too.

"I hope you're both happy about my decision to marry Miss Martin. I know how much you like her, and I think she's going to make you a splendid mother."

The little girl's face split into a grin. "We love Miss Martin, Father. And we're very happy you decided not to marry Miss Whitten. She wouldn't have made a good mother. She doesn't smell as good as Miss Martin."

Brandon nodded, conceding that point.

"And she don't bake cookies. Doesn't," Matt quickly amended, remembering his governess's teachings. "Miss Martin knows how to do all sorts of neat things. She's got a new game she's going to teach us, as soon as she has time."

Brandon caught Jenny's warning glance as she elbowed Matt in his ribs and wondered what the child was hiding. Before he had a chance to ask, Heather entered, a stern look of disapproval on her face as she saw the children.

"You two should be upstairs in bed, not bothering your father, who I'm sure is hard at work." She smiled at Brandon, and her heart nearly stilled when he winked back at her.

"We had important business to discuss with Father, Miss Martin. Didn't we?" Jenny looked at Brandon for confirmation.

"Indeed. The children and I were having the most important of discussions, but I think we're through for tonight."

Matt came forward to shake his father's hand, as Brandon had instructed him to do before exiting a room. Touched by the gesture, Brandon pulled the small boy into his arms and hugged him tightly, then sent him off with a pat on the head. "Good night, son. Sleep tight."

Jenny hung back, pleating and repleating the folds of her nightgown. Shyly, she asked, "Would you give me a hug, too, Father?"

Brandon smiled thoughtfully at the child who bore such a striking resemblance to her mother. The constant reminder of Lydia had been a thorn in his side these many years. He was ashamed to admit that he had kept his distance from Jenny because of it. But now he could finally see his daughter as her own person, see her for what she was: a beautiful, exuberant, loving child. Thanks to Heather, he was throwing off the yoke of grief that Lydia's perfidy had caused.

"Of course I will," he finally replied, wrapping his arms around his daughter's slight body and giving her a hug. He kissed the top of her head. "Run off to bed like Miss Martin says. We'll continue our discussion another time."

The children and Brandon shared conspiratorial smiles. Then Jenny and Matt skipped out of the room, looking happier than they had in a very long time, leaving him and Heather alone for the first time in days.

Rising to her feet, he took a step toward her. "Have you come for a good night kiss, too?" he asked, an erotic smile hovering about his lips.

The question was unexpected, but pleasurable nonetheless, and Heather stepped toward him, smiling. "I guess I can use a hug."

With a bearlike growl, he wrapped his arms playfully

about her and began nuzzling her neck. But play soon turned to passion, and his lips found a path to her eager lips awaiting his kiss.

Brandon caressed Heather's mouth with his, while his hands moved up to cup the fullness of her breasts, palming her nipples into hardened nubs. She leaned into him, moaning in pleasure, trailing her hand along his thigh, hearing his sharp intake of breath when her hand lightly stroked the hardening evidence of his desire.

Breathing deeply, Brandon pulled back to gaze into eyes bright with yearning. "You'll unman me if you continue that, love. I can't seem to control myself when I'm around you, and we have another torturous week to wait."

Heather shocked herself by saying, "Then let's not wait. Let's lock the door and lie before the fire as before." She nibbled kisses along his jawline, tasting his lips with her tongue.

Brandon groaned as if in pain and shook his head. "I will not take you again until we are properly wed. We must exercise control, and, and . . ."

Her hand was cupping his member, stroking it, teasing it. "I know you must think me a shameless hussy, but I want you, Brandon. I want to feel again what you made me feel that night, wild and free, like a bird who's taken flight."

He clasped her hand tightly, and with more conviction than he had ever thought possible he walked her to the door. "You'll thank me for using restraint," he said hoarsely, mopping the perspiration from his brow with the edge of his coat sleeve.

Smiling, she said, "Somehow I doubt that," kissing his lips one last time. "But if that's what you wish, I won't try to weaken your resolve, though mine is already in tatters. Good night, Brandon." And then she was gone, leaving Brandon to wonder if he had gone insane.

He had a warm, willing woman who was eager to make love with him, yet he had turned her away.

He'd spoken of control, when he should have been speaking of climax.

He'd used restraint, when he should have been stripping her naked and bringing himself into her.

"Fool," he told himself, feeling the evidence of that word pressing painfully against his trousers. He was hard, unfulfilled. But at least he had maintained his self-control, his dominance over the situation, he consoled himself.

Crossing to the double-hung window, he pushed it open and stuck out his head to clear his thoughts and cool his ardor. An owl hooted repeatedly as if finding Brandon's present predicament quite amusing, and he withdrew back into the room, wondering if he'd been born a fool or merely developed into one over the years.

CHAPTER 18

"Your secretary said that you wanted to see me, Brandon."

Brandon swiveled about in his chair to find Peter entering his office, holding a thick sheaf of papers next to his chest. "Come in and shut the door behind you," he said, motioning the reporter forward. "We need to discuss the article you're doing on Whitten. I want to be certain you have all your ducks in a row. I don't relish being sued, and that certainly is a distinct possibility. Gerald's not likely to take this attack against him sitting down."

Setting the stack of paper on Brandon's desk, Peter tapped it confidently. "Everything to substantiate my allegations are contained in these documents. There are depositions and sworn testimony, all witnessed by impartial observers. Whitten won't stand a prayer if he decides to go to court against us. Besides, we have the First Amendment of the Constitution on our side—freedom of the press and all that."

Brandon read through several of the papers that Peter presented as evidence, shocked by the allegations made by several prostitutes. There were references to beatings, drug-

215

ging, and thievery of the bordello's customers, and to young, virginal women being sold into slavery.

Shaking his head at his own gullibility, Brandon's lips tightened in disgust at the way he'd misjudged Gerald Whitten. How could someone like him, a newspaper reporter trained to ferret out details, a man who prided himself on being a good evaluator of character and possessing sound judgment, have been so completely taken in by Whitten?

But then, it had happened once before . . . with Lydia.

He wondered how someone as vile as Whitten could maintain such a veneer of respectability and be counted among polite society's own members.

There had been allegations and hints of scandal in the past, especially during the time when the transcontinental railroad was constructed. Stanford, Crocker, and Hopkins's reputations had not gone unscathed when they'd been accused of lining their pockets at other people's expense. But there had been nothing the likes of Whitten's criminal activities. Those men had done nothing to suggest such blatant disregard for human life, all for the sake of the almighty dollar.

"I can see by your face that Whitten isn't quite the man you thought him to be," Peter remarked.

"I'm embarrassed to say that I was completely taken in by him. Jesus! When I think that I almost married into his family, that I would have been his son-in-law . . ."

"I'm sure that was his intention all along. With you and the newspaper in his pocket, he could have done pretty much what he pleased. You provided the respectability he needed. Marriage to Cecelia would have cinched it for him."

His expression hard and resentful, Brandon said, "Glendenning, we need to nail this wily bastard. Nail him to the wall."

"I take it this means that you'd like me to continue with the series after this first article is printed?"

"Yes. We'll turn up the heat on Whitten. I'll contact my friends at the police department and supply them with a few tidbits of information to get them started on their investigation."

"You're a man of honor, Brandon, and I'm proud to be working for your newspaper."

Peter stood to leave, but Brandon stalled his departure. "By the way, Peter, I'm very impressed with the illustrations accompanying your article. I know they've not been done by one of my men. Do you mind telling me who this talented artist is that's helping you out? I'd be interested in hiring the chap for the newspaper."

Peter dusted an imaginary speck of dust off his sleeve, trying to look nonplussed by the question, though his insides were churning in turmoil. He had to protect Heather's identity at all costs, even if it meant misleading his boss.

"I'm afraid I'm not at liberty to reveal any information about the artist, Brandon. It's the agreement we made when this person agreed to illustrate for me. You know how temperamental these artist types are."

"Well, if the man ever changes his mind, let me know. I'd love to have a crack at hiring him for *The Star*."

Peter would have loved nothing better than to tell Brandon that he'd already had his "crack" and had blown it, but of course he couldn't. Instead, he reassured him that he would relay Brandon's interest and admiration to the person the next time they met. He couldn't wait to see Heather's expression when he told her.

"I don't have to remind you, Peter, that if Whitten is as unscrupulous as your article indicates, things could get a bit sticky around here."

"You're afraid of retribution?"

"I'm merely being cautious. I expect you to do the same. We've taken on a very powerful figure. It appears that Whitten is not above using whatever means necessary to achieve his ends."

Peter nodded. "I've dealt with slime like Whitten before. I'll be careful. I have no desire to end up dead."

A high-pitched howl brought Gerald Whitten rushing from his study into the dining room. Cecelia, seated at the head of the long, inlaid-walnut table, was reading the society section of the morning paper. Her face was streaked with tears, her eyes ablaze with fury, making him wonder if her broken engagement to Montgomery had completely unhinged her mind.

"What's going on here?" he asked, storming into the room. "I thought by that horrible sound you made that you'd injured yourself, Cece." He stepped to the end of the table and took the seat next to her.

"Brandon has placed a huge announcement in this morning's paper. They had the audacity, the unmitigated gall, to inform the entire city of San Francisco about their upcoming wedding." She shoved the offending article across the table at him. "How could Brandon be so cruel? All my friends will read this and know that I've been jilted. How can I possibly face them, knowing that the man I was to marry is marrying that redheaded slut of a governess? I'll be made a laughingstock, an object of pity."

It had been shocking enough to hear the news of Brandon's engagement from Lorna Pond, who'd been only to happy to relate the juicy tidbit of gossip with a smirk on her face.

Just knowing that she, Cecelia Whitten, society's darling, had been tossed aside for a governess—a farm girl, no less—was a bitter pill to swallow. The whole thing was just too humiliating. She wouldn't be able to hold her head up again.

Casting a quick glance at the paper, Gerald poured himself a cup of coffee. "I would hardly call Heather Martin a slut. True, she's a bit unrefined around the edges. But I was that way once myself. You're just lucky that my money has afforded you the opportunity to put on airs." He snapped the paper open, and his mouth fell open as he read the headline:

CORRUPTION ABOUNDS AT WHITTEN ENTERPRISES. INVESTIGATION REVEALS LINK TO OPIUM TRAFFICKING AND PROSTITUTION.

"Father, what is it? What's turning your face that frightening shade of purple?" Cecelia pushed herself out of her chair to lean over her father's shoulder. Reading the headline, she gasped. "My God! We're ruined. Totally ruined."

"We'll see about that! Goddammit!" His fist struck the table with such force that it upset the coffeepot, spilling its contents over the table and floor. "I'm not going to take this kind of smear campaign sitting down. Montgomery's going to be facing a libel suit, if he isn't careful."

Cecelia squeezed his shoulder, afraid to ask the question uppermost on her mind, but knowing she had to. "Is the story true? Are you involved in illegal activities? With prostitutes?" She knew he frequented the brothels when his mistress was indisposed, but she didn't think he had a monetary interest in peddling flesh. The prospect was too hideous to consider.

Drawing his daughter down to his lap, he patted her porcelain cheek. Everything he'd done in his life had been for Cecelia. She was his reason for living. She made every dirty deal he executed necessary and worthwhile.

No child of his would be raised without material things, called white trash and cracker, as he had been. Money bought respectability. A lot of money bought position and stature. And illegal business ventures brought in a lot of money.

"Of course not, Cece," he reassured her. "This is all a bunch of lies. This . . . this Peter Glendenning is looking to make a name for himself at my expense." His eyes narrowed as he filed the reporter's name away for future reference. "Wealthy, important men of business are always targets for these types of scandalmongers. It's a disgrace that good, upstanding citizens must defend themselves against such trashy allegations."

Relief flooding her, Cecelia pressed a kiss to her father's cheek. "What will you do, Daddy? What if everyone believes what's printed in *The Star*? Our friends will surely desert us. We won't be invited to any of their parties or other society functions."

"Never you mind about that, Cece. My money and position have secured us a firm place among this town's elite. We'll stare down those questioning minds and show them we're not the least bit guilty."

"But, Daddy," Cecelia whined, her face paling to match her ivory satin robe. "Brandon has practically jilted me at the altar. How can I possibly face everyone? They'll laugh at me, mock me."

Grasping her by the shoulders, he shook her gently. His

tone hardened as he said, "You're a Whitten, girl. You'll hold your head up high and look them straight in the eye. You've done nothing to be ashamed of.

"Montgomery agreed to take the blame for the broken engagement, and this hasty marriage to his governess will merely add fuel to the growing speculation that they had to marry expeditiously. Don't worry, child. Your daddy will take care of everything. Don't I always?"

She rubbed her soft cheek against his bristled one, as she'd often done when she was a child. "Yes, Daddy. You're too good to me. I hope you teach Brandon Montgomery a lesson." *I certainly intend to teach his new wife one.*

Gerald's eyes narrowed as they skimmed over the article once again. "Rest assured, Cece. Brandon Montgomery will rue the day he chose to take up arms against us Whittens. He started a war he can't possibly win. Let's just hope he isn't foolish enough to get injured during the first skirmish."

Cecelia's eyes widen with fright. "You're not planning to harm Brandon, are you, Daddy? I still care for him. And perhaps someday he'll come crawling back to me." To win Brandon back was what she lived for, now.

Lowering his voice, Gerald's tone grew conciliatory. "Of course not, my dear. You know I would never do anything to harm Brandon. I'm much too civilized for such barbaric behavior."

But the feral light in her father's eyes belied his words, sending waves of apprehension up and down Cecelia's spine.

My Dear Sister,
I'm sorry to have waited so long to answer your last letter, but matters here on the farm have consumed my every waking moment.
　　The Englishman has proven intractable. Never in my life have I met anyone so stubborn and foolhardy. Alexander has insisted on learning everything there is to possibly learn about wheat farming, and I have grudgingly agreed to be his tutor. It was the only way

he would allow me to continue living here on the farm. I thought it was a small enough price to pay to be near our dear mama and papa.

We are constructing a new residence. The duke couldn't "abide the hovel"—his words, not mine— we were living in. And he is spending a considerable amount of money to build a fine new house. I must confess that having indoor plumbing isn't all that difficult to accept.

Though the man has made constant overtures, even going so far as to offer me the position of his mistress—Can you imagine such a thing!—I have remained firm in my refusals. It has not been easy, considering the fact that we are now sharing the same bedroom. But I will write more about that later.

I fear our darling Laurel has become overly enamored of her involvement in the temperance movement. Her last letter sounded positively fanatical. Mr. Rafferty must surely have tested her patience, which, as you know, wasn't one of Laurel's virtues.

I hope this letter finds you well. How are your charges faring? Has Mr. Montgomery consented to let you work at his newspaper yet? Men are nothing if not overbearing brutes! Trust me, I speak from experience.

Alexander is due home soon and will expect his supper on the table. I fear I have spoiled him with my cooking skills.

Please do not wait as long as I did to write. I'm eager to hear more of your adventures in San Francisco.

Your loving sister, Rose Elizabeth.

Wiping tears from her eyes, Heather refolded Rose Elizabeth's letter and slipped it back into its envelope. She was unwilling to take the chance that Brandon might happen along and see the reference to her working at his newspaper, though that was closer to the truth than he realized.

What a thrill it had been to open last Monday's edition of *The Star* and see her illustrations in print. She had squirreled the newspaper away, citing an interest in the advertisements when Brandon questioned her as to the reason she wanted her own copy.

With a deep sigh, she glanced around her room, which was a mess. Her trousseau was strewn haphazardly over dressers, chairs, and the window seat, looking like a rainbow of silk and satin.

Nothing would convince Harriet that more clothes weren't necessary, or that a white wedding dress wasn't an absolutely essential requirement for the wedding, now just two short days away.

Two days! Heather's heart beat a little fast whenever she thought about her marriage to Brandon. What would it feel like to be Mrs. Brandon Montgomery? What would it be like to be in his bed every night, to stare at his naked torso while he performed his morning ablutions, and to share in the day-to-day problems of his work?

He was a private man and had shared little of himself up until now, but she hoped that once they were wed, he would feel comfortable enough to confide in her about his past, about his work, about every facet of his life that she would now be a part of.

The knock on the door brought her bounding off the bed to answer the summons. Harriet stood in the threshold holding yet another ribbon-wrapped box, a sheepish look on her face.

"I know you said not to buy you another thing, my dear, but I just couldn't resist this darling nightgown in the store window on Kearny Street this afternoon."

Heather kissed her future mother-in-law on the cheek and ushered her in as she took the gaily wrapped package from her.

"You could consider it an early Christmas present," the older woman suggested.

Shaking her head in dismay, Heather laughed. "You are an incorrigible shopper, Harriet. Brandon will soon be broke if you don't quit charging items to his account."

In truth, the economy was in poor health. Shipping was down, real estate had plummeted 50 percent, and the bottom had dropped out of the Comstock and Consolidated silver mines. It might be only a matter of time, Heather feared, before the present state of affairs started to affect the newspaper industry.

"Nonsense. My son has more money than he knows what to do with. And I feel it's my duty as his mother to help him spend it wisely." She patted Heather's cheek. "I can't think of a better way to spend it than on you, dear."

Pushing aside some of her other newly purchased clothes, Heather sat on the window seat. Raindrops pattered softly against the glass.

Opening the box, she lifted out a sheer black negligee, and her eyes widened. The garment was almost transparent, leaving little, if anything, to the imagination. She looked up, arching an eyebrow at Harriet's naughty smile.

"You constantly surprise me, Harriet. I wouldn't think such a diaphanous gown would be to your taste." Flannel and ruffles seemed eminently more suited to the older woman, but then it wasn't Harriet who would be wearing the scandalous creation.

"I told you once before that Brandon needs something to melt the ice around his heart. That," she pointed to the negligee, "is going to positively incinerate him when he sees you in it."

Wondering just how long Brandon would allow her to keep on the flimsy garment, a soft blush filled Heather's cheeks. "Thank you for your thoughtfulness, Harriet. It's perfectly lovely, if not a bit . . . daring. I'm sure your son will appreciate the gesture to no end."

"I'm so pleased everything is coming together just as I planned." Harriet twisted her fingers nervously. "There is one fly in the ointment, however, that I think we should discuss."

Heather looked at her in confusion. "Is there a problem that I'm not aware of?" With Harriet's penchant for exactness, Heather couldn't believe that any details had been left to chance.

Harriet sighed. "It's that woman . . . Cecelia. I'm so afraid that she'd going to do something to spoil the wedding. I wouldn't put it past her to try to cause a scene. Brandon said that she didn't take the news of their breakup too well."

"You mustn't worry, Harriet," Heather reassured her. "We'll get through the day just fine. I doubt that even Cecelia would humiliate herself to such a degree by attempting to intrude in a wedding that she hasn't been invited to. Anyway, I'm sure her father will keep her in line. He has enough to worry about at the moment. He can't afford to garner any more unpleasant newspaper headlines."

"Ha! Who's going to keep that old goat in line, I wonder? You know Peter's going to be there. Gerald might use the wedding to exact his revenge against both Brandon and Peter."

Heather swallowed nervously at the thought but plastered a smile on her face. "I refuse to let the Whittens mar my happiness or my wedding day. I'm determined to make the best of it. And if either one does happen to show up unexpectedly, we'll just have to handle it."

Harriet took a seat next to Heather, clasping her hand. "Brandon is very lucky to have found you, my dear. Not many people get a second chance at happiness. He was so devastated by his first wife's betrayal. At least with you he won't have to worry about experiencing such pain again."

These continual veiled references to Lydia's betrayal consumed Heather's curiosity. She hadn't thought it proper to ask before, but now she had to know.

"What drove Brandon and Lydia apart, Harriet? He's never confided the reasons for his divorce. And though I don't want to pry into his personal affairs, perhaps knowing will help me understand Brandon better and make me a better wife."

Harriet frowned, as if castigating herself for the omission. "My dear, don't you know? Lydia was determined to have a career on the stage. She wanted to work outside their marriage, but knowing how adamant Brandon was not to have her work, she kept it from him. She pretended to be the perfect wife and mother, all the while leading a second, secret life that Brandon knew nothing about. When he discovered the deception, it nearly destroyed him. And it did destroy their marriage."

A burning pressure had begun in Heather's chest, making it difficult for her to breathe, and she fought against the faintness that threatened to overtake her. Though she wanted nothing more than to block out the hideous thing that had destroyed Brandon's first marriage, she had to face that the same thing could very well destroy her own.

"A marriage based on lies and deceit is doomed to failure, I'm afraid," Harriet went on, failing to notice Heather's distress. "That's why my son is so lucky to have you, my dear. You would never do anything to hurt Brandon," she added, kissing Heather's cheek before exiting the room.

Heather sat as if dazed, tears slowly trickling down her cheeks. *A marriage based on lies and deceit.* She covered her face, sobbing piteously into her hands.

What have I done? Good Lord, what have I done?

CHAPTER 19

The Palace Hotel on New Montgomery and Market Streets was the grandest establishment Heather had ever laid eyes on. It was seven stories of burnished iron and stucco studded with a multitude of bay windows. The gathering place of wealthy San Francisco society families such as the Crockers, the McAllisters, and the De Youngs, it was also the site of Heather's wedding and reception.

"It's so beautiful. I don't quite know what to say," Heather remarked to Harriet, who was seated next to her in the carriage as she gazed out the window. "I've never seen anything so magnificent. If you could see the hotel in Salina, you'd no doubt be as shocked as I am by the comparison." But then, one could hardly call Clyde Boomer's boarding establishment a hotel!

Patting Heather's hand, Harriet smiled with pleasure. "Just say you're happy, dear, and that will be quite enough. Now let's get you inside before Brandon arrives with the children. It's bad luck for the groom to see the bride before the wedding ceremony."

Heather gnawed on her lower lip, worrying that she'd already brought enough bad luck upon herself with her decision to pursue an illustrator's career. If only she'd known sooner about Brandon's opposition to his wife having a career . . .

But could she honestly say that she would have refused the opportunity given her? She was not at all sure.

The carriage pulled inside the front entrance of the building, and Heather was astounded as she caught her first view of the stunning interior. Though the outside of the Palace Hotel was nothing short of impressive, it did not begin to compare with the exquisite beauty within.

Alighting from the carriage, she stepped into the marble-paved, glass-roofed courtyard, where the ceremony was to be held. Because of the great number of people invited to attend, the large hotel had been chosen instead of a church.

Heather had a difficult time keeping her mouth from gaping as she stared at the opulence surrounding her. Potted palms and rare shrubbery lined the flocked paper-covered walls, and as her gaze lifted toward the lofty ceiling, she saw a portion of the eight hundred elegantly appointed rooms, one of which she would occupy with Brandon very soon. Her mouth went dry at the thought.

"Come along, my dear." Harriet nodded at a passing acquaintance as she tugged Heather's hand. "I've reserved a room so that we may change our clothes. I had the driver deliver your gown and everything else we'll need, and Mary is waiting to assist us."

Heather allowed herself to be pulled along, impressed by what this petite, gray-haired woman had accomplished in such a short time and wondering if Harriet Montgomery had missed her calling. She definitely should have been a military leader, or at the very least, in charge of a vast business empire. Harriet was as organized, meticulous, and competent at handling things as most of Brandon's business colleagues, many of whom Heather had had the opportunity to meet over the past two weeks.

And if there was one thing she had learned about the headstrong woman, it was that she wasn't averse to issuing orders.

"Goddammit, Muller! This report holds no surprises. I told you that I wanted information that would discredit Montgomery. Not this drivel about his newspaper enterprise and happy family life. This goddamn report reads like a testimonial to a saint."

The private investigator Whitten had hired swallowed hard several times, his prominent Adam's apple bobbing in rhythm to the pulse pounding at Gerald Whitten's temple.

"Montgomery ain't done nothing illegal, Mr. Whitten. I interviewed people, like you said. I even talked to some of his employees. They all said Montgomery was a fair, honest man. Even the ones he went and fired don't speak bad of the man." Billy Muller mopped beads of sweat from his forehead with the back of his coat sleeve, eager for this interview to come to an end. "I done the best I could, Mr. Whitten."

Whitten made a rude noise, then crossed to the liquor cabinet to pour himself a brandy. He tossed back the amber liquid in one gulp, but it did nothing to quell the burning anger in his gut or the revenge uppermost on his mind.

There had to be a way to get back at Montgomery for the humiliation and embarrassment the news had caused him and Cece. There had to be a way to get even. And by God he would find it, no matter what it took or how much it cost.

He and his daughter had become the object of gossip and speculation since that goddamn article appeared in *The Star*. They couldn't enter a restaurant or attend the theater without hearing rude comments and whispers about that article and about the fact that Montgomery had jilted the Whitten heiress practically at the altar.

Gerald threw his empty glass at the fireplace, and the crashing noise made Billy Muller jump back in fright. The man's hands were shaking so badly that he could barely hold on to the manila envelope Whitten had thrown at him.

Pacing back and forth across his study, Gerald ignored the nervous investigator as he plotted his revenge.

No one treated a Whitten the way he and Cece had been treated and got away with it. And if Montgomery thought he would sit back and do nothing, then he had gravely misjudged whom he was dealing with.

He knew people, the right kind of people, to get things done. There would be hell to pay before he was through with that bastard and his sniveling reporter. In fact, hell would seem a welcome place after he got his hands on them.

"Have I told you what a beautiful bride you are?" Brandon handed Heather another glass of champagne—her third, but who was counting? She didn't need alcohol to make her giddy. The wedding ceremony, Brandon's kiss at the makeshift altar, and their first dance together as man and wife had done that.

"I believe you have," she said, smiling up at him. "But a woman never tires of hearing a compliment."

"I confess that when I saw the bill for that gown my mother purchased, I nearly had a fit. But it was worth every penny." The antique-white satin gown covered with hundreds of tiny seed pearls was a glorious creation, but it paled next to Heather's perfection. "You are without doubt the most beautiful woman in this room," Brandon said, toasting her with his champagne glass.

"That she is," Peter concurred, sidling up to the newly wedded couple. "And I believe it's my turn to kiss the bride. I didn't have the opportunity earlier."

Peter pressed his lips to Heather's for a congratulatory kiss, and Brandon frowned, trying to keep his jealousy under control. The kiss was brief and chaste, but it made his blood boil just the same. "Don't make a habit of that, Glendenning. I'd hate to have to fire my best reporter so soon after hiring him."

"Brandon," Heather admonished. "That's a terrible thing to say."

"But totally true."

"I half expected to see the Whittens here," Peter said. "I'm surprised they haven't crashed your wedding."

"Honestly, you sound just like Harriet. I've never met so many worrywarts in all my life. Obviously the woman has better sense than you give her credit for."

Brandon and Peter exchanged knowing looks, then Peter smiled and said, "Sweet thing, you're too kind. It's best to watch your back when it comes to someone like Cecelia Whitten. I doubt you've heard the last from her. I know we haven't heard the last from her father."

Brandon brushed back an annoying lock of hair that had fallen over his brow. Heather thought the gesture so boyishly endearing that she had a difficult time concentrating on his conversation with Peter.

"You're right. I received a note from Gerald yesterday. He wants to meet with me about the article. Just as I feared, he's threatening to sue. I've put him off until after our honeymoon." Brandon's smile was full of promise as he looked down at Heather, bringing a bright blush to her cheeks.

Peter cleared his throat in an exaggerated manner. "Well, this is where I make my exit," he quipped. "There's nothing more depressing than being a third wheel on a honeymoon."

Heather's smile was heartfelt. "Thank you for coming, Peter. It meant a great deal to me . . . to both of us." Brandon nodded in confirmation.

Kissing the hand she held out to him, Peter grinned devilishly. "I confess to having an ulterior motive, Heather. I've got my sights set on that little blonde over there."

Heather followed Peter's gaze across the room and saw Mary standing beneath a potted palm on the edge of the dancing area. She looked lovely in the blue satin bridesmaid gown Harriet had provided for the occasion.

"You be good to Mary-Margaret, or you'll have to answer to me."

Laughing, Peter left, and Brandon looked down at his wife in amusement. "I see my mother's been a bad influence on you. You've been playing matchmaker."

"Harriet's well-meaning interference hasn't been all that bad, has it, Brandon?" Smiling seductively, she patted his cheek.

He grasped her hand, bringing her palm to his lips for a kiss, nuzzling it with his tongue, making Heather's heart flutter in anticipation. "I think it's time we went upstairs, love. My patience is about exhausted."

"But . . . but we haven't cut the cake yet. Your mother's going to be terribly upset if we leave prematurely."

Leaning down, he placed his lips close to her ear, his warm breath causing gooseflesh to break out over her arms. "Let them eat cake, love. I've got a hunger for something a whole lot softer and much, much sweeter."

A quick, harrowing ride on the elevator brought Heather and Brandon to the top floor of the hotel. Standing before wide double doors that bore a polished brass plate engraved BRIDAL SUITE, Heather waited nervously while Brandon fished inside his pocket for the key.

She didn't mind the wait; it gave her time to compose herself. For some unknown reason, she felt scared. Even though she was no longer a virgin, and she and Brandon knew each other intimately, it seemed different somehow, knowing you were planning to make love, instead of just doing it spontaneously like they had that first time.

The door swung open. Brandon scooped her up in his arms and carried her across the threshold, allowing Heather no more time to think. "I believe it's traditional," he explained, setting her down inside the candlelit room.

A bottle of champagne in a sterling silver ice bucket stood on the foyer table, and there was a profusion of flowers everywhere. Purple hyacinths, purple lilacs, and wild heather filled the crystal vases adorning all the other tabletops and scented the room with their glorious aroma.

Touched by the gesture, a warm glow flowed through Heather, and her voice choked with tears. "It's lovely. Thank you, Brandon."

He kissed the tip of her nose. "They remind me of your eyes, love, though they don't come close to doing them justice. Your eyes are like amethysts—brilliant, sparkling, multifaceted, and rare."

Brandon had just described the beautiful ring on her finger, and Heather gazed down at it, pleased by her husband's eloquent speech. This softer, gentler side of Brandon was new to her. It was hard to equate this thoughtful, considerate man with the harsh, sometimes overbearing one she'd known over the past months.

Perhaps that hard shell he wore around his heart was beginning to crack just a little. She hoped so. If they were to have a successful marriage, they needed to be honest and open with . . .

"What is it, love?" he asked, drying her unexpected tears with his finger. "I tried to make everything perfect."

"They're . . . they're just tears of happiness, that's all."

"Why don't you go into the bedroom and ready yourself?" There was an erotic glimmer in the depths of his dark eyes— a glimmer that promised untold delights—and Heather's heartbeat quickened.

"I'll pour us some champagne and join you momentarily."

She smiled shyly and nodded, and as Brandon watched her walk away his heart ached for want of her. Heather was a rare treasure and different from any other woman he'd known.

Different from Lydia.

It *would* be different this time. In time Heather would come to love him. In time he would trust her enough to confess what was in his heart.

Why then was he still filled with niggling doubts?

Why couldn't he let go of the past, as his mother had often urged him to, and get on with his life?

Hadn't someone once said that time heals all wounds?

That time discovers truth?

Well, he and Heather had all the time in the world. They

had a whole life together. And he was going to make the most of every moment. Starting now.

Heather stood nervously before the fire, waiting for Brandon to enter, and wondering what he would think of the bewitching negligee she wore. It made her feel deliciously wanton and far more naked than if she'd worn nothing at all.

The bedroom door opened, and she turned. Brandon stood in the threshold, devouring her with his eyes, and she felt her cheeks warm at his bold appraisal.

"Your mother bought it," she explained straightaway. "She said you would like it."

His grin was wildly erotic as he stepped quickly to her and lifted the heavy mass of hair off her shoulders, sifting the strands through his fingers. "For once Mother was right. Remind me to give her a big kiss the next time I see her."

"I will. I . . ." He drew her against his chest, cutting off whatever she'd been about to say. And after a moment of his lips exploring hers, Heather completely forgot what that was.

The sweetness of his kiss made her heart sing and her toes tremble. The touch of his fingers on her nipples sent her stomach into a whirlwind of anticipation.

"I need to undress," he said hoarsely, reluctantly breaking his hold while he unbuttoned his shirt and pants.

What was only a few moments seemed an eternity to Heather. She was eager to reach the wide bed, to feel Brandon's mouth and hands on her burning flesh.

Naked, he came to her, his manhood jutting forth proudly, proclaiming his desire and his need. "I must have you now, love. I can't wait another moment to be inside you, to taste your sweet honey."

The gown dropped like a pool of black lace at her feet, and she held out her hand to him. "Your need is no stronger than mine, Brandon. I ache for you; I've thought of little else these past two weeks."

Her words almost unmanned him. He led her to the bed, easing her down on the quilted satin counterpane. Then he kissed her again, unable to satisfy this craving within him, and with his tongue trailed a path down her neck, caressing every inch of her smooth flesh. "You put this coverlet to shame, love. Your skin is much softer, so much sweeter."

Heather felt the familiar tightening in her loins, the ache in her breasts, as he suckled her nipples, then dipped lower to savor her belly button. He brushed his cheek against her pubic hair, blowing gently on the already aroused area, and she thought she would die of the need he created.

"Oh, Brandon . . ."

With gentle hands, he opened her to him, laving at the tiny bud of femininity, tasting the intoxicating honey there. Quivering uncontrollably, Heather clasped his head, urging him on, wanting to feel the exquisite, breathtaking sensations she knew awaited her.

Her breath coming in short, panting gasps, she climaxed into his mouth. *"Brandon!"* she cried, tears filling her eyes as she reveled in the sweetness of the moment.

Easing himself over her, Brandon didn't allow Heather time to recover from the explosion of her senses. He dived into her core, and with long, deliberate pumping motions took her higher.

"Yes!" she said, wrapping her legs around him, drawing him in deeper, matching his frantic thrusts stroke for stroke. With one final, deep plunge he released into her, crying out her name.

Sated, they lay in each other's arms, content in the knowledge that they had pleased each other, and secure in their feelings of love, though both lacked the courage to express what was in their hearts and souls.

CHAPTER 20

A week later, Gerald Whitten stormed into Brandon's office at *The Star,* waving the latest edition of the paper in his face.

"What's the meaning of this, Montgomery?"

"Mr. Montgomery, I'm sorry," said Brandon's flushed assistant, Henry Peoples, as he hurried into the room behind Gerald. "Mr. Whitten refused to wait until I announced him." Casting the bearded man an annoying look, he tugged impatiently at the hem of his plaid jacket, a sign of his indignation.

"It's all right, Henry. I've been expecting Mr. Whitten. You may leave us alone." The harried little man with the permanent stoop to his shoulders nodded, closing the six-paneled door behind him as he left muttering invectives under his breath.

Brandon pointed to the leather chair in front of his desk. "Sit down, Gerald. I had a feeling you'd be showing up about now."

The man's face turned purple in anger, and he plopped

down heavily on the chair. "I can't believe you'd print such lies about me, Brandon. After all, you were engaged to my daughter. I thought we were friends. Where I come from, friends aren't treated so foul."

Leaning back, Brandon steepled his fingers in front of his chest as he assessed the older man sitting before him. Gerald looked weary and tired, as if he carried the weight of the world on his broad shoulders. His confidence had been shaken. There was no trace of the arrogance and self-assurance he usually exhibited when presented with a difficult situation.

Glendenning's second article on Gerald had been even more inflammatory than the first, quoting several prostitutes who'd accused Whitten of trafficking in white slavery and in opium. He could certainly understand why Whitten would be upset by the allegations. But as the facts continued to unfold, Brandon had fewer doubts as to their veracity.

"I'm a newspaperman, Gerald. Impartial and sworn to disclose information regardless of my personal feelings."

"But your reporter has printed lies. I won't stand by and see my good name dragged through the mud and smeared like so much horseshit. This muckraking you've engaged in is cause for a lawsuit, Montgomery. And don't think I won't hire the best goddamn lawyer in the business to represent me."

"*The Star* has had its share of lawsuits over the years, Gerald. It's the unpleasant side of what we journalists do. If the accusations are untrue, as you say, then I'm sure you'll be vindicated, and we'll print the findings."

"I demand that you print a retraction of everything Peter Glendenning has reported. I've heard about him. He's nothing but a scandalmonger out to make a name for himself at my expense. I won't have it, do you hear? It's bad enough that you ruined my daughter's life by jilting her the way you did, but I won't stand by while you ruin mine as well."

Some of Whitten's suppliers had already backed away from deals they'd previously made. At the rate things were going, and if any more articles were printed, he'd be broke and out of business by year's end. And that was something he couldn't and wouldn't let happen.

Brandon purposely ignored Gerald's reference to Cecelia. One thing had nothing to do with the other, as far as he was concerned, and he wasn't going to allow Whitten to muddy the issue by playing on his emotions.

"I can't agree to a retraction at this time, Gerald. *The Star* stands behind the story we've printed."

Gerald mopped his sweating brow with his handkerchief. "You're making a big mistake, Brandon. I'm warning you not to fuck with me. I won't take this abuse lying down. I came here out of past friendship, hoping you would be reasonable. But if you continue printing that trash, I won't be held responsible for what happens."

Brandon's eyes narrowed. "Is that a threat, Whitten? Because if it is, you should know that I don't take kindly to threats."

The older man stood, leaning over Brandon's desk until they were practically nose to nose. "No, goddammit! It's a promise." He stormed out, slamming the door behind him.

A moment later, Henry reentered, holding a stack of correspondence for Brandon's signature. "Is everything all right, Mr. Montgomery? Mr. Whitten seemed quite agitated. I take it he's not happy with the exposé."

"That's an understatement, Mr. Peoples. Have Peter Glendenning report to my office as soon as possible. I need to talk to him about the next article." *And to warn him about Whitten's threat.*

The afternoon rain sheeted against the glass, and Heather wiped the condensation away with the heel of her hand as she stared out the kitchen window. It had been raining for three days straight and didn't look like it had any intention of letting up soon.

Though she loved the rain, the way it cleansed the air and made the house feel warm and cozy, it was taking its toll on the children's usually good behavior. They were fidgety and quarrelsome. Even Mr. Woo's calm temperament had been put to the test. He'd complained an awful lot lately.

"It's still raining cats and dogs," Heather said, mostly to herself, but her comment prompted the Chinaman to abandon the onions he was slicing and run to the window to look out.

After a moment, he declared, "You crazy in the head, missy. I no see cats and dogs coming down." With a perplexed look on his face, he strained his neck to look upward, in case he had missed something.

The children burst out laughing, and Mary-Margaret, who'd been sitting at the table with them, drawing pictures, shook her head in disgust. "She doesn't mean literally, Mr. Woo. Heather's just using an expression. You know, like— 'don't count your chickens before they hatch.' "

Woo shook his head as he cast Mary an annoyed look. "No make sense to Woo. How can chicken come out of egg if they no hatched?"

Realizing that this conversation was going nowhere fast, Heather drew a deck of playing cards out of her apron pocket. For weeks she'd been promising to teach the children a card game, but the wedding had put a hitch in her plans. "I know just the thing to keep us amused on this dreary afternoon. Since Brandon's still at work, and Harriet's taking a nap, there's nothing to keep us from enjoying a friendly game of poker."

All three children squealed with delight, clapping their hands in anticipation. But Mary, who knew what her employer's reaction would be, wasn't quite as exuberant.

"Mr. Montgomery will have our hides if he finds out we're playing poker with the young ones," she warned Heather.

"Oh, Mom!" Jack admonished. "Quit being such a sissy. Nobody's going to tell him, and Miss Heather's entitled to make important decisions now that she's married to Mr. Montgomery."

Heather doubted that Brandon would agree with Jack's assessment. The children's upbringing was very important to him, and she doubted that he would find their learning poker very amusing or instructional. But Brandon wasn't at home, and she didn't see any harm in the pleasant diversion. Her father had taught her and her sisters to play at much the same age, and they hadn't been corrupted by it.

Taking a seat at the table, she motioned for Woo to sit. "Please join us, Mr. Woo. The game is much more fun with a handful of players."

"What are we going to use for money, Miss Heather?" Jenny asked, testing the new informality of Heather's name and finding she liked it. She and Matt had every intention of calling her Mother, but their father had cautioned them to wait a bit longer, until she got used to the idea of being a married lady with children. "Me and Matt don't have any money to play with."

"Mary, if you would fetch that basket of walnuts from the sideboard," Heather said, "I think they would make a suitable substitute for coins."

"I'll fetch'em, but I don't have me a good feeling about this."

Ignoring the maid's dire prediction, Heather gave the children and Mary brief instruction as to how the game was played. Woo, for all his innocent protestations, appeared to be somewhat of a cardsharp, shuffling the cards with a skill that surprised everyone at the table. When Heather commented on it, Woo giggled like a naughty schoolboy.

"Woo play hand close to belly. No varmint get the drop on me."

Everyone laughed, and they all settled down to the afternoon's entertainment. A short time later, Harriet came into the kitchen fully rested from her nap. Her eyes lit when she saw the game in progress.

"Oh, how delightful! Would you mind if I joined in? I haven't participated in a poker game since Charles died."

Hiding her surprise, Heather passed the older woman a pile of walnuts and reshuffled the cards, cutting Harriet into the game. "It's five-card draw, jacks or better to open."

"I used to be quite good at this when I was younger," Harriet admitted, picking up her cards and fanning them out before her. "But Brandon was such a stick-in-the-mud about amusements of this kind that I ceased playing in any of the card parties we were invited to. Hopefully, now that he's married, he'll have a change of heart about some of his opinions."

Woo pushed his cards to the center of the table and rose to his feet. "Leopard no change spots," he said to Harriet.

The older woman blushed, knowing that the opinionated cook was probably right. But she knew also that Heather was a good influence on Brandon. She'd already seen a change for the better in his attitude toward the children and life in general, though she didn't expect any overnight miracles.

"Deal Woo out," the cook added. "I start dinner now."

About to advise Woo as to this evening's menu, Heather paused when Brandon burst through the door. He was smiling widely, until his gaze landed on the poker game in progress and his children's guilty faces.

"What the devil!"

Heather and Harriet exchanged worried looks, and Mary-Margaret shrank down in her chair. Woo shook his head at the irritation evident on Brandon's face.

"Leopard no change spots," he mumbled, turning to face the stove.

"I thought I had made my wishes perfectly clear to you, Heather, about the type of amusements I wanted the children to engage in. Poker is definitely not one of them."

Rubbing the back of his neck in agitation, Brandon paced across the colorful Turkish carpet in their newly redecorated master bedroom, stopping every so often to punctuate his comments with a lethal look in his wife's direction.

"Just because we're married doesn't give you leave to go against my wishes. There's nothing more aggravating or destructive to a marriage than a wife who will not heed her husband's wishes."

Heather's cheeks filled with heat. Brandon was being totally unfair, and all because of a silly poker game. "You're being unreasonable, Brandon. I've always tried to heed your wishes where the children are concerned"—well, most of the time, anyway—"but I saw no reason to deprive them of an afternoon's entertainment. The rain had made the children bored and in need of a diversion. It was certainly harmless enough. We weren't playing for money, only walnuts."

"That isn't the point. There can be only one boss in a family, Heather. I know you think I'm unreasonable about this and maybe someday I'll explain myself more, but until I do, I expect my decisions to be adhered to."

She knew he was thinking of his ex-wife, and the comparison made her stomach knot. She could hardly defend herself, under the present circumstances. But perhaps there was another way to pull Brandon out of his ill humor.

Withdrawing the now infamous pack of playing cards from her pocket, she held them out to Brandon, like Eve offering an apple to the unsuspecting Adam. "I admit my upbringing might have been different from yours, Brandon, but I know a few games we can play that you won't find too objectionable."

His eyebrow arched. "Are you referring to games of chance? I assure you, I am not a betting man. I prefer to know the outcome of whatever competition I engage in."

She smiled seductively, fanning the cards with her fingers. "And have you ever engaged in a game of strip poker?"

He stopped abruptly in his tracks and spun on his heel. "Strip poker?" he repeated, as if he hadn't heard her correctly.

"That's right. We'll play a hand and whoever loses must remove one article of clothing. It's much more diverting than playing with money, don't you think?"

He swallowed. "What I think is that you're trying to make me change my mind about your unorthodox activity this afternoon."

She shrugged. "If you don't want to play . . ."

"Wait!" he said as she began to put the cards away. "I didn't say that." He eyed her layers of clothing. "We'll be here all night with all the paraphernalia you wear."

Glancing toward the window, Heather replied, "The rain is still coming down, the children have no doubt been fed by your mother, and I have all the time in the world."

He began to strip off his tie. "Uh-uh," she cautioned. "You're going to need that bit of clothing before the night is through."

He finally smiled and removed the tie, tossing it on the bed. "You're that positive you can beat me? This should be an interesting match. I don't like to lose."

"I grew up with a man whose motto concerning poker was 'take no prisoners and show no mercy to your opponents.' Papa was very serious when it came to his weekly card game, whether he played with me and my sisters or some of his friends."

Brandon arched an inquisitive eyebrow. "You mean he corrupted your sisters as well as yourself?"

"Papa didn't consider it corruption. He looked upon the things he taught us as broadening our education. We were taught poker, fishing, and shooting. Living on the farm, we learned to be self-reliant and proficient. It was a necessity."

Folding his arms across his chest, an amused expression on his face, Brandon leaned against the bedpost. "And what did your mother think about all this? I can't imagine she was too happy with your father's educational undertakings."

A wistful smile touched Heather's lips as she thought of her parents. "Mama loved Papa to distraction. She would never have thought to rebuke him for teaching us girls something he enjoyed, because she knew he was doing it out of love."

"They sound like wonderful people."

"They were. Oh, don't get me wrong. They had their faults, like most parents do, but children don't have the privilege of knowing that till they're grown themselves. A little part of Papa died when he laid my mother to rest."

Brandon knew that kind of love. It was the way Frank felt about Clara. The way he, Brandon, now felt about Heather.

"Enough of this maudlin talk," he said, pushing himself away from the bed. "You promised me a poker game, Mrs.

Montgomery, and I won't be satisfied until you're stripped completely naked and lying beneath me in that big tester bed."

Heather's hand flew to her throat in mock outrage. "Why, Mr. Montgomery!" she teased. "I said nothing about engaging in the type of activity to which you refer. I merely suggested an innocent game of chance."

"I'll wager a new hat that you'll be naked and willing by the end of the evening. In fact, I'm so confident that I'll win, I'll even throw in a gown to match."

"And will you also wager a puppy for the children?" Jenny and Matt had been begging for a dog, and this seemed like an excellent time to bring it up.

Brandon nodded, and Heather smiled confidently. This was one game of poker she had no intention of winning, but she didn't exactly plan to lose, either.

When Mary-Margaret opened the door and found Peter Glendenning standing on the front porch, she immediately grew flustered. With trembling hands, she smoothed the sides of her hair, knowing she must look a fright.

"Why, hello, Mr. Glendenning," she said, trying to maintain her composure, though the sight of the man she'd been dreaming about since the wedding sent her senses reeling. "How nice to see you again. Won't you come in?"

"You're looking very pretty today, Irish." He grinned, producing a bouquet of yellow daisies from behind his back. "I brought some flowers."

Mary's eyes widened. "Why, I'm sure Mrs. Montgomery will be very . . ."

"They're for you, Irish. I thought maybe you'd like to get better acquainted. Perhaps have dinner with me sometime."

"Well, now, that would be lovely, providing I can find someone to take care of my son, Jack."

Peter swallowed at the woman's revelation. "You have a son? I wasn't aware." A child! That could put a definite twist on his relationship with the alluring woman.

"Does it make a difference?"

"I . . . I . . ."

Disappointment fueled Mary's anger. Men were all the same, out for only one thing. And it sure enough wasn't fatherhood!

"I'll let Mrs. Montgomery know you're here," she said tersely, turning to leave.

"Wait!" Peter grasped her arm, turning her back to face him. *She really does have the loveliest skin and azure-blue eyes,* he thought. "I didn't say it mattered. I was just surprised, that's all. You don't look old enough to have a child."

His compliment appeased Mary, but only slightly. "Jack's ten. And you might as well know, he doesn't have a father. But that doesn't mean I'm easy, Mr. Glendenning. I've got morals same as the next person."

"Irish . . ." He stroked her cheek with his fingertip. "I never thought any differently. There's no reason to get your dander all in an uproar. And don't you think you should call me Peter, seeing as how we're going to be seeing a lot of each other from now on."

Her eyes widened, her heart skipping a beat. "Are we now?" She smiled coquettishly. "And what makes you think so?"

"Just this." Tilting up her chin, he kissed her soundly on the lips, then grinned at the moonstruck look on her face. "You intrigue me, Mary-Margaret Feeney. And that's a fact."

Joy sparkled like diamonds in Mary's blue eyes. "And I think you've been kissin' the Blarney stone, Peter Glendenning. And if you think your boyish grin and sweet-talking ways are going to have an effect on this poor Irish lass, then you just might be right."

CHAPTER 21

"I'm sorry, Gerald, but I don't see how you could win a legal suit against Montgomery's paper," Chester Pickney stated, folding his hands atop his desk as he looked at the man seated before him. He'd been Whitten's lawyer for several years, knew all of the man's underhanded dealings, and he doubted that he, even as good a lawyer as he was, would be able to refute the allegations against Whitten.

Whitten bolted to his feet, slapping the top of the desk with his palms. "What the hell is that supposed to mean? *The Star* has written libelous things about me. Montgomery is ruining my reputation, my business. Surely there must be something you can do. What the hell do I pay you all that money for?"

Not the least bit intimidated by the outburst, for he was used to Gerald's quick temper, Chester leaned back in his leather swivel chair. "Montgomery is an astute businessman, Whitten. He was more than willing to share his proof with me when I visited him yesterday. You know perfectly well that the allegations are true. How am I supposed to pretend that they're not?" He drummed his fingers, deep in thought, then said, "I recommend that you discontinue plans for this lawsuit. It will be a complete waste of my time and your money."

His nostrils flaring, Whitten leaned toward his attorney. "I won't have any money to waste, goddammit, if we can't stop Montgomery. My sources tell me that another article is planned for tomorrow."

"Of course, I can't suggest anything illegal, Gerald." Chester smiled smoothly as he studied his manicured nails. "But if I'd been made aware that another article was being printed tomorrow, I'd be sorely tempted to do something tonight to put a stop to it."

Whitten straightened up, a sinister smile on his face. "I guess now I know why I pay you all that money, Pickney. Your advice has always been right on the mark."

"I'll profess ignorance to whatever it is you're planning to do, Gerald. You realize that, of course?"

"Of course I realize that. You're as corrupt as I am. You just wear better suits and have a bigger vocabulary. You needn't worry that you'll be implicated. From here on out, I'll be handling things my own way."

Staring at the two smashed printing presses, Brandon clenched and unclenched his fists, his face mottled red in anger. Approximately one hundred and sixty thousand dollars' worth of equipment lay scattered at his feet, and it didn't take a genius to figure out who was capable of such wanton destruction.

"I can take a pretty good guess as to who's responsible for this incident, can't I, Frank?" He turned toward the older man standing next to him.

The managing editor shook his head, disgust clouding his features. "My guess is that it happened in the wee hours of the morning, Brandon. The night watchman was knocked over the head and rendered unconscious. He's all right now, except for a large bump on his head."

"Was anyone else hurt? Anything else destroyed?"

"No. It seems the damage was confined to this area, and to Willy Murdock's head. Doc's already pronounced Willy fit to come back to work."

"Thank God for that," Brandon said, rubbing the back of his neck to ease the tension out of it. "Willy's got a wife and four children who depend on him." He studied the mangled presses a few more moments, adding, "We've got to tighten security around here, Frank. I should have taken Whitten's threats more seriously. I'm certain he's the one responsible. From what Peter tells me, this is Whitten's style."

"Well, it did the bastard little good. We've got the article typeset on the other presses, and it'll go out in this evening's edition as planned."

Brandon clasped Frank's shoulder. "This is a minor setback, Frank. Whitten won't win. I'm more determined than ever to see justice prevail where he's concerned."

"Justice can get mighty expensive," Frank reminded him, tugging on his chin whiskers.

Brandon finally found a reason to smile. "But it'll be money well spent. And I'll enjoy spending every penny."

Seated across from Brandon in the carriage, Heather had been waiting for just the right moment to tell him what was uppermost on her mind: that she wasn't about to play an inactive role in their marriage or in his life. Her annoyance had been building like steam within a kettle since this morning when Mary had told her about yesterday's incident at *The Star*.

"I'm sorry you felt it necessary to hide what happened at the newspaper yesterday, Brandon," she began. "I would have thought, as your wife, that I deserved to be taken into your confidence." Crossing her arms over her chest, she waited for an explanation.

Brandon, who had been gazing out the window at a pair of playful brown bunnies scurrying up the trunk of a stately clipped cedar, turned to look at her.

"Yesterday?" He could see by Heather's expression that she was not going to buy his innocent act. "You're referring to the vandalism? How, may I ask, did you hear of it?" He didn't wait for her to answer. "Let me guess—Peter no doubt confided in Mary, who felt compelled to tell you. Am I right?"

"Where I heard the news is not important. What is, Brandon, is the fact that you didn't see fit to tell me yourself. You don't take me into your confidence about anything concerning your work or your personal life. How can we have a successful marriage if I don't know what's affecting you now or what affected you in the past?"

Brandon leaned back against the velvet upholstered seat cushion and sighed. He'd hoped to avoid this confrontation, but he could see by the determined set of Heather's chin that she wasn't about to let him.

"Women have an unending curiosity that I find ridiculously annoying. What happened at the newspaper doesn't concern you or our marriage."

"But that's where your wrong. It concerns me very much. Everything you do or have done in your life concerns me. I'm your wife. I want to be part of your life, share in your sorrows as well as your joys."

His face softened, and he reached for her hand. "You are my joy, love."

Heather would have none of it. Pressing her hands between her knees to avoid the disturbing contact and the chance to weakening her position, she said, "Marriage is more than whispering endearments in the dark and making love, Brandon. It's commitment and responsibility. It's caring and being cared for."

"I care about you very much, dammit."

"Then why won't you share your life with me? I'm not some porcelain doll to be placed upon a pedestal. I want to be a partner in this marriage. Perhaps your lack of faith in a woman's abilities to play an equal role in marriage is what caused your first marriage to fail." She knew she was treading on thin ice, and by the dark look on her husband's face, Heather feared she had overstepped her bounds.

His voice chilled with disapproval. "You know nothing of my relationship with Lydia."

"Exactly. And I should. I'm your wife, the mother to your children. How can I know your desires and dreams, your hurts and failures, if you won't share them with me?"

"You're nothing like her."

She took a deep breath and crossed to the opposite side of the carriage, taking a seat next to him. "How do you know? You've never revealed one thing about your ex-wife to me. But I know, from when I cared for you in your feverish delirium, that you loved her a great deal." He paled, shocked by her revelation, but she pressed on. "You cried out for her, Brandon. You tried to make love to me, thinking it was Lydia."

A knowing light entered his eyes, as if everything that had happened so long ago now made perfect sense to him. ''I thought I was dreaming."

"You were. About another woman. But I didn't care. I'm glad you reached out to me. I . . . I wanted to be there for you. I care for you a great deal." *I love you.*

His shoulders slumped in defeat as agonizing memories washed over him. "I did love Lydia, but she deceived me."

Though she already knew the answer, Heather asked, "With another man?"

"No. I wish it had been that simple. I could have understood an attraction to another man far more easily than the attraction Lydia had for the stage."

"She was an actress?"

"Yes. But I didn't know that when I married her. She hid everything from me. She seemed content in our marriage, in motherhood, but all along she was living a lie."

"Perhaps it wasn't a lie at first, Brandon. Perhaps Lydia tried to be the kind of wife you wanted, the perfect mother to your children. But perhaps it wasn't enough for her. Sometimes people are driven by things deep inside of them. Obviously, Lydia had the need to express herself in some unorthodox way and knew you wouldn't approve of her choice." She could certainly empathize with the woman. Heather just hoped that she hadn't given Brandon too much insight into her own personality."

"A woman's place is in the home. Once the commitment is made to marry, then a wife should cleave to her husband and abandon whatever selfish motivations she might have."

She swallowed her own guilty thoughts. She knew she was being unfair to chastise Brandon for keeping secrets from her, considering that she was doing the very same thing to him. But she wanted to be close to him, to share his problems and sorrows. Soon, when the articles were finished, there would be no more secrets between them. Not ever.

"Sometimes it's not that easy. Sometimes the choices are difficult. A woman might want a husband and children desperately, but feel unfulfilled just the same. You shouldn't condemn Lydia for what happened between you. Her silence in not telling you what she was doing probably stemmed from wanting to protect you because she loved you."

"If she'd loved me, as you say, she would never have deceived me in that way. She would have come to me, confided in me. . . ."

Heather's heart was beating so fast, she thought it might explode. "And if she had, would you have allowed her to continue her craft?"

A brief silence ensued, save for the chattering of the robins and the wind whistling through the treetops, and then he shrugged. "I don't know. Maybe." Hope blossomed in Heather's chest, but soon wilted when he admitted, "Probably not."

Drawing Heather int his arms, Brandon kissed her brow. "Heather, I . . . I . . ."

"Yes, Brandon?" She waited expectantly, hoping and praying that he would finally say what she longed to hear: that he loved her.

His gaze lifted and through the window he saw the familiar stucco house in the near distance. "I believe we're home, love."

"Are we, Brandon?" She couldn't keep the disappointment out of her voice. "I'm not so sure. I think we're a long way from home. A very long way."

He looked at her strangely, but he didn't question her enigmatic remark.

"It was really very sweet of you to accompany me to this month's meeting of The Ladies' Protection and Relief Society, Heather," Harriet whispered, ignoring the annoyed look of the rotund lady seated next to them. The woman stared at them through a gold lorgnette that magnified her eyes and gave her the appearance of an unhappy frog.

"Though the deeds we perform—rendering assistance to strangers, to sick and dependent women and children—are noble, I find most of the members insufferable bores." Harriet nudged Heather with her elbow, nodding toward Cecelia Whitten, who was seated across the aisle from them.

"I'd much prefer to be at home working on my memoirs. It was truly inspirational of you to suggest that I put all my thoughts on paper. I'm having the most marvelous time writing, and I'm going to insist that Brandon publish them when I'm done."

"I'm sure he'll see the value in your efforts. Why, you've witnessed many extraordinary things in your lifetime, and we'll all benefit from reading about them."

Harriet patted Heather's hand. "You're the best daughter-in-law an old woman like me could ever hope to have." She looked across the aisle again, this time smiling spitefully at her son's ex-fiancée. "Gracious, I don't know what I would have done if *she'd* been the one sitting here with me."

"The meeting is about to begin," Heather cautioned.

Elmira Tucker, a reed-thin, bespectacled woman, took the dais, looking sightly flustered as she rummaged through her pockets for her notes. In a voice that sounded like nails raking against a blackboard, she announced, "Today I have the honor of introducing the newest members of our group.

Ladies, would you please stand when I call your name, so our members can get to know you?"

Groaning inwardly, Heather now wished she'd refused Harriet's pleas to attend today's meeting. She hated the thought of standing before this group of gossip-seeking women. No doubt her recent marriage to Brandon had set their tongues to wagging. And she could almost feel their eyes stabbing into her back. It was an uncomfortable feeling at best, and when her name was finally called, she stood with the utmost reluctance.

"This is Mrs. Heather Montgomery, wife of the very prominent newspaper icon, Brandon Montgomery."

There was a brief smattering of applause, and then as Heather was about to resume her seat, Cecelia called out, "His slut, you mean!"

The comment elicited several loud, very shocked gasps, and a definite curse from Harriet, who jumped to her feet. "I would caution you to keep silent, Cecelia Whitten. Your opinions are not sought, nor do we intend to listen to them."

Challenged, the blond woman stood, staring defiantly at the two Montgomery women before she addressed the members at large. "As a member in good standing of this society, I feel it is my Christian duty to point out that there is an imposter in our midst. This woman passing herself off as a respected member of society is nothing more than Brandon Montgomery's mistress. It wouldn't surprise me to find out that he *had* to marry her. Why else would he have chosen her over me?"

Like a rocket being launched, Heather shot to her feet, her violent eyes flashing fire as an ominous hush fell over the room. Sliding down the long row of spectators, excusing herself as she passed by each startled woman, she came face to face with her accuser.

"How dare you publicly malign me and my husband, Miss Whitten! You, who profess to have good breeding and refinement, have shown to this group of ladies that your manners are no better than those of an alley cat in heat." Harriet clapped her hands loudly, but Heather ignored the interruption, as well as Cecelia's outraged, "How dare you!"

"I doubt there's a lady in this room who, having read *The Illustrated Manners Book*—I refer specifically to the chapter on self-control—wouldn't admit that your behavior here today is an unthinkable breech of proper conduct and moral behavior. To quote the author, Mr. De Valcourt: 'The man, or in this case, woman, who is liable to fits of passion; who cannot control his temper, but is subject to ungovernable excitements of any kind, is always in danger. The first element of dignity is self-control. . . .'

"I further doubt, Miss Whitten, that any of these fine ladies have a doubt in their mind as to why Brandon Montgomery chose me for his wife rather than you." Several snickers ensued, confirming Heather's words. "All's fair in love and war, Miss Whitten, and I'm sorry to say that you are the poorest loser I have ever had the displeasure of meeting.

"I can only imagine what kind of model you would have made for two innocent children."

There was a murmur of consensus, then Heather turned toward her mother-in-law, who was beaming at her with pride, and said, "Harriet, I believe I am ready to leave now." And then to Elmira Tucker, who was wringing her hands as if she were holding a wet dishrag, she said, "Thank you, Mrs. Tucker, for your most gracious welcome. I will be happy to lend my support both physically and monetarily to whatever cause your very fine group needs assistance with. Good day."

Arm in arm, Heather and Harriet marched down the aisle to a very unexpected round of applause.

In the midst of all the commotion, Cecelia could be heard shouting at the top of her lungs, "You haven't heard the last from me!"

CHAPTER 22

Heather paced anxiously in front of the library. She gazed down the street every so often, wondering what could be keeping Peter. He was always on time for their meetings; it wasn't like him to keep her waiting, and that made her doubly nervous.

Checking the watch pinned to the front of her dress, she gnawed her lower lip, worrying that Harriet would be home soon with the children. Heather had to be there to prevent any suspicions as to where she'd gone. Questions, no matter how innocent, weren't something she wanted to contend with right now.

Glancing down at the books in her hand, she felt relieved that she'd had the presence of mind to check them out. Though she smiled ruefully when she realized that one of the volumes was on architectural drawing.

A few more minutes passed, and Heather finally decided that Peter wasn't going to come. As she held up her had to waylay a passing cab, she noticed Peter rounding the corner. He looked breathless, as if he'd been running hard, though his face was ashen rather that the beet red she would have expected. His right arm was clutched tightly to his chest.

"Peter, I was so . . ." Heather caught the pained look on his face and paled herself. "What's wrong? Are you injured?"

"Grab that cab," he instructed. "We'll talk while we ride."

Concern had her moving quickly, and after they were safely inside the cab, she gave the driver directions to the Montgomery house.

"You look awful. What did you do to your arm?"

"I think it's broken." He tried to move it to a more comfortable position but the effort cost him dearly, and he moaned. "I was on my way here when I was attacked by two men I'd never laid eyes on before. They were dressed like dock workers, and one had a long, jagged scar on his left cheek."

She gasped. "But why would they want to hurt you?"

"Can't you guess? Whitten's bent on revenge. I suspect he thought that if he broke my writing arm, I wouldn't be able to pen more articles. At least that was the message I was given while my arm was being pulled from its socket." He winced at the memory.

"I'll tell the driver to take you to the hospital."

Peter grasped her arm gently but firmly to forestall the action. "No! I'll see my own physician after I've dropped you off. He's much more discreet about these types of things. Did you bring the illustrations?"

"Of course." She reached into her satchel and withdrew her latest sketches for his article. "I was a bit rushed. Brandon hasn't allowed me much time to myself."

"Neither would I, sweet thing, if I were in his position." Peter winked, despite the pain shooting through him, then looked at the renderings. Obviously pleased, he smiled. "Even rushed, your work is better than most, Heather. Brandon never fails to comment on what a wonderful artist you are. He's still pressuring me for your name, but so far I've been able to put him off."

"I'm growing increasingly uncomfortable about lying to Brandon and everyone else, Peter. I should never have agreed to illustrate these articles. And if Mary discovered we were meeting each other on the sly, there'd be hell for you to pay, as well. She's a jealous woman. She told me so herself."

"Irish has a temper all right." He smiled in remembrance of the last fight they'd had. Over what it had been, he couldn't say, but he distinctly remembered that making up had been one hell of a pleasurable experience.

"I hate to interrupt your romantic musings, but my situation is a bit more serious."

A chagrined look crossed his face. "Sorry. But it shouldn't be much longer. Whitten's actions today merely confirm that we're hitting the nail on the head. I expect the police will soon have enough evidence to bring forth an indictment."

"As if Gerald isn't bad enough. I've had to contend with that loony daughter of his. Cecelia's been following me around. She appears at the oddest times and in the most unexpected places. Just yesterday, Harriet and I went shopping, and there she was in the middle of the department store, pointing an accusing finger at us." Heather shuddered, remembering the incident.

"Well, well, if it isn't the two Mrs. Montgomerys," she had said. "Out spending Brandon's money, I see. Well, you can buy all the pretty dresses and gewgaws you want, but they won't hide the fact that you're as common as dirt. Brandon will tire of your provincial ways soon enough."

Cecelia's spiteful words had infuriated Heather, and she had wanted nothing more than to wipe the nasty smile off her face with the flat of her hand, but she hadn't done so. Instead, she and Harriet had turned on their heels without saying a word and walked in the opposite direction. It had taken every ounce of self-control Heather possessed to ignore the vindictive woman.

"I truly think Cecelia's unbalanced," she told Peter.

His face clouded with unease. "Have you told Brandon about this? Perhaps he can speak to her—warn her off."

She shook her head. "No. And you mustn't say anything. Brandon has enough to worry about right now with Gerald's retaliations. I don't want to add to his burdens by relating Cecelia's crazed actions. Besides, she'll soon tire of taunting me. I'll just keep ignoring her. . . ."

"You weren't too successful at ignoring her at that hen party you attended last week." He chuckled, and Heather's cheeks crimsoned. News of the incident had reached him via his landlady, who had been in attendance at the meeting.

"I was provoked unexpectedly, but I've since learned to control myself." She continually thanked the good Lord and Brandon's library for that book on etiquette from which she'd quoted. For someone who until recently hadn't known a salad fork from a dinner fork, she'd presented a very knowledgeable facade. Harriet, with a great deal of pride in her voice, had commented on it several times over the last few days.

"I'm ignoring Cecelia as much as possible. If I don't acknowledge her presence, she'll grow weary of the game."

"Sweet thing, the Whittens will never tire of the game. People like them thrive on nastiness. Cecelia's spitefulness will only worsen. I strongly suggest that you tell Brandon about these incidents."

"No, I will not. And if you're my friend, you will heed my wishes."

He sighed, favoring his injured arm and shoulder. "If I was truly your friend, I would never have dragged you into this mess in the first place. I'm just grateful that Whitten doesn't know who is responsible for those unflattering, cartoonish drawings of him. I don't doubt for a moment that he would retaliate."

Heather breathed deeply, trying to dispel the nervous apprehension his words had elicited. "He doesn't know, so we have nothing to worry about."

Peter nodded, but the look on his face indicated that he wasn't so sure.

"What is it, Heather?" Mary-Margaret asked, dropping the dish towel and rushing forward. "You look white as a ghost, like you just lost your best friend or something. Did your letter bring bad news?"

Heather looked up, clutching the disturbing missive to her

chest, hardly knowing where to begin the explanation Mary sought. "It's from Laurel," she said barely above a whisper.

"Your sister who's in Denver trying to become an opera singer?" Mary plopped down in the chair next to Heather and waited for an explanation.

"Laurel's written to say that she's in a great deal of trouble, but she doesn't elaborate. I'm terribly worried about her. What if she's sick? What if something dreadful has befallen her?"

"Saints alive!" Clasping Heather's clammy hand, Mary chafed it between her warm ones. "What do you suppose has happened?"

Heather glanced down at the letter again and shook her head in dismay. Knowing Laurel as she did, anything was possible. Her little sister had a penchant for getting herself into trouble.

"Perhaps it concerns her former employer Mr. Rafferty." Heather had been afraid that her sister's involvement with that temperance league was courting disaster, and Mr. Rafferty didn't sound like a man who could be toyed with.

"Mr. Rafferty be the saloon owner?"

Heather nodded. "Yes. And no doubt Laurel has pushed him to the very limits of his patience. I just pray she can handle whatever fate has in store for her."

"Being alone and on your own ain't easy, Heather. I been in the same predicament, but I survived and so will your sister. It sounds like she's got more spunk than most. And she can always go back to Kansas and live with your other sister if she becomes desperate."

Heather doubted that the Duke of Moreland was going to put up with yet another Martin sister, after the way Rose Elizabeth had strong-armed her way into his life. Perhaps Brandon would allow Laurel to stay with them if circumstances warranted, but knowing how he felt about actresses and stage performers, she rather doubted it.

"I've always been there for both of them. I just feel so helpless right now."

"They're both grown women, and you've got other children to mother now. It's time you let them live their lives and make their own mistakes. Brooding over things you can't change won't do you a bit of good. Me dear mother used to tell me that, and she was right. God rest her soul."

"I suppose you're right."

"Of course I am. Mark my words, things will turn out for the best. They always do. Look at me for instance. Who would ever have guessed that I'd be keeping company with a handsome man like Peter Glendenning? I want to pinch myself every time he kisses me." She chuckled. "Course if I did, I'd be black and blue." Heather smiled, and Mary chucked her cheek playfully. "That's better. Now, are we going to finish planning this surprise birthday party for Miss Harriet or not? Putting one over on that snoopy old woman isn't going to be easy. She's got more eyes in her head than a potato."

Stuffing the disturbing letter from Laurel into her apron pocket, Heather nodded. "At least it won't be difficult deciding what kind of cake to make."

"Chocolate?"

"Chocolate!" Heather agreed.

Henry Peoples burst into Brandon's office, not bothering to knock. His shirttail was sticking out of his pants, and his hair was mused, as if he'd been running agitated fingers through it. Brandon and Frank knew immediately that something was very wrong. Henry wasn't given to emotional outbursts over trivial matters, and until this day they'd never seen a hair out of place on his pomaded head. Burnett's Cocaine Hairdressing kept it firmly in place.

"Two newsboys, Simon Curtis and Mike Barrett, have been threatened and had their papers taken away, Mr. Montgomery," he blurted. "I thought you'd want to know right away."

Brandon shot to his feet, his face darkening like a thundercloud. "When did this happen? Are the boys all right?"

The secretary nodded. "Just scared. They're afraid to go back out on their corners. They said they were accosted soon after their bundles had been dropped off."

"Sounds like more of Whitten's shenanigans," Frank said, frowning.

"It sounds like that to me too, Mr. Burnside," Henry agreed, straightening his tie, which he had just realized, much to his horror, was loose.

"Pay the boys their missed wages, Henry, and tell them to take the rest of the day off. I'll expect them back on their corners as usual tomorrow. I want you to explain that they'll be protected from further harm. I'll see to it myself."

Nodding, Henry scurried out the door.

"What are you planning to do, Brandon? Whitten's running scared, and he's sure to step up his vendetta against *The Star*."

Brandon stared out the window. "Our workers must be protected. I want extra men hired and put on the streets to keep an eye on the newsboys. Whitten's men aren't likely to strike if they see the boys guarded by armed men. And I want you to take extra precautions, too, Frank. There's no telling who else Whitten will strike against."

Frank patted his coat pocket, his smile confident. "I've been carrying my own protection for weeks." He pulled out a derringer. "You know I ain't one to take chances, Brandon. And I'd suggest you do the same."

"It's not me I'm worried about, Frank." His thoughts drifted to Heather and the children. If anything happened to them, he'd never forgive himself.

"You don't think he'd harm innocent women and children?"

"Those newsboys aren't much older than Jenny and Matt."

Frank shook his head in disgust, conceding the point. "I guess it's best Clara's staying in that sanitarium. At least I know she'll be safe there."

"Has there been any change in her condition?"

"The doctors are astounded that she's lived as long as she has. Some days are better than others, but they don't hold out much hope for recovery. Her health continues to decline. I guess she's in God's hands now. Funny," he said, shrugging his shoulders. "I was never a religious man before Clara took ill. Now I find myself praying all the time. Strange, how the love of a good woman can change your entire life."

Brandon nodded thoughtfully. "Yes, it is."

• • •

Brandon entered the house as quietly as he could, wishing it weren't so late, since Heather had probably retired for the evening.

Damn Gerald Whitten to hell! he thought, hanging his coat on the hall tree before venturing into the kitchen. He'd missed dinner because of the man's vindictive actions, and he was starved. Though he'd gladly forgo a meal for the chance to sample Heather's sweet fare.

As if conjured up by his provocative thoughts, he found her standing at the kitchen table when he entered, slicing ham onto a plate. She looked up at the sound of his footsteps and smiled, and that smile cut a path straight to his heart. *God, how I love her!*

"Brandon, you're finally home. I was beginning to give up on you."

He kissed her cheek. "Don't ever do that, love."

"You look tired. I thought you might be hungry, so I made some ham sandwiches. It's not much of a dinner, but it's . . ."

His arms pulled her against his chest, and she dropped the knife, her nipples hardening in anticipation of his touch. "I'm starving, love, but not for ham sandwiches."

She turned in his arms, and even though it was dark in the kitchen—only one lamp burned on the counter—Heather could discern the hunger in her husband's eyes. And it wasn't the kind that had anything to do with dining.

She wrapped her arms around his neck. "I'm pleased you missed me."

Holding Heather at arm's length, Brandon frowned, noticing her attire for the first time. "Do you think you should be running around the house dressed like this?" The translucent nightgown rendered the dark areas of her large nipples and the tempting V of her womanhood clearly visible. "If I can see through the material, so can everyone else."

"The children and your mother have been asleep for hours, Brandon. And I wasn't expecting any late-night callers, other than you."

"I want no one but me to feast their eyes on your beauty. You're mine, only mine." Lowering his head, he ground his lips upon her mouth, replicating the motion with his hips.

The familiar ache began again, and Heather moaned aloud. "You have only to touch me and I melt into butter."

"Let me see," he said, licking the whorls of her ear, the long stem of her neck. "*Mmmm.* I see that you do. But this claim of yours may require a more thorough examination."

Remembering his fantasy of months before, Brandon smiled to himself. He'd thought about that fantasy many, many times, and now he was going to live it. "I want you here, now," he said, bending her backward over the table, brushing the sandwiches onto the floor.

Heather's heart thundered as Brandon's meaning became clear. "You want to make love here, on the kitchen table?" She swallowed at his nod. It was a shocking thing to do—shocking and wildly exciting.

He untied the delicate pink ribbons that held her gown closed at the shoulders, and the wispy material fell way. With impatient hands he swept it aside, baring her to his gaze. "I don't want to wait. I can't. I've thought about this all day. No matter how many problems confronted me, the thought of sinking into your sweet warmth saved my sanity."

Brandon's declaration sang through her veins, and Heather tugged at the buttons of his shirt, helping him off with his clothing. When his chest was bare, she pressed her lips to it, kissing him all over, nibbling at his nipples, which were as hard as her own. "I want you, too."

Freeing his hot, hard member from his pants, he spread her legs and entered her quickly, smothering her cries of passion with his mouth. Cradling her soft buttocks in his hands, he pumped into her, hard and fast, until he felt her shudders of release envelop him. With one final stroke, he spilled his seed into her.

He lay motionless, unable to believe the intensity of their joining. In his state of bliss it took Brandon a moment to realize that Heather was frantically trying to tell him something.

"Brandon, quick! Someone's coming. We must hide."

He smiled tenderly at her. "Someone already came, love."

"This isn't funny, Brandon. I heard noises outside the kitchen door."

Hitching up his pants, Brandon helped Heather back into her gown. The back-door bell jingled, signaling that someone was trying to get in.

"In the pantry," he ordered, wishing he had some type of weapon at hand to defend his home and family.

The kitchen door opened just as they ducked into the pantry closet, pulling the door shut behind them.

"I know I left my shawl here earlier, Peter. It's got to be around somewhere."

"It's Mary," Heather whispered.

"Ssh! They'll hear us."

"Will you look at that mess on the floor," Peter commented, staring at the food sprawled beneath the kitchen table. "I don't recall seeing that when we were here earlier."

"I know I cleaned up the place before I left this evening. I hope everything's all right."

"I smell perfume. Do you smell it?"

Heather covered her mouth in mortification. If they figured out what she and Brandon had been doing at the kitchen table, she'd never be able to face either of them again.

"It'll only take a minute to clean up the mess."

"You can get it in the morning. Right now I've got something a bit more pressing for you to attend to."

The moans of passion could be heard distinctly by the couple in the pantry, and Brandon couldn't contain his chagrin at the awkward position his randiness had placed everyone in. Listening to Peter and Mary kiss—and Lord knew what else they were doing—was decidedly uncomfortable, making him feel like a voyeur at a peep show.

However, listening to a couple making love was an erotic sensation Heather had never experienced before. Much to her shame, she felt herself becoming aroused again. Her nipples were engorged, and she had the urge to rub against Brandon's thigh.

"Come on, Irish. If we don't leave now, I'll be tempted to take you on top of the kitchen table."

Mary's gasp was audible. "Shame on you, Peter Glendenning. What kind of a woman do you think I am, to be rutting on top of a table?"

Heather nearly fell over at that remark.

"Well, if I didn't know for a fact that Brandon is much too reserved and respectable to ever do such a thing himself, I'd suspect the old boy had toppled his wife in here. I'm not the best damn reporter in this city for nothing. This place smells like a Tenderloin bordello."

Brandon quickly covered Heather's mouth with his own to smother her gasp.

"It's probably just Romeo," Mary said. "That dog's always leaving puddles and messes everywhere. Come on. Let's go put that imagination of yours to good use."

A moment later the back door closed, and Heather and Brandon chorused sighs of relief.

"Remind me to fire that opinionated smart-ass tomorrow. Too reserved, am I?" Brandon's tone was clearly indignant. "Come on. Let's get to bed before someone else comes in."

"Brandon?" Heather whispered, her voice sultry and soft as mist hovering above a pond on a summer evening. "I'm not ready to leave just yet." She reached for the front of his trousers, and Brandon's member hardened instantly at her touch.

"Are you suggesting what I think you're suggesting, love?"

It was pitch black inside the pantry, and Heather was relieved that Brandon couldn't see the humiliation on her face. Not that she cared, plagued by lust as she was at the moment. "Those flour sacks in the corner might be more comfortable than the table."

Out of the darkness came Brandon's soft chuckle. "An insatiable wench. There really is a God in heaven after all."

CHAPTER 23

As befitting a funeral, it rained the day Clara Burnside was laid to rest. The service had been brief, the interment even briefer. And now, at the Montgomery mansion, the last of the callers to pay their respects to Frank and to his wife's memory were just leaving.

With his arm wrapped around his editor's shoulders, Brandon offered comfort, but knew that at times like these, comfort wasn't easily accepted or particularly well received. "Clara was a fine woman, Frank. She'll be missed by all of us."

"You've been a good friend, Brandon. And you too, Mrs. Montgomery," he said in a choked voice to Heather, who stood silently by her husband's side. "I know it'll take some time, but I'm pretty sure I'll be able to get through this."

The older man was holding up remarkably well, considering the circumstances, Heather thought. Though she had known Clara only a short time, she felt deeply saddened by her death, understanding how much Frank had loved his kindhearted wife.

Patting the grieving man's hand in a consoling fashion, she said, "You're part of our family, Frank, and you will please not call me 'Mrs. Montgomery.' That's Harriet's name. Mine's Heather, and you must feel free to use it."

Frank smiled softly and touched her cheek. "It was a lucky day when Brandon found you, Heather. I know from experience that a good woman isn't an easy thing to find."

Harriet approached at that moment. Having overheard Frank's comment, she clucked her tongue at him disapprovingly. "Really, Mr. Burnside! There are more of us 'good women' than you think. Now I insist that you accompany me into the study. I need to get your opinion on something I'm writing, and my son tells me you're the best editor in San Francisco, aside from himself, that is." She smiled sweetly at Brandon.

Frank cocked a questioning brow at his employer, who shrugged in response. "I'd be happy to be of assistance, Mrs. Montgomery."

"It's 'Harriet,' please. Now come along. We've had enough maudlin conversations for one day. It's time you read something that will put a smile on your face. Your lovely wife, Clara, would have wanted it that way."

Knowing the truth of Harriet's words, Frank followed the determined woman out of the room, and Heather shook her head in disbelief at her mother-in-law's accomplishment. "Well, at least Harriet's done what the rest of us failed to do."

"And what's that?" Brandon pulled her down to sit beside him on the parlor sofa.

"Frank will forget all about his sadness for the time being, if Harriet has her way. And she usually does. By the time she gets done picking his brain about writing, and forcing him to read her memoirs, he'll be too absorbed to mourn over Clara. There'll be time enough for that in the privacy of his home. I expect the nights will be the hardest. They were for me when Mama died."

"I remember when my father died," Brandon said, absently running his fingers up and down Heather's arm. "I put on such a brave front for my mother and the rest of the town, but that night I cried myself to sleep like a baby. As much pain as that old bastard caused me, I still loved him."

"He was your father." That statement seemed to say it all, and Brandon nodded.

"I've wasted years trying to forget my father, trying to pretend that I don't care about him any longer, but I still do. I'll always love the man he was before he took to drinking. I guess I need to try to find the forgiveness for him that my mother's been able to. She never hated him for what he did . . . the mess we had to contend with after he died. I never . . . d her reaction."

". . . . ou love someone, you love them unconditionally. . . . the good with the bad. 'For better or worse,' re . . . ? Harriet confided to me that she felt your father was . . . ng from an illness, something that overtook his body . . . hat he couldn't control. She said his father had suffered . . . n the same affliction, and that she couldn't bring herself . . . condemn Charles for what happened."

Years of sadness shone in the depths of Brandon's eyes. "Death is so final. I don't think I ever really forgave my father for dying the way he did and leaving us. But then, his drinking took him away from us long before God saw fit to take him."

"I'm sure he loved you very much, Brandon. And he would have been so proud to see that you followed in his footsteps and became a successful newspaperman."

Brandon smiled as he remembered. "It was something Father always talked about. 'Son,' he said, 'someday you and I are going to run the largest newspaper in this country. The masses are going to read what we write, and we're going to make a difference.' Of course, I was eight at the time and believed his every word."

"But he was right. You've lived his dream for the both of you. In you, Charles Montgomery will always live on as the man he once was."

Choked with emotion, Brandon pulled Heather into his arms. "God, how I . . ."

"Mr. Montgomery! Mr. Montgomery!" Mary-Margaret cried out as she rushed into the parlor, with Peter, his slinged arm hugging his body, close on her heels. "One of those men you hired just brought word—your newspaper building is on fire!"

It was the longest night the two Montgomery women and Mary had ever spent. And while they waited for word of how destructive the fire had been, they occupied themselves with making sandwiches, preparing bandages, and pacing the length of the kitchen.

"I don't know what Brandon will do if he's lost his paper," Harriet said, laying a rolled bandage atop the pile of gauze on the table. "He's put so much time and money into *The Star*. It's his whole life. Or was," she amended, smiling poignantly at Heather, "before you came along, my dear."

Heather stopped pacing and grasped the back of a sturdy oak chair. "You mustn't worry so, Harriet. We've no reason to believe that the building's been destroyed. I just worry that Brandon, Peter, or poor Mr. Burnside will injure themselves trying to fight the fire." That possibility was all too real, and she didn't know how she would cope if something happened to Brandon.

Mary-Margaret dabbed at her eyes with a piece of gauze. "I told Peter not to go with his arm in that sling. But it's just like a man to be stubborn as a mule."

"Amen to that," Harriet agreed.

"If only Brandon had allowed us to accompany them down to the newspaper. Honestly, men think women are such weak creatures. It's so frustrating!" Sighing discontentedly, Heather plopped down in the chair.

Patting her daughter-in-law's hand, Harriet said, "You mustn't be too hard on Brandon, dear. He would only fret if you were near the danger. And he's got enough to worry about as it is. Speaking of worry, are the children all right? Were you able to calm them down?"

As if Clara Burnside's funeral hadn't been traumatic

enough for Jenny and Matt, news of the fire had nearly sent them into hysterics. It had taken all of Heather's resources and inner strength to calm their fears, despite her own that still lingered.

"They finally fell asleep, after I assured them repeatedly that their father would return home unharmed." She bit her lower lip. "I pray Brandon doesn't make me out to be a liar."

Brandon and Peter arrived at the mansion later that evening, spent and covered with soot, but otherwise unharmed. Heather and Mary practically launched themselves at the two men when they entered the kitchen.

"Thank God you're all right!" Mary said to Peter. "Don't you ever scare me like that again, Peter Glendenning." Covering her face, she burst into tears, releasing her worry and pent-up feelings.

Peter, looking thoroughly embarrassed, but nonetheless pleased by Mary's emotional outburst, wrapped his good arm about the distraught woman's waist and led her into the parlor, where they would have some privacy.

Heather had completed her cursory examination of Brandon's physique. Satisfied herself that he wasn't injured, she insisted that he sit at the table while she poured him a tall glass of water, which he drank greedily.

"Now tell me everything," she said firmly when he set the glass down.

His voice, hoarse from the smoke, rumbled when he said, "The building was only slightly damaged. No one was injured. We lost several hundred pounds of newsprint, but that's easily replaced. Other than that, everything is intact."

Heather breathed an audible sigh of relief.

"Well, praise the good Lord for that." Harriet said. "Did the police find out who set the fire? . . . As if we didn't already know."

Brandon shook his head. "The culprits covered their tracks pretty well. I've placed armed guards within the building and outside of it. I doubt we'll experience any more trouble there."

Fingers of fear crept along Heather's spine, and she swallowed with difficulty. "He's not going to stop, Brandon. Gerald Whitten won't be satisfied until someone is injured or dead."

He grasped her hand, finding it clammy with fear. "You and the children will be well protected. I want you to take extra precautions from now on. Don't leave the house unescorted. I can't take the chance that Whitten might try to harm you to get back at me."

Despite her fear, Heather tilted her chin up defiantly. "I won't have that man make me a prisoner in my own home, Brandon. I refuse to live with that kind of fear."

"And I refuse to allow your stubbornness to get you killed." His harsh voice softened as he added, "Be reasonable, love. The man in unpredictable. He's like a rabid dog who'll attack without the least bit of provocation."

"I promise to be cautious, and I will venture out only when it's absolutely necessary," she said to appease him, though he didn't look at all mollified. And it would be absolutely necessary to meet with Peter in order to supply him with the illustrations.

Harriet rose from her chair, noting the determination on both faces. "I'm not going to take sides in this matter, because both of your arguments are sound. Personally, however, I refuse to allow that boorish Whitten person to dictate where I go and whom I see." This comment produced an angry groan from Brandon, but she ignored it. "Instead of trying to keep us sequestered in this house, my dear, I suggest that you have the authorities lock up Mr. Whitten instead."

Frustrated, Brandon wiped his face with the palm of his hand, smearing the soot that covered it. "What in hell do you think I'm trying to do, Mother?"

"Shouting at Harriet isn't going to solve anything, Brandon," Heather admonished her husband, giving him a disapproving look.

If Harriet was angry or insulted, she gave no hint of it. "Brandon is just overwrought with all that's happened this evening, Heather dear. I'm sure by tomorrow he'll have thought things through and come up with a more practical solution. Good night, everyone. I'm happy you're back safe and sound, son." She kissed his cheek before departing.

Brandon sank down in his chair, looking utterly defeated and miserable. "Women," he declared. "Who can ever figure them out?"

"I wouldn't bother trying, Brandon. Men don't have the capacity for reasoning that women do. It would probably take you several lifetimes." Following her mother-in-law's example, she kissed Brandon's cheek, said good night, and went to bed, leaving Brandon to bear his indignation alone.

Hidden from view within the confines of her carriage, Cecelia Whitten peered out from behind the velvet curtain that covered the window to gaze at the Montgomery mansion, as she'd done almost every day for the past few weeks.

Spying on Heather Montgomery had become her obsession. The disgruntled ex-fiancée was determined to catch Brandon's wife in an act that would discredit her forever in the eyes of her adoring husband. A husband who should rightfully have been hers!

Cecelia had been made a fool of at the Ladies' Society meeting. Who would have guessed that those biddies would have fallen for the gibberish Heather had dished out so self-righteously.

Heather would pay for that, and for everything else she'd done. Cecelia would make damn certain of that! She was positive that her patience would be rewarded if she continued her vigilance in spying on Heather.

There hadn't been much activity in the Montgomery household of late. She'd seen Heather venture forth a time or two with Harriet. Another one of their shopping excursions, she supposed. Of course, who wouldn't shop with all that Montgomery money at their disposal? When Cecelia thought of all the clothes and jewels she could have bought with Brandon's money, it filled her with renewed determination to win him back.

She'd seen the children in the accompaniment of their new "mother"—she nearly choked on the thought—but even Heather's routine trips to the zoo and park had been curtailed.

The reporter Peter Glendenning had been a frequent caller at the house. Though supposedly he was interested in the Montgomery's Irish maid—Cecelia sneered, thinking how common Glendenning must be, even for all his good looks—there was always the possibility that he was really calling on Heather. After all, they'd been an item a while back. Knowing what a little slut the farm girl was, she'd probably spread her legs for the reporter a time or two and was likely still spreading them.

It would be delicious to catch them in the act. Brandon wouldn't be quite so taken with a wife who cuckolded him with his employee.

Once Cecelia had convinced Brandon of his wife's infidelity, he would turn to her in his moment of sadness, and they would take up where they'd left off, before the bitch governess had stolen her place in Brandon's affections.

Tapping her parasol against the roof of the carriage, she signaled the driver to depart. Obviously Heather wasn't going to meet her lover or anyone else today.

But she would soon. And Cecelia would be there to see it.

"Damn shame about that fire the other night, Brandon." Gerald Whitten had sauntered into Brandon's office, ignoring the harassed secretary who followed on his coattails.

"I'm sorry, Mr. Montgomery. He got passed me when my back was turned."

Brandon's voice didn't reflect the inner turmoil he felt at seeing Gerald Whitten. He'd always prided himself on his rigid self-control and had to draw upon that now. "I guess we'll just have to beef up security, Mr. Peoples. We wouldn't want the scum of the earth to float in here, now would we?" Though Brandon's question was directed at his secretary, his tight smile and frigid gaze were solidly fixed on the uninvited caller. "You can leave us now, Mr. Peoples."

When the door closed, Brandon quickly rose behind his desk, all pretense of politeness gone. "You've got a lot of goddamn nerve showing your face around here, Whitten. I should call the police and have you thrown out for trespassing."

Gerald smiled smoothly. "But you won't. Your reporter's inquisitive mind is already thinking up questions as to why I'd beard the lion in his den." The older man chuckled, sitting down without waiting for an invitation that he was sure would not be forthcoming.

"State your business and get out. I'm particular about whom I converse with." Brandon sat hard in his chair.

"There was a time when you were ready to welcome me into your family, Brandon. Are you forgetting that I would have been not only your father-in-law but grandfather to those two adorable children of yours? How are Jenny and Matt, by the way? They're such delightful tykes."

Brandon's gaze turned lethal. "Don't concern yourself with anyone in my family, Whitten. And don't remind me of my lapse of judgment where you're concerned. Being a poor critic of character is a trait I'm doomed to possess."

Suddenly Whitten's polite demeanor changed. "You're going to be doomed all right, Montgomery, if you don't desist in printing those trashy articles about me. I've given you fair warning—"

"If you consider threatening innocent children and burning buildings as warnings, then I guess you have."

Gerald's hand went to his heart. "I'm wounded to the quick, dear boy. I was quite concerned when I learned of the fire." He glanced around. "Doesn't appear that much damage was sustained. Any casualties?"

"No thanks to you. Now get out. We've got nothing more to say to each other."

Leaning back in his chair, Gerald rubbed sweating palms against his thighs, trying to hide his discomfort. If Brandon wouldn't play ball with him, he'd have to take more drastic measures, which he would sincerely regret. He genuinely liked Montgomery, would have welcomed him as the son he'd never had. but all that had changed now.

"I'm a patient man, Brandon, and a generous one. Your articles have put a definite crimp into some of my business dealings. Reputable men don't want to deal with someone they suspect has an unsavory background."

Brandon's snide laughter filled the room. "I doubt you've had many legitimate business dealings, Whitten. But if you have, and they've soured, then that news just might make my day."

"I'm willing to pay to have those articles stopped, Montgomery. If they're not, I'll be forced to take severe measures to ensure that they are. I've been around too long to let some honorable do-gooder like you put me out of business. Don't force my hand, Brandon. I assure you, you won't like the consequences."

With the palms flat against his desk, Brandon pushed himself to his feet again, barely able to repress the anger that simmered just below the surface. "A man like you would never understand honor, Whitten. You're greedy and ruthless. I suggest you crawl back beneath that rock you came from. You're finished in this town. I'm going to make damn sure of that."

Gerald shot to his feet, his upper lip snarling like a rabid dog's. "I can hurt you, Montgomery. I can hurt you in ways you've never dreamed of, without touching a hair on your head. Think about it, before you slam the door in my face."

Coming around to the front of the desk, Brandon hauled a protesting Gerald to his feet and ushered him to the door. "You bother me or anyone else in my family and I'll kill you for the miserable animal that you are, Whitten. Now get out and stay out."

"You'll be sorry. You'll all be sorry." Gerald's threats lingered in the air as he stormed out the door.

"Mr. Montgomery," a wide-eyed Henry Peoples asked, mopping his sweating brow with his handkerchief, "do you think he means to kill us all?"

Returning to his desk, Brandon yanked open the bottom left drawer and removed a brand-new Smith & Wesson revolver. Henry Peoples's mouth dropped open.

Brandon had never had cause to use a gun before, but he wouldn't hesitate to test its accuracy now.

No one would threaten his wife or his children and live to talk about it.

No one.

CHAPTER 24

"This has to be the last meeting, Peter." Heather thrust the manila envelope of illustrations at him, ignoring the reporter's wounded expression. "Brandon was absolutely adamant last night that I not leave the house again. He fears retaliation from Whitten. And who can blame him? The man is as insane as his daughter." Though fortunately she'd not had to put up with any more of Cecelia's antics.

Thinking of the conversation Brandon had related to her yesterday about Gerald Whitten's visit to his newspaper office, tingles of apprehension darted up and down her spine. It was time to end the charade before it was too late.

Standing a few yards from the front of the Montgomery mansion, Peter knew how dangerous it was for them to be seen together, but there was no other way. They couldn't conduct business inside the mansion. Mary was too astute; she was bound to find out what they'd been up to. And Harriet was downright nosy. Not to mention the little Chinaman, who followed Peter and Mary around every time Peter visited, acting as some sort of self-imposed chaperon. His actions had amused Mary, but Peter hadn't found them the least bit humorous.

The series was almost completed. Peter had to persuade Heather to help him just one last time. They were so close to putting that bastard Whitten behind bars; they couldn't quit now. Too much hung in the balance.

"I promise you that after next week, we'll be through with all this cloak-and-dagger stuff." He chucked her under the chin, hoping to alleviate the nervous tension between them. "Sweet thing, I thought you were anxious to be a newspaper-woman."

Heather wrapped her woolen cloak more tightly about her. She was chilled despite the relative warmth of the afternoon, and she didn't think her discomfort had anything to do with the temperature.

"That was before I fell in love with Brandon and married him, Peter. I can't deceive him any longer. It tears me up inside to know that I'm doing the very thing his ex-wife did to him. Brandon would never forgive me if he found out I was deceiving him for the sake of a career." She'd learned that Brandon's love was far more fulfilling and important than any career could be.

Opening the envelope, Peter withdrew the illustrations.

The blond woman seated in the carriage across the street studied the couple through a pair of opera glasses and gasped when she saw the envelope. It didn't take a math wizard to put two and two together and realize that Heather was helping Glendenning with the articles to discredit her father. After all, Cecelia prided herself on having a very calculating mind.

At first, she had thought Heather's meeting with Glendenning was merely a lover's tryst. She had reveled in the notion that she'd be able to go to Brandon with her observations, but obviously their meeting had a much more sinister meaning. Brandon's wife was the one supplying the disgusting, insulting drawings for Glendenning's articles. The unscrupulous bitch was the artist. She would bet money on it.

Her eyes narrowing, Cecelia watched as Peter smiled and shoved the papers back into the envelope. He kissed Heather on the cheek in a brotherly fashion—so much for their supposed love affair—then Heather nodded in assent to something he asked.

That redheaded bitch had been helping Glendenning all along to discredit her father. When Daddy got wind of it . . . Cecelia's calculating smile suddenly turned malicious as she thought of a more ingenious way to get her revenge on Heather Montgomery.

She would exact her pound of flesh for Brandon's betrayal, for her father's ruined reputation, and no one would be the wiser. When Heather Montgomery disappeared off the face of the earth, Brandon would be left a grieving widower with two small children, and Cecelia would be there to comfort him.

That thought was just too, too delicious, and she laughed maniacally, tapping her parasol against the roof of the carriage.

Brandon stared at the group of concerned faces before him and sighed. Even the three children looked frightened at having been summoned so emphatically into his study. Well, it was better that they were frightened now, rather than injured, or worse, sometime later. A chill of foreboding swept through him.

"I've called this family meeting to discuss something of great importance."

Jenny raised her hand, and Brandon frowned in annoyance. "Yes, Jenny, what is it? You know I don't like to be interrupted." The look he cast Heather implied that his daughter's rudeness was probably her fault. Smiling innocently, Heather shrugged in response.

"Are you and Mother going to have a baby?" the child asked.

Everyone in the room began to laugh, save for Heather,

whose cheeks burned in humiliation, and Brandon, who was looking intently at his wife's stomach.

After a moment, he replied, "No, that is not the reason for this meeting. To the best of my knowledge," he cocked an inquisitive brow at Heather, "we're not going to have a baby. But I promise, you and Matt will be the first to know if we are." Appeased, Jenny sat back in her chair.

"Now . . ." Brandon began again, only to be interrupted by his son. He combed impatient fingers through his hair. "Yes, Matt. Do you have an important question to ask too?"

The little boy nodded, looking quite earnest. "You'll still love me and Jenny if you and Mother have another baby, won't you, Father?"

Heather didn't wait for Brandon's answer but reached for the insecure child and hauled him onto her lap. "Of course he will, Matt. We both love you very much. Nothing and no one is ever going to change that. If . . ." she blushed to the roots of her hair as she caught Brandon's gaze, "we're fortunate enough to have a baby, I'd like him or her to be as sweet and smart as you and Jenny."

The twins quieted down, but then Jack yanked on one of Jenny's pigtails.

Realizing how elated he would be if Heather were carrying his child, a lump formed in Brandon's throat, and he cleared it several times before saying, "I believe we've covered that topic quite thoroughly."

"I'd love to be a grandmother again," Harriet blurted out. Then she leaned over to whisper in Heather's ear, "You're not with child, are you, my dear? It would make me so very happy."

Heather shook her head and sighed, wondering if she'd quite told the truth. She could very well be pregnant. If she wasn't, it certainly hadn't been for lack of effort on Brandon's part. They made love almost every night, and often in the morning, too.

She cherished those mornings when it was quiet and the fog hovered silently outside their bedroom windows, and only the sounds of waves crashing against the rocks, a seagull's raucous cry, or a foghorn giving warning to an approaching vessel could be heard.

There were no signs that she'd conceived, but Heather remembered that her mama hadn't had a bit of queasiness or discomfort during her pregnancy with Rose Elizabeth. She breathed deeply, trying to contain the excitement surging through her.

What if she was pregnant with Brandon's child? Her hand went to her abdomen and she smiled softly. A baby. A soft, cuddly, dark-haired brown-eyed baby to call her own.

"Heather, are you listening?" Brandon's voice rudely interrupted her delicious fantasy, and her head snapped up. "I asked you if Mary-Margaret will be joining us? I want everyone in the household to hear what I have to say."

"Yes, she . . ." Before Heather could complete the sentence, Mary and Peter entered, looking downright guilty. Mary's cheeks were flushed, her lips red and swollen, and it didn't take a genius to figure out what she and Peter had been doing in the kitchen. *The Star*'s ace reporter looked inordinately pleased with himself, that was for certain.

"Sorry we're late," Mary apologized as she and Peter hurried to take a seat next to Jack on the sofa.

"Late this afternoon," Brandon began again, trying to keep his temper in check, "an incident occurred that has me very upset and terribly worried for everyone's safety."

Heather glanced at Peter and could tell by his concerned expression that he already knew what Brandon was about to relate.

"One of my newspaper deliverymen was severely beaten and left for dead." He ignored the wide-eyed stares of his children and the women's frightened gasps. "It's more important than ever that we take extra precautions to ensure the safety of this family. You and Jack are included in this, Mary," he said to the maid, who nodded solemnly. He'd already had this same conversation with Woo, who'd taken to carrying a razor-sharp butcher's knife on his person.

"From now on, none of you are to leave this house without letting me or Peter know. I don't want anyone going about unescorted. I will arrange for an armed guard to be with you, if you find it necessary to run errands and the like, though I'd much prefer that you allow Mr. Woo or one of us to handle things from here on out. Until this nasty business with Whitten is concluded, I want each and every one of you to promise me," he looked directly at his wife, "that you will not disobey me on this important matter. Your lives could very well depend on it."

"But what about me, Mr. Montgomery?" Mary asked. "I've got to get to work in the morning and return home at night."

"I can protect you, Ma," Jack piped up, his chest inflating with boyish pride.

Mary paled at the thought of jeopardizing her son's life, and Peter placed a restraining hand on the youngster's shoulder. "You're a man, and that's a fact, Jack Feeney. But your mother needs someone who'll be able to carry a weapon. I'd like to volunteer to take care of both of you, if that's all right."

Jack looked almost relieved. "Sure it is, Mr. Glendenning. I know you and Ma are sweet on each other. And that's all right with me."

Peter ruffled the boy's hair, then kissed Mary, bringing a blush to her cheeks as crimson as Heather's wool dress.

"Mother?" Brandon looked meaningfully at Harriet. "You'll not defy me in this, will you? I couldn't bear it if anything happened to you because of that streak of stubbornness you possess."

Not the least bit affronted, for she knew from whom Brandon had inherited his mule-headedness, Harriet smiled. "If you promise to do everything in your power to give me a grandchild soon, I'll promise to heed your wishes."

Brandon looked at his wife and winked, bringing a soft blush to her cheeks. "I think that can be arranged. Now, you're all excused to leave. Heather, I'd like you to remain behind. There're a few things we need to discuss."

Heather's cheeks crimsoned in earnest at Brandon's remark, for he made it sound as if they were going to embark on this grandchild quest as soon as the room emptied. She was barely able to look at Peter's grinning face when he stood to depart. Harriet, too, had a devilish twinkle in her eyes.

When everyone had gone, Brandon knelt before Heather's chair, clasping her hand in his. "I don't think I've ever been so scared for anyone in my life. If anything happened to you or the children . . ."

She laid a caressing hand against his cheek. "Nothing's going to happen, Brandon. We'll be safe within the walls of our home. Whitten won't be able to get to us."

"And you promise me that you won't go out without letting me know?"

Heather swallowed with a great deal of difficulty, hating herself for having to lie, but seeing no alternative. She'd promised to meet Peter one more time. "I . . . I promise." The falsehood burned her tongue like acid.

Wrapping his arms about her waist, he rested his head on her bosom. "I couldn't bear it if anything happened to you, love. I . . . I'm not very good at expressing myself, except on paper, but . . . I love you, Heather. I love you with all my heart and soul. I never thought to say those words to anyone again, but I mean them. You've become my whole life—my reason for living."

Tears filled Heather's eyes, and her throat tightened with emotion. "Oh, Brandon, I love you so much. I never thought I'd live to hear you say those words. They mean so much to me."

He looked into eyes filled with joy and love and the promise of a lifetime together. "I hadn't dared hope that you felt the same way about me. I know I pressured you into this marriage . . ."

"You should know by now, Brandon Montgomery, that no one can talk me into anything I don't want to do. I admit your proposal was a bit devoid of romance, but you've more than made up for it each night in bed. In fact, you've quite exceeded my wildest expectations in the romance department."

Rising to his feet, Brandon pulled Heather up with him. "I've never been with a woman as exciting and giving as you. I can't tell you how much it means to me that you've given me your heart, your entire self. After . . ."

"Ssh!" she said, placing her finger across his lips. Heather couldn't bear to talk of Lydia's betrayal now. *Not now.* "Shall we go upstairs and get started on your mother's latest project? I fear the woman will be unceasing in her pursuit of a grandchild."

Scooping Heather up into his arms, Brandon crossed to the door, smiling widely. "I think it's the best damn idea my mother's had in quite a while. Second only, love, to my marrying you." He kissed her sweetly, then carried her upstairs to bed.

Sunlight dappled the two naked lovers. Slowly awakening, Heather opened her eyes, still heavy with sleep, and yawned. Stretching like a languid cat, an impertinent nipple thrust dangerously close to her husband's mouth.

Brandon, who was now wide awake, didn't wait for a second invitation. Fastening his lips about the pebble-hard tip, he sucked. "What a delicious way to begin my morning," he said, licking the protrusion as if it were the sweetest bit of candy.

"Shame on you, Brandon." Despite the fluttering in the pit of her stomach, Heather rolled out of his reach. "I'll need to drink a whole bottle of Ayer's Sarsaparilla to build my strength back up if you continue like this. I barely got two hours of sleep last night, and I'm starved. We've already missed breakfast. Mr. Woo is no doubt beside himself because of it." Thank goodness no one had bothered to summon them! As preoccupied as they'd been, she doubted they would have heard a thing.

Ignoring her protests, Brandon hauled her back against him. "I'm just trying to keep the bargain I made with Mother. You wouldn't want me to renege now, would you?"

She laughed, rolling her eyes in disbelief. "I can see where you get your single-mindedness from. You rationalize every bit as well as Harriet."

"Is it my fault that your naked body makes me hard as a piece of granite?"

Heather arched a brow and, lifting the sheet, peeked beneath to find Brandon's maleness jutting up proudly like a flagpole. She giggled. "My goodness! I could hang the wash out on that."

Growling fiercely, he rolled onto her, imprisoning her body beneath his own. "There's only one cure for this particular affliction, my love," he reached down between her thighs to find her wet and warm, "and you've got it." Slipping into her, he swallowed her contented moan with his mouth. As he kissed her long, hot, and hard, Heather's breakfast cravings turned to ones of a much different kind.

Harriet sneezed three times in succession, then dabbed her runny nose with her hankie, an apologetic look on her face. "I'm so sorry I won't be able to keep the children for you this afternoon, my dear. This head cold has made me utterly miserable." She leaned back against the bed pillows and pulled the colorful rose-patterned comforter up to her chin.

The odor of chamomile permeated the room. But the cup of tea Heather had brought up earlier remained untouched on the bedside table.

"You rest and get well," Heather instructed her mother-in-law. "I'll ask Mary to . . ."

Harriet coughed, shaking her head. "She's gone, I'm afraid. Mary asked for part of the afternoon off. I'm not sure when she'll return. I believe she had to purchase new shoes for Jack."

Heather tried not to look disappointed by the news, though it certainly put a wrinkle into her plans. She had counted on Harriet or Mary to sit with the children while she delivered the last of the drawings to Peter. They were supposed to meet at the entrance to the park at one-thirty this afternoon.

She glanced at the ormolu clock on the mantel. She had less than an hour to keep the appointment.

"No matter," she said, smiling reassuringly. "I'll just take Jenny and Matt with me." The children could play while she and Peter talked, she decided. "I shouldn't be gone too long. Mr. Woo's downstairs if you need anything while I'm out."

Woo had been anything but joyful at the prospect of entering a sickroom, though he'd grudgingly consented to check on Harriet every so often. The man really was a dreadful hypochondriac, even despite all the ginseng root and herbal teas he drank to maintain his good health.

As if reading Heather's mind, Harriet said, "You can set Mr. Woo's mind to rest. I'm going to be napping most of the afternoon, so he won't have to expose himself to my illness. You run along and have fun. But be sure to take someone with you. Remember what Brandon said—he was very emphatic. What is it you're planning to do, anyway?"

Hating to lie to the kind old woman, Heather bit her lip, studying the floral wallpaper behind her mother-in-law's bed. Red roses, Harriet's favorite flower, trailed every which way, and Heather made a mental note to bring some back for her; they'd be just the thing to cheer her up and assuage Heather's guilty conscience.

"I'm . . . I'm planning to run a few errands, do a bit of shopping. Perhaps stop by the library. I'll be sure to ask one of the guards to accompany me."

With a nod of her head, Harriet closed her eyes, and Heather was relieved that she wouldn't have to answer any more questions. Silently, she tiptoed out of the room, grateful that today would put an end to her weeks of subterfuge and the mountain of lies she'd been forced to tell.

Tomorrow was another day and a whole new beginning.

CHAPTER 25

There was a spring to Heather's step as she hurried along the cobblestoned sidewalk to meet Peter one last time. Jenny and Matt held tightly to her hands, no doubt wondering about their good fortune at being included in this afternoon's outing, especially since it meant missing their dreaded geography lesson. She smiled, giving their small hands a squeeze to communicate how happy she felt.

The sun shone brightly, warming the air to a delightful degree, and Heather wished her sisters were here with her to experience the marvels of California weather. No doubt it was raining or snowing in Denver and Salina. Both Laurel and Rose Elizabeth were probably still wearing woolen undergarments and heavy coats.

Heather's smile widened as she looked up to catch sight of a blue jay perched on an oak branch. The bird trilled happily sitting atop her nest, and Heather thought that not much could go wrong on so glorious an afternoon.

*   *   *

Cecelia's eyes narrowed as she sighted the two Montgomery children in Heather's company. She hadn't counted on their being along.

Oh well, she decided with a shrug of her shoulders. It couldn't be helped. Besides, the little brats were partly responsible for her breakup with Brandon. She might as well get rid of all the obstacles between her and Brandon in one fell swoop. It'd be sort of like killing two birds with one stone, or three, in this case, she thought, smiling to herself.

Nudging the burly man seated next to her in the carriage with her elbow, Cecelia pointed out the window. "There she is. That redheaded woman with the two children."

The scar-faced man frowned. "You didn't say nothing about involving little children." His frown deepened, making his scar more pronounced, and making him appear even more sinister. "I don't like hurting little children."

Cecelia cast him a lethal look, thinking that he wasn't much brighter than a child himself. But then, what had she expected? Seamen weren't known for their superior intelligence.

"You're not going to hurt them, Dolby; you're just going to make them sleep for a while." She turned to his accomplice, a skinny, dirty-faced man who reminded her of a ferret and who was probably infested with lice. She scratched her arms at the notion. "Did you bring the chloroform?"

"Aye," he replied with a nod. "I know my job, miss. We're to render the woman and children unconscious, then bring them to one of your father's ships."

"Excellent, Mr. Cooper. And you're sure this ship is set to sail soon?"

"Aye. Dolby and me had a pint of ale with the *Voyager's* first mate last night. Soon as their stores are loaded and some minor repairs made, they'll be on their way."

"And you've made arrangements for the additional cargo?"

"I greased a few palms with that money you give us. There won't be no questions asked."

Cecelia leaned back against the leather seat, smiling in satisfaction. "Then what are you waiting for, gentlemen? Your prey awaits."

Peter checked his pocket watch again and frowned, snapping the brass case shut. It was nearly two-fifteen and Heather hadn't yet shown up for their rendezvous. Damn! What could be keeping her? He needed those illustrations for tomorrow's newspaper.

Glancing down the sidewalk, he saw an elderly, white-haired gentleman with a cane, and two uniformed schoolgirls chatting happily as they walked. There was no sign of Heather.

Obviously, something was wrong. Perhaps she'd taken ill. Perhaps she'd been unable to get out of the house undetected. Or perhaps, something more sinister had occurred.

What if Whitten had somehow managed to get his hands on Heather? God! Peter paled at the thought. He'd never forgive himself if something had happened to her.

Calm yourself, Glendenning. She's just late. Nothing's happened to Heather.

Then why did he have that funny feeling in the pit of his stomach? And why were his palms sweating so profusely?

His reporter's gut instincts were sending out signals too strong for him to ignore.

"Shit!" He decided to wait fifteen minutes more. If Heather hadn't shown up by then, he'd go directly to the Montgomery mansion.

She had to be there. She just *had* to.

Brandon entered to find the house quieter than a tomb. Now used to the children's excited greetings when he arrived home and a welcoming kiss from his lovely wife, he wondered where everyone had gone. Probably out back on another fishing expedition, he surmised, chuckling as he thought back to Heather's last fishing fiasco. His eyes warmed as he remembered how enticing she had looked sitting in that pond.

Who would ever have thought then that he'd be married, and in love with his wife?

Romeo bounded into the hallway, wagging his tail and looking overly happy to see him. He bent over to pet the frisky pup. "Where're your chums, Romeo? Where's Jenny and Matt?" The dog barked, as if trying to tell him something, and Brandon wondered when he'd started conversing with animals.

Woo hadn't been able to shed much light on Heather's and the children's absence, saying only that Harriet was upstairs in bed with a serious illness. Knowing his mother had complained of a slight cold when he left for work this morning, and knowing Mr. Woo's penchant for exaggeration, Brandon climbed the steps to his mother's room.

He found Harriet propped up in bed, reading *Wuthering Heights* and munching an apple. She looked up when he entered and her eyes lit with pleasure, obviously glad for the company.

"You look like you're feeling better, Mother. Mr. Woo tells me you've been quiet as a church mouse all afternoon."

"*Hmph!* How would that Chinaman know a thing? He stood outside and shouted questions at me through the closed door. For all he knows, I could be dying."

Brandon smiled. "I'm sure that's just what he thought, which is probably the reason he didn't dare enter." The cook had just left for the day, no doubt to disinfect himself from Harriet's illness.

She glanced at the clock on the mantel. "You're home a bit early, aren't you? There haven't been any more problems at the newspaper, have there?"

"No more than usual." He took a seat on the edge of the bed. "If you're referring to our friend Whitten, no. He hasn't done anything else that I'm aware of."

She sighed in relief. "That's good to hear. Heather's late getting home and I worried . . ."

"Heather left the house?" His face contorted in fear, then anger.

Harriet nodded, hating to be the cause of a disagreement between Brandon and his wife, but she worried about Heather and the children's safe return. "She left with the children a little past noon. I thought they'd be back by now."

"Where the hell did she go? Heather promised me she wouldn't go out unescorted." He rose to his feet. "Damn that woman!"

"She had to run a few errands. I suspect she was getting cabin fever, being locked up inside this house day after day, with no one but me and two six-year-olds for company. But don't worry. She promised to take along one of the guards."

Brandon paled. The guard he had hired was out ill. Heather had obviously lied to his mother.

"Where's Mary? Why didn't she go with her? At least there's safety in numbers." The thought of Heather and the children alone and unescorted sent shivers of fear down his spine.

"Mary asked for the afternoon off. I can't police everyone's activities, Brandon. Besides, you know how strongly I feel about being confined in this house like a prisoner." She could hardly blame Heather for feeling the same way, despite the threat of danger.

Brandon rubbed the back of his neck, trying again to ease the knots out of it. "I can't imagine why on earth I married someone who is a carbon copy of you, Mother. You are infuriating enough as it is."

"Why, that's the nicest thing you've said to me in quite a while, son. Thank you."

With a disgusted sigh, Brandon shut the door on his way out.

Mary was in the kitchen when he entered, and Brandon breathed a sigh of relief, thinking that perhaps she and Heather had been together after all.

"Hello, Mary. Have you seen Heather? Has she been with you today?"

Knowing that she'd probably catch hell for going out unescorted, Mary swallowed, shaking her head. "I'm sorry I had to leave the house today, Mr. Montgomery. But Jack wore a hole clean through the bottom of his shoe, and Peter wasn't available to take me, and . . ."

He held up his hand to forestall the explanation. "Do you have any idea where Heather's gone with the children?"

Mary thought for a moment. "She may have gone to the library. Heather mentioned something about it this morning at breakfast."

Deciding that the library was as good a place to start as any, Brandon turned to leave, then Peter burst through the back door. He had a manila folder clutched to his chest.

"Is she here?" he asked, trying to catch his breath, an alarmed expression on his face.

"Peter, what on earth have you been doing?" Mary asked. "You're sweating like a pig."

Peter, his usually spotless white shirt soaked with perspiration, turned a worried gaze on Brandon. "Is Heather here?"

"No. I was just about to look for her. Why?"

Exhausted from his sprint, Peter dropped down in a chair. "She was supposed to meet me this afternoon. She didn't show up."

Mary covered her mouth and gasped, an accusing look on her face.

Brandon took a step toward the table, his hands fisted in anger.

"It isn't what you think." Peter reached for Mary's hand. "I've got eyes for no woman but you, Irish." Wiping tears from her eyes, the maid sank down in the chair beside him and sighed with relief, silently chastising herself for what she'd been thinking.

"What the hell are you talking about, Glendenning? Where is my wife? And why the hell was she supposed to meet you this afternoon? You knew she was forbidden to leave this house unescorted."

Brandon would be furious when he discovered the truth, Peter knew, and he hated to be the one to betray Heather's trust. But he had no choice. Her safety was what mattered now.

"Heather's been helping me with the Whitten series," he blurted, pushing the manila folder of drawings across the table at Brandon. "She's the one who's been doing the illustrations."

Mary's eyes widened and she crossed herself.

Paling, Brandon shook his head, refusing to believe what he'd just heard, or what his eyes told him as he stared intently at the drawings signed "Martin Heath."

"Heather's been illustrating your articles? I don't believe it. She's been much too busy with the children, with . . ."

"Don't be angry with her, Brandon. I coerced her into helping me. She's an extremely talented artist. I'm surprised you hadn't noticed before now. After all, she did paint that portrait your mother gave you for Christmas."

Jesus Christ! Brandon rocked back on his heels as if struck. *It's happening all over again. Someone I trusted, believed in, has played me for a fool. Heather's been leading a double life, even knowing how I feel about Lydia's deception.*

Raw pain surged through him, then it was replaced by an overwhelming rage. He advanced on Peter and pulled him up off the chair.

"You stupid bastard! Don't you realize that you've put Heather's life in danger? If Whitten knows she's responsible for the illustrations . . . Jesus!" He shook Peter hard.

"Please, Mr. Montgomery!" Mary said, grasping his arm. "Don't hurt Peter. I admit he used poor judgment, but no one could know how Mr. Whitten would act. I'm sure Heather only agreed to help Peter because she knew it'd be helping you as well."

Brandon pushed the reporter from him and checked his watch. "It's nearly four o'clock. What time was Heather supposed to meet you?"

"Half past one. We were to meet at the entrance to the park. I waited until almost quarter to three, then decided I'd better come here and check. I'm worried about her too, Brandon. This is all my fault. I can't tell you how sorry I am. How—"

"Save it, Glendenning." Brandon's words were like icicles, lowering the room's temperature considerably, and Mary chafed her arms. "Your apologies and regrets do little good now. We all have regrets." His heart twinged, but he ignored it. There'd be time later for self-recriminations. "We don't have time to dwell on our mistakes. We've got to find Heather and the children."

"Will you go to the library, Mr. Montgomery?" Mary asked.

"No," Brandon said, shaking his head. "We'll start at the root of the problem. We'll start with Gerald Whitten."

Not bothering to wait for the coffee-skinned maid to summon Whitten, Brandon and Peter barged into the man's private office, startling Whitten as he counted out a stack of money from his safe.

The older man was clearly annoyed. "Montgomery! What is the meaning of this? What the hell do you mean by barging into my home?" He gathered the currency to him like a miser. "And why have you brought that scum with you?" He glared at Peter, who smiled in response.

"What have you done with my wife and children, you scurrilous bastard? I'll kill you if you lie to me."

Gerald's mouth gaped open, his eyes widening in surprise. "I don't know what you're talking about."

Brandon crossed the room in three strides, grasped Whitten's shirtfront, and hauled him up from his chair. "I'm through listening to your lies, you bastard. I told you not to bother my family. You've crossed the line this time and now you're going to pay."

"I don't know what you're talking about, Montgomery. I haven't seen your wife or children. I've been home all day, working on my accounts. You can ask my housekeeper if you don't believe me. Wanda will verify everything I've told you."

"As if I'd actually take the word of anyone in your employ, Whitten. No doubt you've trained them all to lie."

"I'll check with the maid," Peter suggested, heading for the door. "Perhaps she knows something."

Brandon nodded, then turned his attention back to the frightened old man. "You don't look so high and mighty now, do you, Gerald?" Brandon reached back and slapped the man hard across the face, splitting his lip open with the force of the blow. "Tell me what you've done with my family!"

Whitten's arms started to come up to cover his face, but Brandon struck him again. "Tell me, you bastard. Tell me where my wife and children are. If you do, I might let you live."

"I swear on my dead wife's grave: I don't know the whereabouts of Mrs. Montgomery or your children. Please believe me. I'm telling you the truth."

"I doubt you even know what the truth is, you bastard."

Gerald licked at the blood trickling down his lip. "I've been here all day, I tell you. I've been readying myself for a trip. I've decided to leave town for a while, just until things cool off. Thanks to you and your star reporter, I can't show my face around this city without being ridiculed and laughed at."

"You're making my heart bleed, Whitten."

"I swear, Montgomery. I know nothing about your family's whereabouts."

Peter returned a moment later, hauling the crying maid behind him. "The housekeeper confirmed his story, Brandon. She says Whitten's been here all day. I don't believe she'd lie. From what I could discover, there's no love lost between the two of them. Apparently the randy old goat's gotten into her bed a time or two, uninvited."

Brandon pushed the man down into a wing chair, his face a mask of revulsion. :"You're the one responsible for all my troubles of late, Whitten. You started the fire, beat my employees, threatened the newsboys. Why should I believe you or your maid?"

Whitten dabbed at his bleeding mouth with his handkerchief. "Because I'm telling you the truth."

"If you're not the one responsible for my wife's disappearance, then who is? You'd better think carefully, Whitten, for it you don't come up with a suitable answer, you'll be the one who takes the blame. At your age, I doubt you could take many more beatings."

Wide-eyed, Gerald turned to the maid. "Wanda, do you know anything about Mrs. Montgomery's disappearance?"

The black woman began to cry harder. "She said if I was to tell, she'd whip all the skin off my worthless hide."

"Cecelia!" Peter and Brandon said simultaneously, exchanging surprised looks.

"Cecelia?" Gerald repeated, his brow wrinkling in confusion. "Why on earth would she have anything to do with something so sordid? My daughter's a lady of refinement."

Ignoring Gerald's character assessment of his precious daughter, Brandon asked, "What does Cecelia know about Heather's disappearance, Wanda?"

"I afraid, Mr. Montgomery. Miss Cece be powerful mad if I was to tell."

"My wife and children's lives are in danger. Surely you wouldn't want anything to happen to two small children."

The maid began wringing her hands and shaking her head. "Oh no, sir. I loves children. But Miss Cece say . . ."

"Wanda!" Gerald's voice boomed out. "If you know something, tell them, for chrissake, or I'll ship you back to Missouri myself."

The woman's eyes narrowed, and she stiffened. "I only knows that Miss Cece was planning to do harm to Mrs. Montgomery. She hates her 'cause she done stole you away from her, Mr. Montgomery. Miss Cece be a proud woman."

"It nearly killed my daughter when you decided to marry Heather," Gerald added, almost to himself.

Peter clasped Brandon's arm. "Wanda may be telling the truth, Brandon. Heather confided that Cecelia's been following her, tormenting her without the least bit of provocation."

Peter related several of the incidents, and both Brandon's and Gerald's eyes widened in disbelief.

"I had no idea," the older man said. "Though I admit that my Cece has been acting rather strangely these past few weeks."

"Like father like daughter," Peter said, sneering.

"Heather didn't tell me any of this." No surprise, Brandon thought, considering what else she hadn't told him. Her betrayal cut into his heart like a knife.

At the hurt and confusion on Brandon's face, guilt flowed through Peter, and he clasped his arm. "Heather didn't want to worry you, Brandon. I urged her to reveal Cecelia's crazed actions, but she made me promise not to say anything. She said you had enough to worry about with Whitten and the newspaper, and she didn't want to add to your burdens."

Brandon snorted. "How noble of her."

"I'm afraid my Cece's gone and done something terribly dreadful," Gerald muttered.

Peter's voice filled with disdain. "Like I said: like father like daughter. And if I had as devious a mind as yours, Whitten, and I were your daughter, what nefarious plot would I come up with to do away with someone?" Peter began to wander around the study, looking closely at the papers on Whitten's desk, studying the volumes in his bookcase.

While he investigated, Brandon continued talking to the maid, and Whitten slumped down in his chair, looking tired and defeated.

"I have a hunch, Brandon," Peter stated a few moments later, drawing everyone's attention. "I'll need a few minutes to see if I'm correct. Don't let anyone leave. I'll be right back."

It seemed an eternity but was only a few short minutes before Peter returned, smiling in satisfaction. "I had an illuminating discussion with the coachman. It seems he's driven Cecelia to the docks on several occasions."

"The docks?" Brandon repeated.

"After discovering the ship's log in Whitten's bookcase," Peter explained, "I wondered if his deviant interest in prostitution and, in particular, white slavery, might have something to do with this. I'm pretty sure that it does."

"Don't be absurd, Glendenning. My daughter knows nothing of my shipping interests or activities. I've kept her sheltered from that side of my life."

"I want the names of your ships that are engaged in this vile activity, Whitten. Now!" Brandon ordered.

Removing a leather-bound log from the bookcase, Gerald ran his finger down the page. "There's only one of my ships in port that's engaged in that particular commodity. *Voyager*'s captained by Enoch Walters. I'll write out a pass to get you on board."

"Don't think this absolves you of anything, Whitten. Your willingness to help doesn't mean that you won't be prosecuted to the fullest extent of the law. I'll see to it myself."

Peter smiled smoothly at the older man. "It was damned convenient of you to have one of those telephones, Whitten. I've already called the police. They should be here momentarily. Your coachman was only too happy to be of assistance, after I reminded him that he might be considered an accessory to your crimes, as well as your daughter's. He's volunteered to tell the police everything he knows. And I'm sure Miss Wanda will want to do the same."

Wanda dried her eyes on her apron and nodded emphatically, casting her employer the vilest of looks. "I don't relish workin' for no white trash no-how."

Whitten tugged nervously on his beard. "I don't care what happens to me. Just promise me, Brandon, that Cecelia won't be harmed."

Brandon frowned and his voice grew so chilling that even Peter felt shivers run up and down his spine. "I promise you nothing, Whitten. And if any harm has come to my wife or children, I'll gladly strangle the bitch myself."

CHAPTER 26

Heather awoke from her drug-induced sleep to find herself and the children secured in the bowels of a ship. It was dark and dank, smelling of human excrement and bilgewater. Fear clutched her like clammy hands around her throat, rendering her somewhat lightheaded.

She struggled against the rope that bound her hands and feet, but to no avail. She and the children had been tied, but not gagged. They were fortunate not to have been secured to the chains and shackles lining the ship's hull. Obviously they weren't the first prisoners to have been held aboard this vessel.

The rocking motion made her feel slightly nauseated—or was it the effect of the drug that had been used to knock them out? Heather wasn't quite sure.

"Jenny? Matt?" she called out softly, nudging the children with the toe of her shoe as her eyes adjusted to the darkness, trying to determine if they were all right. *Please, dear Lord! Let them be all right,* she prayed silently. If they'd been

298

harmed in any way, she would never forgive herself. Nor would Brandon, who probably despised her now.

Tears filled her eyes when she thought of how he would hate her when he discovered her betrayal, how hurt and confused he'd be by her lies and deception. For she knew that Peter would have had no choice but to confess all.

"Oh, Brandon," she whispered, "I'm so sorry. Please forgive me."

Of course, it was a bit late for regrets. She and the twins were likely to die, if those horrible men she'd caught a brief glimpse of had anything to say about it.

Relief swept through her when the children began to show signs of life. Jenny made whimpering noises, and Matt moved about restlessly as his body threw off the effects of the chloroform.

"Thank God you're all right!" Heather exclaimed, fighting back tears, trying to appear strong for their sake.

"Where are we, Mother? Why are we tied up in here?" Jenny asked, her voice fearful, though she did her best to appear brave.

"I don't feel too good," Matt confessed, looking a bit green around the edges. "I think I have to throw up."

"Try to think good thoughts, Matty. Try not to think about where we are. Take deep breaths. That's a good boy," she said, when the frightened child followed her instructions and soon appeared a little better as his normal skin color returned.

Jenny looked about, confusion evident on her small face. "What is this place? I can't see much. It's so dark in here."

"I'm afraid we've been brought to a ship, children. I don't know by whom, but I have my suspicions."

It wouldn't surprise her in the least to find out that Gerald Whitten was behind their abduction. She knew he owned several ships, and she had little doubt that this was one of them. From what she'd learned from Peter's articles, their abduction followed Whitten's methods of operation. More likely than not, the rumors of Whitten's involvement in white slavery had substance to them. The thought tore at her insides.

"Are we going to die, Mother?" Matt asked in a small voice, hanging his head, sobbing softly into his lap.

"Of course not," Heather reassured him, wishing she could reassure herself as well. "This is probably just some stupid joke being played by Mr. Whitten. Remember how your father told us he might try to cause trouble?"

"But Father said the man was crazy," Jenny reminded her. "Remember?"

Heather nodded, then took a deep breath to calm her fears, and was immediately sorry as the noxious odors surrounding them filled her nostrils. The ship was banging against its moorings, creating a bobbing movement that unfortunately was being replicated in her stomach.

"I promise you both, I won't allow anything or anyone to hurt you."

Suddenly the children gasped in unison, and as Heather followed their stare, she sucked in her breath at the sight of Cecelia being escorted down the steps into the hold by two sinister seamen—the same two who had captured them, she was sure. The larger of the two men, who had a jagged scar on his cheek, stared at the children with something akin to pity. Perhaps he could be persuaded to help them, Heather thought hopefully.

"That's a rather bold statement under the circumstances, don't you think, Mrs. Montgomery?"

Heather held her silence.

"What? No surprise? No screams of outrage. I'm disappointed, Heather." Cecelia laughed maliciously as she gloated over her triumph. Soon Brandon would be hers again, and Heather just an unpleasant memory.

Heather fought hard to keep her crushing rage in check. She wouldn't give this insane woman the satisfaction of knowing how terrified she was, not for her own sake but for the children's.

"Nothing you do surprises me, Cecelia. Though I admit, I

had thought it was your evil father who was responsible for our abduction."

"Daddy?" There was disbelief in Cecelia's voice, and she laughed again. "He's much too softhearted to harm little children. Unlike me, Daddy actually likes children. These two brats were one of the reasons he wanted me to marry Brandon."

"Why are you doing this, Cecelia? What could you possibly hope to gain by abducting me and Brandon's children? Surely you know that he'll hate you for this."

Cecelia flecked an imaginary speck of dust off her gown, pretending not to be concerned by Heather's prediction, though she'd since come to realize that the abduction of Brandon's children would upset him greatly. But Cecelia was certain that she could comfort him once Heather and the children were permanently out of the picture. After all, a man had needs, and Brandon would be vulnerable to those needs. And she aimed to satisfy them in the most elemental way.

"Brandon will probably be upset at first," she admitted. "But in time he'll forget all about you and these little troublemakers." Jenny and Matt started to cry again, but she ignored their wails. "Once we're alone, Brandon will turn to me in his hour of need. I'll be the one to console him, Heather, not you. I'll be the one to share his bed, his home, his life, as I should have been from the start."

"You're insane!" Heather shouted, unable to restrain herself any longer as she lunged toward the woman, fighting wildly against the bonds that held her. But the ropes kept her back.

"The ship's about to cast off, miss," the skinny man named Cooper told Cecelia. "You'd best be getting back to the dock."

"What are your plans for us, Cecelia?" Heather asked, still struggling fiercely against the hemp cutting into her flesh. "Take your revenge out on me, but please, let these innocent children go! They haven't hurt anyone."

"We won't leave without you, Mother!" Jenny cried hysterically, which made Cecelia laugh.

The scar-faced man shot her an angry look. "Stop laughing. You're making the little girl upset."

"Of course, Dolby," Cecelia said, smothering her smile. "We wouldn't want to upset anyone. As for my plans," she said to Heather, "you and the children will be transported to Persia. There's a wealthy potentate there who simply adores American women and children. You'll be a welcome addition to his harem."

Heather's eyes widened in horror. *Persia! Brandon will never find us in such a faraway, foreign place.* "Please, Cecelia, don't do this!" Heather begged, raising her bound hands entreatingly. "For the love of God, have mercy on these children. They won't be able to survive the rigors of an ocean voyage, let alone live in such a heathenish place."

Cecelia walked toward the steps without a backward glance, but the big scar-faced man looked back and shook his head sadly. "I'm sorry about the little ones, miss. I didn't know there'd be children involved when I agreed to take ya."

"Come on, Dolby," Cooper said, knocking his arm. "Don't go getting soft in the head now. We've got lots of money coming to us, ain't that right, Miss Whitten?"

Cecelia looked back, smiling ferally at the bound trio. "That's right, Mr. Cooper. You and Mr. Dolby did an excellent job, for which you'll be amply rewarded. Say good-bye now."

"Pleeease!" Heather screamed as she watched her abductors march up the steps.

Leaning her head back against the timbers, she closed her eyes and whispered, "Brandon, please find us."

It was dark by the time Brandon, Peter, and three of Brandon's armed guards approached the docks and Whitten's vessel, *Voyager*. There was a hubbub of activity as the motley crew made ready to cast off the ropes in preparation for departure.

Running up the gangplank, Brandon and his men were stopped by two menacing-looking crewmen who looked like characters out of a Herman Melville novel. One had a patch over his left eye, and the other was missing most of his front teeth.

"I demand to see Captain Walters. I have a message for him from Gerald Whitten, the owner of this vessel." Brandon retrieved the note from his pocket, waving it under the seaman's nose.

The toothless man looked at it but obviously couldn't read what it said. "Wait here," he demanded. "I'll fetch the cap'n, and you'd better have a damn good reason for delaying our departure. He ain't goin' to like it, the cap'n ain't."

A moment later a large, bearded man appeared. He walked with an uneven gait, but despite that he still exuded an air of authority. In navy pants and pea jacket, he was dressed neater than the rest of the crew and appeared cleaner, as if he actually bathed more than once a year. Brandon knew immediately that this was the captain of the vessel.

"Captain Walters, I'm Brandon Montgomery. I have a note from Gerald Whitten granting me permission to board this vessel." He handed the note to the man, who eyed him with undisguised suspicion and hostility.

"I don't care if you got a note from God himself. This is my ship. I'm her captain, and I don't take orders from Whitten, or from you." He crumpled the note in his fist and threw it to the deck.

"Well, perhaps you'll take orders from this." Before the captain could respond, Brandon pointed a gun at his ribs, pressing the barrel into his side. "My wife and children might be aboard this ship, Captain. And no one is going to stop me from looking for them. Is that understood? If it's not, I can make it understood. But unfortunately, you'll be dead by then."

His tanned, leathery skin paling beneath his beard, Enoch Walters's black eyes narrowed into thin slits as he sized up his opponent. Several of the crew members had stopped what they were doing and turned to see what the commotion was about, but he ordered them back to work with a wave of his hand.

Deciding that the woman and children locked up below weren't worth his precious hide, Walters relented. "Come on, then. But make your search quick. I don't have time for such intrigues."

Feigning ignorance, just in case the angry man took issue with the woman's condition when he found her, the captain asked, "What'd she do? Run away? Can't say as I blame her none, not with your temper."

Peter slid Brandon a knowing look but refrained from commenting on the captain's remarks. He was afraid they hadn't seen the full force of Brandon's temper yet.

But they would. And soon.

Lifting the hatch cover to descend to the hold, Brandon wasn't certain who was more surprised. He, at the sight of Cecelia climbing the stairs toward him, or she, as she stared wide-eyed and openmouthed at him.

Not about to take any chances that her hired thugs might decide to turn heroic—money always proved to be a powerful motivator—Brandon pointed the gun at her midsection, ignoring her shocked gasp.

"Back down the stairs, Cecelia. And tell your dogs to do the same. Your presence here confirms my belief that my wife and children are here. And they'd better be unharmed, or none of you will live to see tomorrow."

"Please, Brandon! Let me explain."

He waved the gun menacingly, and Cecelia and the two men turned, retracing their steps. Peter held them at gunpoint, while Brandon's men bound their hands with rope.

"Brandon! Father!" came the relieved cries from the darkness.

Brandon felt a wild surge of relief as he hurried to his family. Untying Jenny and Matt's bonds as quickly as he could, he then turned to his wife, doing his best to ignore the tears streaming down her face and the elation he felt at seeing her again.

"Thank God you've come, Brandon. I prayed you would."

His voice was every bit as cold as the waters of the Pacific slapping against the hull of the ship when he finally spoke. "I doubt you'll be relieved once we get home. We've things to discuss, you and I, Mrs. Montgomery." He spat the name out like a curse, and Heather flinched.

Releasing her from the rope, Brandon felt a surge of anger when he saw the red welts on her wrists and ankles. "Are you unharmed?"

She nodded. "Yes. We're all fine. Matt was a bit queasy, but he's fine now." She smiled at the child, who looked relieved that his ordeal was over.

Helping his wife to her feet, Brandon supported her elbow with his arm, but Heather could tell by the stiff way he held himself that the idea of touching her now, no matter how casually, was repugnant to him.

Heather told herself she wouldn't cry. There would be plenty of time for tears later.

"I only did it for you, Brandon," Cecelia screamed as Peter dragged the crying, hysterical woman up the stairs. "We were meant to be together, you and I."

"She's insane," Heather remarked as her adversary disappeared from sight. "I almost feel sorry for her. Cecelia must love you a great deal to have gone to such lengths." She chafed her throbbing wrists, but the pain paled next to the stab in her heart at the look of utter contempt Brandon shot at her.

"I doubt most women know the meaning of that word."

Heather's cheeks stung as if she'd been slapped.

"The authorities are waiting to take Cecelia into custody," he continued, giving no thought to how his comment had wounded Heather. "I've no doubt she'll be remanded to a mental hospital where she can receiver proper treatment."

"And the others?"

"They'll have years in prison to ponder the course their lives have taken."

Heather bit her lower lip, noting the rigidness of her husband's expression, and wondered how long she would have to do the same.

•   •   •

"Brandon, please! Let me explain." Heather held out her hands beseechingly, but she could tell by the closed look on his face that there would be no explanations this day.

He took the seat behind his desk, busying himself with the papers there. "I'm not interested in hearing more of your fabrications, Heather. I'm tired right now. Maybe later. By then I'm sure you'll have been able to embellish your tales much more cleverly."

"I realize I deserve your anger. What I did was wrong. But if you'd just let me explain my reasons . . ."

His voice was flat, his eyes cold, and there seemed not an ounce of emotion left in his soul when he spoke. "I've played this scenario before. I'm not interested in doing it again. Please leave me alone. I have work to do."

Heather's cheeks flushed in anger. "I thought you had changed, but obviously I was wrong. You're still the same stubborn, opinionated man I encountered many months ago. You'll never bend. You're too rigid and self-righteous.

He looked up at that, his eyes glittering dangerously. "I did bend for you, and it nearly broke me. You took it upon yourself to endanger my children's lives. You pretended to be something you're not. I've experienced this kind of treachery before. I'll not do so again. Now get out. We've nothing more to say to each other."

As the next three days passed, Brandon remained aloof and detached. He'd virtually sequestered himself inside his study, venturing forth only for an occasional meal or to journey downtown to his newspaper office. He'd taken to sleeping on the sofa in the study. Heather's bed remained off limits to him, but not by her choosing.

Brandon treated her like an anathema. And she couldn't really blame him. She'd brought all this misery and trouble onto herself. But knowing that didn't make it less painful or easier to accept.

Holding her head in her hands, she gave in to her tears.

"Missy's tears make Woo sad. My heart is heavier than bucket of hog livers. You no cry now. I fix tea. Make everything right."

Heather sniffled. Her eyes red and swollen and her nose runny, she was sure she looked as miserable as she felt. Trying to muster a smile for the kind cook, she said, "Thank you, Mr. Woo. But I'm afraid tea won't help what ails me."

Pushing aside the food-laden dishes left over from breakfast, Woo took a seat at the kitchen table. Outside, spring blossoms floated to the ground on gusts of March wind. Spring—a time for new beginnings and the creation of life. Too bad hers was decaying at such a rapid rate, Heather thought.

"Mr. Montgomery no be mad long," he remarked astutely. "He like firecracker. Explode. Make lots of smoke. Then quiet again. You see—things right as rain soon."

"I wish I knew that for a fact, Mr. Woo. I'm not sure things will ever be right again. I'm not even sure I'll be staying on here after what's happened." Brandon hadn't yet mentioned divorce, but it had been the end result of Lydia's betrayal. And, as Brandon had reminded Heather so aptly, she was just like his first wife in the treachery department. "Mr. Montgomery's other wife was forced to leave."

Woo shook his head. "First wife no like you. She no love Jenny and Matt like you do. She no love mister like you do. Mostly, she love self."

Heather's violet eyes widened at the revelation. "I wasn't aware you knew Lydia, Mr. Woo."

"Woo work for mister long time now. Even before first wife. She no like my cooking. You like Woo's cooking. She tell mister to fire Woo. I embarrassment. He refuse. They fight many time. Mister hard man. She stubborn woman."

That sounded all too familiar, and Heather knew that history was doomed to repeat itself. "Mr. Montgomery will no doubt ask me to leave, Mr. Woo, just as he did Lydia."

Woo looked truly horrified. "Missy no go away from here. Children love. Missy make Woo laugh. I make niece, Soon Ye, come and read tea leaves. Tell fortune. She make good fortune."

"I appreciate the offer, Mr. Woo, but all the tea in China

can't make a man as stubborn as my husband change his mind once it's made up."

Woo thought for a moment, then said, "Get flies with vinegar."

Heather looked at the little man strangely, then smiled as his meaning became clear. "You mean to say that you can catch more flies with honey than vinegar, didn't you?"

Woo shrugged. "Same thing. You be nice to mister; he come around. Wife threaten to cut off Woo's pigtail when she mad. I hide for a while. She forget to be mad."

"I'm afraid, Mr. Woo, that there's nowhere for me to hide."

He nodded his head sadly, looking as if he were about to impart the wisdom of the ages, then said, "You really crapped in oatmeal this time, missy."

Wasn't that the truth, Heather thought. The god-awful truth.

CHAPTER 27

"Why, I think Mr. Woo has outdone himself tonight with this chicken, don't you, Brandon?" Harriet asked her brooding son, who'd said not more than three words during the entire evening meal.

"It's fine," he replied gruffly, not bothering to look up from his plate.

Heather cast her mother-in-law an apologetic smile, silently communicating her thanks for Harriet's efforts to bring Brandon back to normal. But that was something which wasn't at all likely to happen. When her husband did speak, it was usually to say something rude or sarcastic. Even the simplest form of dinner conversation had proven too difficult for Brandon of late, making the once-pleasant dinner hour an ordeal to endure.

"Were the children terribly excited about spending the night at Mary's house?" Harriet asked Heather.

"Yes. It's Jack's birthday and . . ."

Brandon's fist came down on the table so hard that it nearly upset the decanter of wine. "What do you mean—

they're spending the night? Why wasn't I made aware of this?"

Heather swallowed at the now familiar look of outrage on Brandon's face. She hadn't consulted him, because trying to converse with him about anything lately had been an exercise in futility.

"I didn't see the necessity," she explained. "It's merely a birthday party. They'll be back first thing in the morning. I discussed it with Harriet, and she said it would be fine."

"*You* discussed it? May I remind you, Mrs. Montgomery, that Jenny and Matt are *my* children. And neither you nor my mother," he cast Harriet a disparaging look, "has the authority to make such decisions."

Heather felt her cheeks warm, but she wasn't surprised. Her blood was about to boil, and she trembled with the heat of her anger. "And may I remind *you*, Mr. Montgomery, that I am their mother, and as such have the right to decide whether or not they can attend a child's birthday party."

"And may I remind you that the decisions you've made concerning my children have not always been the wisest and may have caused them great harm."

Heather's eyes filled with tears. Brandon would never allow her to forget the abduction and her poor judgment in taking the children with her that day.

"Brandon," Harriet admonished, noting the distraught look on her daughter-in-law's face, "you're being totally unreasonable about this. I gave Heather permission to allow Mary to take the children. They're being properly cared for. And they've spent the night there before, in case you've forgotten."

"I forget nothing, Mother," he said, staring straight at his wife, the unsaid meaning quite clear.

Heather's fork clattered to her plate, and she rose from her chair. "Please excuse me. I seem to have lost my appetite."

"Really? How odd," Brandon said, continuing to bait her, though she didn't look back as she exited the room. "And here I thought the chicken was so tasty."

Throwing down her napkin, Harriet glared at her son. "You are an insufferable fool, Brandon. Mind that you don't choke on your own bile, while you continue to eat your 'delectable' chicken alone."

Harriet marched into her son's office at the newspaper the next day, looking like an agitated bull about to charge the matador's red cape. She slammed the door behind her—right in Henry Peoples's shocked face; the man had to jump back to avoid having his nose broken—and approached Brandon's desk.

"I've had about enough of this nonsense, Brandon, and I demand that you come to your senses immediately." She threw herself into the chair in front of his desk, visibly enraged.

Brandon arched an eyebrow at his usually calm and collected mother. Even during his father's illness and subsequent death, he hadn't seen her this upset.

"Is there a problem, Mother?" he asked, though he knew what she was referring to.

"You know damn well and good there is. And don't try to cover things up with your smooth speech and innocent smiles. When are you going to stop this nonsense about Heather and get your marriage in order? It's been two weeks since that horrible woman kidnapped your wife, and you've treated Heather simply abominably. Last night at dinner was a perfect example. I won't stand for it, Brandon. I won't."

Ignoring his mother's fury, Brandon sighed and turned to stare out the window. The sun glittered off the nearby rooftops, the cloudless azure sky as smooth as satin, but the arresting sight wasn't enough to lighten his mood.

He hadn't been able to come to terms with Heather's betrayal. In truth, he didn't know if he ever would. He loved her more than life itself, but he couldn't forgive her. Not for her duplicity. Not for endangering his children. Not for making him fall head-over-heals in love with her.

"Ignoring me will not solve this problem, son. You've got to come to terms with what happened and get beyond it. Heather loves you; you love her. That's more than most people share in a lifetime."

Brandon swiveled about in his chair, doing his best to keep his face impassive and his temper under control. "I refuse to discuss my relationship with Heather. What is, or isn't, between us is none of your business, Mother."

Every bit as stubborn as her son, Harriet refused to back down. "I'm making it my business. You've made your children sorely unhappy. Mr. Woo and Mary-Margaret have been forced to walk about on eggshells, never knowing when you'll explode into one of your rages. Peter is scared to show his face at the house. Even poor Romeo cowers whenever you enter a room.

"I tell you, Brandon, I'm tired of this. You must forgive Heather. She only did what she thought was right. At the time she agreed to Peter's proposal, you weren't even married."

His face darkened at the mention of his reporter. Peter's duplicity had been a bitter pill to swallow. Brandon had severed all personal contact with him, limiting their association to business matters.

"Heather could have stopped her participation once we were married, Mother. She's just like Lydia, wanting to have a career, with no thought to the consequences of how it would affect everyone else's life."

He frowned as he thought of his ex-wife, wondering if she was happy living in England, if she'd found what had been missing from her life. No doubt she'd wooed some duke or earl to the altar with her feminine wiles and charming ways. Lydia was a good actress, after all.

Harriet's cheeks flushed red. "Heather is nothing like Lydia, and I resent your comparing the two women. How quickly you forget that your ex-wife was a controlling, manipulative woman, who bore your children only because you constantly reminded her of how much you wanted a family.

"Lydia was selfish. Heather is the farthest thing from it. I've never seen a kinder, more gentle woman. Children are the best gauge of a person's character. Was it any wonder they despised Cecelia Whitten and her money-hungry father?

"Well, I say good riddance to both of them. I hope Gerald rots in prison for the remainder of his days." She wouldn't speak ill of the dead. Cecelia had hanged herself shortly after her arrival at the asylum.

Brandon took a deep breath and ran his fingers through his hair. "I concede that Heather has more to recommend her than Lydia. But you cannot dispute the fact that she lied and betrayed me in much the same way."

Irritated at her son's continued obstinacy, Harriet said, "You are a blind fool. So, Heather thought she wanted a career. What's wrong with that? You've got one. Why is it so wrong for a woman to aspire to the same thing? She's talented. I noticed immediately . . ."

"And that's another thing. Why didn't you tell me about her abilities as an artist? You presented the painting at Christmas, pretending it was done by a total stranger.

"Where do your loyalties lie, Mother? I am your flesh and blood."

Harriet pushed herself to her feet, impaling Brandon with a look that would have crumpled lesser men. "At the moment, I don't wish to be reminded of that fact, Brandon. And if you chase that young woman away with your stubborn refusal to speak to her or acknowledge her existence, as you've done these past weeks, I will never forgive you.

"Heather is the best thing that's ever happened to this family. I know it. Your children know it. Your hired help know it. Too bad it's escaped your notice."

Turning away in a flurry of skirts and righteous indignation, Harriet fled the room.

"My mother says you might be leaving here, Miss Heather. Is that true?" Jack fished through his pockets for the rabbit's foot Woo had given him. Maybe the good-luck charm would keep Miss Heather from going away. She wasn't nasty and mean like the teachers he'd had before. Miss Heather was neat.

Heather turned from the blackboard to catch the distraught look on the children's faces. It made her heart twinge painfully. Wiping the chalk from her fingers on the apron tied about her waist, she forced a smile to her lips.

"I'm not sure of anything at the moment, Jack. Mr. Montgomery and I have yet to discuss the future." *Or anything else, for that matter,* she thought.

"Please promise you won't leave, Mother. Matt and I love you. We couldn't bear to stay here without you."

Heather came forward to kneel before Jenny's desk. The children had grown so much since her arrival, both physically and emotionally. She couldn't bear it if they reverted to the frightened, sullen little beings they had been. She grasped Jenny's hand and with the other she wiped the tears from her face.

"I'll do everything in my power to stay, sweetheart. But that decision isn't mine to make. Your father is very angry with me right now."

"Because you tricked him?" Matt asked solemnly.

Heather nodded. "That's right. And there's a good lesson to be learned about not being forthright and not telling the whole truth. I shouldn't have done the illustrations for the newspaper without first asking your father's permission. That was very wrong of me."

"But my ma said it was Peter's fault you did them. She's really mad at him." Jack rubbed the fuzzy rabbit's foot harder.

"Peter's not to blame." And she'd steadfastly told Mary that, over and over again. The man was devastated by what had happened. Peter blamed himself far more than anyone else could. But Heather knew it wasn't his fault.

"Mr. Glendenning merely made an offer that I was too weak to refuse. You see, I thought I wanted a career as an illustrator. I thought I had to prove myself. But now I realize that I was foolish to risk my husband's love and trust on something so unimportant."

"But you always told us that our dreams are important, Mother," Jenny pointed out in a most grown-up tone. "I think you should be able to have your dreams, same as everyone else."

She kissed the child's hand. "Sometimes our dreams change, Jenny. My dreams of a career melted the moment I decided I wanted to marry your father and raise you and Matt as my own. But by then I was too caught up in the intrigue of Peter's articles to quit. And I had given Peter my word that I would help him."

"It's important to keep your word. Father always tells us that."

"You're right, Matt. But what I did risked your lives. I should have never taken you and Jenny with me that day."

"That's spilt milk, Miss Heather," Jack reminded her. "My ma says you shouldn't cry over spilt milk. Just clean it up and go on from there." He brushed his hands together several times to make his point.

Ruffling the boy's golden locks, Heather rose to her feet. "Your mother is very wise, Jack."

"Yeah. Some of the stuff she tells me is pretty smart."

"I hope you will always heed her advice. Mothers are known to understand a thing or two." She smiled, hoping to alleviate the tension in the schoolroom.

"We've got the smartest mother in the world," Matt said proudly. "Ain't that right, Jenny? Isn't," he corrected himself quickly, and his impish smile brought an ache to Heather's heart and tears to her eyes.

"Don't you worry about a thing, Mother," Jenny assured her. "Matt and I are going to take care of everything. You'll see."

Not caring to dwell on the depressing topic, for she could see how upset the children were becoming, and she wasn't feeling too happy herself, Heather tried to make light of the moment. "What I see are a few very devious children who are trying to make me forget all about today's lessons." She folded her arms across her chest, tapping her foot in a no-nonsense manner. "It isn't going to work, you know."

"You outfoxed us for sure, Miss Heather," Jack quipped, but Jenny and Matt remained silent, formulating their plans.

•   •   •   •

Taking matters into their own hands, Jenny and Matt entered their father's study quietly. They found Brandon sitting in front of the fire, brooding into the crackling flames, lost in thought. The clock on the mantel ticked its way toward eight o'clock. The leather of Brandon's chair creaked as he settled himself more comfortably.

Jenny approached, clutching to her chest the sketchbook that Heather had given them. She paused by Brandon's chair, waiting for him to acknowledge her presence.

"Matt and I need to talk to you, Father," she said quite matter-of-factly when he looked up.

Surprised, Brandon turned in his chair to give them his undivided attention. "Do you have some schoolwork you'd like to show me?"

"We've come to discuss something important," Matt said, sidling up next to his father's chair, resting his small hand on the arm. "We heard you might make Mother leave, and we can't allow you to do that."

Brandon arched an inquisitive eyebrow. What was all this nonsense about Heather leaving? Surely she hadn't told the children that that was her intention? His stomach tightened at the possibility. Of course, after the way he'd been treating her, he couldn't blame her for wanting to leave.

"What's between your mother and me is our business. I don't want you children getting involved." And he certainly didn't want Heather using his children as a go-between to smooth things out, if that was her intention. "Did Heather put you up to this? Is that why you're here?"

"Oh, no, Father!" Jenny said, her eyes widening as he began to show his irritation. "Mother told us the same thing. That we shouldn't interfere in things we didn't know anything about. But Matt and I decided that we *are* involved, 'cause she's our mother and we don't want to lose her."

"Right!" Matt chimed in. "She's the only mother we've ever had. She plays games with us, and makes us feel good about ourselves even when we don't understand our sums and letters." He crossed his arms over his chest and in a defiant tone added, "If you make Mother leave, then we're going with her."

Brandon was shocked by Matt's ultimatum. Shocked and angered to think that Heather had turned his own children against him. And hurt that they'd let her. Had Heather caused every member of his family to betray him?

"Now wait just a minute! I'm your father," he said, as if that explained everything. "And I love you."

"No one loves us the way Mother does, not even you, Father," Jenny said. "She takes care of us when we're sick. She takes us to the library to check out books, and on expeditions to the zoo and beach."

"And she taught us how to fish. You never taught us how to fish," Matt accused, and Brandon's cheeks colored, not in anger but in embarrassment at the accuracy of his son's assertion.

He patted the boy's head, but Matt pulled away, and a wounded look crossed Brandon's face. "You know how busy I sometimes get with the newspaper. . . ."

Jenny took a step closer and patted her father's hand to console him. "We know it's not all your fault, Father. We know you get busy and don't always have time for us. But Mother does. She makes time. That's because it's her job; she told us so.

"Matty and I have been without a mother too long to lose Mother. She's made us so happy. We do things now that all our friends do, except go to a real school."

"Would you like to go to a public school?" Brandon had never even considered their wishes in the matter. He'd just made an arbitrary decision and stuck with it. He'd done that a lot where they were concerned, he now realized.

Matt and Jenny exchanged glances, then nodded. "We love having Mother for a teacher, but there's not many children to play with here except Jack. It'd be nice if we all went to a public school. Mother thinks we should. She says we'd get a much better education and would be more well-rounded in . . . individuals," Jenny explained.

"I'll think about it," Brandon said, wondering with what other notions Heather had filled their impressionable minds.

Jenny now laid the sketchbook she'd been clutching to her

chest on Brandon's lap. "Mother drew these pictures for us. There's some of me and Matt, Grandmother, and even some of you."

Brandon's eyes widened as he began to flip through the pages. What he saw made the hard shell around his heart begin to melt. The sketches were all of his family, showing the children at various activities, such as playing with the dog and fishing at the pond. There was one of his mother playing cards, a mischievous twinkle in her eyes. And even one of Woo proudly displaying a tin of cloverleaf rolls. The attention to detail was so exacting that Brandon could almost smell the dough.

The love and affection for each person drawn was clearly evident in the artist's renderings. The one of himself, apparently sketched from memory, showed him sitting at his desk, looking austere and businesslike.

He frowned, wondering if that was the way everyone always saw him.

"These are very good," he admitted, more to himself than to the twins.

"The one on the last page is our favorite," Jenny said, smiling.

"Yeah. It's even got Romeo in there."

Suddenly a dog barked, and Brandon knew that the faithful hound was sitting outside the study door, waiting for the children to emerge.

Turning to the end of the book, Brandon found a family portrait. Heather was seated on the parlor sofa, Jenny and Matt flanking each side of her. At Matt's foot was Romeo, looking for all he was worth like another member of the family. Brandon stood behind Heather, and the pride in his eyes and smile brought a lump the size of a grapefruit to his throat.

"That's our family." Matt pointed to the picture proudly, reciting each person's name. "If Mother wasn't here, the picture wouldn't be the same."

"We hope you'll like Mother again, Father. She's wonderful to us. And she told us that what she did was wrong."

Clearly surprised, Brandon looked at his daughter. "She told you that?"

Matt nodded. "Today, during our lessons. She said honesty is always best and that she was wrong not to tell you everything."

"She's real sorry," Jenny emphasized, a pleading look on her face.

"It's always easier to be sorry for something you've done after you've done it," Brandon pointed out.

"Haven't you ever done nothing wrong?" Matt asked, tilting his chin up stubbornly. "Mother always says when we're bad that nobody's perfect and that God loves us anyway. She says nothing we could ever do, no matter how bad, would make her love us any less. Don't you feel the same way?"

The children's eyes burned into Brandon, and he squirmed restlessly in his seat. "Of course I do. But it's different with grown-ups."

"Why?" they asked in unison.

That was the question Brandon spent many hours pondering after the children departed for bed.

Two missives arrived for Heather the following morning. One was postmarked Salina, so she knew it was from her sister Rose Elizabeth. The other had no postmark, but the envelope was imprinted with the logo of *The San Francisco Star,* and Heather's stomach knotted as she tore it open.

The typed letter, which gave no clue to its sender, stated that her presence was required at precisely eleven o'clock this morning at the offices of the newspaper. There was no signature, nothing to indicate the reason for the request.

Obviously it had something to do with her illustrations. Perhaps the art director wished to see her, or perhaps the managing editor.

She hadn't seen much of Frank Burnside since Clara's funeral, and she wondered how he was faring. Though she'd issued several invitations for dinner, he hadn't accepted one. Brandon had said—back when he was still talking to her, that is—that the older man had been throwing himself into his work. At least he hadn't been drinking. And that was a relief to everyone, especially Brandon, who considered the widower a surrogate father.

Pouring herself a cup of coffee from the china pot, Heather settled on the sofa in the family parlor and ripped open her sister's letter. She was immediately filled with frustration and annoyance, not so much by what Rose had to say but what she hadn't.

> . . . and I guess you've heard the news about Laurel. I can't tell you how shocked I was by it.

What on earth was Rose referring to?

> The farm continues to produce, though we've had our share of trials and tribulations, what with the weather, and a certain Englishman's stubborn refusal to listen to reason . . .

Heather scanned the letter hurriedly, hoping to find another reference to Laurel, but there was none, only that enigmatic suggestion of shocking news.

"Good grief, Rose Elizabeth!" Heather said angrily, batting her hand against the pages in frustration. As if she didn't have enough to contend with at the moment, her sister had to write incomplete letters filled with innuendo and mystery!

"May I interrupt, Heather? There's something I'd like to discuss with you."

Heather glanced up to see Mary-Margaret hovering in the doorway. The woman was grinning from ear to ear and looked as if she might burst with excitement.

"Of course. Come in and sit down. Do you want some coffee?" She stuffed both letters into her apron pocket, wishing she could forget about them as easily. "What's happened? You look like the cat that's just swallowed the canary."

"Well, I guess I did. Peter's asked me to marry him, and I've accepted." Her smile faded. "I hope you won't think I'm a traitor because of it. I know Mr. Montgomery's still mad at him."

"Don't be ridiculous!" Heather jumped up off the sofa and hugged the woman to her breast. "I'm so happy for you both. I adore Peter, and I know he'll make you an excellent husband."

"That's what he's always telling me, anyway." Mary giggled.

"Does Jack know?"

She nodded. "Yes. And he's happy as a clam. He's already made Peter promise to take him fishing."

"How is my favorite reporter? I miss him." She hadn't seen much of Peter since the kidnapping incident involving Cecelia. Brandon had made it clear that the reporter wasn't welcome at the house, except for business matters.

"Peter feels the same about you." Mary dabbed at her eyes. "I hate seeing him so miserable. Even though he's still got his job, he says it's not the same because of the way Mr. Montgomery acts toward him."

"Really? I should think Peter would be elated not to have to put up with Brandon's surly moods."

Heather's sarcasm was not lost on Mary. "Has there been any change?"

"If you mean between me and Brandon, no. We hardly see each other. He makes certain he's gone before I come down to breakfast, and he rarely joins us for dinner. He's like a phantom who drifts in and out of the house but is never seen."

Mary clasped Heather's hand. "He'll come around. You'll see."

"That's what Harriet and Mr. Woo think, but I have my doubts." Heather sighed deeply. "I'm not sure how much longer I can go on like this, Mary. It's making me miserable. I love Brandon so much, but I can't seem to reach him. Nothing I've said has made one bit of difference."

"Before I accepted Peter's proposal, I made him promise that he wouldn't try to lure any other unsuspecting females to help him with his investigative articles. He's still terribly upset over what happened."

" 'It's spilt milk,' as Jack would say," Heather said, and Mary smiled.

"I need to go out for a while, Mary. Will you keep an eye on the children for me?"

"Sure I will. Miss Harriet's promised to help me with my wedding, so I was planning to spend the whole morning doing that."

"You'd better plan to spend the entire month doing that. Don't you remember how fanatical Harriet became over my wedding to Brandon?"

"With Miss Harriet busy penning her memoirs and making the wedding preparations, she won't have much time to get herself into trouble. I guess she really let Mr. Montgomery have what-for."

Heather didn't doubt that for a moment. Harriet had barely spoken a civil word to Brandon in weeks, which made Heather feel all the more guilty. She had no intention of coming between Brandon and his family.

"Where are you going, anyway?" Mary wanted to know. "You've been keeping right close to the house since the trouble began."

Heather pulled the letter from her pocket. "I've been summoned to the offices of *The Star*."

Mary let out a shrill whistle. "You don't say? By the mister?"

"I have no idea. It would seem that if Brandon wanted to talk to me, he could do it as easily here."

"That's true," Mary conceded. "But then, Mr. Montgomery hasn't been himself lately."

"Maybe he has," Heather said.

Maybe the man who held her in his arms and confessed his love had been an impostor, or a figment of her imagination. When she thought back to those happy times, it was as if they hadn't really existed. As if it had all been a dream.

Now, she was living a nightmare.

CHAPTER 28

Pacing the length of his office, Brandon felt foolish and nervous. Just the thought of facing Heather after these weeks of contention and discord made his palms sweat, because he knew that he'd been the cause of the disharmony.

He'd done a lot of soul-searching after the children had gone to bed last night. He'd stared at Heather's artwork long and hard and had come to some very astonishing decisions.

But one wasn't astonishing at all—it was merely obvious. The sketches revealed Heather's deep love for the children and the rest of his family. Including him. There could be no denying it. He'd seen the proof before him in black and white. And no decent newspaperman could dispute facts presented in black and white.

She loved him, and that knowledge made his life worth living. No matter what she'd done, he knew she had done it because she loved him. True, her failure to tell him was wrong, but wouldn't he have done the same thing if presented with the same opportunity? Hadn't he lied a few times along the way to get what he wanted out of life?

Telling himself that his marriage to Lydia wasn't doomed from the beginning was probably the biggest lie of all. He'd married her for all the wrong reasons. She was beautiful, witty, charming. She made him laugh. And her ability to draw attention to herself made him the envy of every man who met her.

He had loved Lydia, but not in the total, complete, all-consuming way he loved Heather.

Lydia had never given herself completely to him the way Heather had. She'd always had her own agenda; he'd just pretended it didn't exist. There had always been signs of her unhappiness, her restlessness, but he'd ignored them. He'd been too intent on making her into something she didn't want to be.

He wouldn't make the same mistakes with Heather. He loved her too much. He just hoped it wasn't too late.

The knock on the door proclaimed Heather's arrival, and he quickly took a seat behind his desk, waiting for Henry to announce her. She entered, looking perfectly lovely in a violet and green floral print gown with matching bonnet, like a spring bouquet, but much prettier than any real flowers.

"Come in, Heather." She seemed surprised that he was alone, and she looked around the office as if expecting to see someone else. The police, perhaps? He smiled inwardly at the absurdity of that idea.

"*You* sent the note?" Was that accusation he heard in her voice, or surprise?

"Since this is a business matter, I thought it only fitting that we discuss it here. Is that all right with you?"

"Of course." She took a deep breath, trying to still the nervousness that had built while she'd waited more than fifteen minutes in Mr. Peoples's office.

Brandon was staring down at the papers on his desk, and she immediately recognized her sketches of the Whitten investigation. She swallowed, knowing that her day of reckoning was finally at hand.

"Peter Glendenning has already explained how he lured you into helping him with the articles, so I don't believe we need to go into all that. What I want to know is, why you didn't feel free to confide in me?"

"May I sit?"

"Of course. I'm sorry." His cheeks turning florid, and feeling like a rude, stupid fool, he gestured to the chair in front of his desk.

Crossing her ankles demurely, Heather removed her bonnet to reveal her thick mass of auburn hair, which had been fashioned into a sedate chignon at the back of her head. Clasping her hands together as if to pray, she said, "I know I should have told you what I intended to do, Brandon. In fact, I should have disclosed my intentions to find work as an illustrator as soon as you hired me. But you'd made quite clear what you thought of women working outside the home, as did your personnel director when I applied for a job here"—his eyebrows arched at that revelation—"so I decided to keep quiet.

"I thought what I wanted in life was to be an illustrator and have a career, but now I realize that I was wrong."

Brandon looked at the drawings again, then up at his wife, whose sorrowful countenance made him feel lowlier than an insect. "You're extremely talented. I told Peter so on several occasions. You might find it amusing to know that I wanted to hire you."

"But you wouldn't have, if you'd known that I was a woman. Would you?"

He sighed, hating himself for his male prejudice. "Probably not. Women are new to the workplace. I haven't grown comfortable with the idea of their pursuing what is normally considered a man's job."

"It doesn't matter now. I have no interest in pursuing a career. I only wish to be a wife and mother."

His eyes widened at her declaration, and he felt selfish and small for making her reach such a decision. He knew how much her art meant to her. His mother had been only too glad to acquaint him with the details of Heather's struggles to seek a career.

"You would give up your art for me and the children?"

Heather nodded. "I had already decided that what I wanted most out of life was to be your wife. I love you, Brandon, and I love Jenny and Matt with all my heart. I'll understand if you wish to divorce me, like you divorced Lydia, but . . ."

Jumping to his feet, a look of disbelief on his face, Brandon skirted the desk. "Divorce you! Jesus! What ever gave you that idea? I've no wish to divorce you. I love you, you foolish, talented woman."

Tears formed in her eyes as she rushed into Brandon's outstretched arms. "Oh, Brandon, I'm so sorry for everything. You'll never know . . ."

He kissed her long and hard, silencing her apology with his lips, then said, "I'm the one who's sorry. I've been stubborn and selfish, just as you've accused me of being." She blushed at the memory. "I knew you were nothing like Lydia, yet I tried to force you into the same mold."

"I'm sorry she hurt you so much."

"We were young. We didn't know what true love was."

"And now you do?" she asked, her pulse racing.

"You know I do. I love you with all my heart and soul. I could never lose you. How would I ever face my mother and children again? And Mr. Woo has threatened to quit."

Tears slid down her flushed cheeks. "He did?"

"You're very important to a great many people, love, most of all, me."

She sniffled. "Oh, Brandon."

He held her at arm's length. "There're just a couple of things we still need to get straight."

She nodded.

His smile turned positively erotic. "First, I want you to continue to supply my newspaper with sketches. . . ."

"Really?" Her face lit like a child's on Christmas morning. "You want me to illustrate for *The Star*?"

"You'll work from home as you did before," he continued. "Peter will supply you with the articles. . . ."

"Peter!" She blurted. "You mean you've forgiven him?" Throwing her arms about her husband's neck, Heather kissed every inch of his face. "Oh, Brandon, I'm so happy. Thank you so much. I love you."

"And the second thing, love," he said, pulling her against his stiffening member as he eased her over the desk, "is that I wish to make love to you here and now."

Her eyes widened.

Glancing at the door, he whispered, "I'd better go lock the door, love. We wouldn't want Mr. Peoples to further his education at our expense."

"We're going to make love in here, while Mr. Peoples sits outside and probably listens?" She had the most astonished look on her face as he crossed to the door and locked it. "Why, Brandon," she said, unbuttoning the bone buttons of her gown, "that's the most shocking thing you've ever suggested." She smiled wantonly, tossing the short jacket aside.

Brandon cleared his desk with one fell swoop of his arm. "Come here, love. It's time you learned the newspaper business from the inside out."

She fumbled with the buttons of his shirt. "And will you teach me everything there is to know, Mr. Montgomery?" she asked, trailing her fingers down his chest to toy with the fastening of his trousers.

"Indeed I will," he replied, leaning her over the desk to demonstrate, pulling down her drawers as he did.

Just then Henry Peoples's voice floated in through the closed portal. "Mr. Montgomery? Mr. Montgomery? Is everything all right? I heard strange noises."

There was no answer. Only the sound of muffled laughter, groans of ecstasy, and a very high-pitched *"Oh, Brandon!"*

Please Turn the Page

for a Preview of

SWEET LAUREL

Book Two in the Dazzling

Flowers of the West

Trilogy

Coming Spring, 1996

Chapter One

Denver, Colorado, Late Summer, 1883

"She ain't got no tits to speak of."

"Shut up, Chance!" Rooster Higgins, stage manager of the Tabor Grand Opera House, glared at the tall man seated next to him. "You and Whitey ain't even supposed to be in here during this audition, and you're gonna get me fired. You know if Mr. Witherspoon finds out, I'll be back sweeping up at your saloon again." He mopped nervous droplets of perspiration off his brow with his handkerchief.

Chance Rafferty smiled that winning, self-assured smile that was known to melt the hearts of ladies—well, maybe not ladies—but most women in general. It was a smile that could soothe disgruntled patrons of his first-rate gambling saloon, the Aurora Borealis, and charm angry mamas, whose sons were, more often than not, found drinking and gambling there.

"Pardon me for saying so, Rooster, but if you're going to be showing off your wares at an opera house, and you can't sing worth shit, then you'd better have a pair of hooters the size of Texas to make up for it. That's all I'm saying."

"Well, don't be saying it here." Rooster snorted indignantly, glancing up at the stage and praying that the innocent young woman singing hadn't heard Chance's insensitive remark.

Chance could be pretty thoughtless when he put his mind to it. 'Course, he was so damned good looking most women overlooked that little flaw.

"She sure is purty," Chance's cousin remarked, a child-like smile lighting Whitey Rafferty's face. There was a vacancy behind his sweet smile and sparkling blue eyes that had been there since birth. Though looking at the six-foot four-inch giant, only fools would consider him less than a man. Many had made that mistake, and many had lived to regret it.

Whitey Rafferty wasn't playing with a full deck, as Chance was wont to say. But Chance was as protective as a mother hen when it came to his dimwitted cousin, and didn't tolerate anyone else saying it. Whitey dealt faro and monte at the Aurora with the best of them, but no one was absolutely certain he understood the rudiments of the games he played.

Chance stared intently at the stage. The hairs on his neck were standing straight up at attention—the little blonde had hit a note known only to God and his band of angels—but, as Whitey pointed out, she was a looker.

She had a face that could soothe the savage beast, and there were plenty of them to be found at the Aurora. Most hair he'd seen that particular shade of blond had come straight from a peroxide bottle, but he knew hers was the genuine article.

Chance prided himself on the fact that he could spot a card shark, a con artist, or a virgin at first glance. The little woman on stage had virgin written all over her angelic face.

Damn shame about the tits! A woman needed a healthy pair to interest the customers, especially those inclined to spend their money drinking and gambling, and whatever else took their fancy. Without 'em a woman wasn't likely to get a job anywhere in the bawdy city of Denver, let alone at Tabor's Opera House.

Old man Witherspoon was a stuffy, tight-assed son of a bitch, but Chance'd bet his last silver dollar that old Luther liked a bodacious woman. Or any woman for that matter.

Chance shook his head in disgust. Every gambler knew that a woman was just plain bad luck.

"You guys better clear out now," Rooster told Chance. "Miss Martin's almost finished her song, and Mr. Witherspoon's due back from the bank at any moment." He looked over his shoulder toward the rear door of the theater, peering into the darkness. There was no sign of the old bastard yet, and Rooster breathed a sigh of relief.

Rooster could never figure out what Chance found so damned amusing about these auditions he insisted on attending. It was hard as hell for Rooster to tell all those poor unfortunates like Laurel Martin that he wouldn't be offering them a job with the company.

Mr. Witherspoon had pointed out numerous times that only the finest voices with absolute clarity and resonance would perform at Tabor's Grand Opera

House. He'd heard the cantankerous bastard say it a thousand times, if he'd heard him say it once. "O'course, if the woman auditioning was willing to give Witherspoon a little "extra attention," she'd get the job quicker than Rooster could spit. Witherspoon was a lecherous old goat.

"That's no way to treat friends, Rooster." Chance leaned back against the velvet-covered seat, crossing his arms over his chest, as if he had all the time in the world and absolutely no intention of leaving. "If it weren't for me, and a certain lady opera singer who shall remain nameless, you wouldn't have your present job."

Rooster looked chagrined. "I know that, Chance, and I try to accommodate you and Whitey as best I can. But this here ain't no meat market. You come in here every week, inspecting these sweet young things like they was sides of beef hanging in Newt Lally's butcher shop.

"That ain't right, Chance. Even Whitey knows it ain't right, and he don't know a whole hell of a lot." The stage manager smiled apologetically at the big man, but fortunately Whitey had taken no offense at the comment.

Shooting Rooster a disgusted look, Chance made a rude noise, muttered an invective under his breath, and stood to leave; like a shadow, Whitey followed his movement.

At that precise moment the lady on stage hit the final note of her arpeggio, and Chance covered his ears against the screech.

"Jesus, Mary, and Joseph! You'd better shut that woman up, and quick, Rooster," Chance said loud enough to be heard above the wail, "or you're gonna have every goddamn cat and dog within a fifty mile radius in here."

From her position on the stage, Laurel peered out over the footlights and could barely make out the men who'd been talking during her performance. The rudest of the three had even covered his ears. Of all the nerve!

The slight built man she knew was Mr. Higgins, the stage manager in charge of hiring for the theater, so she couldn't very well find fault with him. But the other two were as unwelcome and loud as they were big, and she just wished they'd leave.

Nervous as she was, auditioning for the very first time in her life, Laurel sure as heck didn't need an audience. And a boisterous one at that. Not at this stage of her burgeoning career.

She'd arrived in Denver two days before, weary but determined to get hired on as an opera singer. She hadn't taken the time for lessons, but felt certain that she'd be able to perform adequately enough without them. Her many beaus back home had told her that her voice was a gift straight from Heaven.

For as long as Laurel could remember singing was all she wanted to do. Her father's death last May had been the impetus for her journey west. And she was finding Denver a far cry from the sleepy farming community of Salina, Kansas, where she'd spent the last twenty years of her life living on the prairie in a ramshackle soddy.

All three of the Martin sisters had tried to respect their father's deathbed wish that they leave the farm to pursue rich husbands, though none had the least desire to do any such thing.

The eldest sister, Heather, had gone to San Francisco to find herself a job as an illustrator. Rose remained on the farm awaiting the new buyer before attending a finishing school back East. Heather had arranged for her enrollment, much to Rose's dismay.

Laurel doubted Mrs. Caffrey would have much luck "finishing" Rose Elizabeth. With the amount of rough edges Rose possessed, Laurel thought it more likely that it'd be Rose who finished off Mrs. Caffrey instead!

Her song at an end, Laurel stood waiting nervously and watched with no small amount of disgust as Mr. Higgins pushed the shorter of the two men out the door. A shaft of sunlight poured in as the door opened, and she caught a glimpse of dark hair and broad shoulders. She thought she heard the men bellow something about cats and dogs, but she couldn't be certain.

Mr. Higgins' effusive apology about not hiring her to join the opera company hadn't made the rejection any easier for Laurel to swallow. She'd been so positive that once he'd heard her sing, he'd be falling over himself to get her signed to a contract.

Though the man hadn't said as much, she thought his reluctance to hire her might have had something to do with her lack of experience. She wouldn't try to fool herself into thinking that her first audition hadn't revealed a lack of polish.

Practice makes perfect. Her mama had always said so. It seemed Mama'd had an adage to suit every occasion.

Having worked up an enormous appetite, Laurel entered the Busy Bee Cafe to eat lunch. Her large appetite was incongruous with the smallness of her frame, and her papa used to remark teasingly that filling her up was like filling a silo with grain. Smiling sadly as she remembered her father's words, Laurel seated herself at one of the blue gingham-covered tables by the window. A terra cotta vase graced the center, holding a lovely bouquet of wildflowers.

The restaurant was fairly crowded and hummed with the noise of enthusiastic diners and idle chitchat. If the delicious odors she smelled were an indication of the food, she was in for a treat. Fresh brewed coffee filled the air with a heady aroma, and the scents of cinnamon and nutmeg held the promise of apple pie for desert. Her stomach growled loudly at the thought, and she glanced about to make sure no one else had heard it.

Laurel had just taken her first bite of steak and gravy-covered mashed potatoes when a nattily garbed gentleman in a garish green suit approached her table. He had a thin black mustache, and a gold watchfob attached to his red brocade vest. And he was staring down at her with the most peculiar look on his face, like a predatory animal on the prowl. Immediately she chastised herself for the unkind thought.

"Excuse me, ma'am," he said in a very nasal way. "But I was wondering if we could chat for a moment?"

Laurel had been warned about talking to strangers, but this man looked harmless enough. He had asked politely, and she was in a very public place. Deciding to throw caution to the wind now that she was on her own, Laurel inclined her head and smiled. "Of course. Please have a seat. I hope you don't mind if I continue eating my lunch, but I'm absolutely famished."

From across the room, Whitey caught sight of the pretty lady from the Opera House and knocked

Chance in the arm. "Look at that lady over there. It's the purty one from the thee-a-ter."

Chance looked over his shoulder, his eyes narrowing at the sight of Albert Hazen, Denver's most notorious pimp. No doubt he'd smelled the woman's virginity from clear across the restaurant. She'd make an attractive addition to the slimy bastard's stable of whores; there was little doubt about that.

Hating to be interrupted during the best fried chicken dinner he'd eaten in a month of Sundays, Chance heaved a deep sigh and shook his head. An aura of bad luck suspended around him. Like pond scum skimming the surface of water, it needed removing at once.

If there was one thing a gambler didn't need, it was bad luck.

"I doubt that little gal knows what she's letting herself in for, Whitey. We'd best go over and get rid of the creep."

Approaching the table, Chance placed a warning hand on the man's shoulder, touching the brim of his hat with the other in greeting to Laurel. "Beat it, Hazen. The lady's eating her supper, and I don't believe she wants any company."

Laurel stared wide-eyed at the giant who accompanied the handsome dark-haired man. She'd never in all her born days seen hair as white as that before. It was as if the sun had bleached all the color out of it, like wheat left too long in the field.

"That's all right," she said, realizing she was quite rude for staring. "I was just explaining to this gentleman that if he wanted to talk, he'd have to do it while I ate. I'm quite hungry."

"Who I talk to is really none of your damn business, Rafferty. Now why don't you . . ."

Whitey took a menacing step forward. Al Hazen shut his mouth and pushed his chair back, trying to ignore the nervous drops of sweat trickling onto his mustache. Turning toward Laurel, he bowed his head in apology. "Sorry about the intrusion, ma'am. Perhaps we'll meet another time."

"Over my dead body, Hazen." Chance's voice rang cold and deadly as the derringer in his coat pocket.

"That can be easily arranged, Rafferty." The man smiled maliciously before walking away, and Laurel gasped aloud, her hands flying up to cover her cheeks.

"My goodness gracious! I guess I should thank you, Mr . . . Rafferty. But that man wasn't really bothering me. He just wanted to talk. I realize I shouldn't have spoken to someone I hadn't been properly introduced to, but he seemed harmless enough and very polite."

"So you won't make the same mistake twice, ma'am, my name's Chance Rafferty and this is my cousin, Whitey. And you're?"

"Laurel . . . Laurel Martin."

"Now that we've been properly introduced, Miss Martin, I thought you might like to know that the man you've been conversing with so politely is the biggest pimp in the state of Colorado."

"Pimp?" Laurel stared blankly, shaking her head. "I'm afraid I don't . . ."

Chance looked up at Whitey, shrugged his shoulders in disbelief, then sat down at the table, lowering his voice an octave. "Ma'am, a pimp is someone who procures whores." When there was still no reaction, he said, "You know—prostitutes? Women who sell themselves for money."

11

She gasped, covering her mouth. "I had no idea. Why . . . how dreadful." At the implication of his words, Laurel's big blue eyes widened even farther. "You mean that nice man thought I was . . ." She felt intense mortification redden her cheeks.

Chance shook his head. "No. He was hoping you'd want to come to work for him, though."

"But that's preposterous! Why on earth would I want to do that? I don't even know how to be a prostitute. And besides, I've come here to sing at the Opera House."

A virgin, just as I figured, Chance thought.

"We know," Whitey blurted before Chance could signal him with a kick in the shins. "We heard you singin' today."

Laurel studied the two men closely. She couldn't recall having met them before, but there was no mistaking the massive width of Chance Rafferty's shoulders. She was positive she'd seen them before, and she suddenly knew where.

"That was you!" There was definite accusation in the tone, and her eyes narrowed slightly.

Chance had the grace to look embarrassed. "That your first time auditioning at the Opera House?" he said, trying to change the subject.

The comely blonde was definitely not cut out to be an opera singer. Her voice was too grating—earthy even. He could picture her belting out a barroom diddy. But an aria from *Aida*? He thought not.

"You sure sing loud," Whitey remarked and received a scathing look from his cousin.

"You'll have to excuse Whitey, Miss Martin. He tends to speak off the top of his head."

"I guess that's better than covering his ears during a

performance." She pushed her plate away, her appetite suddenly gone. Somewhere on the other side of the dining room a waiter dropped his tray of dishes, and his curses could be heard above the clatter of broken glassware.

"Yeah. Well . . . You new in town? I don't recall seeing you around before."

"I arrived two days ago."

"Where're you staying?"

"I fail to see how that's any of your business, Mr. Rafferty." Laurel was beginning to like this handsome man less, the more she got to know him.

Chance turned on a winning smile, but it didn't erase the frown off Laurel's face. His brows drew together as he filed her very unorthodox response away for future reference. Rejection wasn't something Chance was accustomed to when it came to members of the opposite sex.

"We just thought you might need an escort back to your hotel, Miss Martin," he explained. "Sedate as it's become, Denver can still be a pretty rough and tumble place. A lady should take heed where she goes unescorted, especially in this neighborhood."

Laurel'd already had that lecture from Heather before leaving Kansas, but had totally disregarded it, knowing of her sister's overprotective nature. Perhaps there'd been some truth to Heather's warning after all, she decided. And she couldn't help that she'd been forced to seek accommodations near the Opera House, which sat just a few blocks away from the vice dens of the city. Funds were limited, and she certainly couldn't afford to put herself up at the ornate and expensive Windsor Hotel.

"There does seem to be an inordinate amount of saloons in this town," she said, her lips pursed. "I can't believe people don't have better things to do with their time than sitting in a saloon all day long. When on earth do those men have time to get their chores done?"

Chance swallowed his smile at her naivety.

"Chance's saloon is the best one."

Laurel arched a blond eyebrow at the big man's comment. "You have a saloon, Mr. Rafferty?" She stared at the impeccable cut of his black broadcloth suit, the flashy gold and silver rings on his fingers, the ruby stick pin in his tie, and wondered why she hadn't put two and two together before. "You're a gambler, aren't you, Mr. Rafferty?"

Chance grinned, and her heart nearly flipped over in her chest. "Hell, yes, little lady. I'm the proud owner of the Aurora Borealis, the finest gambling and drinking establishment in the whole state of Colorado."

"Chance is honest."

Chance patted his cousin's shoulder affectionately. "Thanks, Whitey." He told Laurel, "I pride myself on running a straight game, ma'am. I don't water down the drinks, and my dealers don't cheat the patrons. If a man loses his hard-earned winnings in my place, it's because he's not good enough to beat the house."

"And do you also pimp, Mr. Rafferty?" Her stare was wide-eyed and innocent as she waited for him to answer, and Chance nearly choked on the water he sipped.

"No, ma'am." He shook his head, the dark strands of hair glinting like brown satin in the sunlight streaming in through the window. "The Aurora ain't a brothel, just a gambling house and saloon. Of course,

14

what the customers do on their own time is their business." He wasn't a policeman.

And if the women in his employ wanted to make a little extra money on the side, then who was he to interfere? It was hard enough making a living these days, what with those do-gooders from the temperance league breathing down everyone's neck.

The Denver Souls in Need League, they called themselves. A bunch of self-righteous, teetotalling hags who had nothing better to do than harass a hardworking saloon owner, his employees and patrons.

Laurel took a moment to digest all Chance had told her. After a moment she said, "If you'll excuse me, Mr. Rafferty . . . Whitey," she smiled kindly at the dimwitted man, "I'd best be on my way. I have hours of practice ahead of me, if I'm to audition for Mr. Higgins again."

"Did Rooster . . . Mr. Higgins offer you another audition?" Chance was damned surprised to hear that. After all, he'd heard the woman sing, and he knew Witherspoon would never hire her. Not without bosoms to recommend her!

On the other hand, he could use another songbird. Even if Laurel Martin's voice was as grating as sandpaper and shrill as a cat's in heat, most of his patrons would be too busy gambling and drinking to notice. And her looks would add a breath of fresh air to the place. Most men were suckers for the sweet, innocent-looking types. Most men. But not him.

"Well . . . no," she admitted, her smile so sweet he could fairly taste the honey of her lips. "But my mama always said that practice makes perfect, and I know he'll want to hire me just as soon as I'm able to perform a little better."

Hell'd freeze over before that ever happened.

Wondering how any one woman could be so innocent, Chance took Laurel's hand in his own, and the jolt of electricity shooting up his arm at their contact startled him. Enough to make him say, "Good luck to you, Miss Martin. And if it don't work out with Rooster, you come see me at the Aurora. We can always use a pretty gal like you to sing for the customers."

Whitey nodded enthusiastically, but Laurel was anything but. Her mouth unhinged at the shocking suggestion, and she yanked her hand away as if she'd been burned. Which she had. Her fingers still tingled from the brief touch.

"I am a respectable artist, Mr. Rafferty, not some dance hall girl. I would never consider working in an establishment such as yours."

"Never's a long time, angel. I'm sure you and me will be seeing each other again." In fact, he'd been willing to place a pretty hefty wager on it.

"I wouldn't hold your breath, Mr. Rafferty."

"Chance holds the record for breath holding," Whitey informed her proudly, looking at his cousin with unconcealed adoration. "Last year at the Fourth of July celebration he held it for two and one-half minutes."

Chance smiled smugly at Laurel, tipping his hat before he walked back to his table and left the little want-to-be opera singer staring openmouthed after him.